The Darkest Evening

BY ANN CLEEVES

The Vera Stanhope Series
The Crow Trap
Telling Tales
Hidden Depths
Silent Voices
The Glass Room
Harbour Street
The Moth Catcher
The Seagull
The Darkest Evening

The Shetland Series
Raven Black
White Nights
Red Bones
Blue Lightning
Dead Water
Thin Air
Cold Earth
Wild Fire

The Two Rivers Series
The Long Call

ANN CLEEVES

The Darkest Evening

MINOTAUR
BOOKS
NEW YORK

First published in the United States by Minotaur Books, an imprint of St. Martin's Publishing Group

THE DARKEST EVENING. Copyright © 2020 by Ann Cleeves. All rights reserved. Printed in the United States of America. For information, address St. Martin's Publishing Group, 120 Broadway, New York, NY 10271.

www.minotaurbooks.com

Library of Congress Cataloging-in-Publication Data

Names: Cleeves, Ann, author.
Title: The darkest evening / Ann Cleeves.
Description: First U.S. edition. | New York : Minotaur Books, 2020. | Series: Vera Stanhope ; 9
Identifiers: LCCN 2020016421 | ISBN 9781250204509 (hardcover) | ISBN 9781250204523 (ebook) | ISBN 9781250796585 (signed edition)
Subjects: LCSH: Women detectives—England—Fiction. | GSAFD: Mystery fiction.
Classification: LCC PR6053.L45 D37 2020 | DDC 823/.914—dc23
LC record available at https://lccn.loc.gov/2020016421

Our books may be purchased in bulk for promotional, educational, or business use. Please contact your local bookseller or the Macmillan Corporate and Premium Sales Department at 1-800-221-7945, extension 5442, or by email at MacmillanSpecialMarkets@macmillan.com.

Originally published in Great Britain by Macmillan, an imprint of Pan Macmillan

First U.S. Edition: 2020

10 9 8 7 6 5 4 3 2 1

For my new friends in the North.

Acknowledgements

Thanks, as always, to the teams of publishers, editors, copy-editors, marketeers and reps who support my writing and bring the books to readers. They are too many to acknowledge in person, and now they're based all over the world, but they have become friends, they make the books better and I couldn't have the fun of storytelling without their hard graft. They know who they are. A special mention to Angela McMahon and Jill Heslop, who joined us last year. And of course, the team wouldn't be complete without my fabulous agents, Sara, Moses, Rebecca and Jill.

Thanks to Anna and Charlotte at Pan Mac, for supporting my whim to target a new audience, and to Lou and her Bristol bus drivers for making it possible and sharing their stories. Let's hope we can use *The Darkest Evening* to spark equally exciting projects. With the support of the Old Low Light in North Shields and the Literacy Trust, this has already started.

Constance Browne, Karan Pabla and Joanne Simmons Wright either gave large amounts to charity or won a competition to allow me to use their names in the novel. Thanks to them for their generosity.

I wouldn't still be published without the support of public libraries and independent book shops. Again, there are too many to mention, but please know how much I appreciate your hard work and enthusiasm.

This is a Vera book, and in the tenth year of the TV drama I'd like to share my appreciation for the people at Silverprint who have brought the character to the screen: the execs, producers, cast and crew, and most especially the magnificent Brenda Blethyn.

Of course, a huge thank-you to my fellow crime-writers. We joke that people who write crime are the friendliest and most welcoming people in the business, and it's true. Many have become close friends. Again, I can't mention everyone, but Louise Penny provided help, support (and a rather lovely bed for the night) when I most needed it and has been there during the bad times. Also, this is the twentieth anniversary of Murder Squad and we continue to do what our founder Margaret Murphy intended, to raise the profile of individual members and the genre in general, to enjoy each other's company and lift the occasional glass to the craft.

Finally, a shout-out to the readers who pay our wages and encourage us to continue writing. We need you a lot more than you need us.

The Darkest Evening

Chapter One

Lorna lifted Thomas from his high chair and held him for a moment on her knee. She still couldn't quite believe he was real. In the darkest days of her illness, she'd been warned that a child of her own might never be possible. Now here he was, more than a year old, walking a few steps, the centre and the love of her life. She tickled his tummy to make him giggle and held him tight. She would fight for him, with all the weapons she had. She'd fought the illness and come back stronger, done that by herself, and this was far more important.

Outside, the light had almost gone, and in the street light's beam she saw flakes of snow. In a house further along the street, there was a tree in the window, artificial, strung with gaudy baubles. Soon, it would be midwinter, the longest night of the year. There was a temptation to stay where she was, to turn up the heating and decorate the room for Christmas. She'd bought sticky coloured paper to make old-fashioned paper chains, silver foil to turn into stars. Perhaps she'd invite her parents to come for wine and mince pies. It was the time of year for reconciliation.

She knew, though, that any sense of celebration would have to wait. Still with the boy on her knee, she pulled on his snow suit and his little red wellies, then set him on the floor while she found her own outdoor clothes. She took a set of keys from a hook on the kitchen shelf, looked around the room, distracted for a moment by thoughts of decoration, the presents she still had to buy for her son, then she stepped out into the cold.

Chapter Two

IT WAS DARK AND FREEZING and Vera was starting to panic. Halfway home, she'd known the journey was a mistake. She should have listened to the team and spent the night in Kimmerston, waiting for the storm to blow over, but she'd thought she knew better. She'd mocked her colleagues for their anxiety, told them that extreme weather was unusual this early in the winter, even in rural Northumberland. And when was the weather forecast ever accurate?

She'd left the police station in a light dusting of snow, a gusty wind blowing it away from the street and into tiny drifts at the kerbs and in shop doorways. Now, on the higher ground, there was a blizzard and the flakes were so big and so thick that she had to lean forward and peer through the windscreen in an attempt to see her way. There were no lights, and even with four-wheel drive she was anxious that she'd come off the narrow road. She'd seen no other traffic since leaving the last village and felt completely alone, disorientated. She drove this route most days, had told her sergeant Joe Ashworth she could do it blindfolded, but now she was lost and felt bewildered and scared.

She came to a crossroads and changed gear, preparing to stop, so she wouldn't have to use the brakes and cause a skid. There was a finger sign but the village names were covered with snow. She had a moment of real fear then, a complete lack of recognition. In her headlights she saw trees on one side of the road, a thick plantation of spruce. She must have missed a turn earlier. She left the engine running but climbed out to clear the signpost. In one direction was Sawley Bridge and in the other Kirkhill. Kirkhill would bring her closer to home, so she turned right. The road started to rise and her wheels spun. The snow was so deep here that she worried she would get stuck, but there was one set of tyre tracks for her to follow now. Some other foolish soul had been here not long before her and must have made it through.

She seemed to reach the top of a low hill and, in the distance, saw a light below her, almost hidden by the blizzard. The outskirts of Kirkhill village, perhaps. There was a pub in Kirkhill, and she had a feeling that it did food and had rooms. There were worse places to spend a night. The team need never know she'd made an arse of herself. Already she was starting to relax; she could feel the fire warming her bones and taste the first pint of beer. But when she turned the next bend, she almost drove into a car that had slewed off the road and come to a stop just before hitting a five-bar gate. The vehicle was white, almost camouflaged in the snow. The foolish soul hadn't made it through after all. Vera pulled slowly past the car and came to a stop. The driver's door was open and it was possible that someone had fallen out. She found a torch in the dashboard and climbed down from the

Land Rover. The wind eased for a while and everything was very quiet and still.

Any footprints had been covered by the blown snow, but it seemed that the driver had been able to walk away from the crash. There was no sign of a casualty nearby and, now she was close to it, Vera could see that the car was unharmed. She was about to return to the Land Rover and continue her drive, when she heard a noise. A cry. She shone her torch into the back of the car and saw a toddler, strapped into a seat. The child was wrapped up in a red snow suit and wore small red wellies. It was impossible for her to guess gender or age. Vera's experience of small children was limited.

'Hello!' She was aiming at jolly, friendly, but the child started to whimper. 'What's your name?'

The child stopped crying and stared impassively.

'Where's your mam, pet?'

Nothing. Vera pulled her mobile phone from her pocket. There was no signal. Not unusual here in the hills. She supposed the driver had walked away to see if she could get better reception to call for help. Vera had already decided that the car had been driven by a woman. A small woman. The seat was pulled right forward towards the steering wheel. She must have left the child, knowing she wouldn't get very far carrying it. Even if the toddler, staring at Vera from the seat in the back of the car, was old enough to walk, the snow was so deep that it would be impossible for the child to move through it. The red boots were so small that they were more fashion statement than practical bad-weather footwear.

But Vera was troubled. Wouldn't a mother have shut the door, to keep out the bitter wind? She felt the prospect of a fire and beer disappearing. She lifted out the child's car seat and strapped it beside her in the Land Rover, struggling to slot the seat belt to hold it firmly in place. It seemed a complicated sort of set-up. Parenthood must be a challenging business these days.

Vera jotted down the white car's number plate on the back of a receipt she happened to have in her bag, then scrabbled for a clean scrap of paper. She wrote a note and left it inside the white car's dash. 'I've got your baby. It's safe.' With her phone number. Then she thought again and put her work business card beside it. The last thing she needed was an accusation of kidnap.

She drove on, even more slowly than she had before, hoping to catch a glimpse in her headlights of a struggling woman. She'd thought she'd come across her sooner than this. Vera swore under her breath. This was going to take longer than she'd expected. At least the child beside her was quiet, asleep and breathing gently.

The snow thinned and then stopped. The clouds broke and a slight crescent moon appeared. Vera drove round a bend in the road and suddenly she knew exactly where she was. There was a long wall covered with frozen ivy, two pillars marking the entrance to a drive which once must have been very grand, a sign with a coat of arms, faded and covered with snow. But Vera knew what was there. One word: Brockburn. The coat of arms would belong to the Stanhope family.

The light she'd seen from the hill must have come from here. At the entrance she paused and the memories came tumbling in. She'd been dragged here a few times by her father, Hector, when he'd been on his uppers and demanding that the family recognize that he too had a claim to a place in the sun. Each year they'd gatecrashed the gathering before the New Year's Day hunt. Hector would be in his element, chatting to the local farmers who remembered him as a boy. The black sheep returned to the fold, to drink whisky out of a small plastic glass, while the hounds grew restive and the glistening horses paced outside the big house. Proving that he too honoured tradition.

The family had been unfailingly polite. That branch of the clan used politeness as a weapon of mass destruction. But Hector had always come away humiliated and angry. Vera, who'd never felt any obligation to be loyal to her father, had understood the family's point of view. Hector would be rude and demanding, usually halfway drunk on the most recent visits. She'd been hugely embarrassed and they'd been kind to her.

On the last visit Vera had been a teenager, perhaps fifteen years old, already a little overweight, awkward, defensive. She couldn't remember now why she'd been there. Hector had no qualms about leaving her home alone, even as a young child. Perhaps he'd been more nervous about the encounters than she'd realized and had seen her as some kind of shield, or perhaps he'd thought the family would be more sympathetic if they saw he had a daughter to support. It had been a summer afternoon, the sun full and warm, flooding the place with light. They'd sat on the terrace drinking tea, eating thin sandwiches that disappeared in two bites. There'd been meringues. Even now Vera could remember the meringues – all at once crisp and chewy, the intense sweetness contrasting with the soft, bland double cream – more clearly than she could recall the other people who sat at the table. The background sound had been the call of wood pigeons and the faint strains of Bach, coming from a radio in the house.

Sitting with them had been three generations of women: Elizabeth, white-haired and wiry, wife of Hector's elder brother

Sebastian; Harriet, the very glamorous wife of Hector's nephew Crispin; and her daughter Juliet, a toddler with blonde curls and a knowing stare. If the men were in the house, they'd kept well away. There'd been a conversation, which must have been about money, but which was so hedged around with euphemism that Vera hadn't been able to work out what was being said. Besides, she'd been focused on the meringues, wondering if it would be rude to take the one which remained on the plate. As always, Hector had left empty-handed and bitter, swearing revenge all the way home.

Now Sebastian and Elizabeth were long dead. Even Hector's nephew Crispin had passed on. Vera had seen the notice in the local paper but hadn't gone to the funeral; she'd known it would be a showy affair and anyway, she wouldn't have been welcome. Only the two women, Harriet and her daughter Juliet, were left, and by now Juliet would be an adult, approaching middle-age.

The baby in the car seat stirred and Vera was brought back to the present. The heating in the Land Rover had never been very effective and she was starting to feel cold. She turned into the drive. The snow was churned by tyre tracks; she hoped that didn't mean her smart relatives had left the house. She felt strangely anxious about seeing them again, but they would have a phone and the child's mother might have made her way here. It was the closest form of habitation to the abandoned car. Besides, Vera thought, if she could face murderers and rapists, she wasn't going to be intimidated by a few weak-chinned minor aristos.

There were more cars than she'd expected parked on the long drive. Some were covered with snow, so had been there for a while, others had clear windscreens. It seemed the

Stanhopes had guests. Vera looked at the sleeping baby, lifted out the car seat and made her way to the house.

The sight was like something from a fairy tale. Magical. The flurry of snow had passed and there was moonlight, and a sky flecked with stars. A large cedar stood close to grand stone steps, which were lit from below. The tree had been decorated with hundreds of fairy lights, all white, all twinkling. The ground-floor curtains had been left open and Vera saw a huge Christmas tree, decorated completely in silver. A handful of people, most of them young or very well-preserved middle-aged and all grandly dressed, glasses in their hands, were gathered around an open fire. She checked her watch. Only seven o'clock. Too early in the evening for a party surely? A gathering before dinner perhaps. The house was big enough to accommodate all the guests and this branch of the family might be wealthy enough for lavish entertaining. She wouldn't know. Some of them had turned out for Hector's funeral but, since then, there'd been no contact. She paused for a moment, Cinderella looking in: the fifteen-year-old girl again, excluded. Suddenly aware of a different, more glamorous life which would never be hers.

Chapter Three

WHEN THE DOORBELL RANG, clanging and tuneless, Juliet couldn't think who might be there. Her guests had come early, freaked out by the weather forecast. Two couples had cancelled but six people had made the journey, each carefully chosen by Mark for their wealth and professional standing, and then the vicar and her husband for local colour. Had there been another invitation? Someone she'd forgotten? She felt a return of the panic that had been lingering all day, fended off in the last hour by supermarket champagne and a sense that things hadn't turned out as badly as she'd feared. Earlier, the day had been a bit of a nightmare, to be honest, because people had started to arrive before she was ready for them, anxious about the forecast of snow. Full of apologies: 'So sorry, darling! Don't mind us, we won't get in the way.' But wanting to be made comfortable, to be given tea, obviously shocked that the bedrooms were so cold.

They managed to heat the reception rooms downstairs – wood from the estate was free and the ancient boiler just about managed to work down there – but upstairs it was fucking

Arctic. That was what Mark said, laughing it off, because the whole lord-of-the-manor thing was still a novelty to him; in her more depressed moments it occurred to Juliet that this stately pile had been a major influence on his proposal of marriage three years before. She could tell, though, that there were times when he thought longingly of his single life, the smart apartment, which he still held on to, on Newcastle's quayside, his work at the Live Theatre, the easy access to bars and good restaurants. She'd loved Mark so much when they'd married. Now the relationship seemed complex and fraught, and she wasn't sure how they'd move forward. She thought that somehow, she'd failed him.

When the doorbell went, she excused herself from her guests and made her way into the hall. Dorothy would be up to her ears preparing dinner and her mother Harriet, deep in conversation with Jane, the priest from the village, still seemed to believe that they had staff to respond. Harriet had blossomed after her husband's death, taken to the solo role of lady of the manor with aplomb and seemed hardly to miss Crispin at all. Away from the fire, the hall felt chill. Juliet thought again about the bedrooms and made a mental note to remind Dorothy about hot-water bottles. Juliet hoped that their city friends might see them, and the electric blankets she'd put on some of the beds, as charming, a part of the country-house experience. Dorothy was brilliant and almost certain to remember, but it was the small details that counted. This was about business more than friendship.

Juliet opened the door and felt a blast of icy air. The snow had stopped and it had started to freeze. There was a moon and the park looked glorious, a fairy-tale setting with the circle of black forest as a backdrop. She had a sudden moment of cold exhilaration, of love for the place. After all, Mark was right: this effort was worthwhile. On the doorstep was a woman. Definitely not a late-arriving friend who'd been forgotten. This woman was large and shabby. She wore wellingtons and a knitted hat. She reminded Juliet of the homeless people she encountered occasionally outside Newcastle Central station, wrapped in threadbare blankets, begging. Then there was a flash of recognition. She remembered a funeral. Her great-uncle Hector's funeral. Hector, her grandfather's younger brother, a mythical black sheep of whom stories had been told in whispers when she was growing up. It had been a bleak, rainy day and she'd been surrounded by strangers. She'd been sent along to represent their side of the family, because in death Hector could be forgiven. He would no longer be around to cause trouble.

'Vera, we weren't expecting you!' She realized immediately that she'd let dismay creep into her voice. How rude that must sound! Was it possible that her mother, who was becoming ever more eccentric, had invited the woman without letting Juliet or Mark know? 'I'm sorry, do come in out of the cold.'

'Hello, pet.' Vera came in and stamped her boots on the mat to get rid of the snow. 'I'm not gatecrashing, honest. I've got a bit of a situation.'

'What sort of a situation?'

'Well, there's this.' Vera looked down and Juliet saw a sleeping child in a car seat. 'Do you think I could bring it in? It's freezing out here. It's asleep at the moment.' She looked at Juliet as if her opinion mattered.

Juliet felt a tug in the gut. She'd wanted children ever since she could remember, but it hadn't happened and she was approaching an age when perhaps it never would. Sometimes she couldn't help an overwhelming feeling of jealousy when children were mentioned. *If it's not mine, I don't care if it freezes to death.* Sometimes a gentler longing, which was just as desperate. 'Of course, bring him in. Or her. Which is it?'

'Good point,' Vera said. 'I haven't checked.'

Juliet, who looked at mothers' forums on the Internet in secret, with shame, as if she were accessing pornography, thought it could be about twelve months old. It might just be walking. Not properly talking. But really what did she know? In the drawing room, she heard the sound of voices, a sudden shrill laugh. It was clear that they weren't missing her. Mark and Harriet would keep things going. She looked again at the baby and found herself unclipping the straps and lifting it out into her arms. It smelled of fabric softener and baby oil. And poo. 'I think it needs changing. We might have nappies some-where. Dorothy, our housekeeper, has a baby.'

Duncan. Fourteen months old. Soft dark hair and round cheeks.

'You must be Juliet,' Vera said. 'You were at Dad's funeral. We didn't really have a chance to speak.'

'No.' Juliet felt defensive. These days she often felt defensive. 'I'm sorry. I had to rush away.' Then, in an attempt to assert herself:

'What's the story behind this child? Why are you here?'

'A car came off the road in the blizzard,' Vera said. 'I found this in the back. No sign of the driver. I need to use your phone, see if we can track down its parents.'

'Oh, of course. You must.'

'I don't want to get in the way.' Vera nodded towards the sound of laughter.

'There's a phone in the kitchen.' Juliet found herself becoming decisive, useful. 'You can use that. It's warmer in there anyway. And we'll get a nappy from Dorothy, make him more comfortable.' Because, despite the gender-neutral colour of the clothes, Juliet had decided that this was a boy.

In the kitchen there were good smells; they'd decided on pheasant, cooked slowly with red wine and shallots. Lots of pheasants, because they were cheap as chips here, and the city people would love them and find the dish exotic, authentic at least. And a vegetable casserole for the vegans and veggies. Roast potatoes and parsnips and sprouts because it *was* nearly Christmas. A variety of puds, hot and cold, because even the skinny women liked dessert and that way nobody would go to bed hungry. Dorothy was in charge, calm and capable, and Juliet felt a rush of gratitude. She wasn't quite sure now what she'd do without the woman.

'Dorothy, we've got a bit of a crisis.'

Dorothy turned away from the pan she was stirring. Real custard made with eggs and cream. 'Just give me a minute. I don't want this to catch or separate.' It *was* just a minute, then she looked at Juliet. 'Sorry about that. What can I do for you?' She was wearing jeans and a hand-knitted jersey. Her long hair was tied back with a red cotton scarf. Dorothy didn't need to frock up, because she never went front of house, except in an emergency. That was part of the deal.

'This is Vera, my cousin. Sort of. She's found a baby in an empty car that ran off the road. We think the parents might have gone to find help. But he definitely needs changing. Do you have a spare nappy we might borrow?'

'In the cupboard in the hall.' And because Dorothy was efficient, there was also a changing mat and lotion and wipes. Juliet came back into the kitchen with the bag. She still had the child on her hip. Dorothy smiled. 'Shall I do it?'

'No,' Juliet said. 'You've got enough to do. I'll manage. I'll just take him upstairs.' She was aware of Vera watching her.

'Can I use your phone?' Vera said. 'Let the office know I've got an abandoned child in tow. See if we can track down the parents.'

'Of course!' Dorothy nodded to the extension on the dresser.

Juliet saw that the baby was awake, staring at her. 'I'll be back in a moment.'

She walked past the drawing-room door but it seemed that still nobody had noticed that she was missing. Mark had a crowd around him and she heard him give a sudden guffaw, head back. Either it had been a very good joke or he was trying hard to impress. She looked at her watch. Another half an hour and they'd all go through to dinner.

Upstairs she put the changing mat on their bed and the child on the mat. She wished again it wasn't quite so cold. She would have liked to take her time over this. She took off the boots and snow suit and then a pair of dungarees, pulled off the nappy. She'd been right, it *was* a boy. When the child was dressed, she lingered again, standing by the window, the boy in her arms, looking out at the snow which had started to fall again, silent and relentless. It occurred to her that Vera wouldn't get out now, even in the old Land Rover, and that the baby would be hers for the night.

'Jules! Where are you, darling?' It was Mark, shouting up the stairs. That false, loving voice he put on for strangers. The actor in him made it entirely credible to his listening audience, but she knew him well enough to hear the irritation. She set the thought aside. Mark was tense, that was all. He'd put so much effort into this evening. It mattered to him and she couldn't spoil it.

'Just coming! We've got rather a mysterious guest. Look,

everyone!' She was halfway down the stairs and through the open door; they all stared at her, at the child in her arms.

'Where did you get that?' The question hadn't come from Mark, but from Harriet. Juliet's mother had got up from her chair and moved out into the hall. Even in her late sixties, she was the most beautiful woman in the room. Silver hair, immaculately cut. Eyes icy and blue. A dancer's grace and a model's instinct for the clothes that most suited her. She was looking up at Juliet. 'Is there something you haven't been telling us, darling?' The bad joke took the edge off her original question and the tension in the room dissipated.

'Nah.' It was Vera, who'd emerged from the kitchen and was standing on the edge of the crowd in the hall. 'It belongs to me. Sort of.'

'He.' Juliet turned to Vera and smiled. 'It's definitely a boy.'

'Well, why don't you hand him over then, pet? You don't want your dinner spoiled. Dorothy and I can take care of him. I've put the word out. We should have the car owner traced in no time and your mystery will all be sorted.' Vera turned to face Harriet. 'You probably don't recognize me. I was just a bairn myself last time I was here, or not much more than.' Vera smiled. 'Vera Stanhope. Hector's daughter.'

For a moment Harriet didn't move. Juliet even wondered if there might be a scene, or as close to a scene as her mother could ever contemplate. A snide and disparaging remark about Hector, perhaps, or some comment about Vera's appearance. Instead she decided to be gracious and reached out her hand. 'Vera, what a lovely surprise. No, I didn't recognize you, though I should have done. There's definitely a family likeness. Something about the chin and the forehead. Will you join us for dinner?'

Juliet thought Vera might do the unforgivable and accept the invitation, just to be mischievous, but the woman shook her head. 'I need to find out what happened to this little one's mother. It's not a night for anyone to be traipsing around outside.' She sounded genuinely concerned.

Mark took over then and led the guests into the dining room, where there was another fire. Juliet handed over the baby and followed them in. It did look magnificent. Shadows thrown by candlelight and firelight hid the shabby corners, and the heavy curtains kept out the draughts, which made their way through the ill-fitting sash windows even on the warmest of days. The tablecloth was starched and white and the silver heavy and gleaming. Dorothy had hired in a couple of sixth-formers, daughters of a tenant farmer, to wait at table, slender young women in black dresses and black ballet pumps. According to Dorothy they were Goths during their spare time, so the black clothes hadn't been a problem, but this evening they seemed willowy and charming, insubstantial, more ghost than vampire. Juliet thought of the snow; perhaps they too would need a bed for the night. Thank God for Dorothy. She would already have thought of the problem, had probably even phoned their parents. Without her, this would be a logistical nightmare.

Mark didn't begin his pitch until the meal was almost over. There was port on the table and the remnants of a North-umberland cheese board. They'd decided that everything should be as local as possible. If the Wylam Brewery had made port, they'd be drinking that too. Everyone was relaxed. He stood up and threw a couple more logs on the fire. Juliet watched him from the far end of the table and thought how easily he'd slipped into the role of country gentleman. It was hard to believe that he'd been brought up in a modest semi in one of the suburbs of Newcastle, and that he'd been educated in a state comprehensive. He even looked the part in his rather shabby clothes but fine, handmade shoes. He'd always been a quick learner and had known how to research a character.

His voice was deep and musical; it had been the first thing to attract her. 'Thanks to all our friends for turning out in this beastly weather. I'm sure you can see what a beautiful place this is, even in midwinter. We've decided it's unfair to keep the house to ourselves. How can we justify all this space just for three people?'

Four, Juliet thought, *if you count Dorothy.* She thought it rather unfair of Mark not to have counted Dorothy, then realized she'd drunk a little too much, because Dorothy of course had a family of her own.

He was still speaking. 'We've come up with the idea of a novel project that would allow the space and the beautiful landscape to be enjoyed by more people. A theatre, we thought, here in the heart of Northumberland. Opera has Glyndebourne, so why shouldn't we have an artistic space in the North?'

'Because up here, it rains all the bloody time!' A shout from one of his college friends, the words slightly slurred.

'We're not talking outdoor performance.' Mark smiled, but again Juliet could pick up the irritation. He wasn't a stand-up comedian to be heckled. 'Not necessarily, though of course with these gardens that would always be a possibility. We're thinking an auditorium within the main house, as well as a studio space. We'd look to attract good touring companies and to support new local writing. We're already looking into grant applications, but of course we need match funding. And that's where you come in. This is your opportunity to invest in this project, to become sponsors and have your name or your organization involved right at the beginning.' He paused and looked at them all. 'You didn't think we'd invited you here just for your company, did you?' His grin grew wider. 'Of course not! We need you to give us your money!'

He had them hooked. Juliet could tell that right away. Now he was moving round the table, squatting so he was level with each individual, his face at once earnest and passionate, waving his arms as he described his vision, his grand idea. Charming his guests, making them believe they were special, that they could buy into a piece of the whole thing: grand house, grand family, a piece of history: the Northumberland Reivers. Of course, he did have a vision; it was for a theatre, away from the city. But he'd been truthful when he'd said it was really their money he was after. He'd seen within his first few months in the house that it was crumbling beneath them, and, by then, he'd come to love it as much as she did.

Harriet got to her feet and waved to the room. 'I fear I'm feeling my age. I'll see you all in the morning.'

Juliet watched her go. Her mother still had the stamina of a marathon runner. Harriet knew they had to do something to keep the house going, but she thought this talk of money was vulgar and wanted not to be a part of it. Mark was writing names in a notebook. He seemed pleased with the response he was getting. Juliet slipped quietly out of the room and made her way to the kitchen.

Chapter Four

VERA SAT AT THE KITCHEN TABLE and looked at the mound of pheasant bones, which was all that was left of her meal. The baby was back in the car seat close to the Aga, awake but drowsy. Watchful. Two black Labradors were curled together in a basket. They raised their heads occasionally then went back to sleep. Vera wondered what Hector would have said about her sitting here, in the servants' quarters, with the house-keeper and the dogs. He'd probably have been affronted and made a scene on her behalf. Vera wasn't sure what *she* made of it. Perhaps she should have accepted Harriet's dinner invitation and sat with the bright young people in the grand dining room, but then she wouldn't have been so warm or so comfortable. She'd never much seen the point of pride for its own sake. Besides, much of the time she'd been on the phone and she wouldn't have wanted all those people listening in. Bad enough that she'd been forced to talk in front of Dorothy.

Dorothy intrigued her. The housekeeper had a posh accent, more clipped and regal than Juliet's. Tall with a rather long horsy face and big feet, but with a certain style and confidence.

Perhaps because of that, it was hard to age her. Late thirties? No more than that despite the old-fashioned name. Vera carried her plate to the bin and threw away the bones. Dorothy was already loading the dishwasher with plates from the first course. The teenage lasses had carried through the mains to the dining room and were outside the kitchen door smoking an illicit tab. Vera nodded in the direction of the closed door. 'They must be bloody freezing.'

'They're young. They don't feel it.'

'Juliet said you had a bairn. Boy or a girl?' The one thing Vera knew about parents was that they liked talking about their offspring.

'Boy. Duncan.'

'What have you done with him then?'

'He's with Karan, my partner.' A pause. 'We've got a cottage on the estate.'

'You didn't recognize him?' Vera nodded towards the toddler in the car seat. 'I don't know, from playgroup or mother-and-baby club? He might be local. You wouldn't be driving around in this if you weren't on your way home.'

'No,' Dorothy said. 'I've never seen him. But I don't socialize much. Karan would be more likely to know. He does the toddler group. He's the main carer.'

Then she was back, bent over the big double sink, up to her elbows in water, scrubbing out the giant pans. The young women floated in from outside, their arms wrapped around their bodies. They'd been standing in a covered porch so their feet were dry, but in the moment that the door was opened there was a blast of freezing air and Vera saw the falling snow, as heavy as it had been earlier, caught in the light from the kitchen.

'Can you clear the plates, girls?' Dorothy looked away from the sink for a moment to speak, but her back was turned to Vera. It was obvious that she was in no mood for conversation with the strange woman who'd blown in with a baby. 'Then come back for the puddings. They can go on the table so people can help themselves. And leave the cheese on the sideboard. Juliet or Mark will deal with that. Then you can get off.'

'Will they *get* home?' Vera thought she didn't need more dramas tonight.

'Their dad farms the land around Brockburn. The Home Farm. The house isn't far and he's coming with a tractor. The girls can squeeze in the cab with him. He's already on his way. That's why I've told them to leave the desserts for Juliet and Mark to serve.'

The phone rang. Vera looked at Dorothy for permission to answer it. The housekeeper nodded. 'Vera Stanhope.'

It was Holly, her DC. Vera had caught her still in the office and had left a list of instructions. 'I've got a name for you. The registered owner of the car.'

'Hang on.' Vera scrabbled in her pocket and found a scrap of paper and a pencil. 'Go ahead.'

'Constance Browne. Aged sixty-seven. Address in Kirkhill.'

That was the last thing Vera had been expecting. Not the address. Kirkhill was just over the hill. But the age. Was this kid, eyelids drooping now, almost back to sleep, a grandchild? And was an older woman wandering around in the snow? Surely someone of that age would have been more cautious about driving in bad weather. More sensible. 'I don't suppose the car has been reported stolen?'

'No record of that.'

'Have you got a phone number for her?'

'Just a minute.' Holly rattled off a landline number and Vera scribbled it down.

'Are you OK to hang on in the station for a while? I don't know what the weather's like there, but it's a nightmare here and I don't like the idea of an elderly woman out in it alone. We might need to get some sort of search under way. Mountain rescue maybe. People who know the area.'

There was a pause. Holly always thought she was taken for granted within the team, that Vera made allowances for the others when it came to putting in extra hours, because Joe had his family and Charlie had experienced problems with depression in the past. Holly felt hard done by.

'If you've got anything planned for tonight,' Vera said, 'I'll get the duty team on to it.' She knew this was playing dirty. Holly very rarely had anything planned. The job was her life.

Another pause. Holly wasn't daft. She knew she was being played. But she was like Vera. A natural detective. Curious. She'd regret leaving with the story still untold, and if it did develop into a more interesting case, she'd want to be in at the beginning.

'Nothing special,' Holly said. 'I can stay for a bit. The snow's not so bad down here and the ploughs are already out keeping the main roads clear.'

'Let me just give this woman a ring. If she's made her way home, you'd think she'd be on to us about the baby. She'd want to know it was safe. I'll give you a bell when I've called her.'

'Yeah, that's fine. Want me to do anything while I'm here?'

If Dorothy hadn't been listening, Vera might have asked Holly to find out about *her* and her partner. In fact, everything that there was to know about this branch of the Stanhopes. Arriving at Brockburn had been like wandering into a world that was alien – apart from those occasional visits with Hector she'd had nothing to do with this branch of the family – yet it was part of her own history, and she was intrigued. Fascinated. Instead, she said, 'Give the hospitals a call. See if anyone's been brought in with hypothermia, anyone at all, not just our Constance.' She still couldn't rid herself of the notion that the baby's mother had been in the car.

She'd just replaced the receiver when the waitresses came in. Now they were wrapped up in thick duvet jackets and looked like ordinary young women. Solid. At the door they pulled on boots.

'Your dad should be here any minute,' Dorothy said. 'He said he'd come around to the back door, so just keep an eye out for him here. No point freezing outside.' She dried her hands on a towel that was hanging over the range and pulled an envelope of cash for each of them from a drawer. 'If there are any tips, I'll give you a shout.'

Vera was on the phone again. She dialled the number Holly had given her for Constance Browne. The snow had piled onto the outside window ledge, but the top panes were clear and she could see headlights; the tractor must be on its way.

At the other end of the line a voice gave the number Vera had dialled. An older voice, a little prim but firm, confident, with the hint of a question when she added, 'Hello.'

'Is that Constance Browne?'

'Who's calling?'

'Vera Stanhope. Northumbria Police.'

A moment's pause. 'Yes, this is Miss Browne.' Another pause. 'Is anything wrong?'

'It's about your car, Miss Browne. It was found abandoned near Brockburn. It had come off the road.'

'I don't understand.'

'Has it been stolen?' Vera wished she was in the same room as the woman. She always found it hard to judge a person's reaction on the phone. 'Or have you lent it to someone?'

There was no reply and Vera continued. 'There was a child in the car. A little boy. A toddler. He's quite well. I have him with me now in the big house at Brockburn. But I'm anxious about the safety of the driver, who seems to have left the car to get help. There was no phone signal out there, you see.'

There was another pause and then Constance Browne spoke. 'I let Lorna use my car sometimes. Lorna Falstone. She assured me she was insured to drive it.' This seemed to trouble the woman. 'I'm sorry. Perhaps I should have checked.'

'You're not in any trouble, Miss Browne, and neither is Lorna. We're just anxious about her. Does she have a baby?'

'Yes. Thomas. A lovely little thing. But Lorna didn't ask to borrow the car today and she would never take it without my permission.'

'Is there some way you can check if your car is there, Miss Browne?' Vera was starting to lose patience. Her colleague Joe Ashworth was much better with witnesses like this.

'Just a moment.' The woman returned almost immediately. 'I've just looked out of the window. You're right, Inspector. The car isn't where I parked it.'

'Who is Lorna?'

'She's a neighbour. Her parents are farmers. I taught her in the village first school here and I've known the family for years.'

'Is there a husband? A partner? Someone we should contact about Thomas?'

The question was followed by a silence that stretched so long that Vera wondered if Constance Browne had hung up.

Eventually she spoke. 'Lorna has been very unfortunate in her choice of men, Inspector. She's a very gentle soul.'

'Could you give me a name of her most recent partner? An address?' Vera wondered if, after all, somebody else had been in the car with Lorna. This might turn out to be more than an unfortunate accident. She still couldn't believe that a caring mother would leave her child with the vehicle door wide open to let in the cold.

It seemed that this question was too direct for the woman on the other end of the line. 'This is very difficult over the telephone. But no, I'm afraid I can't give you any contact details for her child's father.'

'What are the roads like there?' Vera said. 'If it's possible to drive I could ask one of my officers to talk to you in person.'

'Oh, no! That wouldn't be sensible at all. We've all been advised to stay indoors.'

'If Lorna was in trouble,' Vera asked, 'is there anyone she might go to? Her parents? Could she have been making her way to them?'

Another moment of silence, but now Constance seemed to have appreciated the need for frankness. 'Really, I don't think so, Inspector. They had very little in common. Robert Falstone is a rather unforgiving man and it seems his wife hasn't the courage to stand up for herself. I like to think that if Lorna was in trouble, she would have come to me.'

'She didn't, though. Not today.'

'But I was out all afternoon! The old folks' lunch club was holding their Christmas tea in the church hall. I'm on the committee and of course I was there to help out. Perhaps she did try to come and I wasn't there for her.' Now, Constance sounded distraught.

Vera's attention was caught by the tractor headlights, right outside the window. She expected the girls in black to run out to their father and disappear into the night, but before they could move, the door opened and a man in overalls and a heavy jacket came in. He banged his boots on the floor and took off a balaclava so Vera could see his face. It was red with cold. He filled the room with the outside chill, so the warmth from the range and the girls' cheerful chatter seemed overwhelmed by it. The conversation fizzled out like hot coals doused with water. They looked at him as if he was a stranger. Usually, she could see, he didn't behave like this. He stared at Vera. 'I need to use that phone.'

'Sorry, pet. This is important.'

'There's a woman out there. A dead woman. I doubt what you have to say is more important than that. The police need to know.'

Vera returned her attention to the woman on the other end of the line. 'Constance? Sorry about this. I'll have to get back to you.' She ended the call. Then she turned to the man. 'I *am* the police.' She saw his incredulity, allowed herself to enjoy it just for a moment, then introduced herself properly.

Vera pulled on her coat and followed him out into the night. He'd parked the tractor so the headlights shone out into the garden. This was a competent man who thought things through. A practical man, not given to shock, though she could tell this had shaken him. 'I wouldn't have seen her if I hadn't nearly driven over her. She was almost covered in snow. But the wind must have blown some of it away, because I could see her face.'

They were at the back of the house. Vera wouldn't have seen her when she was walking from the Land Rover to the impressive front door. There was a track from the Kirkhill road, which the tractor must have taken, nowhere near as grand as the front drive. As Vera remembered, there was nothing to mark the turning but two cottages, owned by the estate, once let to workers. Vera supposed Dorothy and her partner lived in one. Perhaps the other had been sold off, or was rented out to provide income. Had the dead woman walked that way? If so, she must know the house, the lie of the land.

The snow was fine and powdery. She could see how the wind might have caught the tiny flakes. It was deep enough to trickle into her boots. Thank God for fat legs so there wasn't much of a gap. The man in front of her stopped.

'Sorry,' Vera said. 'I don't know your name.'

'Neil Heslop.' It came out as a mutter. His focus was on the mound of snow ahead of him.

'Can you just move away now? Let me see what we've got.'

He nodded and backed away, stood to the side so he wasn't blocking the light.

'Did you get down from the tractor to look?'

'Aye. I couldn't believe it and I had to check she wasn't still alive.'

'You did check?'

'I'm a voluntary first responder. We've had training. To check for a pulse. And you'll see the wound on the side of her head. She'll have had no chance.'

Vera didn't get any closer to the body. She'd do that when she was on her own. There was no sign of the man's boot prints. The wind and the snow had cleared any mark that he'd made. Any marks that had been here before. There was no way to tell if the woman had walked here with the person who'd killed her or if she'd been dragged.

'Did you recognize her?'

'I'm not sure. Hard to tell when I could only see part of her face, but it could be Robert Falstone's girl.'

Of course. We're not going to have two young women disappearing into the night. Vera wondered how she'd let Constance Browne know. The woman was already guilty and distressed, and now it seemed that her neighbour, the 'gentle soul', was dead. She turned to Heslop. 'Go back into the warm and wait with your girls. It's time for me to take over. But if you could leave the engine running and the lights on? So I can see what I'm about?'

He nodded and turned away. The flurry of snow had passed and the night was clear again. So icy that Vera struggled to breathe. She walked towards the woman, then moved beyond her, so the tractor headlights wouldn't throw her shadow on the body. As Heslop had explained, the face was only partly clear; a layer of hoar frost gleamed on the woman's forehead and chin.

She reminded Vera of a child, buried in sand, but a beach scene would have been vivid and noisy and this image was monochrome, drained of colour and sound. Vera took photos on her camera. Heslop had said there was a gash on her head, and it was as he'd described, just above her left ear. It was more brutal than she'd expected: the bone and the brain exposed. Blood. Vera wondered if they'd find blood spatter under the top layer of snow to indicate that the woman had been killed here. She was glad that wouldn't be a job for her. She needed Paul Keating, the pathologist, and Billy Cartwright, the crime-scene manager, here before the evidence melted away, and the difficulties of getting them to Brockburn preoccupied her for a moment.

From the house came the faint sound of music. A heavy bass line. The guests were partying, maybe they'd be dancing until dawn. The notion seemed disrespectful, obscene, but how could they know that a dead woman was lying here? Unless one of them was a killer.

Chapter Five

JOE ASHWORTH WAS AT HOME when the call came. They'd got the younger kids to bed and Jess was in her room on her phone. She spent more and more time hidden away from them these days. Sal said Jess was nearly a teenager now, only a few weeks to her birthday, so what could they expect? Sal said it was the age that caused the attitude too: the rolled eyes, the sullen silences, the slammed doors. 'It's all raging hormones. She'll come through it.' Joe missed the old Jess, though. The daughter who held his hand and giggled a lot, and lost herself in Harry Potter.

They'd decided to have a late supper on their own and to open a bottle of wine. He'd just poured the first glass. Sal had made a casserole that had been in the slow cooker all day, but they were relaxing for half an hour before she dished it out. There was a movie they wanted to catch on the television. When his work mobile rang, he didn't recognize the number.

'If that's bloody Vera . . .' Sal didn't finish the sentence.

He shook his head. 'It's a landline I don't recognize. Best answer it.'

Only of course it *was* Vera, shouting as if the phone had never been invented and she needed to yell to make herself heard. So Sal, stretched in front of the fire in the same room, could pick up every word.

'We've got a body. I need you here. Brockburn House, just outside Kirkhill.'

He wondered what Vera was doing already at the crime scene, but looked at Sal's face and knew better than to ask. 'I'm not on duty tonight.'

The boss pretended she hadn't heard that.

'You might have a bit of trouble getting here with the weather, so I've arranged for a tractor to pick you up from Kirkhill. You and Holly.' A pause. 'Paul Keating reckons he'll be able to get through with his fancy four-wheel drive and winter wheels and he'll bring Billy Cartwright with him.'

Joe began to speak but Vera ignored him. 'So, you'll sort out the details with Holly? She's got the contacts and knows what's happening.'

And before he could say anything else, the line went dead.

Joe knew he should be angry at the way Vera treated him, but deep down he thought she was doing him a favour. She knew what she was doing. If she'd asked him if he minded putting in the extra shift, he'd have had to say, yes, he *did* mind, with the food almost ready and Sal already angry with the hours he'd put in this month. This way he had no choice and Vera would be considered the villain, not him. In his heart, he'd rather be out in the freezing night investigating a murder, than here in his comfortable suburban home with his family. The notion scared him – what sort of monster did that make him – and he pushed it away while he dug his wellington boots from the cupboard under the stairs and placated his wife. 'I'm sorry, but you know what she's like.'

'It's time you moved from that team,' Sal said, mouth in a straight line, sullen as her nearly teenage daughter, 'find a boss who appreciates you.'

But Joe knew he would never move while Vera Stanhope was in charge of his team. Because she *did* appreciate him and that's why he'd been summoned in this way, with Vera putting herself in the firing line. And, anyway, she needed him; she'd go ape without him to talk sense to her. She'd never really understood the difference between her own morality and the constraints of the law. He walked to the end of the street to the main road where the snow had already been cleared, to wait for Holly, feeling shit for abandoning Sal when she'd been planning the evening for days, but experiencing too the thrill of excitement and exhilaration that compensated for the boredom of family life, and made it possible for him to be a reasonable husband and father at home.

When they arrived, it was midnight. The last couple of miles had been weird and disorientating. No street lights. A scattering of stars, hidden when the cloud blew across them again, or by a flurry of snow. The only sound the crunch of the tractor's giant tyres flattening the snow beneath them. The cab was open on either side. Holly was crouched on the seat next to the driver and he was perched on the wheel arch. The cold had seeped through his down jacket and gloves. It seemed to find any gap where there was bare skin: his wrists, his neck. Holly was wearing a ski suit and hat. He'd teased her when

he'd first seen her getting into it. 'You about to climb Everest?'
Now he envied her.

They swung around a corner and suddenly there were lights
reflected in the snow. The downstairs rooms of the big house
still seemed to be lit. The tractor stopped. 'That's the kitchen
door. Your boss is waiting for you in there.' They climbed down
and Joe pushed his way in. The tractor drove away.

Inside there was a wall of heat and noise. Voices talking and
a child crying. That high-pitched scream that gets under your
skin and makes you want to yell back. Or do anything to stop
the noise. Joe was confused by the sudden contrast with the
dark world outside. A stylish, slender woman in a black dress
and heels scooped up the baby from a high chair. On the tray
there was an empty pot of yoghurt and a plastic spoon, a
couple of toast fingers. 'I'll take him upstairs, try and get him
settled.' When she left the room, the other voices faded and
everyone was looking at the arrivals.

Now he'd adjusted to the new environment, Joe realized that
he knew most of the people there. Keating the pathologist and
Cartwright the crime-scene manager were sitting at the table,
hands clasped around mugs of steaming coffee. Joe could smell
it. And there was Vera, in her element and her stockinged feet,
at the head of the scrubbed pine table, beaming. The only
stranger was a woman, angular and tall, of indeterminate age.
She moved a large kettle back onto the hotplate of the range,
scooped more coffee into a jug and poured on the hot water.
It was as if she'd guessed what Joe was dreaming of. She pulled
a tin from one of the shelves and lifted pieces of flapjack onto
a plate. They oozed syrup and the pieces stuck to each other.
She set the jug and the plate in the centre of the table.

'I need to go home.' She had a deep, educated voice. Not

local. Not what Joe had been expecting in a housekeeper. 'I told Karan, my partner, I'd get back. *My* baby's playing up. He needs me.'

'Will you be okay to go on your own?' That was Vera.

'Of course. I can walk. The cottage is just at the end of the track, where it meets the road. I have a head torch.' She looked at Vera. 'That is all right with you? I won't be . . .' she paused, '. . . contaminating evidence?'

'No, you get off.' Vera thought for a moment. 'Billy, you go with her. Make sure she's safe. You can mark where she's been walking. Set up an access path a good way from our body.'

Cartwright seemed about to object but thought better of it and drained the last of his coffee. 'Just leave me some of that flapjack. I know what you buggers are like.' The kitchen door opened and the two disappeared. Joe and Holly shed their outer garments and took their places at the table.

'So.' Joe found a clean mug. 'Are you going to fill us in?'

Vera looked at him. 'I got a bit lost in the snow. There was more of a blizzard than I'd been expecting.' She sounded sheepish, but moved on before he or Holly could get anywhere near *I told you so*. 'A car had come off the road up the bank not far from the main entrance to this house and there was this bairn on his own in the back.' A pause. 'I know the folk who live here. At least, I know Harriet, who must own it since her husband Crispin died, and her daughter Juliet, the lass who took away the baby just now. They're distant relatives. On Hector's side.'

Joe was astonished. Vera lived in the cottage which had once belonged to Hector, her father. It was small and scruffy, a hovel perched on the edge of a hill. There'd never been any indication that she might belong in a place like this.

'You can shut your gob,' Vera said. 'You just look gormless, staring like that.'

Joe heard Holly snigger beside him, but he sipped his coffee and waited for Vera to continue. There was no point talking to the boss when she was showing off.

'So, there was a kiddie in one of those child seats. I thought the mother must have gone to get help or a phone signal. But what worried me was that the door had been left open. I couldn't see that a woman would do that.'

'You were sure it was a woman driving?' Holly asked. Holly saw it as a mission in life to challenge Vera's outdated sexist assumptions. 'It could have been the father.'

Vera shook her head. 'The driver's seat was pulled right forward. It must have been a small woman. I drove on and brought the baby here and arrived in the middle of a social gathering. A kind of weekend house party. There are three couples staying overnight . . .' Vera looked down at her notes, '. . . the Blackstocks and the Wallaces, and Jennifer Abbot and Peter Little. Juliet gave me a list of names and addresses. The only locals at the party were the priest and her husband and they left straight after dinner, before the body was found. We can get someone round in the morning to take a statement. We can chat to the others tomorrow too, see if any of them has any connection with the dead woman.' She paused and eyed up the remaining pieces of flapjack. 'Then of course there are the family – Juliet, her husband and her mother Harriet – and Dorothy Felling, the wonder woman who's been feeding and watering us.'

Joe shifted in his seat. 'What's the husband's name?'

'Mark Bolitho. I don't know him. He arrived on the scene long after I had any contact with this side of the family.

According to Dorothy, he ran a theatre in Newcastle before moving out here, still does, part-time. He's a writer and director, apparently. She thought I should have heard of him . . .' Vera's voice tailed off.

'I know his work,' Holly said. 'He's done some film and television too. I heard him speak at the Tyneside Cinema.'

Of course you did, Joe thought. Holly saw herself as the office intellectual.

'Well, you can do the interview with him in the morning then, pet.' Vera's voice was bright. 'It seems he's dreaming up some scheme to set up a theatre here and the party last night was all about tapping his mates for cash to support it.'

Holly nodded. 'Did you speak to the car owner? Was it stolen?'

'Nah. It belongs to a retired woman, a former schoolteacher called Constance Browne. She thought a neighbour called Lorna Falstone might have been driving. Apparently, they had an arrangement. A kind of informal car share. Neil Heslop, the farmer who gave you a lift, found the body and thought he recognized her as Lorna too. We'll need confirmation – her parents live at Broom Farm further across the valley between here and Kirkhill – but all the indications are that it's her. It wasn't an accident or hypothermia. There's severe blunt-force trauma to the side of the head.'

'That couldn't have happened when the car came off the road?' Holly had been taking notes and looked up, pen poised.

'I've looked at the body too.' Keating was an Ulsterman, precise and a little dour. Sentimental when nobody was watching. 'There's no way anyone could have staggered nearly a mile from where her car left the road with an injury like that.'

'And there was no sign of damage to the vehicle.' Vera reached for a flapjack. 'The kiddie wasn't hurt at all and nor was the car. It just seemed to have slid off the road. It can't have been going at any kind of speed.'

'So definitely murder then?'

'Oh, yes,' Vera said, and Joe caught the gleam in her eye. 'Definitely murder.'

Chapter Six

Juliet sat in the bedroom she shared with Mark and looked out at the garden. She'd heard Vera talk about bringing in a generator to light the patch of lawn where the body had been found, but there was no sign of that yet. No rumble of the engine or intense white light. Already a tent had been erected, flimsy enough for Juliet to see a shadow of a person inside, backlit by a torch.

Their room was on a corner and she could see both to the front – the formal garden – and along the side track that led up to the cottages on the Kirkhill road. She watched a small group of people at work, lifting equipment from the back of a large SUV. Everything was lit by the security light fixed to the wall above the kitchen door. It felt unreal, like wandering into one of Mark's film sets. She could imagine him following the action from a distance, completely focused, shouting the occasional note, before someone yelled, 'Cut.' Now, he was still downstairs in the drawing room drinking with his friends, more interested, it seemed, in their promises of money than in a murdered young woman.

Thomas was on her knee, wide awake, squirming. Juliet put him on the carpet and he scuttled away, exploring. It was a strange crab-like crawl; the child used his feet rather than his knees.

Your mother's dead. What will happen to you now?

Vera had spoken of grandparents living in the valley, people who might take the child in. 'The Falstones. An old farming family. You must know them? They're nearly neighbours.'

Juliet had muttered something about Robert Falstone being a tenant. 'They've farmed our land for years, but they keep themselves to themselves.' What else could she say?

Then Vera had persisted, poking away with her questions, like a disturbed child picking at its skin. 'You'd have known Lorna though? She was younger than you and I daresay she went to a local school, not that fancy place in Newcastle where you were sent, but in this sort of community you'd all know each other. The New Year's Day meet, everyone turns out, don't they? She'd likely have had a pony when she was a bairn.'

'She was a lot younger than me.' Juliet had tried to be firm. 'By at least ten years, maybe fifteen. I was aware of her, bumped into her in the Co-op in Kirkhill. As you say she came to the meet from time to time. But I've not met her recently.'

'Heard any rumours? Apparently, she was a gentle soul. Given to depression perhaps. Anxiety.'

'I try not to listen to rumours, Vera.' And that, at least, was true.

'Ah, rumours are what my job is all about.' And the woman had given a little laugh, making Juliet wonder what she might have heard about *her*.

Dorothy had found an old camping cot, which they kept in the house for guests with babies, and at last, it seemed, Thomas was ready for sleep again. Juliet laid him in the cot, wrapped up in a blanket, and climbed into bed too. She was awake for a long time, waiting for Mark to appear. At one point she considered going downstairs to see what was happening there, but what would that look like? A harridan wife in her dressing gown chasing a recalcitrant husband to bed. Mark would be mortified. In the end, she took a sleeping pill, an over-the-counter remedy that would have no real strength to it but might help a little. She slept fitfully and didn't properly wake until she heard Thomas muttering to himself. He wasn't crying, but making odd soft noises that could have been the beginning of speech. Mark was in the bed beside her, still in his socks and underwear, his other clothes and shoes scattered over the floor.

It was dark and she looked at the bedside clock. Six forty-five. She got out of bed, opened the curtains and stared out of the window. A uniformed officer she didn't recognize stood by the tent, lit by the light inside it. He was wrapped in a heavy jacket, but she thought he'd be freezing: there'd been no more snow, but it was still and clear and there was ice on the pane. She dressed quickly – a bath could wait – and took Thomas downstairs. They'd told the guests there'd be breakfast at nine and she hoped none of them would be ill-mannered enough to emerge before then. She'd left kettles and tea in the rooms. Dorothy had said she'd be in at eight, but surely Vera and her team would need hot drinks and food now. Juliet felt the old need to please, to make herself useful.

Vera was in the kitchen where Juliet had left her the night before. She was asleep, her head on her ample chest, snoring lightly. There was no sign of the younger detectives, the pathologist or the crime-scene manager. Vera woke up when Juliet came in. 'Morning!' Bright as if she'd had a good night's sleep in her own bed.

'I didn't mean to disturb you. I was going to make some tea.'

'Oh, Juliet, my love, you're a life-saver.' Vera nodded to Thomas. 'How's the little one?'

'He seems fine.'

'I called the duty social worker last night,' Vera said. 'She's going with one of my colleagues to tell Lorna's parents first thing this morning. Before the news gets out. I'm assuming her relatives will want to look after the kiddie. We should be able to take him off your hands by lunchtime.'

Juliet didn't know what to say. She put Thomas on the floor and started making tea. 'Where are the others?'

'Crashed out in your lounge. Sofas, armchairs. I didn't think you'd mind. We left one poor chap to mind the scene and he'll need a hot drink as soon as. I'll rouse the others when the tea's ready. They did what they could last night, but they'll start again this morning when it gets light. We'll have reinforcements then if the weather holds up. The forecast says no more snow.'

'I hope all our guests can get home.' Juliet was aware of an edge of desperation in her voice.

'Had enough of them, have you? I don't blame you. I can't abide my space being invaded. We'll need to have a quick word before they disappear, but as long as we have names and addresses, we'll be happy to let them go.'

Juliet put a big brown china teapot on the table.

'You'll have to put up with us for a little while longer, though.' Vera smiled a wide wolf's smile. 'I'm afraid you won't get rid of *us* quite so easily.'

★

The rest of the morning passed in a blur, leaving Juliet with a sense of mild panic and disengagement. She felt a need to concentrate in order not to lose control. It was a sensation close to seasickness and certainly she couldn't eat. The smell of frying bacon made her nauseous. Strangers drifted in and out of the kitchen. Dorothy arrived early and coordinated the whole scene like a choreographer, making sure everyone was fed and watered, skipping through the crowds with a mound of toast or thermos flasks of coffee.

The invited guests sat in the dining room. Most looked wan and hungover, but still excited about being in their very own country-house murder mystery. They didn't seem in any hurry to rush off. Mark looked remarkably fresh, just out of the shower, hair still damp. He came into the kitchen to find her:

'Come on, darling. You must have breakfast with us. They're *your* friends too and we do need them if we're going to keep this crumbling pile in your family.'

What family? she'd wanted to ask. *I'm the only one left. Officially. Apart from Vera and I doubt she has any offspring hidden away, ready to inherit.* But of course Juliet said nothing. She left Thomas with Dorothy and followed him to the dining room, where she drank coffee until the caffeine gave her a headache.

There was an awkward moment when Harriet arrived. She stood in the doorway, immaculate in a tweed jacket and tailored black trousers, a silk scarf round her neck. Demanding attention.

'What *is* going on in the garden?' She looked at Juliet for an answer, and Juliet saw that of course she'd slept through everything, the discovery of the body and the arrival of Vera's team.

'There's been some kind of incident, Mummy.' Burbling. Harriet always made her nervous. 'Neil Heslop found a dead woman when he came to pick up his girls last night.'

'What do you mean by "incident"?'

'It looks like murder, Harriet.' Mark stood up to speak across the table to his mother-in-law. 'There are police all over the place.'

'And nobody thought to tell me!' She didn't wait for an answer. 'Who is the supposed victim?'

'There hasn't been any confirmation yet, but they think it's Lorna Falstone, and that it was her baby that Vera brought in last night.'

There was a moment of silence. No expression of grief or shock. But Harriet hadn't expressed grief even after finding her husband dead in the drawing room, early one morning. He'd had a heart attack the night before, but she hadn't found him until breakfast time. By then they were no longer sharing a bedroom. 'How did Lorna get here? To the house?' As if it was the height of bad manners to appear without invitation.

'We don't know, Mummy.' Again, Juliet felt herself to be a gibbering teenager again. 'That's what the police are trying to find out.'

At that point, Vera appeared, crumpled, still wearing the clothes in which she'd fallen asleep, but so full of life and energy that she pulled the room's attention away from Harriet.

'I think you all deserve a bit of an explanation. Come on in and sit down, Harriet. Dorothy's just bringing in some fresh coffee, and then we'll start.'

Harriet, astonished, did as she was told.

Vera stood at the head of the table and leaned towards them. 'First, the good news. The plough's been down the lane and

44

cleared from here to Kirkhill, so as long as you take it easy up the drive, there's no problem about getting you all home. My colleagues, Joe Ashworth and Holly Jackman, will join us when I'm done. They'll take a quick statement from each of you, asking if you saw anything unusual when you drove in. We're interested in a white Polo that went off the road about a mile from the house. We think the dead woman's name is Lorna Falstone. She lived in Kirkhill. Does that mean anything to you?' She paused, looked at them, was met with blank faces and shakes of the head, except from Harriet, who seemed about to intervene. And a young couple, the Blackstocks. The woman was about to speak, but the man touched her arm, warning her to stay silent. Juliet saw that Vera had noticed that too.

'Of course we'll talk to the family later, Harriet,' Vera said, meaning, *so shut up for now.* For a moment Juliet was lost in admiration. She would never have the nerve to talk to her mother in that way.

And so the morning rolled on. Mark played the jovial host, flirting with the women, joking with the men. The younger female detective took him off to his study for a chat, but he emerged smiling as if he'd enjoyed the encounter. Juliet thought he always enjoyed the opportunity to perform. It was as if the body in the garden had been laid on just for their entertainment: *See what a marvellous backdrop to drama we have here!* There was no sadness, no sense of a tragedy unfolding, but then he was an outsider. Lorna Falstone's death wouldn't have the same meaning for him.

The younger detectives took over from Vera and led each of the guests into a corner of the drawing room to ask their questions. It seemed straightforward enough, though Sophie

Blackstock seemed to warrant more attention than the others. Juliet recognized her as one of Mark's team, one of the bevy of admirers who supported him in his artistic endeavours. Sophie was his job-share. One of the women who always made her feel inadequate.

Chapter Seven

Holly thought this was one of the strangest cases she'd ever worked. She was slightly thrown by it: by the big house, the suspects trapped by the weather, the snow. It reminded her of the TV dramas her parents had forced her to watch when she went home for Christmas. They expected her to solve the mystery before they did and were disappointed when she showed no interest.

'You must know who the killer is, darling. It's what you do for a living.'

She sat in a small room with Mark Bolitho. A Calor gas heater sent fumes, but not much heat, into the space. It was furnished with a desk and office chair, and three scratched leather chairs grouped around a coffee table. On the wall hung gloomy portraits of people Holly assumed were Stanhope ancestors. There was a computer on the desk, a printer and a pile of scripts next to a landline phone. The view from the window was of an outhouse and the bins. Bolitho was soft, just a little flabby. He might once have been fit, but the beginning of middle-aged spread meant his jersey was stretched tight across his stomach. He had the face of an overgrown, enthusiastic schoolboy.

Holly took one of the leather chairs. Bolitho sat opposite. 'This is your office?'

He grimaced. 'Not much, is it? But yes, this is where I have all my grand dreams for the house.'

'And the dinner last night was the first step to make the dreams come true?'

He nodded. 'I need an indication of local support before I can go cap in hand to the major funders. A commitment to sponsorship would help the project on its way. I chose a select number of people who might be prepared to contribute.'

'You don't find it awkward asking your friends for money?' Holly would have disliked the idea, found it embarrassing, and the notion of being in debt to anyone made her squirm.

'If you work in the arts in this philistine nation, you can't afford to be squeamish.' He paused for a moment. 'Harriet thinks I'm a grubby little oik, demanding cash in return for a part of all this.' He waved a hand. 'And of course, she's right. That's just what I'm doing. I'm giving my city-dweller pals the illusion that they can play at country-house living, and the chance to buy into the romance and the snobbishness of it all. But what Harriet also realizes is that if we don't do something to bring life to the place it'll crumple around her ears. She might pretend to have nothing to do with it, but she's not stupid. She's a realist. It suits her to make me out as the mercenary bad guy, but she wouldn't want me to stop.'

'And Juliet?' Holly asked. 'What does she make of it?'

'Jules trusts me.' His voice softened. 'Like her mother, she despises all talk of money, but she'd hate to lose the house even more. This place is in her blood. When we first got together, I knew they came as a package. Brockburn and Juliet. I would never have her if I wasn't prepared to take the house on too.'

'How did you meet?'

'At a party in Newcastle. Friends of a friend. You know how it is. I could tell she wasn't having a good time and she didn't really know anyone. She looked very lost, very fragile. I went to rescue her.'

'You're her knight in shining armour?' Holly didn't believe in those kinds of fairy stories.

He gave a sad little smile. 'I do try, but I'm not sure I'm terribly good in the role.'

'Did you know Lorna Falstone?'

He shook his head. 'I still work part-time in the city for Live Theatre. More than part-time now my job-share is away on maternity leave. I don't ride and I don't particularly like dogs, so I don't fit in too well with the social scene here.'

'Tell me what you did yesterday.'

'I was in here all morning. Keeping out of the way. Jules has a kind of social anxiety. You'd think she'd be used to entertaining, living in this place, but it's not really her thing. Because of the weather, there weren't even that many overnight guests – the vicar and her husband didn't really count because they weren't staying – but she was getting herself into a panic. Dorothy had it covered, of course, and I knew she'd deal with Jules better than I would.' He frowned. 'I do worry that my wife's a bit dependent on Dorothy. You know, they've been friends for years.'

'And later in the day?'

'Because of the weather warnings, everyone began arriving much earlier than any of us had expected. Soon after lunch, I started getting emails from them saying they were on their way. That didn't help Jules's mood – she's not good at dealing with the unplanned – so I went out to help. To meet and greet. Show them to their rooms. Make tea.'

Holly nodded. She thought Mark would be good at that. Pleasant, hospitable. He'd been an actor. He'd pretend to be pleased to see his guests even if it was inconvenient. 'What time did people start arriving?'

'About three-thirty. Two couples cancelled, but otherwise, everyone was here by five-thirty, an hour before we'd organized to start.' He paused. 'It was a bit of a pain, but actually, I thought that was a good sign. For the project, I mean. If people were prepared to change plans and battle against extreme weather to have a bit of the action, then they'd surely make the effort to see brilliant theatre out of the city.'

Holly wasn't sure that followed. The fund-raising party had offered food, booze and an overnight stay in a special house. Theatregoers would be expected to pay for their tickets and for their interval glass of wine.

'Did you notice anything at all unusual during the evening? The sound of a vehicle perhaps? We think Lorna would prob-ably have been killed where she was found. It was a brutal attack. There might have been screams, cries for help.'

'Good God, no. If we'd heard anything like that, we'd have gone out to help. Of course we would. But it was a party. There was music. Laughter.' He paused. 'A house like this, you don't have to worry about disturbing the neighbours, so there's no need to keep the noise down.' He paused again. 'The most unusual thing to happen was your boss turning up with that kid.'

'Did you recognize the child?'

The question seemed to irritate him. 'No. I've told you.

I don't mix much with the locals. And really, one child looks much the same as another to me.'

Holly sent him back to the others and joined Joe, who was interviewing the party guests. They sat, grasping mugs of coffee, picking at the home-made shortbread Dorothy had supplied. Holly looked over the room.

'Anyone still to give a statement?'

A tall, elegant woman raised her hand. Something about her, a tension, a reluctance, made Holly turn back to Mark. 'Is it okay if we use your office?'

Perhaps the woman was shy or perhaps she had information to share, but Holly sensed this interview would be better done in privacy. Mark had switched off the gas heater and the room was even chillier than it had been previously. The woman was wearing a long thick sweater, which reached almost to her knees, over leggings. She was wearing make-up; too much make-up, Holly thought, for this early in the day.

'Could I take your name?'

'Sophie Blackstock. I'm here with my husband Paul. He's already been interviewed by your colleague. I'm not sure why you need to speak to me.'

Holly smiled, an attempt to reassure, to put the woman at her ease. 'These are just a few routine questions. You're here at Brockburn because you're a friend of Mark and Juliet?'

'Of Mark,' Sophie said. 'I'd never met Juliet. Mark and I were very close at one time. We went to university together.' A pause. 'We job-share now at the theatre, though I'm on maternity leave at the moment.' There was another hesitation. 'It's the first time we've left the baby for a night. When I saw the weather I wanted to cancel, but Paul said it would do us good to get away.'

Perhaps, Holly thought, this was the cause of the anxiety: a new mother separated from her child, even more delayed now because of the murder.

'This won't take long, I promise, and then we'll let you get home.' Holly had taken a dislike to Paul Blackstock, although she'd never met him. 'Could you take me through your movements yesterday?'

'We arrived at about five-thirty. Paul wanted to set off even earlier, but he couldn't get away from work until four. We were probably some of the last to arrive.'

'Did you see any cars on your way?'

Sophie thought. 'We followed a tractor for the last mile or so. That was great because it cleared a path in the snow, but it turned off before we came to the house and then the drive was really treacherous.'

'You didn't see a smaller, white car? It had been driven by Lorna Falstone, the young woman who was killed.'

'Lorna Falstone? That's the name of the victim?'

'Yes.' Vera had given out the name when she talked to the group. Sophie must have heard it.

Holly saw that Sophie was very pale and that her hands were trembling. 'Did you know her?'

There was a moment of silence.

'Sophie?' Holly pressed.

'I've met someone with that name and it would be too much of a coincidence not to be the same woman. She said she came from the wilds of Northumberland.'

'Where did you meet her?'

'In a private hospital in Cumbria. I was working there, running some drama workshops. The clinic specialized in treating people with eating disorders and Lorna was a patient. The workshops were part of the therapy.'

'Are you saying that Lorna had anorexia?' Holly's spirits lifted. This was new information, and she'd been the person to discover it.

The woman nodded.

'When was this?'

Sophie spoke immediately. 'Five years ago. Nearly five years. I know because it was where I met Paul, my husband.'

'Was he a patient too?'

Sophie gave a little smile and shook her head. 'God, no! He'd hate it if anyone suggested he had a mental illness. His little brother Nat was there. Paul was a regular visitor.'

'So, Paul might have met Lorna?'

'He might have done. Visitors were encouraged to mix with the patients. There were social evenings. Some even joined in the drama sessions, which is how we got together. Not Paul's thing at all, but he'd have done anything to get Nat eating again.'

'Did it work?'

Sophie shook her head again. 'No. Nat did enough to get home, but then he became ill again.' She paused for a beat. 'He had a massive heart attack and he died.'

Chapter Eight

At midday, just when Juliet was wondering if they'd be expected to provide lunch, Vera was back in the dining room to say that the party guests could all leave. Once they'd cleared snow from windscreens, they drove off with waves and shouted words of thanks. The house seemed suddenly very quiet and Juliet had a moment of intense relief. Harriet had retired with some dignity to her room. The forensic experts were in the tent by the body. Thomas was pottering around in the kitchen, occasionally pulling himself up on a chair and walking a few steps before looking around, expecting applause. The house felt as if it belonged to the family again. With the child in the kitchen, like a real family.

Dorothy had made soup and they sat round the big table to eat. Not Harriet. When Juliet went to tell her that lunch was ready, she said she'd rather eat in her room. 'Could you bring me something up, darling? I really can't face Vera just now. Whenever I see her, I'm reminded of the odious Hector.' So Juliet had trotted up the stairs with a tray, and for one moment thought she was being treated more like a maid (in the time when they did have real staff in the place) than the woman running the house. Then she told herself not to be such a snob and to get over herself.

The experts came in from the cold, rubbing their hands to bring them back to life. There was a tall stern serious one, the doctor, and a little jolly one. Neither of them talked about their work, though earlier, when they were leaving their boots in the scullery, Juliet had seen them whispering to Vera. They'd just finished eating and there was more tea, more coffee, then the front doorbell went. It was cracked and discordant and always reminded Juliet of a bell ringing for a funeral. She went to answer and saw a woman standing there: she was cheerful, dressed for the weather in boots, down jacket and a hand-knitted bobble hat. Late thirties maybe, but still with the look of a student. Red-faced, no make-up.

'Hiya. I'm Helen Clough. Social worker. I think you're expecting me. I'm here for Thomas.'

Juliet should have been expecting her, but she'd put the inevitable arrival of the social worker to the back of her mind. 'Of course. Come in. We're all in the kitchen where it's a bit warmer.'

Then it happened very quickly. Dorothy found more nappies to go on the journey, Thomas was laid on a mat on the floor and zipped into his snow suit. The boots were put on his feet.

'Where are you taking him?' Juliet tried to bring a tone of polite curiosity to her voice.

'To his grandparents. They know about Lorna's death. I was there with a police officer this morning.'

'And they're happy to take him in?'

The social worker hesitated for a moment. 'Mrs Falstone wants to give it a go. We'll be keeping a close eye.'

'And one of my colleagues is going too,' Vera said. 'To chat to them, see if we can find out a bit more about what Lorna was doing here. They'll make sure Thomas settles well.'

Juliet had expected the young female officer, Holly, to accompany Helen Clough, but in the end, it was Joe Ashworth who went.

'He's got a family of his own,' Vera said. 'He's soft as clarts when it comes to kids.'

The door closed behind them and it felt to Juliet more like a tragedy than when she'd heard about Lorna Falstone's murder.

Chapter Nine

Joe sat beside the social worker, with the baby in the car seat behind them. Helen Clough drove carefully up the Brockburn drive, following the tyre tracks of vehicles that had left earlier in the day. Out between the grand pillars, the road was almost clear and Joe felt that he'd been allowed some kind of escape. He hadn't realized how oppressive the atmosphere in the house had been until he left it behind. It was something to do with the discomfort he felt in the company of the upper classes. A sense that he didn't quite know how to behave. He always admired Vera for not seeming to care.

Everywhere was white and the sunlight reflecting on the snow hurt his eyes. There was nobody else about.

'What are they like then, these Falstones? You said you visited them before coming here.'

Again, she paused before speaking. He'd noticed the same hesitation when Juliet had asked if the family was happy to take on the baby.

'Not the easiest,' she said at last. 'But that could be grief.'

'But they will take the bairn? Surely, if they're his grand-parents.'

'I'm not sure they know him,' Helen said. 'It's all a bit confusing. There seems to have been some falling-out with Lorna. They say they haven't seen Thomas since he was born, though I have a sense that the mother might be hiding some-thing. I'd like to speak to her when her husband's not there. I'm still not convinced it's the best placement, but like I said to your boss, we'll keep an eye. Better than a temporary foster placement and having to move him around.'

'But one of my colleagues has discovered that Lorna had been poorly. Anorexia. Surely the parents would have wanted to look out for her, to stay in close touch.'

'Ah,' Helen said. 'Sometimes the parents are the problem.'

Joe didn't know how to reply to that. He'd been expecting a longer drive, but they came to the farmhouse very quickly. It was no more than four miles away from Brockburn, solid, grey, stone. Once it might have stood against the Reivers, the raiders from the north. Because these had always been border-lands, debatable lands, places of clans and shifting allegiances. There was a walled garden to one side and a field of hardy sheep leading to a slow-running river fringed with ice. Joe had been expecting something a bit scruffy and run-down – weren't hill farmers supposed to be going through hard times – but this was tidy, the barn new and well maintained. To one side, there was a stable, a horse with a rug looking out over the door. The yard had been cleared of snow, and it was lower here, a little warmer. The field by the river was already showing patches of green. In the distance, hills and to the west, the sweep of the forest.

They were greeted by barking dogs and a middle-aged man

in overalls. Joe stayed where he was and turned to the back of the car to play peek-a-boo with Thomas. They'd already decided that Helen would take the lead. She was out of the car, hand outstretched.

'Hello again, Mr Falstone.'

'The wife's in the kitchen. You'd best go on in.' He gave a quick glance at the baby, then turned away, the dogs at his heels. When Joe looked after him, he'd disappeared round the side of the barn.

Helen turned to Joe and shrugged. He could tell she was disappointed by the man's reaction. Joe got out of the car and lifted Thomas from his seat. He was thinking of his own parents and how they loved his bairns to bits. If anything happened to him and Sal, they'd be there for the children. It was so obvious to them all that the family had never discussed it. Now, he wondered if they *should*, so there'd be no awkwardness with the authorities, no questions. He was still thrown by the notion that parents could be the problem.

Helen tapped at the back door of the farmhouse and let herself in. After the reflected light on the snow and ice, it seemed suddenly dark, gloomy. There was brown lino on the floor, a proggy mat in front of the range, grey with coal dust and dog hairs. A pine table and a couple of ancient armchairs. No photos of Lorna, even as a baby. No pictures at all, except one of a ram, taken at an agricultural show, a young man and young woman standing either side of it. The man's hairstyle suggested the photo had been taken in the eighties, but the woman's image drew him in and took him by surprise. She was dressed like her husband in jeans and a sweater, but she was pale and willowy, lovely. Not at all Joe's image of a farmer's wife. The photo looked quirky, posed. He thought it could have been the design for an album cover, the old folk rock that Sal claimed to like. The woman had the look of a hippy music star of a different era, the sixties or seventies.

While the yard had been pristine, the house looked uncared for. Joe wouldn't want a child of his crawling around on this floor, but perhaps Thomas would come to no harm. Vera always said he was obsessive about cleanliness.

The woman had changed since the photo had been taken, thickened round the waist. The blonde hair had been cut. Now she looked grey, and brown too, and had merged into the background, but it was clearly the same woman. The same cheekbones, the same eyes. She was sitting at the table peeling vegetables. She stood up.

'Look who's here.' Helen's voice was gentle. 'It's little Thomas come to see his grandma.' She took a seat next to the woman. 'Joe, this is Jill Falstone. Jill, this is one of the detectives looking into Lorna's death.'

The woman didn't reply. She held out her arms and Joe put Thomas into them. 'I'm so sorry,' he said, 'about your daughter.'

She nodded her acknowledgement, but still she didn't speak.

'If this is too soon,' Helen said, 'there's no pressure at all to take your grandson now. We can arrange for foster care for a little while. It'll be a hard time for you both, coming to terms with Lorna's death. Thomas could come to visit for days until you feel ready to look after him full-time.'

'No!' The answer was sharp and immediate. 'No, this is where he belongs.'

'And your husband feels the same way?'

'He does.' There was a pause. 'He says we have a second chance with Thomas. We got everything wrong with Lorna. We lost her. Now we can give a better life to her son.'

Joe thought of the man in the yard, hardly looking at the baby, turning his back on him. Perhaps he'd wanted to hide his grief from strangers, but it was hard to believe that he really wanted a second chance with a child. He thought Jill Falstone was talking for herself. Guilt was in there somewhere, and a longing to be close to the child when she'd grown apart from Thomas's mother.

'I need to ask a few questions,' he said. 'Just to understand Lorna a bit better, to understand what might have happened to her.'

The woman nodded to show she appreciated that questions would be inevitable. 'You'd best sit down.'

'Would your husband like to join us?' Joe thought they might get more out of the woman if they spoke to her on her own, but he didn't want to alienate Falstone, to make him feel more excluded than he already seemed to be.

'He's busy,' Jill said. 'The farm won't look after itself just because our daughter died. This weather, the sheep need feeding.'

Her husband's words, Joe thought. 'What happened with Lorna? Why did you lose touch?' Holly had explained about her conversation with Sophie Blackstock and the possibility that Lorna could have had an eating disorder, but surely, Joe thought again, you wouldn't cast out your child because they were ill.

There was silence, broken by the growl of a tractor. Jill Falstone sat on the other side of the table from him, Thomas on her knee. The child sat calmly looking around at them, then started playing with a couple of teaspoons.

'We'd almost given up having children when I fell pregnant,' Jill said. 'He never said, but I think Robert was hoping for a boy, someone who might take on the farm. I know a girl can be a farmer too, but he's old-fashioned that way.'

'So, he was disappointed when you had a girl?'

'No!' The surprise Jill must have felt at her husband's response showed in her voice now. 'He doted on her. I was the one who found it hard after all those years of independence, of working with Robert to make a success of this place. I love farming. It's in my blood. I took Lorna out with me as much as I could but she wasn't an easy baby.' Jill stroked Thomas's hair. 'His mother would never have sat like this. Lorna was always grizzling and demanding attention.'

'So how did it go wrong?' Joe asked. 'If Robert loved her so much?'

There was a moment of hesitation. Joe thought she was deciding how open she should be. She glanced at the social worker. He wished he was there on his own. Social workers had the knack of making the best parents feel anxious, guilty.

'When Lorna was growing up, her dad spoiled her to bits,' Jill said. 'She was horse-mad from a tot and he bought her a pony, then a better horse, put up jumps in the lower field, drove her all over the county when she wanted to compete.'

Joe heard the edge of resentment in her voice. Perhaps Jill had been the one to feel excluded, at least when Lorna had been a girl.

'And later?'

'It started going wrong when she was a teenager, thirteen or fourteen. She'd moved to the high school in Kimmerston then. It was a long day, eighteen miles each way in the school bus, longer if the weather was bad and some of the lanes were closed. She never really settled there. Of course there were other country kids, but she was an only child. She'd only known the bairns in the school in Kirkhill, and they were never very close. There were just a couple the same age as her and they were girly, you know, giggly. Not like our Lorna at all, though she was as pretty as any of them. Prettier, if anything. I think that made them jealous. And it must have been hard settling into the big school, all the noise, rough boys, strange faces.'

'She was bullied?' Joe asked. He'd worried about that when Jess moved on to the comprehensive. Sal said she'd give as good as she got, but still, the anxiety had kept him awake at night.

'I don't think they cared about her enough to bully her. Not at first. She shrank into herself. Later they noticed her, started with the names and the whispers behind her back. She didn't come to us about it though. I only guessed later what had been going on.' Again, Jill shot a look at the social worker before continuing, and again Joe thought there were things she wasn't saying. 'She'd always been a quiet little thing, but she turned nervy, withdrawn. She still had the horse but she wouldn't go hunting any more and she didn't bother with the other local girls who were into riding. She turned pale and skinny.' Jill paused and tried to find the words. 'Like a ghost. Like she didn't want anyone to see her, to know she was there.'

'And your husband couldn't cope with the change in her?'

'No!' Jill raised her voice. Thomas turned and stared at her before squirming away onto the floor. He sat under the table banging the spoons on the quarry tiles. 'It wasn't that. He was just as worried as me. We tried everything to get through to her. We went to the school and tried to explain, but she was well-behaved and did her homework. They couldn't see there was any problem. In the end I dragged her along to the GP.

She was losing so much weight and we thought she might be ill. Cancer. Leukaemia. Something like that.'

Joe nodded. He'd had those fears in the middle of the night too and his children had been fit and healthy.

Jill was still speaking. Now she'd started, it seemed she couldn't stop. 'He said there was nothing physically wrong with her. Not the sort of thing we were imagining. But he thought she might have an eating disorder. He said he could refer her to the child and adolescent mental health services, but there was a waiting list. We couldn't make any sense of it.' She paused for a moment. Helen the social worker reached out and touched her hand. 'That was when things really started going wrong.'

'In what way, wrong?' Helen asked. She shot a look at Joe, but he gestured for her to go on. This was her territory more than his and it was just as important for her to get a handle on the family.

'Robert couldn't understand it. Why would Lorna starve herself? It made him frustrated, angry.'

'Had you noticed that she wasn't eating?'

'We were never the sort of family where everyone had their meals together. I'm not a domestic goddess.' Jill allowed herself a small smile. 'I've always been happier outside than in the kitchen. I suppose I thought she was helping herself to stuff from the pantry or the freezer, like we, Robert and I, did. She was spending more and more time in her room, becoming more isolated, and when she wasn't there she was out walking. She walked miles. She said she needed the exercise, but I think that was all about losing weight too. She was always counting calories.' There was a moment's silence. 'In the end she was so poorly that she had to go to hospital. We went for a private place in Cumbria. We thought she'd get better care there. They specialized in teenagers with an eating disorder.' Another pause. 'Lorna didn't want to go, but they said if she stayed at home, she might die. That her heart might just pack up.'

Now Joe could understand why Robert Falstone had taken himself away to feed sheep, why he wouldn't want to be here for this conversation. It would bring back the bad times, the anxiety that his daughter was starving herself to death, the helplessness that he could do nothing to save her. The guilt that now he'd always live with.

'But she got better,' Helen said. 'She must have done if she was able to have a baby. That's impossible if you're anorexic.'

Jill nodded. 'She was months in hospital because she was so poorly. They had to get her weight up and for a while she was lying in bed, too weak to move. They put her in a wheel-chair just to use the toilet. A nurse would sit by her at meals, to make sure she was eating, and still she couldn't accept that she was ill. I visited from time to time, but there was no real response – some days she just turned her back on me – and I could tell all she wanted was for me to go. When she *was* well enough to leave the clinic, she refused to come home. Maybe she'd convinced herself that it was all our fault, that we were to blame for the way she felt about herself.' Jill Falstone's words were bitter. She turned to Helen Clough. 'Your lot didn't help. You egged her on, helped her make the break. You set her up in a house in Kirkhill. She was eighteen by then, isolated, vulnerable.'

'I don't know the details.' Helen sounded defensive. 'I haven't been able to access her files. But if what you say is true, we couldn't force her to live with you and she couldn't stay in the hospital indefinitely.'

'They said she'd have support!' The words came out as a cry. 'But nobody checked on her. Not after the first few weeks. I asked my doctor. She was left in that council house in Kirkhill on her own, day after day.'

'But she stayed well,' the social worker said. 'Maybe that was what she needed – to stay in control of her own life.'

'Who's the baby's father?' Joe felt he had to break in. He was finding the recriminations unbearable and this wasn't helping. Not now. It was time to move on.

'She would never say.'

'So, you did see her? You did keep in touch?'

Jill Falstone nodded. 'She'd been out of hospital for a month or so when I got a text suggesting we meet. Her choice. That made the difference, I suppose. We had coffee in a place in Kimmerston, out of the village, away from the gossips. After that, I went around to her house once a week. Fridays. Friday was my day for going into Kirkhill to stock up for the weekend. She didn't want to see her dad and I never told him I was visiting. He'd have been so hurt that she was prepared to see me, but not him. Maybe she thought she'd disappointed him, I don't know. By then she seemed to be holding things together. She'd got herself a little job, working in the pub in the village, and she'd got the house nice. It was one of the council places on the edge of the village and she was lucky to get it. Tiny, but it suited her. She even started having driving lessons – she'd never had the confidence for that before. I noticed that she was putting on a bit of weight. She was still skinny. It still looked as if her wrist would break if she picked up a cup of tea, but she was getting better. I was so pleased.' She paused. 'For the first time in years I was able to relax for a bit.'

'And then you found out she was pregnant?'

'Yes, that was later. A year or so later and by then she was well. I went one day and she was throwing up in the bathroom. That had never been part of her eating disorder. She'd never done the binge thing. She just starved herself. She was due to work that evening and I said they wouldn't want her in if she had some sort of stomach bug. She said it wasn't a bug.' Jill looked over the table at them. 'I didn't believe her at first. When she was younger, she was given to fantasies. I wondered if she wanted to shock me, to make herself more interesting.' Jill paused. 'As far as I knew, she'd never even had a boyfriend. There was no one when she was at school. She'd never had the confidence, though she was a bonny little thing. And I thought I would have heard if she'd been seeing someone. A place like this, there's gossip.'

'She never mentioned a man?' Helen asked.

'No, but we didn't talk much about her private life on those visits. That's why she let me go every Friday. Because I didn't intrude. She needed to be private to be healthy, she said. She held her small secrets to her like a kind of comfort blanket. She wrapped herself up in them. She knew her dad would want to pry, because he was so anxious about her, because he loved her so much.'

'But you must have asked about the baby's father,' Joe said. 'You'd have wanted to know.'

Outside, the sun was already very low in the sky, red behind a windbreak of trees, throwing long shadows, showing the smears on the kitchen windows.

'Of course I wanted to know!' Jill Falstone had raised her voice. 'When she told me she was pregnant, I had this dream, a kind of vision – that Lorna had found a man who'd take care of her and make her happy, that they'd be a real family in the little house in Kirkhill, that her dad and me would go some nights to babysit. That we could stop worrying about her because she'd have a man to do that. I saw myself sitting there, with the baby on my knee.'

'But it never worked out that way?'

Jill shook her head. 'Lorna was always more complicated than that. I should have realized.'

'What *did* she tell you?'

'Only that she was pregnant, and that she was going to keep the baby. She made that very clear. She said she was an adult.' Jill looked straight up at them again. 'I wouldn't have tried to persuade her to do otherwise. I was thrilled to have a grand-bairn and I don't care what people round here think. Besides, things have changed now. There are more kids in this village born outside wedlock than within it.' She paused. 'I told her I'd support her, whatever happened. And so would her dad.'

'Would he have done?' Again, Joe thought of the man they'd met briefly outside, closed and stern.

'Of course.' Jill Falstone sounded surprised. 'I've told you – he loved her to bits.'

'You must have asked about Thomas's father?' Helen bent down and gently tickled the child's belly and made him chortle.

Jill took some time to answer. 'I did. But gently. It was as if I was walking on eggshells. The last thing I wanted was for her to think I was prying. I didn't want to make her ill again, to get her anxious and stressed. I was worried that she might just run away. She was that jumpy.'

'She didn't tell you about the father?'

Jill shook her head. 'And so I stopped asking. I thought it must be a married man. Or maybe she'd had a fling one night.

The bar where she worked could get a bit rowdy at weekends. She made it clear it would be just her and the baby.'

'When did you tell your husband that Lorna was pregnant?' Helen straightened and took her attention away from the baby.

Jill flushed. 'It never seemed like the right time . . .'

'So, how did he find out?'

'In the pub one night. Usually he never goes to the Pheasant, the pub just down the road from here. And never into Kirkhill at night. But he just fancied a drink on his way back from Hexham and he called into the Pheasant. One of the blokes who farms up the valley shouted across the bar to him, for everyone there to hear. 'What does it feel like to be nearly a granddad, then?' She paused. 'He's a proud man. How could he admit he didn't know his own daughter was pregnant? When he came back, he was furious. I could hear it in the way he walked from the Land Rover, the footsteps, the slammed door.'

'Was he angry with you?'

There was a moment of silence. 'I couldn't tell him that Lorna had told me, that I'd been going to see her behind his back.'

'You're frightened of him?' Helen asked.

'Not in that way! Not thinking that he might hit me. He's never been violent. But sometimes I'm frightened of hurting him even more, of his moods.' Another pause. 'Of his silences. I feel guilty when I see how much I've hurt him.'

'Was that when you stopped going to see Lorna?' Joe could see how torn the woman was, her allegiance split between the man and the daughter.

'I didn't stop seeing her. I was there when the baby was born, in the hospital. She wanted me there so of course I went.

It was a long labour and Lorna was so brave. Hardly a whimper. And then Thomas was born. Tiny and perfect. The midwife let me hold him for a moment while she tidied up Lorna. It was seven in the morning. Nearly this time of year. Just starting to get light and I carried him to the window to see the world outside. There were tears running down my face.' Jill looked out of the window. 'But I thought it was the happiest day of my life. Better even than the birth of my own girl, because then I was so full of painkillers that it was a bit of a blur. That morning Thomas was born, I was sharp and clear. I still remember it. Every bit of it.'

'Had you told your husband where you'd be?'

Another silence. 'No,' she said at last. 'Not before I went. He was out when Lorna called to say her waters had broken. I left him a note here on the table, but he'd been to Edinburgh to watch the rugby and it was late when he got in. He'd been drinking with his friends. He dumped his bag on top of the note without seeing it and took himself to bed. So drunk, he didn't even notice I wasn't there. Or didn't care. The next morning, he got himself into a panic, wondering where I was because the car had gone and he still didn't find the note.'

'He thought you'd left him?'

'Aye. He was probably wondering how he'd manage the farm by himself. Thinking what it would cost to hire in some help.' She stared at them across the table, gave a little smile. 'That's not fair. I'd made him feel foolish. There are some men who hate to feel foolish. And it was my fault for not telling him that I was seeing Lorna, that she wanted me there for the birth.' Another moment of silence. 'I came home, so excited to tell him about the baby, but he didn't want to know. "I don't care about the bastard child. I never want to see it." Of course he did, desperately, but once he'd said those things, it was impossible for him to change his mind. He's stubborn. Afraid of seeming weak.'

'You must have gone to see them, though.' Joe thought she wouldn't have left her daughter alone and unsupported in a house with a new baby.

There was another smile. 'Of course I did. I think Robert knew where I was going those Fridays – he's not daft – but he didn't ask. That pride again.'

'When was the last time you saw them?' Joe said.

'A week ago.'

'How did Lorna seem?'

Jill seemed to choose her words carefully. 'I've thought about that since they came this morning to tell me that Lorna was dead. She was a bit quiet, withdrawn, but she could get like that some days. I tried not to read too much into it – no point in getting anxious. I never asked if she was still seeing Thomas's father, but maybe that was it. The relationship a bit rocky. Often the next time I'd go, she'd be brighter, talking about the future.' Joe noticed she was pleating the wool of her jumper with her fingers, compulsive. 'I was supposed to be going to see her yesterday. Friday, my usual day. But it had started to snow and the forecast was dreadful, so I texted her to say I wouldn't make it.'

'Did you hear back from her?' *When did we all start texting?* Joe thought. *When did we stop actually speaking to each other?*

The woman shook her head. 'But that wasn't unusual. She didn't communicate much and when she did it was on her own terms. She didn't seem to think that I wanted to know she was safe. But I'd stopped worrying about her quite so much. She'd made a friend. An older woman, who used to teach her in the village school. Constance Browne. A good woman. Lorna seemed able to talk to her.'

'Didn't that make you a bit jealous?' Joe didn't know how he'd feel if his Jess found other adults to confide in.

Jill Falstone seemed astonished. 'Of course not! I was pleased there was someone kind to look out for her. As I said, Connie Browne is a good woman. She even let Lorna use her car if she needed to do a big shop in Kimmerston or take the baby to the health visitor.'

'She was driving Miss Browne's car yesterday. She was about a mile from the entrance to Brockburn, the big house on the edge of Kirkhill. Any idea why she might have been there?'

Another pause, before Jill shook her head.

'There's a woman who works there, Dorothy, quite a bit older than your Lorna but with a baby about the same age. Could they have been friends?'

'I've explained, Sergeant, I didn't know anything about Lorna's life. She needed to be in control, just as she needed to be in control of what she was eating when she was younger. So, she held her secrets close. It was her way of surviving.'

'Do you have a recent photo?' he asked.

Jill got up and went to the dresser, pulled out a folder with half a dozen photographs. 'I took these on my phone last summer and they were so lovely I went to a place in Kimmerston where they print them out.'

They'd been taken in a small garden, presumably outside Lorna's house. Thomas was sitting on a rug. Lorna was staring at him, smiling. She had the same startling beauty as the younger Jill, still model skinny, high cheekbones, long, elegant neck. He took the folder. 'We'll take copies and make sure we get them back to you.'

Helen, the social worker, seemed fidgety. Joe saw her glance at the clock on the kitchen wall.

'Do you need to be away?' His voice was sharp. He could think of nothing more important than settling this baby in her new home.

'Sorry, my life is one constant rush. This afternoon it's a child protection plan core group session. I need to be there. And if you need a lift back to Brockburn . . .'

'Sure,' he said. Jill Falstone was staring at them, confused by the exchange. He thought, now, that she would look after the baby well enough.

He waited for a moment by the car while Helen made arrangements for future visits to the farm. He was hoping that Robert might reappear so he could talk to him, but there was no sign of the man.

Chapter Ten

Vera knew the village of Kirkhill. It was where she came on a Saturday morning if she wanted a sense of belonging to the real world. She'd stock up in the Co-op, visit the butcher and have a bit of chat with the women who ran the greengrocer's. No matter that the village shops were a little more expensive than the supermarket on the retail park outside Kimmerston. She'd have a coffee in the cafe, not the posh one looking out over the river, but the one in the square which pulled in elderly farmers talking about sheep. The coffee was just as good and they cooked their own ham for the sandwiches, saw nothing wrong in putting a pile of chips on the side. It was run by Gloria, who knew Vera by name and always had her coffee ready by the time she reached the counter, even if there was a bit of a queue.

Vera knew where Lorna Falstone had lived. There was a terrace of council houses on the slope that led out towards Brockburn. The road ran on to some old folks' bungalows further up the bank. Vera thought the houses would mostly be privately owned now, but the local authority must have held on to one or two: the small ones in the middle of the terrace, with a strip of garden so narrow that it felt like you could stretch your arms and touch the fence at each side. Vera didn't go in. The crime-scene investigators were already there: Crime-Scene Manager Billy Cartwright's bright young things. He seemed to attract the bonny young women, despite his flirtatious reputation. These days perhaps he knew better than to try it on, and he'd always been a charmer rather than a lecher or a groper. The house was cordoned off, blue-and-white tape flapping in the westerly wind. The air was a little warmer and felt as if it might carry rain, not snow. Vera thought all the bairns who'd been hoping for a white Christmas would be disappointed, though there was still time. Just a week to go. They were only a few days away from the winter solstice. There was still an edge to the breeze that penetrated clothes and chilled the bones.

Constance Browne lived on the other side of the road, down the bank, closer to the village centre, in a small private development of detached bungalows. So, Lorna hadn't been a next-door neighbour. Not close enough to chat over the garden fence. But of course they'd already known each other because Constance had taught the girl in primary school. It would be interesting to find out what Constance had made of her then.

Joe had been on the phone to Vera as soon as he'd got back from Broom Farm, filling in more details of Lorna's early life, but she wanted to understand more. There had been times, growing up, when *she* had wanted to shrink away from the world, to become invisible, but that had never stopped her eating. If anything, food had always been her comfort, her means of escape. Her own private addiction.

The teacher's garden had been tidied for the winter, shrubs

pruned, dead leaves swept. Vera rang the bell. The woman who opened the door was fit, spry and looked younger than her sixty-seven years. She wore jeans and a sweater, long earrings. Arty in a restrained kind of way. She made Vera, who was still wearing the clothes she'd slept in, feel lumpish and unkempt.

'You must be Inspector Stanhope. Do come in. I've just made a pot of tea.'

There was a hall with hardwood floors, a sideboard completely clear of clutter, on the wall a photo of a young woman in cap and gown at her graduation.

Vera nodded towards it. 'Your daughter?'

'Oh, no, my niece. We're very close all the same.' A pause. 'I never married.' Another beat. 'Too picky, my mother said, but I think it was more that I valued my independence. I never met a man who was worth giving that up for.'

'No,' Vera said. 'Nor me.' *Though it might have been nice to be asked,* she thought. *Just once.*

They sat in a living room with two windows. One had a view to the side of the house and across the valley to the forest beyond, the other looked up to the road. There was no Christmas tree to drop needles, but a holly wreath had been fixed to the wall, and holly and ivy spread along the mantelpiece. Cards with snow scenes and penguins had been stuck underneath. Everything was tasteful, ordered and in its place. Bookshelves had been built on each side of the chimney breast, the books neatly aligned: the sort of novels which won literary awards and slim volumes of poetry. Vera looked at the spines while Constance was in the kitchen organizing the tea. Competent watercolours, painted presumably by Constance, hung on the walls. The house was pleasant enough, but there was nothing startling to give away the owner's secret preoccupations.

Nothing that leapt out. Vera wondered if she'd manage *her* life in this way if she was retired. Would she clear out her house in the hills? Dust and declutter? Start home-baking and take up a hobby? She knew the answer before the thought was fully formed and restrained a laugh. She'd hate retirement. She needed her work and she needed her team. And she'd never take to housework.

Constance came in, carrying a tray, interrupting Vera's thoughts.

'Tell me about Lorna,' Vera said, once the ritual of tea-pouring was over. 'You must have known her very well.'

'I taught her of course. She was one of those quiet, shy little things. Not particularly academic, but certainly not a child who struggled. A reader. I hoped she might blossom later. Some children do. She was stunning to look at, but had no confidence at all. She was passionate about animals and I assumed she'd join the family farm when she grew up. Many of my pupils had their lives mapped out for them in advance. Even the rather grand ones from the big house. They might have a spell of freedom – university, travel, work – but then they'd be pulled back to take over the reins on the estate.'

'Did you teach Juliet from Brockburn?'

'Yes, but only for a couple of years. Later she went to an independent day school in Newcastle. I think she stayed with a friend of her mother's or a distant relative during the week so she didn't have to travel every day. But she was at the village school in Brockburn before that.' Constance paused. 'She's older than Lorna though. They wouldn't have been there at the same time.'

Vera nodded.

'You might be related to Juliet and her mother.' Constance

spoke as if this was a joke because surely it couldn't possibly be true. How could there be a connection between the smart people in the big house and this scruffy middle-aged cop? 'The same name. I just wondered.'

'We are actually,' Vera said. 'Distantly. Round here, if you go back far enough, we all have the same ancestors.'

'Not me,' Connie said. 'I came to Newcastle as a student from Sussex and I never went home.'

'You caught up with Lorna again when she came to live over the road from you?'

'Yes.' The light had gone now and Constance got out of her seat to switch on a standard lamp and close the curtains. Vera saw this was a ritual too, which would be performed at the same point every evening. 'I'd heard she'd been ill, of course. Anorcxia. A place like this there's always gossip. Then I saw her across the road and invited her in for tea. I thought she'd refuse at first – I'd seen her a few times in the village and she'd always hurried away as if she was ashamed – but she came. Perhaps I was a familiar face and I reminded her of a time when things were easier.'

'You must have put her at her ease.'

'I hope so. I like the company of young people. I enjoy talking to them. She was an interesting woman.'

In the dim light, sitting in a comfortable chair, Vera felt relaxed, almost sleepy. 'In what way was she interesting?'

There was a moment of silence. A tabby cat pushed through the half-closed door and settled on the arm of Connie's chair. The woman reached out to stroke it.

'I thought she was brave,' Connie said, 'to fight the illness and come back from it stronger. She wanted to learn. She was interested in life away from the village. We talked about art, travel. I gave her books. She'd been an only child of two doting but not terribly emotionally intelligent parents. They were practical – if she asked for something, they gave it to her. But she couldn't ask for what she really needed. She didn't know how.'

'And what did she really need?' Vera wasn't sure about the turn this conversation was taking. It seemed to her a lot of waffle and guesswork, amateur psychology of the worst kind. Had Connie seen Lorna as a surrogate daughter? The child she'd never had? But maybe that was psychobabble too. She reached out for another home-made biscuit and looked at the woman for an answer.

'Confidence,' Connie said. 'Reassurance. A close friend of her own age. Permission to talk about the things that were worrying her when she got to the high school. I don't think anyone talked very much at all in that house. Unless it was about sheep prices and horses. Robert would have hated a discussion about anything more intimate.'

'When I phoned to ask about the car, you said that Jill Falstone did just what her husband told her. Did you ever suspect domestic abuse?'

Another silence. 'Not physical violence,' the woman said at last. 'I think he was just one of those men who assume that within the house their word is law. He'd grown up in that sort of home and had never changed.'

'Did Lorna ever talk to you about Thomas's father?'

'No.' The answer came quickly. Too quickly? But it was an obvious question and perhaps Constance had been expecting it. 'I didn't ask. She'd have been subject to enough prying in the village. I didn't want to be just another nosy old woman.'

'When did you last see Lorna?' As comfortable as she was,

Vera knew it was time to move the conversation on. She needed a bath and sleep before an early briefing the next day.

'The day before she died. Thursday. She phoned first thing to ask if I'd look after Thomas for a couple of hours. Something urgent had come up.'

'And did you?'

'Yes. I'm a busy woman, busier than I ever was before I retired, but I was free that morning and the child's a delight. Very sunny and even-tempered. A credit to his mother.' Constance broke off. 'Where is Thomas now?'

'With his grandparents.'

Constance stroked the cat once more. 'I suppose that's for the best. To be with relatives.'

'You don't sound too sure. You don't think they'll make the same mistakes twice?'

'No,' the woman said. 'I'm sure that they won't.'

'Did Lorna tell you where she was going? Why she needed you to babysit?'

'No, and I didn't ask. As I said, I tried not to intrude into her private life. I was her friend, not her mother. And certainly not her teacher any more.'

Vera lay back in her chair, was tempted to close her eyes, just for a moment. 'Did she borrow your car when she dropped Thomas off?'

'No.'

So, wherever Lorna had gone that day it had been on foot or public transport. They would need to track her movements.

Before Vera could ask another question, Connie continued.

'She texted me at about eleven-thirty to say she'd been a bit delayed. Would I be okay to give Thomas some lunch and she'd be back at one-thirty at the latest? It was a little inconvenient because I had plans for the afternoon, but I said it would be fine. Usually she was always on time. She never took advantage of me. I knew it must be something important.'

'How was she when she came to pick up Thomas?'

'I don't really know. She was back at exactly one-thirty, but I was all ready to go straight out. I even had my coat on and the baby's things all packed. Not to make a point, but because I was worried that I'd be late. I'd planned to meet a friend in Corbridge. An author we both enjoy was talking in the book-shop there. So, it was just a question of doing the handover.' Connie sat very still. 'I should have taken more time to ask if everything was well with her. To give her the chance to talk. I have this ridiculous compulsion to be punctual. What would a couple of minutes have mattered?'

'The next day . . .' Vera had never bothered about punctu-ality unless she was the person doing the waiting. 'The day that Lorna died. Did you see her then?'

Connie shook her head. 'Friday's one of my busy days. I help at the over-sixties lunch club. We take it in turns to cook, and I was on the rota. It was our last meeting before Christmas, so a little bit special. We gave them afternoon tea.'

'Did you notice that the car wasn't there when you came back?' That would at least give them a timeline, an idea when Lorna had set out.

'No, but I wouldn't. I came up the lane at the back of my house and the car was parked on the road in front of the bungalow. I wouldn't see.'

'But when you drew the curtains, you would have realized it was missing?' Because Vera had seen the cars parked in the street through one of the windows when she'd first come into the room.

'I'm not sure that I would have done. It was snowing by then and the visibility was poor. The street lamp is further down the road. I was thinking about the weather.' Connie paused. 'I'm afraid I just can't be sure whether it was there or not.'

'Did Lorna have her own set of car keys?'

'Yes, it made sense. I never thought she'd abuse it. She never had. And it was reassuring to know that somebody had a spare.' Again, Connie paused. 'It must have been urgent for Lorna to take the car without asking. Very, very urgent. You have to understand, Inspector, that wasn't like her at all.'

When Vera arrived back at her house, it was freezing, much colder than the milder wind that had been blowing in the valley. Her hippy neighbours, who lived in the smallholding next door, had cleared the track, but there was still snow here, and ice on the cottage windows. Hector had never seen the point of central heating when the house was so small. He'd been brought up in the big house at Brockburn with its draughts and temperamental boilers and had been sent to a boarding school where it had been a point of honour never to complain about the cold. Until he was expelled.

Vera had considered installing central heating when her house had been damaged by fire, earlier in the year, but in the end, she'd decided against. She'd had to move out for a few weeks when the builders were bringing the place back to life. She'd stayed next door with Joanna and Jack, camping out in one of their spare rooms, eating supper with them at the cluttered table in the farmhouse kitchen, drinking too much of Jack's homebrew. She'd been grateful. The alternative would have been a B&B and that would have been worse. But still, she'd longed for the chaos to be over and to move back into her own space, so she'd told the plumber not to bother with the central heating and just to replace the hot-water boiler. Moments like this, she wondered if that had been a mistake.

She kept her coat on while she lit the fire, had a moment of panic when she thought she'd run out of kindling, but got it going at last. Joe Ashworth was always telling her she should get a log-burner, because the fire stayed in longer and gave out a better form of heat. His Sal had got one installed in their suburban house in Kimmerston; Sal had loved the idea of it, seen them in the fancy interior-design magazines she read, though Vera suspected the couple only lit it when friends had been invited for dinner and they wanted to impress. She couldn't see Sal emptying ashes. Now, as most of the heat seemed to disappear up the chimney, Vera wondered if it wouldn't have been a bad idea to take Joe's advice while the house was being renovated.

She heated a tin of soup in the tiny kitchen, leaving the door wide open so she could keep an eye on the fire, then ate it in the sitting room, the bowl on a tray. The bread was stale so when the soup was finished, she toasted two slices, one after another, using the long-handled fork that again held childhood memories, holding it towards the flames, squatting on the hearth until her cheeks were red and at last, she could take off her coat.

All the time she was thinking of Lorna Falstone, trying to understand her, feeling some sympathy. They had things in common, after all. Lorna had been a girl with a difficult man as a father too. Vera thought *her* mother would have been different from Lorna's: more sociable, livelier. While Jill Falstone was a farmer, Mary Stanhope had been a teacher in a village school, like Connie Browne. If she'd lived long enough, not been taken away by cancer, Mary might have painted watercolours in her spare time too. Hector had always said she was a brilliant artist. Hector had adored his wife and had disliked Vera because she was nothing like her mother, no possible sort of substitute. That, at least, was how it had seemed to Vera.

She allowed herself a moment of self-pity, while she thought how different her life would have been if her mother had lived. Because her mother would have loved her, wouldn't she? Unconditionally. She would have taken her into town and bought her the sort of clothes the other girls wore, had tea ready on the table when she got in from school, taken an interest. All the things that Hector had never managed to do. It occurred to her that with a mother like that, *she'd* have grown into a different woman. Softer, weaker. Not so good at her job. All the same, she thought, maybe that would have been a price worth paying.

In contrast to Vera, Lorna Falstone had had two parents who doted on her, at least according to Joe Ashworth, and he usually got families right. But wouldn't loving parents have noticed that she was miserable, that she was starving herself, apparently hoping to disappear? Vera thought they needed to speak to an expert, someone who would understand these things. What sort of man might be attracted to a young woman like Lorna? Someone compassionate, who wanted to rescue her? Or a bully who'd see she was easy to dominate?

Vera carried her tray back to the kitchen and left it on the wooden draining board. She made instant coffee and poured a small whisky, then went back to sit by the fire.

Since she'd got in, she'd been immersed in thoughts and memories of Brockburn past and present. That had been Hector's home and had shaped him. She knew he'd never got on with his elder brother, Sebastian, and that he'd turned his back on Crispin and Harriet, only visiting when he needed cash. He'd scarcely spoken of the family. Now, she thought, there was one person who'd know everything about her Brockburn relatives. It still wasn't late, only early evening, but she was too knackered to go out again. She reached for the phone and dialled.

Chapter Eleven

By late afternoon, all the guests had disappeared and Brockburn was quiet, but Juliet thought the place still didn't feel like home. Though Vera's people were no longer working in the main house, they were still outside, some searching the garden, others hovering over the body in the thin white tent, like raptors taking their fill of a dead lamb. Juliet had no idea how long they would stay. Soon it would be dark. The black crescent of the forest beyond the high stone wall was already shadowy and indistinct.

Dorothy had taken charge of the arrangements with the investigating team. She'd suggested that the officers could use an outhouse, an old workshop, as their base. It had a lavatory and small hand-basin, and power points for a kettle and for computers and phone chargers, though there was little reception for either. Dorothy had taken out old mugs, teabags, milk and sugar for them. The forensic boss with the grin and the cheeky smile had protested, said they could do a run to Kirkhill for supplies now the roads were clear, but Juliet thought Dorothy had been right to make them comfortable. Surely it was better to keep these people on side and make friends of them.

Dorothy had left the big house just over an hour ago; Karan and the baby had walked down to meet her.

'I hardly need a bodyguard.' Dorothy had nodded towards the figures in blue overalls moving slowly through the trees. 'Not with all these people about.' But she'd smiled and tucked her arm into her partner's, so when they'd moved down the track, they'd looked like one very large person, not a family of three. Watching, Juliet had felt the familiar stab of envy.

Now, she stood for a moment, feeling a little alone and without support, like one of the saplings they'd planted in the park, which needed a stake to hold it up. Mark said she was becoming reliant on Dorothy: 'I know she's brilliant and all that. In an old-school kind of way. But I'm not sure she'll have a role in the new regime. We'll need a different kind of staff then and we won't have the cash to employ everyone we want.'

Juliet hadn't replied to that. She still wasn't sure what Mark had against Dorothy, except that she'd been to school with Juliet, then off to Cambridge, and it made him insecure to have an employee who was better educated than he was. Or because Dorothy wasn't young or beautiful and she didn't shower him with compliments like the women with whom he worked. She was just thinking she might wander up to Dorothy and Karan's cottage, because it was always warm there, and she hadn't really had the chance to talk all this through, when her mother appeared. Juliet saw she'd reapplied her make-up, though there was nobody to see, nobody but the family to perform for.

'Darling.' Harriet spread her arms wide. 'Isn't this the most terrible mess?' There was a hint of reproach in her voice as if

Juliet and Mark had somehow been responsible for Lorna's dead body being found in their grounds.

'What do you want, Mother?'

The tone of her mother's voice had rankled and Harriet rarely ventured into the kitchen *unless* she wanted something. Certainly not to help stack the dishwasher or put laundry into the machine.

'Well, tea would be lovely,' Harriet said, 'and perhaps we could plan something a little more substantial than soup for dinner, but now we have the house almost to ourselves, I thought we should discuss what's happening and decide how we should deal with it. Some sort of meeting. Just the three of us. Where is Mark? I suppose he should be there while we have our little chat.'

Juliet didn't say that he'd gone to sleep off the results of last night's drinking. As soon as their friends had left, he'd dropped the bright and cheery act and collapsed. 'I'll find him. Why don't you put the kettle on, while you're waiting for us?' She walked up the stairs, surprised that she'd found the courage to suggest her mother should do such a menial chore.

Later, they gathered in the small drawing room, just the three of them. Dorothy had laid a fire in the grate before she'd left and Juliet put a match to it, but the place still felt damp and chill. She drew the curtains to shut out the gloom and the memories of Lorna, who as far as she knew was still lying outside. Harriet had surprised Juliet by making the tea and had carried it through; the tray was on a small occasional table. While they spoke, they sat with cups and saucers finely balanced on knees and chair arms, like actors in a pre-war farce.

'So, what has been going on?' Harriet had obviously decided to take the lead. She looked at her daughter and son-in-law, her eyes icy and her back straight. She looked almost excited. 'And what should we do about it?'

'I don't think there's much we can do about it.' Mark had been churlish since Juliet had gone to summon him. She suspected he still had the hangover. 'Except to let the police get on with things and hope that they find the killer quickly.'

A silence. Juliet thought she might be expected to fill it, but she was thinking, *just no. I'm too exhausted. And they never listen to me anyway. They'll fight it out between them and do want they want.* She finished her tea and reached out to put the cup and saucer back on the tray.

'I think, Mark, that whether we like it or not, we are involved.' Harriet was talking as if he was a backward child. He'd hate that. There was nothing he disliked more than being patronized. Juliet couldn't blame him. She wanted to tell him not to take it personally. Her mother spoke to everyone like that. Harriet continued speaking. 'The girl was found dead on our property, her parents are our tenants and we've known her since she was a girl.'

'Do the police know that you're the family's landlady?' It seemed that he was too curious to be aggrieved by her tone.

'You make me sound like the owner of a seaside guest house.' Harriet looked at him as if he was a worm. 'They're tenant farmers. Nearly all the people who farm in the valley are our tenants. Of course the police will know. Whatever I think of Vera Stanhope, she's a countrywoman. She understands how these things work.'

'So, you both knew the dead woman?' This time he looked at Juliet for an answer.

'I knew her a bit when she was younger. We were both mad about horses, so I saw her around. She was younger than me.'

'She was a nervy little thing,' Harriet said. 'She had an eating disorder when she was at school.' A pause. 'The GP didn't seem to be doing anything. She ended up in a specialist residential clinic.'

'You seem to know quite a lot about her.' Mark's surprise came across as manufactured. He took every chance he could to have a dig at Harriet. Juliet found the continual spats, the need to take sides, childish and exhausting.

'The family has always felt a certain obligation to the people who live on our land. Of course we take an interest.' This was Harriet at her most imperious; she brooked no argument. Which, Juliet thought, was just as well. She didn't want Mark poking around into their private lives either.

'You know there'll be press interest in the case,' Mark said. 'I'm surprised they haven't been here already. Perhaps the snow put them off, but according to the lunchtime forecast, it'll all be gone tomorrow. I think we should provide them with a statement.'

'They've been on the phone.' Juliet had fended off a couple of calls, then made sure they went straight to voicemail.

'Obviously, we'll be careful what we say to them.' Harriet turned to Mark. 'Why don't you draft a statement. I'm sure you're good at that kind of thing.' A pause. 'Of course, run it past us before you put it out.'

'I could do that.' He seemed almost pleased though Juliet knew that Harriet hadn't meant the comment as a compliment. She despised the press. 'We might be able to slip in something about the theatre project. It'd be great to get something into the nationals.'

Harriet shot Juliet a look that said, *couldn't you really do better than him?* But at least she managed to stay silent. 'So, we're agreed then. Of course, we're courteous to the police and answer their questions, but we don't volunteer unnecessary information, and, apart from supplying them with the statement which Mark will write, we'll have no communication with the press.'

Harriet stood up and left the room, leaving the tray and cups behind her. Juliet was left, as always, in awe of her mother's ability to get just what she wanted in every situation.

Mark looked up. 'Has she got something to hide?'

'You don't think she killed Lorna?' Juliet thought humour was the only response to this ridiculous situation. 'That she went out into the snow while we thought she was dressing up for the party and bashed the woman on the head?'

He smiled. He had an adorable smile and she remembered why she cared so much for him. 'I wouldn't put it past her. She's the most ruthless woman I know. And I've met a few in the theatre. All those divas.' He took Juliet's hand and pulled her down to sit on his lap. 'Are you okay? I realize I've not been much help.'

'I might go out,' she said. 'I feel as if I've been stuck in this house for days. Just to clear my head. I might wander up to Dorothy's.'

'Sure,' he said. 'If that's what you want.' But she heard the distance in his voice and knew she'd disappointed him again. He didn't offer to go with her, to make sure she was safe.

Outside there was the sound of melted snow dripping from the trees in the park, a tawny owl close by, and as she walked around the corner of the house the chug of the generator used by the crime-scene team to power the lights in the tent. It was already quite dark, but she could see perfectly. The police officers had shown them the route they should use, a path well away from the crime scene, but the lights were so fierce that they lit the track all the way to Dorothy's place.

The cottage was low, single storey, one of a pair. The other, larger house had been sold off by her father when the estate was short of cash and the tax man was getting heavy. Now it was a holiday home, owned by a businessman in the south, only used in the summer, but quiet and dark at this time of year. Dorothy's curtains were still open and Juliet looked inside and felt again a tug of jealousy. The baby, Duncan, must just have been in the bath. He was lying on a towel in front of the fire. Karan was drying him. Everything seemed so compact and simple. So manageable. Karan looked up and saw her. He smiled and waved her to come in.

There was a glass porch at the front of the house where they sat on summer evenings drinking tea or wine looking out over the valley. Juliet left her boots there and walked straight into the living room. Karan had scooped the baby into his arms. Through an open door to the back, Juliet saw Dorothy in the small kitchen.

'I'm sorry to intrude. I just needed to get away.'

'I don't blame you. What a nightmare it must be.' Dorothy was folding laundry.

Still working. Still doing what she's been doing for us all day.

'It would have been worse without you to take charge.'

Karan stood up, the boy in his arms. 'I'm taking this one to bed. I'll be back soon.'

In the kitchen, Dorothy reached into a cupboard and pulled out a bottle of wine. It would be better, Juliet knew, than any of the stuff she and Mark drank. Dorothy opened it deftly, poured a glass and took a moment to taste it before pouring one for Juliet. 'I see they're still there.'

'According to Vera, they hope to have taken the body away this evening.' Juliet paused. 'I guess things will get back to normal then.'

'I don't think they'll be anything like normal until the police find the killer.' Dorothy lifted the pile of laundry into a basket. 'We were here when she died. The snow was so thick it's unlikely anyone else could have got in. Of course, they'll be asking questions.'

Karan came in and heard the last comment. He poured himself a glass of wine. He was Glaswegian, of Indian heritage, calm, easy. He and Dorothy had met at university; he'd trained as an accountant to please his parents and had given it up to become a teacher. The plan was that he'd start training in the autumn. There were times when Juliet found herself comparing him with Mark, wishing she'd ended up with someone like him.

'But you didn't have anything to do with her,' Karan said. 'The idea's crazy! You didn't even know her.' He looked at them. 'Did you?'

'This is a small place,' Juliet said. 'We know everyone.'

Chapter Twelve

HOLLY JACKMAN WAS AT HOME IN her clean, white flat, with its view of the city graveyard, when Vera called. The boss had sent her away at lunchtime, soon after Holly had interviewed Mark Bolitho and Sophie Blackstock, and when the guests were allowed to leave Brockburn. 'Get on off. I doubt you got much sleep last night. I'll give you a shout if we need you.' And now, it seemed, Vera did need her.

'I hope you managed some kip this afternoon.'

'A little.' Holly wasn't sure what she was letting herself in for. She'd been for a run and then dozed for a while, but didn't pass on those details. With Vera, it was best to be cautious, to give nothing away.

'If you're up for it, I'd like you to go back to Brockburn. The roads are clear there now. I've not long got back. I don't need you at the big house, but it's been niggling me that nobody's really spoken to Dorothy Felling, the housekeeper. I don't know anything about her, except that she's a good cook and she's got a partner and a little boy. I'd rather someone talk

94

to her this evening. I couldn't quite work out how she ended up working there.'

Holly didn't answer immediately. She'd changed into pyjamas after the run and a shower, and there was nothing appealing about going out again.

'No worries if you don't fancy it.' Vera's voice was chirpy. 'I'll ask Joe. He's always glad of an excuse to escape the family.'

'No,' Holly said. 'I'll go.'

'Maybe phone first. It's a long way for a wasted journey.' And before Holly could answer Vera had replaced the receiver.

It was only an hour's drive from Newcastle but it could have been a world away. It was already dark when Holly left home – this close to the winter solstice there seemed to be hardly any daylight – and out of the city there were no street lamps. The old Roman road that led west was straight but hilly, a roller coaster of sudden stomach-dropping dips that left her feeling seasick. Occasional headlights appeared suddenly over the brows of the hills, blinding her. Snow was still piled on the verges, but the tarmac was clear. She followed her satnav to the address Dorothy Felling had given her, and she arrived at the cottage before realizing quite where she was, without any sight of the big house.

When she'd phoned Dorothy had said they'd be in, but sounded a little reluctant. 'If you really think it won't wait until tomorrow . . . Please don't ring the doorbell though. Our son will be asleep.'

Now Holly stood in the garden, tapping at the window. The

curtains seemed heavy, and there was no view inside. She hoped they would hear her and let her in.

The door was opened. All she could see was the silhouette of a man, backlit from the room beyond. He moved into a wide front porch where jackets had been hung and boots stood in a line, where split logs had been neatly stacked and two wooden chairs looked out to the garden. There must have been a sensor, because the porch light came on, making her blink.

'You must be the detective. Do come in.' A Scottish accent. He stepped aside and she saw he was dark, slender, movie-star good-looking.

The living room was small but tidy. Bookshelves had been built on each side of the chimney breast above low, white-painted cupboards. The shelves were packed but ordered, no stray copies piled on top of other books. Holly liked that. There was a small sofa and a large armchair facing the fire. No television. A wicker basket full of toys was tucked away in a corner, and next to that a box of board picture books. Dorothy sat on the sofa with a glass in her hand. The woman got to her feet. 'Come in. I'm sorry if I sounded grumpy on the phone. It's been quite a couple of days. I don't suppose you'd like a glass of wine?'

'I'd love one, but I've got to drive home.'

The man held out his hand. 'Karan Pabla. Do sit down. I could make some coffee?'

'Oh, yes,' Holly agreed, because she could tell it would be good coffee. 'That would be terrific.' She thought that if these weren't witnesses, she'd like them as friends; she suddenly felt strangely lonely.

She sat in the armchair, felt warmed by the fire, comfortable.

'I'm sorry to disturb you so late,' Holly said, when coffee

was made, biscuits offered. 'But the first few days of a murder investigation are so important.'

'And we do live close by . . .' Karan smiled.

'Well, yes. Dorothy, were you in the big house all day on Friday?'

'It was an important day for the family,' Dorothy said. 'Mark has this idea for saving the building, keeping it in the family, making it a focus for cultural tourism in the North-East. It was his chance to pitch it to their friends, influential people in the regional arts scene. Well, I suppose they were mostly his friends. His acquaintances. Juliet didn't know many of them. It was all a bit of a nightmare for her. Mark was hoping for enough sponsorship to allow him to make a big match-funding bid. We all wanted things to go well. When the weather closed in, we wondered about cancelling, but by then some people had already turned up, so we decided to go ahead.'

'You help them all out there?'

'She's the only person who keeps it together,' Karan said. 'It would fall apart without her.'

'Really? I hardly think so.' But Dorothy gave a little laugh and Holly could tell she was pleased.

'What brought you there?' Holly wasn't quite sure how to phrase the question. *What's an obviously intelligent, well-educated woman doing being a skivvy for a bunch of entitled people?*

'I'm Juliet's friend.' Dorothy seemed to understand what Holly wanted. 'We were at school together. I went on to Cambridge. Crispin, Juliet's dad, was already in failing health, so she came back here to help her mother on the estate as soon as she'd done A levels. She was never very interested in the academic thing anyway. But we kept in touch. After university, I started in law, got a place in chambers, all set to be a barrister, but I hated it. London and the work. Really, I'm much happier here in the country and I love bringing order out of domestic chaos. Karan wants to train to be a teacher, and we didn't have much money after he gave up his job in the city, so when Juliet offered us the cottage rent free, it all came together. Karan's been tutoring some of the local teen-agers. It's experience and a bit of extra income.'

Karan pulled a face. 'For my sins. At least it's made me realize I made the right choice when I plumped for primary teaching. No way could I do high school!'

Dorothy continued, as if he hadn't interrupted. 'This is a great place for Duncan, our son, to grow up. When he's older he'll have the run of the garden. Imagine the freedom . . . We'd like to buy this place later if the family agree. It would give them a bit of extra cash and be some security for us. We're saving frantically for a deposit.'

'What do Mark and Juliet say about that?'

'Juliet loves the idea,' Dorothy said. 'They could use the money. Mark's more ambivalent. He says they might need accommodation for visiting actors. I don't know where he expects us to move to, if that's what he's planning.' She frowned and for the first time since Holly had met her, the woman sounded a little rattled.

Karan reached out and touched his wife's arm. 'I'm sure the detective doesn't want to hear about our domestic prob-lems.'

'Of course.' Dorothy smiled. 'Sorry.'

'Did you know Lorna Falstone?' Holly directed her question to the woman.

'No, your boss already asked me that. I went to school in Newcastle with Juliet. I didn't grow up here. I came to stay for weekends but I don't remember meeting Lorna. She'd have been younger than me.'

'You never met her in Kirkhill?'

'I don't think I'd know her. Karan has been doing the house-husband thing until his teaching course starts in September. He's been taking Duncan to the toddler group and Rhythm and Rhyme in the library. He's more likely to have met her than me.' Dorothy looked at her partner. 'Did you ever come across them?'

'The little boy is called Thomas.' Holly looked at Karan.

He seemed to think for a moment before shaking his head. 'Sorry, that doesn't mean anything to me.' There was a quick grin. 'I find the toddler group pretty hard going actually. I'm the only bloke. I tend to take a paper, sit in a corner and read.'

Holly smiled. She wasn't quite sure she believed him. Wouldn't a charmer like him be the centre of attention among a group of bored women? Because Holly couldn't imagine that a woman with only a house and a child to occupy her would be anything *but* bored. Surely Karan wouldn't be allowed to sit apart, reading his paper, even if he were the retiring type? And besides, she sensed he'd enjoy the banter, would see nothing wrong in a little harmless flirtation. Here, though, with his wife listening, she didn't feel she could push him. 'If you could quickly take me through your movements yesterday, I can leave you in peace to enjoy the rest of your evening.'

'I was at the big house all day,' Dorothy said. 'I was there by seven in the morning to start prepping. It wasn't just the food, but most of the guests had been invited to stay over. Mark wanted to make it very special, a real country-house weekend. I'd made sure that the bedrooms were all clean the week before, but they needed the extra touches to make them welcoming. Juliet helped, of course, but we were all thrown when people started turning up early because of the weather.'

'You didn't come back here during the day? To see your son perhaps?' Holly knew this might be important. Lorna's body had been found not far from the track between the big house and the cottages.

Dorothy shook her head. 'Really, I didn't have a minute to breathe. I phoned here early evening, about six, to say hello to Duncan before he went into the bath, just so he wouldn't forget who I was, but apart from that it was head down all day.'

'Like I said,' Karan broke in, 'they couldn't run that place without her. Sometimes, I think they take advantage.'

'Juliet's a friend,' Dorothy said, 'and I love it.'

'You didn't hear anything unusual?' Holly was still talking to Dorothy. 'It would have been early evening, after the snow had settled.'

'It was manic there. Guests arriving every ten minutes, needing tea, to be shown their rooms. I'm not sure I'd have heard a rocket being launched from the front lawn.'

'And did they all arrive at the front of the house?' Holly asked. 'Nobody came down the back track where Lorna's body was discovered?'

'Oh, no! Mark was very definite about that. He'd staged the whole thing as if it was a piece of film. He wanted their first view of the house to be grand, beautiful – the big cedar on the lawn with the lights, the steps lit from below. There were directions on all the invitations to make sure the guests came to the right entrance.'

Holly nodded and turned her attention to the man. 'And you, Mr Pabla, how did you spend your day?'

'Duncan and I went into Kirkhill to do some shopping in the morning. I wanted to go early because the forecast was bad for the afternoon. We just did a quick trip to the Co-op to stock up on essentials. Duncan was well wrapped up in the pushchair, but it was already freezing. When we came back, he went down for his nap and I split some logs. We get given logs from the estate, but they're whole, too big for the woodburner. Besides, I quite enjoy it. It's exercise and it keeps me fit. By mid-afternoon the weather had really closed in and we stayed indoors. Duncan played and I read – I'm catching up on stuff for the teaching qualification. It's pretty intensive once you start.'

'Did you see anyone in Kirkhill? Anyone you knew?'

'Lots of people to wave to in the shop. Everyone uses it, so it's a kind of social hub. I'm pretty distinctive. The only person of colour in the village.' He seemed easy, slightly amused to stick out.

'Anyone specific?'

'I had quite a chat with Connie Browne. She's a retired primary headteacher and she's been giving me some advice on possible voluntary placements before I start the course.'

Holly said nothing. She recognized the name. Miss Browne was Lorna Falstone's neighbour, the owner of the car which had ended up in the ditch. Was it plausible that Karan Pabla could be so close to the retired teacher, but know nothing of Lorna? Especially if everyone used the same shop? It seemed unlikely.

'Did you hear anything in the late afternoon or early evening? A vehicle driving down the back track? It is very quiet here. Surely you *would* hear.'

Karan thought for a moment, then shook his head. 'I'm

sorry. It's very quiet now, but it's not when Duncan has all his toys out. I didn't notice a thing.'

Holly got to her feet. She had a suspicion that she was being played, that these people were too pleasant, too charming. She imagined secrets cleverly hidden, stories still to be told. Then she told herself she spent too much time with rude, aggressive and ignorant people, and that she'd lost any sense of perspective. She was standing just inside the door, when something else occurred to her, the sort of question that Vera would have asked.

'Juliet and Mark. Are they happy?'

The couple seemed surprised, almost shocked, and there was a moment of silence. In the end, it was Dorothy who answered. 'They come from very different worlds,' she said. 'Mark's a city boy. It must be hard for him here. I struggled at first too with the whole feudal, lord-of-the-manor thing. It seems so outdated; that sense of history must weigh the family down. I think the theatre project will help. It'll give him his own identity – he won't just be Juliet's husband and Harriet's son-in-law.'

'What did Harriet make of the match?'

A pause. A little smile. 'I don't think Mark would have been her first choice. She'd have preferred someone with a similar background, someone who understood the responsibilities. A member of the Northumberland landed classes. Mark didn't even have any money. But at least he was willing to move to Brockburn to make it his main home. If Juliet can give her a grandchild to inherit the estate, I think Harriet will tolerate Mark as a son-in-law.'

'I think they're happy,' Karan said. 'Not as happy as we are, obviously. We're ridiculously in love still. Horribly soppy. But I think they'll make a go of it.'

He put his arm round Dorothy's shoulder and she looked up at him and smiled. Holly felt as if she were intruding on a moment of intimacy and again there was a flash of envy. What must it be like to have a relationship like this? She couldn't imagine it ever happening for her; she wasn't sure she'd have the confidence to let anyone get that close. Perhaps she'd end up like Vera, wedded to the job.

The thought still haunted her as she drove home down the straight, empty roads.

Chapter Thirteen

It was Sunday morning, still dark, and the roads were quiet. On the outskirts of Kimmerston, a couple of elderly women were going to the early service in the Catholic church on the edge of town, huddled into coats, heads down to face the raw weather. Vera got to the station before the rest of the team and put the kettle on. She was still thinking of the phone conversation she'd had the night before.

She'd called a former colleague, a man who'd been based in the police station in Kirkhill when there were still village bobbies. Ernie Moorland had lived in the police house and knew everyone in the village and the surrounds. He'd been a passionate conservationist, a ringer of birds and surveyor of the uplands' natural history, for a while the county's police wildlife liaison officer, dealing with all things rural from poaching to badger baiting. His particular interest had been animal welfare and the theft of raptors from the wild. So, Hector's natural enemy. Vera had gone to him for advice when she contemplated joining the police force and he'd encouraged her, more, she'd realized even then, to annoy Hector than because he thought she'd be any good. He'd retired years ago, but she bumped into him occasionally in Kirkhill. He was in his late eighties now, but still a force of nature.

'You'll have heard about the murder at Brockburn, Ernie?'

'Aye.' Ernie had never been one for wasted words.

'What can you tell me about the lass?'

'Not a lot. I don't have much contact with the youngsters. Not these days.'

'Anything you can tell me about the Stanhopes then? I haven't had much to do with my relatives recently.' *Not that I ever did, much.*

'You know I never thought much of that family.'

Ernie would never have thought much of any major landowner. If he'd been born a bit earlier, he'd have been one of the ramblers marching on a mass trespass to get rights of access to the uplands.

'I need details, pet.' Vera had started losing patience at that point. 'I didn't get any sleep last night and I'm ready for my bed.'

'Crispin Stanhope was a randy goat. He thought it was part of his laird's privilege to have sex with his workers.'

'Eh, man, that was years past. When did he die? I read it in the *Journal*. Three years ago? And he'd have been ill before that. Have you nothing more recent to tell me?'

A pause. 'I've heard word that the new man in the house treats his wife with the same lack of respect as his father-in-law did Harriet.'

'You're saying that Mark Bolitho has affairs? With the tenants?'

'Well, maybe not so close to home. But I understand he's a bit of a lad. He's been seen in the city with another woman.'

'With Lorna Falstone?' Her imagination had been running wild at that point.

'Nobody's put a name to the lass,' Ernie had said. 'You know that the dead woman had a kid, though.' At that point, he'd said he needed to be away to his bed too.

Now, in the police station, Vera looked down at the street and replayed the conversation in her head again. She thought there'd been little substance in it. They needed more than gossip and rumours.

There'd been rain overnight and it had cleared the remaining snow. She carried her tea into her little office and wondered how she'd explain the set-up at Brockburn to her colleagues. Even the ones who'd grown up in the country would find it difficult to understand the place of the big house in a community like Kirkhill. They'd be thinking it was all about money and class, *Downton Abbey* for the modern world: servants downstairs slaving for the rich above them. The rumours about Crispin Stanhope and Mark Bolitho's adultery would feed into the myth.

Vera understood life in the country was a bit more nuanced these days than the plots of a costume drama, but she suspected the Stanhopes would still be pulling the strings. They owned the land the tenants farmed and the houses where they lived. People depended on them for their homes and their work, so life for employees could be precarious. The landed classes had the confidence that went with generations of living in the same place, knowing every inch. But still, there were obligations and responsibilities. Ownership would bring stress. She was glad that Hector had offended them all and been cast out, and she had no part of any of that.

People started to drift into the operations room. Holly arrived first, although she had furthest to come, then Joe, then Charlie; this was Vera's core group, the people she relied on. Soon the room was full.

Vera took centre stage in front of them, stood for a moment looking out, waiting for the chatter to die down so that she had their full attention.

'Our victim is Lorna Falstone. Rather a sad young woman, at least when she was growing up. She had an eating disorder and a long spell in a psychiatric hospital. I've checked that out. It was a private clinic in Cumbria called Halstead House. No information about how her family afforded it, but it'd be good to find out who paid the bills. Maybe her family got themselves into debt to do the right thing by her, but they're tenant farmers and there's not a lot of cash in sheep these days.' Vera paused for breath and again she wondered how many of the team would understand the context. Most of them had come into the region from outside. Joe was brought up in Northumberland, but in a former pit village in the south-east of the county. There, the chapel and the union had shaped his life. He wouldn't understand how tough farming was at the moment. Charlie had been born in the West End of Newcastle and probably hadn't seen a sheep until he was an adult. For him, lamb came from the Indian takeaway in a korma.

Holly took advantage of Vera's pause to stick up her hand and speak. 'A couple of the party guests had links with the hospital. Sophie and Paul Blackstock. Sophie ran drama work-shops for the patients – some sort of therapy – and Paul's brother Nat was a patient. He died several months later.'

Vera nodded. Holly had passed on the information the day before, excited by the connection. Vera couldn't quite see that it was important after all this time, but of course it had to be followed up. 'They live in Tynemouth. Joe, can you go this afternoon? See if they have any more information about Lorna and if they've seen her since.'

Joe nodded. Holly seemed put out. She'd feel more at home in the smart coastal village of Tynemouth than in the Northumberland hills.

'What about the other two couples who were overnight guests? Any links to the murdered lass?'

'None that they're admitting to,' Joe said, 'and I can't see that they could have killed her. They were with the others the whole evening, apart for a few minutes to use the bathroom. Sophie and Paul Blackstock took themselves off for longer just before dinner – they've got a new bairn and they wanted to talk to the babysitter. Juliet let them use the phone extension in her bedroom, because they had no mobile signal in the house, but it would have been a stretch to go outside, kill Lorna and then come back. It's not as if they'd been dressed for it.'

Vera thought about that. 'We'll be checking the Brockburn phone records anyway. Let's just make sure that's what they were up to when they disappeared from the rest of the group.'

She looked back at the faces turned towards her and continued. 'There've been rumours that the husband of Harriet and father of Juliet, Crispin Stanhope, who died a few years ago, had a number of affairs in the village. It seems possible that Mark Bolitho has been continuing the tradition. It would be interesting to know if Lorna Falstone was one of Mr Bolitho's conquests. Let's make some discreet enquiries. No need to wreck a marriage unless we're forced to.' Another pause to check she still had their attention before she went on.

'Lorna was a single mum. Her little boy Thomas was

strapped into his car seat, but the vehicle had skidded off the road. It belonged to retired headmistress Constance Browne and had been taken without her knowledge. Not stolen. She wanted us to know that. They had an arrangement and Lorna was allowed to borrow the car when she needed it. The father of the little boy remains a mystery. We need to track down a name. The registrar won't be working today, but first thing tomorrow, let's see if there's anything on the baby's birth certificate, any clue that might give us a link to Bolitho.'

Once more, Vera paused. 'The body was found in the grounds of Brockburn, a big house belonging to a family called Stanhope.' There were a few giggles. 'And yes, they are relatives, but only distant and I haven't seen them for years so I don't see any conflict of interest.' Another pause. 'Anyone got any problem with that?'

No response.

'Joe here's been to see Lorna's parents. What did you make of them?' She thought they'd all be sick of her voice by now and it was time someone else did some speaking.

He stood up. One time he'd have been a bit nervous giving any kind of opinion, but he'd gained in confidence. Vera thought that was down to her. She'd trained him well.

'I thought the father seemed cold, a bit distant,' Joe said. 'I was there with the social worker, when she was handing over their grandson. Their daughter had just died and this little scrap was all that was left of her. But Robert just took himself off when we arrived. Maybe it was just too much for him and he wouldn't want strangers to see him emotional.'

Vera ignored that. 'And the mother?'

'There was a lot of guilt there. Like you said, Lorna had an eating disorder and they hadn't done anything about it until it was almost too late. The mother, Jill, had kept in touch with Lorna but always felt the need to handle her carefully. No prying questions. They didn't speak for a while and Jill was worried about losing her again.'

'So, Lorna's mother had no idea who the child's father might be?' Vera tried to imagine again why the dead young woman might have been so keen to keep the man's identity to herself. Could it just be that she needed secrets to feel in control of her life once she'd started eating again? She looked out at the room. 'So that's the first priority. We have to find the man and at the moment Bolitho is prime suspect as lover or father.' She paused for a moment before shaking her head. 'I'm not sure I see him as capable of it, though. This looks like rage. She was hit over the head where she was found, according to Keating. I think she must have been chased from the car. I can't see her leaving the child on its own with the door open otherwise. And, anyway, could Bolitho have left the big house, battered the lass to death, and then gone back to the party? Even if he'd managed not to get blood on his clothing, he'd surely not have been in the mood to have intellectual conversation over dinner.'

Vera tried to put herself in the dead woman's head and wondered if the car had been shunted from the road. Though she hadn't *seen* any damage, she hadn't looked closely. That could explain some details of the scenario. Perhaps Lorna had got out and run, heading for the nearest house. She must have been terrified if she hadn't even stopped to shut the door.

Surely that meant she'd known the person who had chased her, been scared from the beginning, because a simple bump in the snow wouldn't provoke that kind of flight. You'd just talk, wouldn't you? Exchange phone numbers and insurance details?

Vera imagined the effort, the exhaustion and the panic as the slight young woman had run up the hill, seen the lights of the big house and headed towards it. But the shortest route would have been via the track to the back of the house, where she'd been found, and that would have taken her past Dorothy and Karan's cottage. Why hadn't she stopped there? Karan had claimed to be in all evening and there'd have been lights on, so why hadn't she banged on the door, demanding sanctuary?

Vera was aware that the people in the room were staring at her. She must seem like a gaga old woman, standing there, lost in thought. Frozen. But she needed to go over these details again in her head. This was important.

Vera shook her head once more to clear her mind of the dark night, the panic, the ice, and turned back to the room. 'Holly, you chatted to Juliet's husband Mark Bolitho. What can you tell us? Do you think he's capable of murdering a young woman?'

Holly stood up. The young detective was a mystery to Vera: always so cool, so immaculately dressed. Her private life never spoken of. If she had any kind of private life.

'Bolitho grew up in Newcastle, went to university in Durham and came home to do an MA in theatre at Northumbria. He wrote and directed an independent film that did very well here and in the US, and he ended up as Creative Director at the Live, down on the quayside in Newcastle. He and Juliet married three years ago. He still works at the Live and spends a couple of days a week in the city. He's kept a small flat there.' Holly paused.

Vera thought this was all very well but she could have Googled the information herself. 'Go on, Hol.'

'His big plan is to bring theatre to Brockburn. He talks about the importance of arts for rural areas, but admits that his main motivation is to provide an income to maintain the big house. The party on Friday night was a way of tapping his arty and business friends for donations.' Another pause. 'He says that he'd never met Lorna Falstone.' She looked up at them. 'Really, I believed him. He might live in Brockburn, but I had the sense that all his work and his friends are still in the city.'

'*Could* he have killed Lorna?'

'It depends on time of death, but, like you, I really don't think so. Guests started arriving mid-afternoon because of the weather and they were mostly people that he knew, so he did all the meet-and-greet and schmoozing. He could have slipped away, but it seems very unlikely.'

Vera took a moment to consider this. 'Bolitho might not be the killer, but he still might be the father of Lorna's child. We need to confirm that either way to save ourselves a wild-goose chase after the other men she knew.' A pause. 'You spoke to Dorothy and her partner last night, Hol. What did you make of them?'

'I thought they were lovely,' Holly said. Vera was surprised by the warmth in her voice; Holly was usually such a cold fish. 'They seem like a happy couple who've made the decision that they want a simpler life. So, a few months ago, she gave up her career in the law and he stopped being an accountant and they came to live in the country with their son. Juliet was an old schoolfriend and she gave Dorothy the cottage. A tied cottage that goes with the job of housekeeper. The couple are hoping to buy it eventually if the family will agree. They definitely see their long-term future there. Karan is going to start a post-graduate teaching course in September. He's become friendly with Connie Browne.'

'That's the woman who owned the car.' The names were all up on the whiteboard, but Vera wanted to make sure the whole team understood. 'Perhaps that's just a coincidence though. A community like that, everyone knows each other. It's not on the tourist route, too far from Hadrian's Wall, the coast or the Pennine Way to attract visitors.' *And that's just as I like it.*

'It did seem odd then,' Holly went on, 'that neither Dorothy nor Karan admitted to knowing Lorna. You'd have thought they'd at least have heard of her.'

'You think they're hiding something?'

Holly shrugged. 'Maybe. Or perhaps I was just getting a bit hypersensitive.'

'Eh, pet,' Vera smiled, 'that's just what we need at the start of a case like this.' A pause. 'Did either of them see or hear anything on Friday?'

'They claim not. Karan Pabla was in all day after a quick trip to the shops in the morning.'

And the man on his own in the cottage with the bairn surely would have heard a young woman, banging on the door screaming in panic. Vera still couldn't understand how the woman wouldn't have stopped at the first house she came to. Did that mean she wasn't being chased? That she was heading to the big house because she knew the family and was attacked in the grounds just as she was getting there? It was possible that Vera was making too much of the open car door. It was too soon to get hung up on the details.

'Actions for today. Joe, after you've spoken to the Blackstocks, I'd like you to check out the clinic where Lorna was treated for the eating disorder. They might have a record of the people who visited her and I want to understand more about it. I always thought it was tricky for sufferers of anorexia to get pregnant, but I don't want to rely on guesswork and myth. Holly and Charlie, let's have you back in Kirkhill, canvassing the neighbours. Sunday lunchtime, there'll be a few old boys in the pub having a pint before their Sunday lunch. That'll be for you, Charlie. Get them chatting. We want all the gossip about the Falstones.'

Vera looked around her. 'The rest of you, the important things. Facts. Chase up the technicians who are working on the car. There won't be CCTV on the roads around Brockburn but there might be in Kirkhill, and there are speed cameras on the road out of the village. There's a chance they might have picked up the car Lorna was driving. And I want to know where Lorna was on the day before she died. She went somewhere on her own on the Thursday morning because she asked Connie to babysit. It was a last-minute thing so it might have been urgent. A GP's appointment? A meeting with the baby's dad that might have triggered the events of the following day?'

'What about you?' Holly. Cheeky mare. She added too late, 'Boss. Where will you be?'

'Me?' Vera gave her one of her special smiles. 'I'll be back at my ancestral home.'

Chapter Fourteen

VERA WANTED TO RETRACE HER JOURNEY of Friday night in the light. The weather was grey and gloomy and there were sharp bursts of hail that rattled on the windscreen of the Land Rover like the spatter of shotgun pellets, but at least she could see where she was going. She parked close to where Connie's car had been. The lay-by where it had ended up was no more than an entrance to a field gate, muddy and pocked with puddles. Shards of ice still floated on the water and blades of discoloured grass poked through the patches of snow.

She'd realized quite clearly driving here where she'd taken the wrong road in the blizzard. There were two right turns very close to each other and she'd missed the first, the road not taken, which would have led her home. On the opposite side of the road to the gate, the forest came almost to the side of the road, the trees thick and tall, but here, where the car had been, there was open farmland, surrounded by a drystone wall. Vera thought now that car might have ended up there by design rather than accident. She had assumed it had skidded off the road, but it was impossible to tell if that was the case.

She climbed out of the Land Rover and stood for a moment, looking across the field to the valley. There was a view to the big house. Brockburn was looking very grand at this distance with its pillars, its symmetry and its extensive parkland. It was too far away to see the crumbling stone and peeling paint. In a blizzard, Vera suspected, even the lights would be hardly visible; she'd seen something there, but had thought it marked the edge of Kirkhill village. Lorna must have known where she was going. It would surely be too much of a coincidence for both of them to have taken the wrong road and ended up in the same place. Vera left her Land Rover where it was and started to walk.

On the Friday evening she'd driven up the hill until she came to the crossroads with the signpost to Kirkhill. That road had taken her in a wide semicircle to the main entrance of the big house. She saw now that only a couple of hundred yards from the parked Land Rover was the track that led to the back entrance to Brockburn. It was very narrow and hidden by a spinney of bare deciduous trees, in the upper branches an old rookery: large, untidy nests spilling twigs. Two cottages were tucked behind the spinney; in one of these lived Dorothy Felling and Karan Pabla. Vera stood at the junction. In the dark and a blizzard, she would have missed it. She felt a moment of guilt.

If I'd been more careful, I would have seen the turning. I might have caught up with the lass before she was killed. Instead, I was intent on getting warm and out of the weather. When a young woman was being attacked, I might have been chatting to Juliet and drinking tea.

Vera turned down the track, which was sunk between two steep banks. It was more sheltered here, the wind broken by the trees. The ground beside the lane flattened and she reached the cottages, which were low, single storey, stone, with small front gardens and a longer strip at the back leading on to a field full of sheep, the only boundary a rickety wire-mesh fence held up by wooden posts. Vera wondered who farmed this land. Not the Falstones. They were on the other side of the valley. Perhaps the tenant was Neil Heslop, the father of the lasses who'd helped out at the dinner on the Friday night. The first cottage was blank, dead-eyed, the windows misted. This must be the holiday home. In the back garden of the attached cottage, she saw a small child's swing, a hen run, evidence of gardening: some frosted sprout stalks and leeks gone to seed. No sign of life inside though and no car parked outside. In a place like this you would need a car. She stopped by the small gate and listened for a child, music, voices, but everything was quiet.

Vera hesitated outside for a moment, tempted to go in and snoop. Somewhere like this, they'd likely not be too bothered about security and the door might be open. She was driven by curiosity, not by any sense that the couple might be guilty of Lorna's murder. Holly might have suspected that they had secrets, but the constable's description of them didn't suggest hidden rage or a need for revenge, and the attack on Lorna had been brutal and violent. They were outsiders and this felt like an insider's crime.

In the end Vera heard Joe Ashworth's disapproving voice in her head warning her against intruding – he'd never been a rule-breaker – and she walked on. She was pleased that she'd listened to his unspoken advice, because just as she passed the cottage there was the sound of an engine coming towards her and a quad bike with a collie perched next to the driver emerged round a bend in the track. It would have been embarrassing to be caught breaking into a witness's home. The driver was slight, but wrapped in a heavy jacket on top of blue padded overalls, a knitted hat pulled low over the face. It was only when the quad pulled to a stop that Vera recognized one of the young women who'd acted as waitresses at the dinner on the night Lorna was killed.

'Can you switch that thing off for a moment?' Vera was yelling over the engine sound and the collie was barking.

There was sudden silence apart from rooks in the distance.

'I'm Vera Stanhope, investigating Lorna's murder.'

The girl nodded. 'Nettie Heslop.'

'Aye, I met you at the big house Friday night. Are you the younger or the older daughter?' Vera thought they'd looked similar and it'd been hard to age them. She didn't bump into teenage lasses often enough to tell, only ones dressed up to the nines on a Saturday night in the Bigg Market in Newcastle and they all tried to look older than they were.

'The oldest. Cath will be seventeen next week. I'm eighteen.'

'You're both at the high school in Kimmerston?'

Another nod. A quirky little smile. 'A levels this year for me.'

'You'll both have known Lorna Falstone then. You'll have been at school together.'

'She's five years older than me. I didn't really know her.' A pause. 'We hung round with a different crowd. You know.'

'All the same, you'd have gone into Kimmerston on the same bus every day. You'd have seen her around.' Vera was wondering if it was possible for a young lass to be as isolated as Lorna had seemed, in a place where everyone was aware of everyone else's business. *If I was that way inclined, I'd imagine some sort of conspiracy of silence.* 'Both from farming families in the valley, I'd have thought you'd have some things in common.'

'No,' Nettie said. 'Not really. Our parents weren't friends or anything. Mam and Dad like a bit of a laugh – Dad plays fiddle and there are always folk in the house. The Falstones aren't ones for socializing.'

'You heard she'd had a baby? The bairn I took into the kitchen on Friday night. You didn't recognize him?'

A shake of the head. 'Like I said, we didn't mix with them much.' Another small smile. 'Besides, we were rushed off our feet that night. I didn't take much notice.'

Too much information? Too many excuses?

'There must have been gossip, rumours about who the father was. You'd have heard folk talking.'

This time there was a pause. 'A place like this there's always gossip. I try not to listen.'

Vera thought this was harder work than getting info from some of the tough lads they picked up peddling drugs on the coast. She scrabbled in her bag for a card, but couldn't find one. 'Look, if you think of anything that might help, give me a ring. Kimmerston police station. They'll put you through to me if you say who you are and ask.'

'Okay.'

There was an awkward silence when they stared at each other, Nettie thinking there might be more questions, Vera not able to come up with anything further. In the end she gave a little wave of her hand. 'Off you go then. I don't want to keep you.'

The engine roared into life again and the quad bike bumped away down the track. Vera watched it go. She contemplated going back to the Land Rover and driving the long way around to the house. There'd be coffee there and perhaps a bit of flapjack left at the bottom of the tin. Besides, she'd never seen the attraction of walking for its own sake. But this time curiosity *did* get the better of her. Where had Nettie Heslop come from? Was there some sort of shortcut from Home Farm to the track that led to the cottages and the road? Presumably her father farmed this land. Vera suspected that Nettie might have been curious too, and had wanted a neb at the spot where her father had found Lorna Falstone's body. The CSIs were still working the crime scene and the young had a taste for the ghoulish. It didn't hold any fear for them, because they thought that death was so far away.

Vera walked on down the track, which, away from the cottages, became even more potholed and rough, bordered on one side now by a high stone wall, marking the boundary of the walled vegetable garden. Vera had a brief memory of being brought here by Harriet to pick soft fruit on one of the summer visits. She'd been very young then, so it hadn't been that last visit, the one that had burst into her mind when she'd approached Brockburn on Friday night. She'd been a small, plump, sullen child, led away, no doubt, so Hector and Crispin could shout at each other without an audience. The men had always disliked each other, and Vera suspected both had enjoyed an argument.

At the end of the wall, Brockburn came into view. The track forked. One path, just wide enough for a quad bike, led west into the forest. Vera watched it twist away into the distance, tantalizing and mysterious. She couldn't imagine where it might lead, but certainly not to farmland. Nettie Heslop must have been checking the sheep in the field behind the cottages. The other led towards the house. From this angle it could have been the back of any shabby country-house hotel: bins full of bottles waiting for the recycling lorry, an outhouse that had obviously been turned into a laundry because, even from here, she could hear the churring of a tumble dryer. Vera could understand why Mark had wanted his party guests to use the grand front drive.

The search team and CSIs had been using another outbuilding as a base. Inside, Vera could see boots on a rack and overalls hanging on pegs. A few officers sat round a trestle, drinking tea. Billy Cartwright was outside on the lawn, inside the tent, though Lorna's body had been removed. The area was still cordoned off and only the track and the concrete yard by the kitchen door were free for use. The post-mortem would take place the following morning; Paul Keating, the pathologist, was a religious Ulsterman who preferred not to work on the Lord's Day. There was no rush, Vera thought. The cause of death had been obvious from the start. Billy emerged from the tent and she waved for him to join her.

'Anything?'

He shrugged. 'I'm not sure you really want to know.'

'H'away, Billy man, I'm no shrinking violet. I'll not faint at the sight of blood.'

'As the snow melted, we were able to collect brain tissue, pieces of bone. She might have looked peaceful lying in the snow, but it was a brutal attack.' He looked up. 'One of the worst I've seen. At least it would have been quick.'

She wasn't sure how to reply. Billy was the least squeamish man she knew, given to black humour and tasteless jokes. Either he was developing some respect in his old age or this had been a horrific assault. 'Murder weapon?'

'Nothing yet. We're still looking.' He nodded towards the

blue-suited team, who'd moved away from the immediate area of the locus. 'Doc Keating thinks something smooth. A mallet? Even a heavy rock.'

'So she was definitely killed here?'

He stretched. She thought he looked exhausted. Maybe he was just feeling his age. 'Killed yes, but Doc Keating found a bruise on the other side of her head too. He thought it possible she was knocked out, stunned at least, elsewhere and carried here to be killed. He'll know more after the post-mortem.' He paused. 'Even if she was battered by something to hand, this was planned, Vera.'

'Why would anyone move her? It'd be tough going to carry her such a distance in that weather. Were they trying to make a point? Linking her death to the big house to implicate the folk there?' Vera shook her head. 'It makes no sense.'

'It makes no sense to kill a young mother.'

She nodded her agreement. There was another sharp shower of sleet but the team worked on. 'You deserve a medal,' she said. 'The lot of you.'

'Dorothy's looking after us very well,' he said. 'It could be worse.'

Again, Vera wondered at the change in him. Usually he was full of complaint, sardonic and only half-joking. 'She's in there today?' She was surprised. For the last couple of days Dorothy had been working flat out. Surely she deserved a day off. When she'd found the cottage empty, Vera had imagined the family had escaped for a while.

'Aye, she was already in the kitchen at first light when we arrived. She had tea and bacon stotties organized in minutes. A wonderful woman.' For a moment, Billy sounded like his old self. He gave a little wave and moved back to his work.

Again, Vera paused, wondering whether she should return to the Land Rover or go on. She wanted to be surer of her facts before she confronted Mark with rumours that he had another woman, and now she was here, so close to the big house, she couldn't face Harriet and Juliet, the politeness, the stabbing, elegant words that said so little. She'd done what she wanted and had a clearer sense of the geography. She was sure that Lorna had taken the track past the cottages towards the big house. Besides, Vera thought, her role was back at the station, monitoring the investigation as it developed. Here, there was scarcely even any mobile signal. She was effectively out of touch. She'd made up her mind to return to the Land Rover when Dorothy came out through the kitchen door, carrying a laundry basket full of bedding on her hip.

'Hello! I'm afraid the family is out. Harriet insisted on church in the village and then they've been invited to friends for lunch.' A pause. 'As I'm sure you can imagine they're very popular at the moment. Everyone's desperate for news.'

'Ah, well, I'll head back then. I've left my vehicle on the road.'

'There's coffee made if you fancy some. I'll just stick this in the machine.'

So, Vera found herself back in the Brockburn kitchen, drinking good coffee and eating home-made shortbread, not part of the family, but a hired help, brought in to clear up the mess. Because that was surely what Harriet wanted: for the drama to be over and the killer to be a stranger.

Dorothy poured coffee and sat at the table with her.

'Did you ever meet Juliet's father, Crispin?' Vera had only seen the man fleetingly, had an image of a straight back walking away from her, a spaniel at his heels. He'd been Hector's nephew, but not very much younger than her father. Hector must have been an afterthought. Or a mistake.

'Oh, yes, he was still alive when Juliet and I were at school together.'

'What did you make of him?'

'He was very much the gentleman, courteous and pleasant. My parents were professional people, both lawyers. Very successful in their field, wealthy, but really, city people. This world of shooting parties and country sports seemed very alien and old-fashioned to me. It was like walking into the pages of *Brideshead Revisited*.'

Vera took another slice of shortbread without quite realizing what she was doing. 'I'd heard rumours that Crispin was a bit of a ladies' man. Did he ever try it on with you?'

Dorothy threw back her head and laughed. 'No! But then he wouldn't. I was a gawky schoolgirl, all feet and teeth. I can see how women would have found him attractive, though. He had a way of making one feel special.'

Vera was trying to frame a tactful question about Mark, but the woman was already on her feet. 'Do you want to wait for them? They might be a while.'

Vera shook her head. 'No, but I'll be back. I'll keep coming back until all this is over.'

Chapter Fifteen

JOE HAD PHONED THE BLACKSTOCKS IN advance and they were waiting for him. They lived just off Front Street, in a large 1930s corner semi, with stained glass in the porch and mellow red brick. An estate agent would have described it as having 'original features'. Meaning a tiled fireplace and Bakelite door handles. Joe suspected that there'd be a shiny kitchen and central heating and they'd definitely have been more recently installed. As soon as he got out of his car, Joe saw Sophie standing in the bay window, a baby in her arms. When he rang the bell, she didn't move, and a dark-haired man he'd seen at Brockburn on the night of the murder answered.

'You're the detective.'

'Joe Ashworth.' He held out his hand.

'I don't know what this is about.' Blackstock was thickset. The accent was local. 'We've already given our statements.'

'You both knew the murdered woman,' Joe said mildly. 'You might be able to help. We didn't want to keep you at Brockburn when you had a baby to come back to. It seemed kinder to speak to you at home.'

'That *was* very kind.' Sophie had moved into the hall to stand behind her husband. 'Come on through. We can talk in the kitchen and I'll make some coffee.'

Holly had described her as anxious and tense, but here in her own home, she seemed relaxed, in charge of the situation. It was the husband who was reluctant, almost truculent. The kitchen had been extended. At one end of the room there was a long dining table and chairs and the men sat there. It felt very formal, as if they were at a meeting for work. Sophie put the baby into a wicker crib and set off an elaborate coffee machine. Joe would have preferred tea, but didn't say so. The kitchen looked like something people would drool over in a women's magazine. There was no shortage of money here.

'You both met Lorna at Halstead House, the hospital where she was being treated for an eating disorder?'

'I didn't know her, though,' Paul Blackstock said quickly. 'I mean, not really. Not to talk to. I was there to visit my brother.'

'Did he speak about Lorna?'

'Sometimes,' Sophie said. 'They seemed friendly. In a situation like that, people get close very quickly. All the relationships are intense.'

'Was it a romantic relationship?'

'No!' This time Paul answered. 'No, I don't think so. They were friends. Close friends.'

'Did they keep in touch with each other when they left hospital?'

This time there was no immediate answer. 'I don't know,' Paul said at last. 'Nat had been allowed home. I thought that was it – he was cured. I didn't understand the illness properly. I'd moved on. I'd taken over the family business – we run a haulage company – and I'd started seeing Sophie. All the time

Nat was in hospital it was as if my life was on hold, ruled by him, the visits, the worry. Then he came home to live with my parents again and I thought everything could go back to normal. It was selfish. I let him down. I didn't want to see that he was as thin as ever. I thought Mum and Dad were on top of it.'

'I'm sorry,' Joe said.

'Lorna came to Nat's funeral.' Sophie looked up from the counter where she was setting out cups.

'Did she?' Paul seemed surprised.

'I wasn't part of the family then.' She brought coffee to the table, with a plate of mince pies. 'I was sitting at the back. Lorna came and sat beside me.'

'Did you talk?' Joe asked.

'No, she slipped off straight after the service.'

There was a moment of silence before Joe asked, 'You work with Mark Bolitho?'

'Yes. I soon realized I wouldn't make it as an actor.' Sophie smiled. 'I'm not sufficiently thick-skinned. All the auditions, all the rejections. I enjoyed the residency at the hospital, but that was stressful in its own way too. I moved into admin at the Live Theatre, starting out as Mark's assistant. When he married Juliet and moved out into the wilds, he offered me a job-share.'

'That suits you better?' Joe took a mince pie while he was waiting for an answer.

'I love it! We make a good partnership. Mark's very creative and I'm more organized, better at the figures and the finance.'

'You were already friends?'

'Yes,' she said. 'It was shameless nepotism that got me the job.'

'Mark was Sophie's first boyfriend,' Paul said. 'The love of her life.' He gave a little laugh, but there was an edge of jealousy in his voice. 'And now he's trying to tap me for sponsorship for his project.'

'I was only his girlfriend when I was eighteen.' She smiled and put her hand on his shoulder. 'And I was at Brockburn as his colleague. I'm sure he didn't see us as potential donors.' There was a pause. No response from the husband. 'You do know that I wouldn't swap what I have here for anything.' Joe thought she'd said that before. Paul Blackstock was a man who needed reassurance.

'What's Mark like as a boss?' Joe asked.

'Great! Really understanding and supportive. Not every manager's as flexible about maternity leave in a small company.'

Joe wondered what it must be like to have a boss who was so helpful, then he thought he'd rather work for Vera than Mark Bolitho any day.

The baby in the crib began to grizzle. Sophie got to her feet, picked her up and stroked her head. Joe stood up too. He thought he'd done all he could here. Vera always said she didn't believe in coincidence, but the link between the couple and Lorna Falstone was so tenuous that he couldn't believe it was important.

Chapter Sixteen

HOLLY WASN'T COMFORTABLE IN PUBS. She'd never seen the attraction, even when she was a teenager and it had been a rite of passage to con an underage drink in the bars that weren't too fussy. The chaos and the shouting, the loud and raucous laughter, the closeness of strangers had unnerved her. The worst were the city pubs with TV screens showing endless snooker, blaring music competing with the beeps of slot machines, but even here in the Stanhope Arms in Kirkhill, she had a moment of panic. In the bar, a large screen was showing a Premier League football match and a group of middle-aged men had pulled chairs into a semicircle to watch it. There were occasional groans and at one point they all got to their feet and cheered. The lounge had started serving early Sunday lunch and though it was quieter there, the acoustics made it seem as if all the diners were shouting.

In contrast, Charlie seemed entirely at ease. He stood behind the football fans and cheered with them when a goal was scored. He must have sensed Holly's discomfort.

'Why don't you leave me here? You take the old people's bungalows on the edge of the village. They're in the same little estate where Lorna had her house. The old gadgees will find it easier to chat to a woman and if anyone knows the village gossip it'll be them.' Charlie gave a sudden grin. 'You'll probably have to drive back, like. I'll not get this crowd to talk to me if I've not got a pint in my hand.'

Holly nodded and found herself outside, looking down the grey empty street. The shops seemed shut and the hills beyond were covered in cloud. When it lifted a little, she saw that there was still snow on the ground on the tops. She walked down the main street, past a butcher advertising home-made pies, and a greengrocer. Only the Co-op was open and that was empty. She knew Lorna's address and the layout of the village. Basic research. Vera had never been able to fault her on that. Sometimes, Holly wondered what it would take to get her boss's admiration, her approval even.

Charlie had been right. There was a small terrace of council houses, a few already decorated for Christmas, with a glowing Santa on one wall and flashing fairy lights on another. Further down the slope towards the village stood four detached bungalows, smart, tidy. Holly knew that in one of these lived Constance Browne, and Vera had already been there. Past the house where Lorna had lived, the road curved up and led to six more bungalows, older, semi-detached, obviously designed for elderly or disabled people. Some had ramps and some had grab rails. They were not at all smart.

Holly rang the bell of the first house and heard it sound, very loud, inside. A light seemed to have been triggered on the other side of the door and when it opened, she saw that the elderly man wore hearing aids.

'Who are you?' The tone was pleasant enough, but he was making it clear he would take no nonsense.

She showed her warrant card.

'Ah, you'll be here about the poor lass down the street. I'm not sure I can help you, but come away in. You'll not have to mumble, mind. I canna bear mumblers.'

In the end, if she spoke clearly and faced him, he heard her well enough. They sat in a small living room. No sign of Christmas here, except for four cards on the mantelpiece. He was Matty Fuller, a retired shepherd, and he'd moved to Kirkhill when his wife had died. 'I thought it might be lonely out there in the old place, with no company but the dog. I've been here three years though, and I'm still not sure I like it. I'm a coun-tryman at heart.'

To Holly, this village was as *country* as she thought it could get, and she didn't know how to reply. 'Did you know Lorna?'

'She was a canny little thing. Bonny. She called in every now and again with the bairn. Company for me and I think she was glad of the change of scene. Other times we'd meet up in the village, usually in the Co-op. It can take half an hour to get through the checkout with everyone chatting. She was a skinny little lass. A good gust of wind and she'd blow away.' He paused. 'I knew her parents. I worked that way for a while.'

'On the Brockburn estate?'

'A long time ago. In Sebastian's day. Before he gambled away all his cash and when he could still keep his staff.'

'Sebastian?'

'Crispin's father. Crispin's gone too now. His widow rules the roost. The Lady Harriet we used to call her, though there was never any real title. She had that air about her. Snooty.'

Holly couldn't help herself. 'Did you ever know Hector Stanhope?'

Matty chuckled. 'Aye. He was Sebastian's younger brother. Not a great one for rules and responsibility. Married a school-teacher out Wark way when we thought he'd never find a woman to take him on. He seemed to be settling down – he loved her to bits, they said, worshipped the ground she walked on – and then she died and he went back to his wild old ways.'

So, the Stanhopes of Brockburn weren't such distant relatives of the boss after all. Holly thought Vera wasn't a great one for rules either.

'What are Lorna Falstone's parents like?'

'Solid. Hard-working. A bit proud maybe.' He paused. 'Some folk round here think they're unfriendly because they don't mix. They run a good farm, though. Anyone will tell you that.' Another pause. 'I did a bit of work for them when Jill was pregnant with the lassie and she couldn't help with the lambing. Robert didn't chat much – there was no joking to pass the time – but he was fair. Paid the going wage.'

'There must have been a bit of gossip when Lorna got pregnant. She was living in Kirkhill by then.'

'Aye.' He smiled. 'There was a bit of talk in the Co-op queue when she started showing.' He looked up at her. 'You know she'd been ill? Anorexia, do they call it? Starving herself.'

Holly nodded.

'There'd already been people giving their opinion about Robert and Jill letting her live by herself here. They thought she should be at home where they could look after her, make sure she was eating properly.' He paused. 'I thought it was something she had to do for herself. The last thing you'd want would be your parents running your life. You'd want a bit of control.' A pause. 'And then they didn't stop her being ill when she *was* living at Broom Farm.'

'Yes,' Holly said. 'I think you're right.' She looked up at him. 'There must have been some speculation about who the father might be.'

'Ha! Speculation is right. Too many people with too much time on their hands making up stories. Nobody knew.'

'What were the stories?' Holly thought Lorna must have had some courage, living here, walking down the village street, knowing people were watching, walking into a shop and facing a sudden silence.

'I don't know,' Matty said. 'I never listened. There are times when it's a good thing to be deaf.'

'We need to know, though.' Holly leaned forward. 'Because we have to find out who killed her. And besides, there's a child without a mother. Maybe it would help Thomas to know his father.'

Matty looked at her. Through the wall to the adjoining bungalow came a woman's voice, someone shouting that dinner was ready.

'I don't know,' he said at last. 'The talk was that there was some fancy man in the city. She was seen taking the bus to Newcastle a few times. That was all it needed to start the rumour.'

'She didn't mention anyone when she came to visit?'

He gave a little laugh. 'Nah, we weren't on those sorts of terms.'

'Thanks.' Holly stood up. 'You've been very helpful.'

Now Matty seemed reluctant to let her go. 'Why, I've never offered you a drink. Would you like some coffee?' She saw that even here, on the edge of the village, he was lonely.

'What happened to your dog?' she asked. 'The one that kept you company before you moved in here.'

'Oh, I had to have her put down. She was a working dog and she needed space and exercise and I can't walk so far these days. It would have been a prison for her, to bring her here.' He looked up. 'I miss her, though. I miss them both.'

It was only as she was leaving the bungalow that Holly realized he was talking about his dog and his wife.

The other people who lived in the street were eager to help, excited that a detective should want to ask them questions, but they could tell Holly little more about Lorna than Matty Fuller. A large, blowsy woman, who'd struggled to the door with the aid of a walking frame, mentioned the fancy man from Newcastle too. 'They say he runs his own string of businesses and he's minted.' But when Holly asked for details and to know who'd actually started the rumour, the woman couldn't tell her. She'd kept Holly chatting on the doorstep and when Holly had asked for some form of corroboration to the story, she took offence. 'Are you saying I'm a liar? I'm only trying to help, to tell you what some neighbours are saying.' The door was firmly shut.

Holly walked back to the Stanhope Arms, hoping that Charlie had had more success. It was quieter now, the football match over; the families in the lounge eating lunch were concentrating on their food. Charlie was at a table in the bar with a pint and an open packet of crisps; he was chatting to a couple Holly would have described as the actively retired. The woman was slight, gym-fit, with tinted hair and competent make-up. The man had a paunch, but carried it with a confidence that showed he still believed he was attractive to women. Charlie jumped up when he saw Holly. 'I've been chatting to Geoff and Veronica here. What can I get you?'

'I don't suppose they do a decaff coffee?'

'I can try.'

'Oh I'm sure they do,' the woman said. 'You wouldn't believe how much things have changed since we first moved here. I'm a veggie and when we first arrived the only thing on offer *anywhere* was an omelette.' An educated voice but a little slurred. A large glass of red stood on the table. The wine glass in front of the man was empty; he'd moved on to whisky.

Holly thought they'd moved here on retirement with dreams of an idyllic lifestyle, of becoming leading lights in the community, running it perhaps as they had their business or office, but now they were bored. 'How long have you been here?'

'Five years,' Veronica said. 'Geoff took early retirement and we thought, *why not?* We could practically buy a mansion with what we got for our house in Newcastle. And really we've never looked back.' But her voice was wistful and Holly thought she was still hankering for smart coffee shops and the friends who shared her interests.

'I'm sure my colleague has already asked, but did you know Lorna Falstone?' Charlie was taking a suspiciously long time at the bar. Perhaps he'd thought Holly would be more on this couple's wavelength. *What does that make me? A snobby cow?*

'We met her a couple of times, didn't we, Geoff? Through Connie Browne. Connie set up a watercolour class, persuaded a very talented local artist to come along as tutor. We get together in the village hall on Monday mornings.'

'And Lorna came to the class?'

'Not regularly. I suppose it was hard with the baby. But Connie thought she had talent and persuaded her along.'

'What did you make of her?'

There was a pause. 'She was a shy little thing. Pretty enough, but she didn't make much effort with her appearance. I think she loved the class. She seemed to lose herself in the painting.'

Holly saw Charlie heading her way with her coffee, a biscuit covered in a plastic wrapper in the saucer.

'Did she have any special friends in the class? Perhaps there's someone we might talk to who knew her better.'

Veronica seemed to take a long time to think about this. She drank wine. Her lips were stained with it. She made Holly think of a vampire. 'Well, the tutor took an interest in her. She was the only person under fifty in the group, so I suppose they had more in common. I must say, I wasn't desperately impressed by her art. Rather gloomy I thought. All black forests and glowering skies.' She must have realized how churlish she was sounding, because she gave a little smile. 'But what would I know? I'm only an amateur. I'm sure it's very good.'

'What's the name of the tutor?'

'Josh Heslop.' His parents farm in the valley near Brockburn. 'He's not long out of art school and he's struggling to make his way. Good, though. He's already got a little gallery in Kimmerston to stage an exhibition. He's back at home, helping the family out.'

Holly drank her instant coffee and thought about this. Josh must be brother to the teenage girls who acted as waitresses in Brockburn the night of the murder. His father had found the body. The boss was always interested in coincidence and Holly looked forward to passing on the information.

Charlie had his phone out and was checking messages. Still

he seemed happy to leave the interview to Holly. 'Josh must be about the same age as Lorna,' she said. 'They would have gone to school together?'

Veronica seemed bored by the conversation now. Perhaps she only enjoyed talking about herself. She shrugged. 'I suppose so. All the secondary kids go to the high school in Kimmerston.'

Charlie got suddenly to his feet. 'Sorry, folks. We need to get on. Thanks for your help.'

Holly followed him out of the pub. It was only mid-afternoon but the light had already drained away. She thought of Veronica's words about a glowering sky.

'There was a message from the boss,' Charlie said. 'The CSIs have finished in Lorna's house. She wants us to take a look, see if we can find anything that might give us a name for the baby's father or some kind of link with Mark Bolitho.'

Chapter Seventeen

ON THE WALK TO LORNA'S HOUSE, Holly phoned Vera with the information about Josh Heslop running the art class to which Lorna belonged. Charlie was listening in. He grinned and stuck up his thumbs when he heard the tutor's name, mouthed, *Well done, lass.*

'Well now, that *is* very interesting.' Reception was poor and Vera's voice seemed a long way off. 'It's definitely worth a visit to that family.'

'Do you want us to go when we've finished up here?'

'Nah,' Vera said. 'I bumped into one of the Heslop lasses this morning, so I've got a bit of a relationship. And it's almost on my way home. I'll go.' A pause. 'Good work, Hol.'

Holly wished that didn't mean so much to her, that she didn't feel as she had when she'd just been given a gold star at school as a five-year-old.

A crime-scene investigator was waiting for them outside Lorna's house with a key. 'We've done what we can. There are a few fingerprints, but nothing on the database. We've taken DNA where we can but we won't get a result back on that for weeks. You know about the backlog and until you've got a suspect, I'm guessing there's no rush. You won't want to blow your budget by fast-tracking.'

Holly thought Vera had never been over-concerned about budget, but she just nodded. Charlie was already at the front door, with the key in his hand. He turned back. 'Where did you get the key? Was it on the body?'

'There was a key in the victim's jeans pocket but that's still with her. We got this spare from a woman who lived over the road.' The CSI nodded towards Connie Browne's bungalow, then pulled up the collar of his jacket. 'Bloody freezing out here in the hills, isn't it? I'm off back to civilization.'

It was cold in the house too. The front door led straight into the compact living room, where a small sofa, covered with a fleece blanket, faced an armchair that must have come from a charity shop. A plastic box of toys sat under the stairs, which led to the first floor. Through an open door in the far wall, Holly saw a kitchen large enough to contain a table, a couple of stools and a plastic high chair. The living space was similar in size to Dorothy and Karan's cottage, but she thought the place felt very different. Less warm in terms of decor and furnishing as well as temperature. Tidy and clean enough but utilitarian. Perhaps Lorna had inherited her taste in interior design from her parents. An electric storage heater stood against one wall. Holly reached out to touch it: switched on but tepid. She imagined Lorna curled up on the sofa, wrapped in the fleece.

'No telly or radio,' Charlie said. 'Isn't that a bit odd?'

'She probably accessed media through her laptop.' Holly paused. 'Did the CSIs take that?'

'I guess so.' Charlie shivered. 'Do you want to look upstairs? I'll do down here.'

Holly nodded. There were two bedrooms but Thomas had obviously shared the bigger room with his mother. There was a cot under the window, a pretty duvet with an elephant print, a mobile hanging from the ceiling. Lorna had slept next to it. She'd had a double bed but there was only one pillow. If she'd still had a secret boyfriend, it seemed unlikely that he stayed here very often. Methodically, Holly went through the drawers in the pine chest. The top two contained the toddler's clothes. Brightly coloured dungarees and jackets, woolly jumpers.

Again, Lorna's clothes seemed purely functional; there was little pretty or indulgent. Holly wondered about that. Had Lorna been so confident that she hadn't felt the need to dress up to impress? Or had she believed she didn't deserve anything beautiful or glamorous? Holly thought this wasn't a theory she should share with Vera, who had very definite views about psychological guesswork. Holly looked at the labels of the underwear, T-shirts and jerseys and all came from bargain chains or supermarkets. Perhaps the explanation was simple: this was a household where money was tight and any spare cash was spent on the son. Lorna had given up her job in the pub once the baby was born, so presumably she'd been living on benefits and handouts from her mother.

On top of the chest of drawers there was a wooden box with a mother-of-pearl pattern on the lid. Holly opened it to a scent of sandalwood and laid out the contents in order on the bed. Lorna's birth certificate and GCSE certificates. A passport, medical card and details of the baby's inoculations. And Thomas's birth certificate. Holly flattened it out. No father's name. She'd bag them all up, but she couldn't see that they'd help find the man who'd made Lorna pregnant, unless the GP could give them any information.

Holly moved on to the bathroom. An avocado suite that must have been installed in the eighties. Along the edge of the tub, a row of plastic toys, a bottle of bubble bath, a supermarket brand of shampoo and a cake of soap. Nothing to help Lorna relax at the end of a busy, child-centred day. Holly looked in the cabinet over the sink, hoping to find scented bath oil or body lotion, but all she saw was spare toothpaste and a packet of ibuprofen.

The smaller bedroom was at the back of the house and Holly was expecting a storeroom containing the hoarded detritus of family life: sleeping bags, suitcases, Christmas decor-ations waiting to be hung out. Because surely Lorna would have planned to celebrate Christmas for the sake of the toddler. Holly thought there'd be nothing useful to the investigation. The door opened towards her, she reached in and felt for the light switch. It was scarcely bigger than a box room, but there was a desk under the window, stretching across the whole width of the space. On it, a jam jar containing various thick-nesses of paintbrush, and a pile of good-quality watercolour paper. This was Lorna's treat to herself. This was where she escaped. There was a single bookshelf fixed to a wall. A few paperbacks offering self-help and instruction in mindfulness and a couple of novels, which Holly had read and enjoyed. One volume had been left on the desk: the collected works of the poet Robert Frost. It seemed an odd choice for a farmer's daughter, who'd left school before taking A levels. Holly looked inside. There was a note in beautiful handwriting: *To Lorna. Happy Christmas 2017. Love from Connie.* This wasn't new so it must be a favourite. Holly had studied Frost for GCSE and had the same book at home.

Lorna's art was displayed on the walls here. Downstairs the only painting on show had been created by Thomas, obviously with help from his mother: a collage made up mostly of glitter and glue. These were quite different. As Veronica had said, they were dark, almost abstract landscapes. Holly felt pulled into the bleakness. Occasionally there was a mark which might represent a figure, but in most the scenes were empty. Holly felt close to tears. She thought nobody but the art class had ever seen these and most of the work had been done in secret, here in the tiny room. They had a sense of despair. Holly stood back and thought that was ridiculous. How could she judge Lorna's mood from the tone of her art?

More paintings were leaning against the wall. Holly pulled them out one by one. They looked as if they'd been painted in acrylic on some kind of board. The subject was always the same. A stone cottage almost derelict, surrounded by pine trees, with ivy covering most of the wall and growing through one of the window frames. It was like something from a fairy tale and Holly wondered if Lorna was trying her hand at illustration, or perhaps there'd been a specific commission. The roof was rusting corrugated iron and that was almost lovingly painted. Lorna seemed to have enjoyed the texture, the variety of colour. Each was neatly signed in the corner but only one had a title. It was of the cottage in winter, the grass frosty, the one at the top of the pile, so probably the most recent. It was labelled 'The Darkest Evening'.

In some of the paintings the scene was almost dark and there was a light in the window. A pale light from a candle or lamp. In others the cottage was shown in full daylight. Sunshine slanted through the trees onto the building, changing the colour of the stone to silver. Clover and buttercup grew in a meadow in front of the house, bringing splashes of colour, making the scene feel almost joyous.

She called down to Charlie. 'What do you make of these?' She heard the sound of his footsteps on the stairs, then he was standing behind her, peering at the pictures on the wall.

There was a moment of silence. 'Are we sure that she did these?'

'Yes, your friend Veronica in the pub told me she went to a community art class.'

'Poor lass,' he said. 'Poor troubled soul.'

'Then there are these.' Holly stood aside so he could see the cottage paintings. She'd leaned a number against the wall, facing out. 'All of the same place. Any idea where it is?'

He shook his head. 'Somewhere out here in bandit country. The boss might know.'

Holly nodded and started taking photos. 'Why so many paintings of the same place? Some kind of obsession? A place where she was once happy?'

Charlie shrugged and repeated his earlier words. 'Poor troubled soul.'

Chapter Eighteen

VERA KNOCKED AT THE DOOR OF the Home Farm house, where the Heslops lived, but there was no answer. There were lights on inside, though, and she thought the family must be around. She moved to the side of the building and looked through a sash window into a long living room. The view was partially blocked by a giant Christmas tree, a Scots pine. It was hung with ancient, home-made decorations and fairy lights shaped like flowers. On the top was a star, a child's creation, years old, covered in glitter. She thought that the tree had been recently cut and decorated because there was no sign of dropping needles. No sign of people either. No fire in the grate.

The house was quiet, but Vera became aware of music, drifting from somewhere beyond it. She continued moving around the building towards the yard and the music got louder. Vera was mystified. It was dark and cold and, even if the Heslop young people had been willing to brave the elements for an impromptu party, this was hardly rave material. This was the traditional music she remembered from her childhood.

There had been a pub Hector had frequented when he'd

felt a sudden need for company, or he'd run out of booze in the cottage. As a small girl, she would be left outside in the car with crisps and lemonade, and occasionally, when the door opened, she'd see two elderly men by the fire, one playing fiddle and the other the Northumbrian pipes. The music brought the image immediately to mind now.

Moving on, she came to a square wooden barn facing a yard, where half a dozen cars were parked. Bunting was strung outside, along with more fairy lights, as if for a celebration. The timing seemed odd, almost as if the family was responding to the death of Lorna Falstone in the most inappropriate way possible. A wake before the funeral. The wide barn door slid open and the two Heslop girls came out. They walked into the shadows and shared a roll-up. For a moment, before the door closed behind them, Vera glimpsed people gathered inside, a long trestle table loaded with food, bales of hay forming makeshift seats.

'Hiya! What's going on here?'

She must have startled them, coming out of the dark, but Nettie seemed to recognize her voice immediately. 'Cath's birthday party.' She shivered dramatically. 'A family tradition. All birthdays celebrated by a bash in the barn, whatever the weather.'

'All right if I gatecrash? I was hoping to speak to your brother.'

Cath answered. She was rounder and softer than her sister. Gentler, with less attitude. 'Of course. The more the merrier. Josh is in there.'

She put out the cigarette, put the stub carefully back into the tin of tobacco and led Vera into the barn.

Their father, Neil Heslop, was standing at the front on a low stage formed of bales, playing a violin. An older woman, sitting beside him, leaning forwards, was on guitar. Vera hadn't seen Heslop properly on the night he'd found Lorna's body. Then he'd been wrapped up against the cold, hood up, a scarf around his face. She thought now there was something of the Viking about him: sandy-haired, blue-eyed.

The place was surprisingly warm and filled with people of all ages. A small child was asleep on a blanket laid on a bench in the corner. A middle-aged woman with grey curly hair was supervising the laying out of the food. Nettie went up to her, while Cath joined a group of girls who were passing round a bottle of Prosecco.

'Mam, this is the detective who's investigating Lorna's murder. She wants to speak to Josh.' Then Nettie too wandered away to join the other young guests, without waiting for her mother to respond.

The woman held out her hand. 'Rosemary Heslop.' She looked out at her daughters and grinned. 'Sorry about that. You bring them up to be polite, then they turn into teenagers and all the manners disappear.'

'It's your youngest's birthday? Eh, pet, I'm sorry to intrude. I wouldn't have bothered you if I'd realized.'

'Yes, my baby's turning seventeen very soon. The years have gone by in a flash. We thought about cancelling. Neil's been that upset since he found the lass's body – he's hardly slept since it happened – but it was all organized and the girls wanted to go ahead.'

The tempo of the music changed, became slower. It must have morphed into a tune Nettie and Cath knew, or perhaps they'd been expecting it, because they started singing along and the others joined in. The girls' voices were sweet and clear and Vera could see that Rosemary was almost in tears.

The song ended and the musicians laid down their instruments. 'Time for supper,' Neil Heslop said. 'And make sure it all gets eaten, or we'll be having it all week.' The humour sounded forced and Vera could see the dark shadows under his eyes.

He'd seen Vera and came up to her. They stood apart while the guests queued up for the food. 'Is there any news?'

She shook her head. 'I came hoping to speak to your Josh. It seems Lorna went to an art class he taught.'

'Oh, aye. Connie Browne bringing culture to the masses.' He gave a little smile but still he seemed distracted.

'How are you getting on?'

There was a moment's hesitation. 'It all seems like a dream.' He spoke very slowly as if he was reliving the nightmare. 'The snow. The dark. I was just keen to get our lasses safely home out of the weather. I was thinking I should never have let them go to the big house at all. Then suddenly to see that face in the ice.'

'Of course. And you were able to identify her for us. It's always harder if it's someone you know.' A pause. 'Though when I bumped into Nettie, she said you weren't close friends with the family. Is that a bit strange when you both farm estate land?'

Rosemary had joined them and it was she who answered. 'They're not really sociable, the Falstones. It's not that we've ever fallen out. Nothing like that. We help each other professionally, but I wouldn't just call in for a coffee if I was on my way to Kirkhill, like I would some of my other neighbours. I know they wouldn't welcome it.'

'They might welcome it now,' Vera said. 'Just losing their daughter and with a kiddie to look after, it's a lot to cope with on your own.'

That appeared to knock the breath from Rosemary and she

seemed mortified, anxious that Vera might consider her unsym-
pathetic. 'You're right, of course. Poor souls! I'll go in tomorrow.
When Lorna was ill, they made it clear they didn't want any
interference. They cut themselves off from the village. Before
that, Jill would come to the WI if there was a topic that caught
her fancy and I'd see her occasionally at church, but after
Lorna went away to the clinic for help, they shut down all
contact. I don't blame them. The Kirkhill gossip can be brutal.
But I'll pop in. See if there's any way we can help.'

'I was hoping to chat to your lad.'

'Apparently Lorna went to that art class of his,' Heslop said.
Vera wasn't sure if that sounded like an explanation or a
warning. He called out to a dark-haired young man with soft
eyes and lashes that a girl would envy. 'Josh, this is Inspector
Stanhope. She'd like a word.'

Josh joined them. The parents stayed, one on each side,
protective as guard dogs. Vera would have liked to take him
back to the house and chat to him there on his own, but she
didn't want to upset the family. She might be glad to have
them onside later.

'Lorna came along to the class you ran for Miss Browne in
the Kirkhill hall?'

Josh nodded. 'She came along to a couple of sessions.'

'Was she any good?'

It wasn't the question he'd been expecting and it took him
a while to answer. 'Yes. Better than any of the others, certainly.'

'You must have known her from school. You'd have been
the same sort of age.'

'We were in the same year, but I didn't really know her.'

Vera wondered again if they'd find anyone who'd admit to
any kind of intimacy with Lorna.

Josh was still speaking. 'You know what it's like. You keep to your own little groups, people who share your own interests.'

'And with you it was art?'

'Art and theatre.' He gave a shy grin. 'I was always up for making a fool of myself in the school play.'

'But Lorna was into art too. She wasn't part of your group?'

Josh shook his head. 'She was a bit of a loner. I was surprised when she turned up for the class in the village hall. I think she was only there because Connie Browne dragged her along.' He paused. 'She didn't make it into the sixth form because she was ill, anorexic. I made most of my strongest friends then.'

Vera had never made it to the sixth form either. By the time she was sixteen she'd had enough of school and enough of Hector. She'd joined the police force as a cadet and found her own family. She'd been a loner too and felt an increasing sympathy for Lorna Falstone. 'Did you see her away from the class?'

'Once. One evening. I just bumped into her in Kirkhill. She had the baby in the pushchair and was walking around to try to get him to sleep. Apparently, he was teething. I'd just gone to the Co-op for something Mum had forgotten. Lorna asked me into her house for a coffee.'

'And you went?'

'Yeah, sure. Why not? I was curious, I suppose. There'd been all that talk about her in the village. She showed me some of her paintings. I think that was why she asked me. She wanted me to give her some feedback.'

A silence. Neil moved away to gather up plates, but Rosemary stayed to listen.

'Did you talk about anything else? Other than art?' Vera

wished again that there wasn't an audience. She should have asked to speak to Josh Heslop on his own, even if it had annoyed his parents and disrupted the party. She'd been seduced by the warmth of the family, had thought this would be a routine chat. Now, looking at him, at the tense little smile, the leg that couldn't quite stay still, she wasn't so sure.

'Probably. We looked at her paintings first. They were in a small room upstairs. Then she made me some coffee. The baby was asleep by then and Lorna put him into his cot, so I was alone for a while, but when she came back, we chatted. I can't really remember what about. Old schoolfriends, probably. That's a standard when you get together with someone you've not seen for a while.'

'You must have asked about her? Her life?'

'A bit. She wanted to go to art school too. She asked what it was like. I suggested places for her to do her foundation year.' He looked up. 'It was just chat. I was surprised because she was good company. Intelligent. Fun.'

'Did you get the impression that she was in a relationship?'

He shrugged. 'Not really. She didn't mention anyone.'

'She didn't tell you about the father of her child?'

'No! And I didn't ask. I knew better than to pry.'

'Where were you on Friday night?'

Vera asked the question in the same tone, and it was Rosemary who realized the implication first. 'You can't think Josh had anything to do with Lorna Falstone's death?'

'I don't think anything yet, pet. That's why I'm asking all these questions. We'll be asking everyone who knew the lass.' Vera turned back to Josh. 'So? Where were you?'

'In Newcastle with some mates. Friday night in the pub. It had been arranged ages ago, a kind of university reunion. Our own version of a Christmas bash. I stayed over. That had always been the plan, even before the snow.'

She nodded to show she accepted the reply. 'I assume you drive?'

'Sure. Everyone does. It'd be impossible out here without a vehicle.'

'Lorna didn't have a car,' Vera said. 'Witnesses say she used to go into Newcastle occasionally on the bus.'

'Connie Browne let her borrow hers. And lots of us use the bus for Newcastle. That's how I went in on Friday. It's cheaper than paying for parking.'

'I don't understand where you're going with this, Inspector.' Rosemary was ready for battle, protecting her son again.

'No, well, nor do I really.' Vera smiled. 'That's what it's like at the beginning of a case. 'We're all groping in the dark.'

Vera thought she'd been seduced by her first sight of the Heslop clan, by the party, the music and the singing. The party that was far more enticing than the fund-raising bash at Brockburn had been. Of course, they'd have their secrets; every family did. She pictured the two lasses as she'd first seen them, standing in the cold for a sneaky cigarette. She'd bet their parents didn't know they smoked. There'd be other things going on too, with bonny lasses of that age. Vera imagined them in an upstairs bedroom at the farm with their mates, giggling, smoking weed out of the window to get rid of the smell, letting in lads when nobody else was in, escaping to wild parties but telling their parents they were doing revision at friends'.

Now the conversation with Josh was over, Rosemary was hospitable again. 'Stay and have a bite to eat.'

'That's very kind,' Vera said, 'but it's been a long day and

I'll be glad to be home.' A pause. 'I wouldn't mind using your lav, though, before I go.'

'Sure,' Rosemary said. 'The back door's unlocked and there's a cloakroom before you get to the kitchen.'

Vera was crossing the barn when the door opened again and Dorothy Felling came in with a man who must be her partner Karan Pabla. They were carrying a present for Cath and they waved to Rosemary. The mood in the room seemed to change. These were welcome guests. The girls went to greet them.

'Sorry we're late,' Karan said, in a voice that was loud enough to take in the whole room. He could have been some kind of celebrity. Perhaps it was the glamour of the big house rubbing off on them. 'Juliet offered to babysit and we wanted to get Duncan settled before we left.'

Neil was still standing close to Vera. 'Pals of yours, are they?' she asked.

'Karan's been tutoring Cath. She's been struggling with English and history.' He smiled. 'She takes more notice of him than she does of her teachers.'

Vera thought about that. She could understand why Holly had been so taken with the man – he had a presence that lit up the room – but wondered why he'd taken Cath Heslop as a pupil. Because he needed the money? To feel valued in the community?

And then there was dark-haired, dark-eyed Josh, the artist. What secrets might he have about Lorna Falstone? Could he be her secret lover, the father of her child?

Vera slipped unnoticed from the barn and headed for the house. She could have waited for a pee until she got home, but she'd been itching to get inside, to get a real sense of the family. A corridor led from the back door into the kitchen. As Rosemary had said, there was a cloakroom to one side, the light on, for guests who needed it. Along the corridor photos had been fixed to the walls, memories of family life: Neil and Rosemary's wedding, the bride and groom in ridiculous nineties clothes, the kids as babies and growing up, local views and places where they must have taken holidays, moody silhouettes against sunsets and sunrises.

'Did you find it okay?' Rosemary must have come into the house without Vera noticing.

'Yeah, fine, thanks.' Vera paused. 'Sorry, I couldn't help nebbing. It goes with the job, I'm afraid.'

'You do know Josh would never harm a fly,' Rosemary said. 'We're a close family.'

'I can see that, pet.' Vera looked again at the photos and let herself out.

Back in her cottage, Vera lit the fire and sat for a while at the table. She took a large sheet of paper and began drawing a chart, all circles and lines. A way of making sense of the complex relationships. There were three families all linked. The Falstones: Robert and Jill and baby Thomas, tied by blood to Lorna, but tied, it seemed, by little else. The Heslops, the happy family: parents Rosemary and Neil and the kids, Josh, Nettie and Cath. They were linked to Lorna in more ways than Vera had first supposed. Neil had found the body, the girls had been in Brockburn when Lorna had died, and Josh had become a recent friend. Then there were the Stanhopes at the big house. Because Mark had become a Stanhope by marrying Juliet, whatever name he called himself. Mark had a girlfriend, according to rumour, and Lorna took the bus occasionally to Newcastle to meet up with a wealthy man. Also linked to the Stanhopes were Dorothy Felling and Karan Pabla, and Paul and Sophie Blackstock. Too many people.

At the centre of the circle sat Lorna Falstone, the lost little girl who seemed to be growing in confidence, taking tentative steps out into the world, exploring her feelings through art. Making new friends. But just as life was getting better, as she was getting stronger, she was killed. Vera wondered if there was any significance in that. Had the shrinking, cowed Lorna been allowed to live, while the more confident Lorna posed a danger and had to die? But why *then*, in a blizzard in the grounds of Brockburn? Could it be so the Stanhopes would be implicated? *Were* they implicated? Surely, that was a ridiculous idea.

Vera got to her feet and tipped more coal onto the fire. She poured herself a glass of whisky and raised a silent toast to the young woman she'd never known, but with whom she felt an unlikely affinity, the woman who would haunt her thoughts and dreams until the investigation was over.

Chapter Nineteen

MONDAY MORNING AND JOE WAS ON his way to the private hospital where Lorna had been treated as an inpatient for anorexia. The website said Halstead House was the only place specifically treating inpatient adolescents with eating disorders in the UK. The medics specialized in the physical and psychiatric effects of the illness and there were counsellors and complementary therapists. Joe supposed Sophie Blackstock had been involved with that group. As far as he could tell, the place wasn't part of a large private health organization, but had been founded by a psychiatrist whose daughter had died from anorexia and the bereaved doctor had made treatment and research into the disease her life's work.

The website showed a beautiful country house bathed in sunshine. Joe found this suspicious: the place was just over the border in Cumbria and whenever he'd been to the county it had been raining. The photos showed smiling staff, but few patients. The fees listed made his eyes water. A month's stay would cost almost as much as the deposit on his house.

His phone call the day before had been answered by a

Scottish woman, who had been polite and professional, even friendly, but had managed to give him no information at all about Lorna. She'd said that there was nobody else he could talk to: 'Many of our patients have family visits on Sunday, or they're out on a day's home leave. Because of that, there are routinely few clinical staff on site. No, I'm sorry, I really can't pass on our colleagues' home phone numbers.'

Joe had supposed she must be used to dealing with tense and anxious parents. He'd fumed gently and made an appointment to visit the following day.

He'd set out early. The weather had changed again; the wind was back from the north, but the sky was cloudless. He'd woken to a frost, ice on the windscreen. When he'd checked his phone before setting off, there'd been an email from Vera, with details about her trip to the Heslops' farm. *We need to check out the arty boy.* The royal 'we'. Still giving her orders, even at a distance and in the middle of the night. Vera having Wi-Fi installed at the cottage had been a very mixed blessing. He'd messaged her back to remind her that he'd be at the clinic for most of the day and received no reply. The sun came up behind him just as he crossed the Northumberland border.

There was a discreet sign by the gate: *Halstead House Private Hospital*. The building was hidden from the road by a line of poplars and came into view as he drove round a curve in the drive. The place was built of weathered red brick, large but not grand or imposing like Brockburn, more domestic in scale. Joe thought it might have been built by a Victorian mine owner who'd wanted an escape from the grime of the Northumberland coalfields. A veranda ran around the front of the house, looking down over the gardens and a tarn in the distance. It was pretty now; in the spring and summer it would be spectacular. There was a visitors' car park at the back of the house and he left his car there. Beyond it, there was a new building, all glass and pale wood, but with the same grey slate roof. Another sign, with the same lettering style as by the front gate: *Well-being Centre*. Joe thought it was possible to explain how those extortionate fees had been spent. This looked like an upmarket spa.

A double door into the older building led to a reception area: country-house scruffy, scratched wooden floors, with a boot rack and coat hooks then a couple of ancient sofas. An open door in the opposite wall showed an office beyond. A middle-aged woman stuck out her head. 'Can I help?' She was Scottish, the implacable woman on the phone. Around her neck a lanyard and a pass with a name. Elspeth.

Joe showed his warrant card. 'We spoke yesterday.'

'Of course. Joanne is expecting you.' A couple of teenage girls came through the door. They were dressed in jackets, hats and scarves and they were laughing. It was only when they took off their coats that Joe saw how thin they were, bony and gaunt. He tried not to stare. Elspeth gave them a wave and continued talking. 'You're a little early and Mrs Simmons Wright is still tied up with the patients. Can I get you some coffee?'

He was still drinking the coffee when Joanne Simmons Wright came in, bursting through the door so it banged on the wall behind. 'I'm so sorry to have kept you waiting.' She was skinny too, but tall and fit. The same age as the receptionist but ungainly, like a tall kid with too much energy. She had short hair streaked with grey. No make-up. She could be a runner and was dressed like one in Lycra leggings and a long sweatshirt. 'I take the yoga class on a Monday morning, over in the well-being centre.'

'Yoga can cure anorexia?'

She recognized the scepticism but wasn't offended. 'Well, not on its own, but anything that helps patients feel more relaxed and more at ease with their bodies is going to help. Shall we go to my office? It'll get a bit crowded here when they all come through.'

The office was on the first floor at the front of the house, looking down over the garden to the tarn beyond. There was a desk against one wall, three easy chairs. Joe took one. Joanne was leaning with her back to the windowsill, drinking from a water bottle.

'You were Lorna Falstone's doctor?'

'I'm not a doctor. I'm a psychologist, but I was her key worker.' Joanne took a seat opposite to him. 'Poor Lorna. How did it happen? Did she get ill again? Suicide?'

'No.' He looked at her face. 'It was murder.'

There was a stunned silence. He waited for the psychologist to speak, but she turned her head away. 'You do remember her then?' he said at last. 'It was four years ago and you must get a lot of kids through here.'

'Of course I remember. This isn't a place where people come for a few days. Some of them stay for months. We have to make sure they're physically stable, build their weight up slowly, insist on bed rest, before we make a start on any psychological problems. We form relationships here. It's important. Most anorexics feel entirely alone.' Still, she saw he was sceptical. 'This illness has real and distressing physical symptoms. The girls' periods stop, patients' hair falls out, such weight loss can even trigger a heart attack. This is more than the self-indulgence of teenagers who want to look fashionable.'

'And Lorna needed that? The bed rest? The feeding?'

'She was very ill when she came here. She weighed less than six stone.'

'Hadn't her parents noticed?' Joe was horrified. 'Why didn't they do something before?'

'Anorexia is a sly disease. It creeps up on the sufferer. In the beginning, the parents might have encouraged the exercise, the decision of their child to cut out apparently unhealthy food. Weight can seem to drop away slowly at first. The sufferers are sly too. They hide. Throw away food when nobody's looking. Exercise in secret. You have to know that this is all about control. Control and compulsion. In chaotic and uncertain relationships, food is the one thing over which sufferers feel they have any power.'

'You're saying she was in a chaotic and uncertain relationship?'

'I'm saying that her relationship with the world was uncertain. She felt friendless at school. I have the sense that her parents' marriage was shaky. I'm pretty sure she'd never had a boyfriend if that's what you're asking.'

'Why did she need to come here? What was wrong with the NHS?' Joe's grandfather had been a miner, a union man. He and Sal might live in a smart house on an executive estate now, but this still felt all wrong. Whatever Joanne might say, he thought these were rich kids who just needed to pull themselves together and stop agonizing over their appearance.

'I worked in the NHS for ten years. I'd still be there if it had given me the resources to do my job properly. But it didn't and this is work that can't be rushed.' She looked up at him. 'I still feel bad about leaving. I still feel that I've deserted a sinking ship.' She paused and when she continued her voice was more even. 'Some health authorities pay for patients to come here. They recognize that ultimately, we provide good value for money. It's not cheap to keep an adolescent as a long-term inpatient in any hospital and we have a decent rate of success.'

'Tell me about Lorna,' Joe said. He wasn't here to argue politics with a woman who was cleverer than him and knew more about the issues.

'She was bright. Painfully quiet at first. Her refusal to speak was about control again, I think, like her refusal to eat. She was confused. But she did eat and she did put on weight slowly – then we could start the real work.'

'Which was?' Out of the window Joe saw a young man in a wheelchair being pushed down the path by a carer.

'Building her confidence and self-esteem. Giving her choices about her treatment and her future.'

'She went from here into her own place, not back to her parents. Was that her choice?'

'Yes. By the time she left us, she was eighteen. Officially an adult. We worked with social services locally to find her somewhere suitable.'

Joe was impressed again that the woman could remember the details so clearly. He forgot most of the cases he'd worked as soon as they went to court. 'Do you know why her relationship with her father had broken down so dramatically? Her parents are looking after Lorna's son now. Is there something we should know? Any possibility of safeguarding issues?'

Joanne looked up sharply. 'You're asking if there's any possibility that the father abused her as a child?'

Joe nodded.

'No,' Joanne said. 'I didn't pick up anything of that kind. There was more a coldness from the father, I think. A lack of communication. At least once Lorna had passed early child-hood.'

Joe felt frustrated. He'd already gained that information from Jill Falstone. He'd driven all this way and he felt as if he'd come away with nothing to help him explain the young woman's death. No little gem to carry back to Vera as a gift.

'I didn't know she'd had a child,' Joanne said. 'She kept in contact with me for a while – the odd text or call – but I've not heard from her for a couple of years. Pregnancy could have come as a surprise. Former anorexics often struggle to conceive.' She paused and professional curiosity seemed to take over. 'Was she depressed after the birth? That sometimes happens.'

'I don't think so. She seemed to be getting on with her life. She saw her mother regularly. I don't think they were particu-larly close, but at least they kept in touch.' Joe paused for a moment. 'There was a patient called Nat Blackstock here at the same time. Were he and Lorna friends?'

Joanne seemed confused by the question. 'Yes, close friends. I was Nat's key worker too. But he can't have anything to do with Lorna's murder. He died several years ago.'

'Do you remember his brother, Paul?'

'He was an older brother. Very protective.' She shut her eyes briefly in an attempt to recall the details. 'He spent a lot of time here. Too much time, I sometimes thought. Nat needed to be allowed to make his own decisions.'

But in the end, Joe thought, *Nat decided to die.*

'Would Paul have met Lorna?'

'I'm sure he did. As I said, she and Nat were very close friends.'

'Paul went on to marry someone working here,' Joe said. 'A drama therapist called Sophie. Do you remember her?'

'I do! We've had a number of artistic residencies over the years. I hadn't realized the two of them knew each other.'

'They say that this is where they met.'

There was a silence. Joe looked out over the tarn. Still, he was reluctant to leave without some gem to pass on to Vera. 'You say that Nat Blackstock's brother came here often. Did Lorna have any frequent visitors? Apart from her parents?'

'Her parents didn't come often. Lorna's choice, not theirs. A couple of pupils from her school turned up once, driven by their parents. I had the sense they were there out of duty – or guilt – rather than because they really wanted to be. And there was an older man, a relative I presume.'

'Would you have kept a record of their names?'

She shook her head. 'This is a hospital, Sergeant, not a prison.'

At last, Joe did get to his feet. 'Is there anything else you can tell me?'

Joanne considered for a moment. 'This is about Lorna as a woman, not a patient. She was hugely creative. She painted and she wrote. Stories and poetry as part of occupational therapy, but she kept a diary too. She said that one day she'd turn it into a book. To help other kids on the verge of anorexia.'

Joe made a note about that. He wondered if she'd continued writing the diary and where it was now. The CSIs hadn't mentioned finding anything like that in Lorna's house and they'd have been looking.

He was at the door, looking forward to heading east again, and back to proper policing. This was all too close to home. His Jess wasn't much younger than Lorna had been when she'd started starving herself and Jess was always complaining that she was too fat; she could get faddy with her food too.

He'd talk to Sal and make sure she was keeping an eye. He turned back to Joanne. 'Was Lorna one of the patients who had their care paid for by their health authority?'

Joanne shook her head. 'We don't have a partnership agreement with Northumbria. It must have been self-funded.'

'You *would* keep a record of that, wouldn't you?'

'Of course. It'll be in the office. Ask Elspeth to help you.'

And the efficient Elspeth, tapping on the computer, found the answer he needed very quickly. 'Lorna Falstone's fees were paid by a third party.' A pause. She'd been working on a laptop and turned it so Joe could see the screen. A pro-forma bill, the name at the top: Crispin Stanhope. 'Shall I print out the address?'

'No, thanks,' Joe said. 'I already have it.' His soul was singing. After all, he did have a little something to take back to Vera.

Chapter Twenty

TEN IN THE MORNING, AND VERA was back in Kirkhill, walking the streets, drinking Gloria's coffee, listening to gossip. The village hall was on the edge of the settlement on the road that led to Brockburn. It was wooden, and looked to Vera like a Scout hut, as if a strong puff of wind would blow it over. She got there before the art class arrived, but the building was already unlocked, the door on the latch. Inside it was cosier. The electric heaters on the wall must have been on for some time and a well-preserved blonde woman was filling a giant urn in the tiny kitchen. She turned when she saw Vera.

'Have you come to join us? It's only three quid a session and you get tea and biscuits for that as well as the tuition.'

This must be Veronica, Holly's informant.

'Ah, pet, I haven't got an artistic bone in my body. I'm Vera Stanhope, Detective Inspector. You spoke to one of my colleagues in the pub yesterday.'

'You're a Stanhope?' The woman was more curious about any relationship with the family in Brockburn than about Lorna's murder.

Vera waved her hand. She wondered how often she'd have to explain. 'A very distant relation to *your* Stanhopes. I understand that Lorna was a member of your group.'

'She came occasionally if she could persuade Thomas to time his nap to coincide with the sessions. Then she'd wheel him across in the buggy and join us.'

'Constance Browne is one of your members?'

'Oh, Connie's our leading light,' Veronica said. 'The group was her idea. She's usually here by now to help set things up.'

'What needs doing?'

'It's just a case of putting out the furniture. Some of us have our own easels, but everyone else uses the folding tables and they're stored under the stage. We could set up in our sleep now.' Veronica hadn't stopped moving while she was talking to Vera. Now she plugged in the urn and began to root in a cupboard for cups.

'And Josh Heslop? I suppose he gets here early too?' Vera had been hoping to speak to the tutor before the session started. Overnight, she'd formed the questions she'd have been unable to ask in front of his family.

'Nah, he rocks up just before we start. I don't think he takes us very seriously. It's not the most glamorous of gigs, is it, for an up-and-coming artist? Or maybe he thinks shifting tables is beneath him. I suspect he only does the class because Connie twisted his arm. And for the cash, I suppose.'

The other members of the art group started drifting in. Vera realized that her presence had lowered the average age in the room considerably. Most were in their sixties and seventies; a few were much older. No wonder Lorna only wandered in on occasions. What could she have in common with these elderly people with their chat of bargain cruises and brilliant grandchildren? Why had she attended at all? Perhaps she had felt some form of obligation to Constance Browne. Or, if Josh Heslop *was* her lover, it provided an excuse to see him without the rumour machine firing into action. Then Vera thought this gentle group of people probably provided her with the kind of warmth that her parents had seemed unable to give.

Josh Heslop came in, just as a couple of the students were starting to mutter disapproval about his being late. He was flustered, apologetic, full of excuses about his car not starting. Vera thought the group had probably heard it before, but they were indulgent. Really this was a social, rather than an educational, activity. A few of them were already working on a painting and he encouraged them to continue. 'I'll come around and take a look.' He set an earthenware jug, containing bare twigs and a spray of holly, on the table in front of him. 'Shall the rest of us start on this?'

Vera saw it would be impossible to talk to him now. The artists would feel short-changed if she dragged him away. She'd come back at the end of the class.

She stood behind Veronica, who was sketching out a landscape from a photo propped on the top of the easel. 'The view from my kitchen window. Isn't it joyous?'

Vera supposed it was, but this was her home, this space and these skies, and she took it for granted. 'Have you heard from Constance?'

'No. I tried phoning but I don't have any signal in here. Perhaps she didn't feel she could come so soon after Lorna's death. They were very close.'

Vera nodded, but decided she'd find out what had kept the teacher away. Connie would have decent coffee and home-made biscuits, and Vera was interested to know why the woman hadn't mentioned Lorna's attendance at the art class or her friendship with Josh Heslop. She must have understood that the information would be important. 'I'll be back before you finish.'

They were all so focused that she didn't think any of the others had noticed her leaving.

She left her car outside the hall and walked back to the village. There was ice on the river still and the wind was from the north again. Perhaps the bairns would have snow back for Christmas after all. She'd forgotten her gloves and kept her hands in her pockets, tried to pull her hat down over her ears, before realizing that her head was too big. Or that the hat was too small.

The curtains were open in Constance Browne's bungalow, but looking through the window, Vera saw the woman wasn't in the living room. Vera rang the bell. No answer. She tried the door. As she had expected, it was locked. She was about to turn away when she remembered she'd taken the car keys from Constance's car when she'd found it on the Friday night. The automatic response of a police officer. There had been other keys on the ring. Connie hadn't needed them and Vera had intended to pass them over to Billy Cartwright to go to the lab. She had her work bag with her and, pulling on a pair of nitrile gloves, she tried the keys one by one in the lock. At last the door opened.

Vera stood inside the door and shouted. Perhaps the woman was in the bath or the shower and the sound of an intruder would scare her. Still there was no response. Vera stopped, pulled shoe covers from the bag and put them over her boots, wobbling in the attempt. She was probably overreacting and she'd look like a proper twat if Connie bowled in from the Co-op with a bottle of milk, but she was feeling uneasy. Connie had been distressed by Lorna's death, but not over-wrought. She wasn't a woman who missed appointments. And she'd told Vera that she had an obsession about punctuality. She wouldn't have missed the art class without telling Veronica.

A corridor led down the length of the house with doors leading off. Vera opened them one by one. The living room was much as Vera had seen it on her previous visit. Tidy. She continued. To the left a big bedroom, bed made, a couple of garments folded on a chair, a wicker laundry basket, its contents waiting to be put away. A faint scent of talcum powder and washing powder. Connie's smell. The woman had slept there the night before.

Next to it a bathroom, empty. Then a smaller bedroom, cold, impersonal, seldom used. At the end of the corridor was a large kitchen, an extension built out into the garden, with a view over the village and across the valley to the forest beyond. It seemed clear that this was where Connie spent most of her time. A couple of easy chairs had been placed by the window. Over the hills on the horizon more clouds were gathering and the light was turning grey.

This was the last room left to search and Vera paused on the threshold before walking in. A Tupperware box of muesli stood on the table, next to a bowl, a tub of yoghurt, a supermarket container of blueberries. Of course, Constance would be a woman who went for a healthy breakfast. But the bowl and the spoon were clean. Constance had prepared her breakfast but not eaten it. A cafetière stood on the workbench close to the kettle. Coffee had been spooned into the glass jug, but no water had been added.

Vera saw these details from the doorway. Again, she told herself that she was being ridiculous, but she couldn't help considering this as a crime scene. In her head, she was talking to the woman. *Oh, Connie, if you'd told me everything you knew, everything you suspected, when I drank your tea and ate your biscuits, would you still be here, eating oats and fruit, drinking your upmarket coffee?*

She couldn't see the whole room from where she stood and now she moved in, so she could see the floor beyond the counter. In her head she'd pictured another body, more blood, bone and brain spilled onto the quarry-tiled floor, a confident older woman reduced to an interesting corpse for Paul Keating to pick over. In the end there was nothing. The room was empty. She was turning back to the rest of the house when a noise made her start and sent a shot of adrenaline through her body, but when she turned it was the big tabby pushing through the cat flap in the kitchen door. There was food for it in a bowl on the floor.

Vera was flooded with relief, a physical sensation that felt like drowning. Then came anticlimax, then suspicion. What had sent Constance Browne hurrying away from home before she'd eaten breakfast? Who had she been running away from? A killer who thought she knew too much, or the team who were investigating Lorna's death?

Chapter Twenty-One

IT WAS MONDAY MORNING AND JULIET thought Brockburn was returning to a semblance of normality. A team of officers was still searching the grounds, but they'd moved further away from the house now and seemed less intrusive. Mark had left early for Newcastle and his work at the theatre. Sometimes he went to the city on Sunday evening and slept in the flat he rented on the quayside, but this week she'd persuaded him to stay the night at Brockburn and leave first thing on Monday. She'd needed his company. By the time they'd returned after church and had lunch with the Charltons, Dorothy had retreated to the cottage, and Juliet had thought she couldn't bear an evening on her own with Harriet. Church and lunch had been ordeal enough.

In the end, she and Mark had spent the evening in Dorothy's cottage, babysitting Duncan while the couple went to a party at the Heslops' place. With all the drama, Juliet had quite forgotten she'd promised to look after the boy. She and Mark had passed a peaceful evening, enjoying the warmth and the quiet of the cottage, sharing a bottle of Dorothy's wine. Once,

Juliet had gone into Duncan's room to breathe in the scent of him, to stare at him in the dim light. It had been a restful evening after a fraught and unpleasant day.

Mark didn't have a religious bone in his body, but he always rather enjoyed the ritual of attendance at church in Kirkhill. Juliet thought it made him feel grand. He had images in his head of the royal family, turning out from Balmoral or Sandringham to spend an hour worshipping with the common people. But perhaps that was doing him an injustice – he would have hated to be considered that kind of snob – and it was the ritual he liked. Church was theatre of a kind too. He had a beautiful tenor voice and he joined in the hymns and the responses with great gusto. After the service, the weather had been too bad to stand talking in the churchyard, so there'd been an excuse to run straight back to the car, without having to discuss the drama at Brockburn with the other parishioners.

Sunday lunch with the Charltons had an element of ritual too. It had been a fixture every month since Crispin's death. Margaret Charlton was Harriet's second cousin, so it was considered a gesture of support to a widowed relative. It was also an opportunity for Margaret to boast about her children and for her husband Henry to drink more than he would normally be allowed. This wasn't one of the Sundays on the schedule, but when Margaret had phoned with the invitation, Juliet had accepted. The Charltons were gentle souls, and Juliet had thought it would be an excuse to get away from Brockburn, to eat a meal cooked by somebody else, and to escape having to deal with Lorna's murder. However, there had been no escape. Margaret and Henry Charlton had been desperate to talk about the killing, had leaned over the table, demanding information. They had reminded Juliet of the hounds from the

Brockburn kennels on hunt day, red tongues out, noses thrust forward in search of prey.

Now, it was Monday and Juliet could almost believe that nothing dramatic had occurred. Dorothy was upstairs, still stripping beds and cleaning bathrooms after the party on Friday. The hum of the hoover was reassuring, almost hypnotic. Harriet had taken herself off immediately after breakfast. 'I might park in Hexham and get a train into the city. There's an exhibition at the Laing Gallery that I rather fancy.'

Juliet thought any examination of the art would be superficial and quick. Harriet adored shopping, but would have thought it undignified to admit to browsing the city's clothes shops as a form of therapy. The exhibition provided an excuse. She would have lunch or afternoon tea with one of her friends. Usually Juliet was anxious when Harriet disappeared to Newcastle – she had an ability to spend money that was close to addictive, and Mark became almost puritan when Harriet came back dripping with upmarket clothes bags – but today she was delighted to be free of her mother.

Juliet was setting out a simple lunch for herself and Dorothy – the remains of the cheese and fruit left over from the Friday party – when the doorbell rang. Though there was a police officer on the gate, the previous day some journalists had found their way into the grounds and now Juliet answered the door with a little trepidation. She found it hard to be rude and to shut the door in the faces of the reporters, even when they'd climbed over a wall to intrude, so when she saw Vera standing there, it was almost with a sense of relief.

'Come in!'

Vera walked past her and made her way, without being asked, into the kitchen. She stood with her back to the Aga. 'It's still bloody freezing out there. I wouldn't be surprised if there was more snow.' She looked at the places set at the table. 'Just the two of you today?'

'Just Dorothy and me. Mark's at work and Mother has gone into Newcastle to get her monthly fix of the shops.'

'Have you and Dorothy been in all morning?'

'I've not left the house. Dorothy drove into Kirkhill first thing to pick up bread and milk. I thought we had some in the freezer, but your forensic chaps cleared us out.' Juliet couldn't see where this was leading. She wondered if all Vera's conversations sounded a bit like an interrogation.

Vera sat heavily on one of the wooden chairs by the table. 'Stick the kettle on, pet. I'm parched and this might take a while. It's not a courtesy call.'

'You've found out who killed Lorna?' *Then this might be over,* Juliet thought. *We can go back to how things were, worrying about money, Mark's project, the need for a new boiler, but not thinking about a killer who might be lurking in the trees in the park. Not worrying that someone we know is a murderer or that all our family secrets will spill out.*

'No.'

The kettle squealed and Juliet moved towards it to make tea. There were footsteps on the stairs and Dorothy appeared in the doorway carrying the hoover as if it had no weight at all. She looked at Vera. 'I thought I heard the door.'

'It's Constance Browne,' Vera said. 'She's disappeared. I wondered if you had any idea where she might be.'

'What do you mean, disappeared?'

Juliet poured boiling water into the teapot and carried it to the table.

'She left home suddenly, without telling anyone.' Vera sat

heavily on the nearest chair. 'Anyone else, whose car had been involved in a murder, and who disappeared off the face of the earth, we'd think of them as a suspect.'

'You don't believe Miss Browne killed Lorna?' Juliet thought this was so ridiculous that she wondered if Vera meant it as some weird joke. She felt herself begin to giggle, the rise of hysteria. She turned away to fetch mugs from a cupboard and only looked back when she'd composed herself.

'Why not? She was fit, strong. We only have her word that Lorna had borrowed the car last Friday. She could have been driving.' Vera reached out to pour tea into her mug before waiting to be asked, stared at Juliet. 'Or don't you think an older woman could be capable of planning something like that? Don't you think she'd have the nerve?'

'Constance had plenty of nerve,' Juliet said. 'But couldn't she just have gone off to Newcastle for a day's Christmas shopping? Or off to visit relatives for the holidays?'

'A day's Christmas shopping, maybe,' Vera conceded, 'but not the holiday. As far as we can tell, she didn't take anything with her. We're checking taxi firms and bus companies now. We still have her car, so she'd not have been driving.'

Dorothy fetched milk from the fridge and set another knife and plate for Vera. Lunch, it seemed, would be eaten, despite the new mini-drama.

'Constance might have the strength,' Dorothy said, 'and she's certainly intelligent enough to plan something like that, but why would she? There's no reason at all.'

'No skeletons in her cupboard?' Vera asked. 'Some secret Lorna might have discovered?'

'Of course not!' Juliet felt the hysteria bubbling again. 'This is ludicrous. Like some dreadful TV crime drama. In real life, retired village teachers don't go around hitting people over the head.'

'You're probably right, pet. She'll turn up at teatime and I'll look a right fool for having half of Northumbria police on the lookout for her.' Vera turned her attention to Dorothy. 'Did you enjoy the party at Home Farm last night?'

'Very much. It was kind of Mark and Juliet to babysit. We don't get out much.'

'And your fella's helping the Heslop girl with her exams?'

'Cath's struggling a bit. It can't be easy having such a bright elder sister.'

'So, Nettie's the brainy one?'

'According to Neil and Rosemary.'

'A bit like you and me, Dorothy.' Juliet couldn't help joining in. She tended to babble when she was nervous. 'I always felt a bit stupid compared to you.'

Vera took no notice of that and carried on speaking before Dorothy could comment. 'Nice that you're both settling into the community.'

'It is,' Dorothy said. 'We both feel very much at home already.'

Now Vera turned back to Juliet. 'There's something I need to ask you. It's a family matter. Perhaps we should discuss it on our own.'

Dorothy stood up. 'Of course. I'll leave you to it. There's plenty to do upstairs. Lunch can wait.'

The last thing Juliet needed was to be left alone with Vera. 'No, no. Please stay. Dorothy's my friend, Vera. I would tell her anyway, once you've gone.'

Vera nodded again and Dorothy returned to her chair. 'My sergeant's just been to Halstead House, the private hospital where Lorna was treated for anorexia. It's a pricey business being ill, it seems, if you don't want to queue with the NHS.' She paused, seeming reluctant at first to ask her question. 'Lorna's bills were paid by your father, Juliet. Did you know about that? Was it some kind of loan to the Falstones?'

For a while, Juliet said nothing. So, after all, the family secrets would leak out. Harriet's efforts over the years to keep a lid on things, to smile as she walked into church, to host garden parties for the Women's Flower Guild and the WI, to pretend that there was no gossip, had all been in vain. *Poor Mother. It was such a strain. Perhaps it'll be a relief not to have to pretend any more.* But she knew Harriet would be mortified.

'I didn't know about *that*,' she said at last. 'I knew my father had relationships with other women. He was famous for it. Nobody talked of it, of course. When he was younger it was almost as if he were admired for it, for his ability to charm.'

'He'd had a relationship with Lorna?'

'No!' Juliet was horrified. 'She was still a child when he became ill. He died not long after she left the clinic.'

'So it was Jill Falstone he had the affair with?'

Again, Juliet took a while to answer and wondered how much she should tell. But Vera was a witch; she'd find out anyway. 'Jill was different from the others. I think she got under his skin.'

'How do you know? You'd only have been a bairn.'

Another silence. The deep dense silence that could only be experienced this far from neighbours and a road. 'I was an only child,' Juliet said. 'I spent a lot of time listening to conversations I wasn't supposed to hear. When my mother was out of the house, my father made telephone calls to Jill. He loved her, I think.' A pause. 'Once, I went into his office and he was crying.'

'Was Lorna his daughter?'

'No!' This time there was no hesitation. 'No! My father could be reckless when it came to his own safety. He rode like a madman and drove like a maniac. But he wouldn't have allowed anything like that. Not something that would have affected the reputation of the family.' There was a pause and Juliet considered the question again and pushed it away. Just as she had since she'd first met Lorna when she was still a child, riding a horse that was just too small for her.

Now, there was another silence, and when Vera spoke it was very gently. 'You do know we'll be able to find out,' she said. 'We'll ask to take a sample of your DNA and compare it to Lorna's.' Another pause. 'Of course, we'll be discreet.'

This was much worse than Juliet had been expecting. 'My father felt an obligation to Jill Falstone. When her daughter was struggling, he wanted to help. I think he would have acted in the same way for any of his tenants who were in trouble, for Nettie or Cath Heslop at Home Farm, for example.'

'But he never had an affair with their mother? With Rosemary?'

'No!' Juliet imagined her father falling for Rosemary Heslop, so domestic and practical, so physically ordinary, and couldn't help smiling. 'She wasn't his type at all.'

Dorothy shifted in her seat. 'I'm sorry, Inspector, but I don't quite see how this might relate to Constance Browne's disappearance.'

Vera smiled. 'Good question. I've been wondering about that myself.' She turned back to Juliet. 'You'd have needed someone to talk to while all this was going on. You'd still have been in the primary school when Lorna was born, when your dad was losing his head over a bonnie lass. You wouldn't have known Dorothy here then. It occurred to me that you might have confided in Connie.'

Juliet blinked. For a moment she was back in the little school, in the playground surrounded by fields, the sound of sheep. There was a climbing frame where the brave girls hung like bats, their knees round the bar, skirts falling over their heads, so the boys screamed that their knickers were showing. She'd never been one of the brave girls. It must have been April because there were new lambs in the field and someone in the village had been cutting grass. She couldn't remember how old she'd been. Not in the top class, because one of the older girls came over to her and started jeering about her father. Using words Juliet had never heard before. She'd cried and run inside and had found Miss Browne drinking coffee from a flask she must have brought with her. Even now Juliet could remember the smell of the coffee with the back note of floor polish.

Somehow, it had all spilled out. 'I think my father's going to leave us.'

Miss Browne had said seriously:

'That wouldn't be the end of the world though, would it? It would be sad, of course, but not worth crying about. Other pupils in the school have had parents who've divorced. You'd cope, Juliet. I promise.'

That hadn't been what Juliet had wanted to hear. She'd wanted reassurance, for Miss Browne to laugh and to tell her how stupid she was being. Because, deep down, Juliet had known she wasn't like the other pupils, she'd known that people gossiped about her family in a way that they never did about anyone else, that as Mummy was always saying, they had a position to maintain. She'd been brought up to believe that she was different.

Juliet stared back at Vera. 'I didn't tell Connie anything that the rest of the village hadn't guessed. I really can't see how it might have prompted any drama after all this time.' She managed a little smile. 'We're old news now. It's three years since my father died.'

Vera drank her tea. Nobody had eaten anything. Juliet cut a few slices of bread to start them off, in the hope of bringing things back to normal. Vera reached out for a slice, buttered it, cut a lump of cheese. 'If Lorna *was* Crispin's daughter, would she be entitled to anything from the estate?'

'No,' Juliet said. 'Absolutely not! I would be the oldest child. Whatever happened, it comes to me. It *has* come to me. Mummy's entitled to live here until her death, of course, but I inherited.'

'There was a will then?'

'A very old one. My father made it soon after I was born.' Juliet wondered if Vera was thinking she might be due some kind of inheritance, but Hector had never been in the running and he'd died several years before Crispin.

But Vera only seemed mildly amused. 'Eh, it seems very old-fashioned, doesn't it? This talk of wills and inheritance. Very genteel. As you say, it's hard to believe they could have anything to do with the brutal murder of a young woman.' She bit into a doorstop sandwich. 'Would it make any difference that Lorna had a son? Don't boys matter more in situations like this?'

Juliet kept calm. 'Not if there was a will. Besides, the house is already mine.'

Vera turned her attention to Dorothy. 'You were in Kirkhill this morning? You didn't see Constance?'

'Yes, I was in the village. We needed a few things from the shop, but I was only gone for twenty minutes. Juliet will tell you.' Dorothy looked at Juliet, who nodded. 'No, I'm afraid I didn't see her.'

'I'll have to speak to Harriet and Mark,' Vera said. 'Are you expecting them home today?'

'Mother will be back for dinner. Mark will stay another night in the city. He has meetings all day tomorrow.'

'You're sure he didn't know Lorna?'

'Quite sure.' Juliet managed a little laugh. 'They didn't move in the same circles at all.'

'Oh, I don't know. Apparently, Lorna was quite arty. Perhaps they had more in common than we'd think.' Vera didn't seem to expect a response, which was just as well. She finished the food on her plate. 'Very tasty. I don't think I've got any more questions now. But if you think of anything, you will be in touch?' She got to her feet.

'Of course.' Juliet stood too. She walked with Vera to the door. In the far distance, the blue-suited officers were still in the woodland, moving so slowly that they could have been motionless, some strange art installation. Antony Gormley, perhaps. Vera reached out and touched Juliet's shoulder. 'Someone will be back to take that DNA sample. You just take care.' Then she disappeared into her Land Rover without a backward glance.

Later, when Dorothy had gone back to the cottage to spend an hour with Karan and Duncan, Juliet slipped upstairs. Again, she remembered being a child, snooping, listening. She'd gone through her parents' letters then, looking for anything that would make sense of what was going on around her. Now, she paused outside her mother's room and wondered if it was time for her to search again.

Chapter Twenty-Two

HOLLY SPENT THE MORNING IN KIMMERSTON police station. She was there when Vera called through Constance Browne's disappearance, and still at her desk in the early afternoon, answering calls from the public, staring at blotchy CCTV picked up from the main street in Kirkhill. She thought the boss had lost it big style this time and that she was seriously overreacting. Constance Browne had been close to Lorna Falstone, so surely it wasn't beyond the bounds of reason that she might change her routine a little, decide she wanted to escape the village for a day. If Holly lived in Kirkhill, she'd want to escape. And so what, if it was a spur-of-the-moment decision and she'd left before breakfast? Perhaps Connie had suddenly lusted after eggs Benedict for brunch in one of the classier coffee shops in Newcastle. That would have been Holly's idea of heaven. As the morning wore on, though, and Connie still wasn't responding to her phone or her email, Holly began to understand Vera's disquiet.

It was two o'clock when Vera phoned again.

'Can you go into Newcastle and have a chat to Mark Bolitho?

Apparently, he left home at six this morning to get into town before the morning rush hour. If he has witnesses to say he was in the theatre that early, I can't see how he could have been involved in Connie's disappearance. But you know there are rumours in the village that Lorna made trips into Newcastle to see a wealthy fancy man. And Bolitho has a reputation as a bit of a womanizer. That could tie up. After all, there's nobody else who could meet the description. He and Connie might even have been friends. Two arty souls among the philistines of Kirkhill.' Vera gave a little laugh. 'He might have an idea where she's run off to.'

Despite the laugh, Holly sensed Vera's anxiety. Was it because Connie was a spinster of a certain age and she felt some affinity for the woman? Was Vera hoping that people might look for *her* if she suddenly did a runner?

But at least chatting to Bolitho would give her an excuse to get away from her desk. 'Doesn't Josh Heslop spend time in Newcastle too?'

'Aye, he does and he was a student there until recently. He and Lorna could have arranged to meet in the city away from prying eyes if they were having a fling. I'm not quite sure why they'd feel they had to keep that relationship secret, though, unless Lorna had that obsession to be in control of things again. Secrets are a sort of control, aren't they?' The boss paused, seemed to be thinking. 'You're right, though, Hol. We need to check. While you're in the toon, talk to Heslop's mates, the ones he claims can confirm he was partying on Friday night. I'll forward the names and numbers he gave to me yesterday.'

So Holly drove back into the city that felt like home. As much as anywhere did. She parked close to the Quayside and watched the Tyne blown into waves, the reflection of the Sage

Music Centre chopped and cut by the wind. The famous bridges. Then she turned her back to the river and made the short walk to the Live Theatre, the wind in her face.

It was early afternoon and a school party was watching a kids' matinee, an adaptation by David Almond of one of his own novels. She'd loved the books as a child and was almost tempted into the auditorium. Music and children's laughter seeped out. Holly stood by the box office, waited until a woman had bought a couple of tickets for the evening performance, then asked for Mark Bolitho.

'I'm not sure if he's free. Can somebody else help? If it's about a role in the new show, you'll have to arrange an audition through your agent.'

'I'm not an actor.' Holly showed her ID.

'Oh, it'll be about that terrible murder in his house out at Kirkhill. I'll give him a ring.' There was a whispered phone conversation, then the woman turned back. 'He'll be down in a minute.'

Mark took Holly into his office at the top of the building and made her coffee. There were posters for shows she'd been to see on the walls. A shelf full of plays and books about theatre. He was pleasant enough, but she sensed his impatience. The phone rang. He frowned but left it unanswered. 'I really don't think I can help you. I told you everything I know at the weekend. I am very busy.'

'Has your wife called you since you left home?'

'No,' he said, 'but I've just come out of a lunchtime planning meeting and I haven't had a chance to check my phone.'

'A woman called Constance Browne has disappeared. Lorna was driving her car the night she was murdered and we're starting to get a little concerned.'

'You think Lorna was killed by mistake? That they were after Connie Browne all the time?'

This had never occurred to Holly. It seemed unlikely – even in the dark a retired teacher couldn't be mistaken for Lorna Falstone and the woman hadn't been killed in the car – but it was something she might suggest as a possibility at the evening's briefing. Vera liked her detectives to show initiative and Constance seemed to be the focus of her attention at the moment. 'You know Miss Browne?'

'Yes. Juliet's very fond of her. She even invited her to our wedding. We hold occasional fund-raising events in the gardens – the church fete, that sort of thing – and Connie's always one of the main movers. She seems to run every committee going in the village. I've talked to her recently about becoming involved in my theatre project. She'd make a brilliant volunteer and a kind of advocate in the village for my plans. She seemed very keen.'

'What time did you get to the theatre this morning?'

'Just before nine.'

'According to your wife, you left home just after six.' Holly felt awkward about the way the conversation was going, the inevitable tone of accusation in her voice. Mark Bolitho was an influential creative, at least here in the North-East. She couldn't imagine him abducting an elderly woman, or helping her to flee from justice. 'It wouldn't take you three hours to get here.'

'Of course not. I went to my flat first and dropped off some of my stuff. I'm staying there tonight. Then I had breakfast in the place close by. I'm a regular. They'll remember me.' He smiled at her, as if he understood the position that she was in. 'Avocado on sourdough with a poached egg and a double espresso to kickstart the day. Always the same.'

'We think Lorna Falstone came into Newcastle sometimes on the bus. We're trying to find out what she did in the city, who she met. Are you sure she never came here?'

'I told you, in Brockburn, I didn't know her.' His tone was frosty.

'There are rumours in Kirkhill that the two of you were friendly.'

For a moment, Holly thought Bolitho was furious. He stared at her, his body still and tense. Then he threw back his head and laughed. 'They believe I'm the father of her child? You do know that's completely ridiculous.'

Holly wasn't quite sure what else there was to say. She couldn't accuse him of lying about a potential relationship with Lorna without any evidence at all. She remembered her last conversation with Karan and Dorothy. She'd asked them if Mark and Juliet were happy. Now she reworded the same question. 'It must be hard splitting your time between the theatre and the big house in the country. Doesn't it feel . . .' she paused to find the right words, '. . . a bit schizophrenic?'

He laughed again. 'I suppose it does. But in a good way. I think I'd go a bit mad if all I had was the life of a country gent. The house, the dogs, Harriet playing lady of the manor. This way I can escape the *Brideshead* myth for a couple of days a week.'

'You don't have to be here full-time?'

He shook his head. 'I job-share with a woman who's just had a baby. Sophie Blackstock. You met her, I think, because she was one of the guests at the party. I'm covering her maternity leave at the moment, but I'll go back to part-time in a few months. It suits us both. Even now, I can work a lot from home. I've got an office at Brockburn. But if the new project works out, I'll have the best of both worlds. Bringing theatre to rural Northumberland is something I'm passionate about and there's something pitifully indulgent about that huge place standing almost empty.'

'Juliet and Harriet don't mind?'

'Juliet's as excited by it as I am and Harriet realizes it's the only way to stop the roof falling in, unless she turns the place into a hotel or has glampers in the garden, and she'd hate that. Besides, she doesn't really have much say. The place is Juliet's. Her father gave it to her when she was still quite young. Some wheeze to avoid inheritance tax. So, Harriet can like it or lump it.' Mark sounded gleeful. A schoolboy.

Holly got to her feet. She'd check the cafe where Mark had claimed to have breakfast – Vera insisted on rigour, on not making assumptions – but she couldn't see that Bolitho would have murdered anyone. And what reason would he have to lie if he'd helped Constance to run away?

The cafe was on the ground floor of the block where Bolitho had his apartment. The building was stylish and cool with a view of the Tyne and the Blinking Eye bridge. Holly wouldn't have been able to afford a place here and she could see why some Kirkhill residents might consider him minted. The cafe was busy. It was near the Crown Court and there were smart lawyers in suits and business people having a late lunch, women who'd escaped the busy pre-Christmas town centre for tea and cake. Holly ordered coffee and waited for a lull in the service before going back to the counter and introducing herself.

'You know Mark Bolitho?'

'The theatre guy? Sure.' He was in his twenties, confident in ripped jeans and black T-shirt, but still with a trace of adolescent acne, a teenager's inability to keep still. 'He's a regular.'

'Was he in for breakfast this morning?'

'Probably.' He started wiping down the fancy coffee machine.

'You don't remember specifically?' Holly wanted to shout, to tell him to pay attention, to focus. 'It's important.'

'Look, it's crazy here at breakfast time. I don't have time to look at the faces. I see the hands with the debit cards, swiping through contactless, the coffees, the orders.'

'He always has avocado on sourdough.'

'Ah, he can't have been here this morning then. We couldn't get any avocado. There was nearly a fucking riot.' Now he did look up at her. 'First-world problems, huh?'

Oh, Mark, she thought and she smiled. *Why did you lie?*

She was walking away when she turned back. 'Have you ever seen him here with a woman?'

'Tall? Skinny? Yeah. Not recently though. Not for a while.'

Joshua Heslop's friends both worked in the same place, the Baltic Gallery on the south side of the river. Once it had been a ruined flour warehouse, now it housed contemporary art, strange installations, interesting sculpture. Holly tried to imagine Vera here and failed. Oliver worked in the gift shop and Jonnie was an outreach worker, planning projects to hook in kids. They were a couple and they'd both been at university with Joshua. There was a bar overlooking the Tyne and she met them there. They'd just finished their shift and were drinking beer. She ordered a mint tea; any more caffeine and she'd be as jumpy as the barista she'd just been interviewing.

The light had drained away and now the reflections in the

river were street lights, the neon signs advertising the bars and restaurants on the north side of the Tyne. There was a hooter and the Millennium Bridge slowly swung open, the eye blinking not to let through a ship but just to show that it could.

'Joshua stayed with you on Friday night?'

'Yeah. It was a party, a kind of reunion of the gang we were at uni with.' Oliver was pale, slender, still. He could have been a sculpture, carved from white marble. 'Josh was always going to stay. He wouldn't have been able to get back to the farm by public transport. In the end, of course, the weather made it impossible and he was with us until Saturday afternoon.'

'You're close friends?'

'The best,' Jonnie said. 'We shared a student house when we were at Northumbria Uni.'

'Tell me about him.' Holly looked at the clock on the wall of the bar. She had plenty of time before the evening briefing. There was no need to rush this.

'He's not complicated,' Jonnie said. 'There's no artistic angst. He likes the simple life, his family, the farm. He loves his art too, of course, but that's all related.'

'In what way?'

'He does meticulous watercolours, which draw you into the painting, into the detail. They're not photographic, I don't mean that. You'll have to see them to understand. His work is different from anyone else I can think of. He captures his place in the landscape.'

'Where could I see them?'

'Well, not here. They'd get lost in a gallery this size. There's an exhibition in a little place in Kimmerston.'

Holly nodded. 'I'll go and look out for it.' A pause. 'Has he got a girlfriend?' There was a silence. It didn't seem a hard question and she couldn't understand why they couldn't answer immediately. 'Well?' She was losing patience with them, then realized the assumption she'd made, found herself blushing. 'A boyfriend?'

'Nah.' Jonnie laughed. 'He's not gay, but he's got this secret woman, someone he won't tell us about. We thought he might bring her to the party on Friday – he hinted that he might. Then he turned up on his own.'

'And drank himself stupid all night,' Oliver said. 'We thought he might be broken-hearted, that maybe he'd just been dumped.'

'You don't know anything about her? A name?'

'Nope. I wondered if she was married, someone his family might disapprove of. He's always been very close to his parents and sees his dad as a kind of hero. He'd hate to upset them.'

Holly looked at the clock again. Now it was time to drive back to Kimmerston to the evening briefing. She'd go right past her flat on the way there and for a moment, she wondered if she could go home, just phone in what she'd discovered during the day. Then she thought that she had important information, information that Vera would value, and she didn't want to miss being there for that. But there was something in the flat that she wanted to collect, so she just called in briefly and was on her way.

Chapter Twenty-Three

Joe Ashworth was halfway home from Cumbria, had just crossed into Northumberland, and was following the line of Hadrian's Wall, feeling a sense of relief at being back on familiar territory, when his phone rang. He'd already had a call from Vera to tell him about the disappearance of Constance Browne, but this was a number he didn't recognize. He answered it anyway.

'Sergeant Ashworth? It's Joanne Simmons Wright.' *The psychologist from Halstead House.*

He pulled into a lay-by. The car was buffeted by a northerly wind and there was a view of bare moorland. If he got home at a reasonable time tonight, they'd get the wood-burner going, the curtains drawn, spend a bit of time with the kids. His vision of board games and hot chocolate around the fire never seemed to work out in reality – the children got bored, distracted, and started demanding their screens back and Sal was ultra-competitive – but in the middle of this bleakness, the idea was appealing. Joanne started talking and he had to make an effort to listen.

'I had a few days' leave at the end of last week, and then there was yoga and my meeting with you, so I've only just had the chance to check my voicemail.'

'Yes?' He was still planning his idyllic evening in. Perhaps they'd get takeaway pizza. The kids would love that and it would save Sal cooking.

'There was a message from Lorna Falstone.'

Now she had his full attention. 'When did she phone you?'

'Thursday morning.'

Thursday was when Lorna had left Thomas with Connie because she'd had something urgent to do.

'What did she say?'

'It's rather a long message,' Joanne said. 'In fact, she called twice. Would you like to come back to hear it?'

He hesitated for a moment. He was halfway home and the over-heated, familiar office in Kimmerston nick seemed very attractive. 'Of course. I'll be there in less than an hour.'

The psychologist was waiting for him in the reception hall. Joe could tell she was restless, distraught. She'd changed from the Lycra and sweatshirt into a long skirt over boots, a jersey the colour of chestnuts. 'I keep thinking that if I'd been here to answer her call, she might not have died.'

She took him back into the same office. There was a filter coffee machine on a sideboard, the jug still almost full, and she poured out two mugs, offered him a little carton of UHT milk. He shook his head. He would have liked sugar, but that didn't seem to be on offer.

'This was the first call.' She pressed a button. Joe had already taken out his phone and set it to record. Lorna seemed to come back to life for a moment, to became more real to him than she had at any time during the investigation. She sounded very young, her accent the gentle rural Northumberland lilt of the hills. It was very similar to Vera's, but Lorna's voice was panicky, in places almost shrill.

'*Joanne, I need to talk to you. I thought I was doing fine. I was doing fine. But something's happened. I need to talk to someone. It feels like it did before, as if it's all unravelling. I'm losing control. I worry that I'll be ill again, that I won't be fit to care for Thomas. That I might hurt myself. Can I come in to see you? I could borrow a car, come over tomorrow. I know it's early and you probably won't be in yet. I'll try again later.*'

'Couldn't she have asked to speak to another counsellor?'

'She could,' Joanne said, 'but it's a long time since she was resident here. Staff move on. She couldn't have guaranteed speaking to someone she knew.'

'You said there was a second message.'

'Yes, that came a couple of hours later. The first call came through at seven-thirty in the morning.'

While Joanne reset the phone, Joe put himself in Lorna's place. Had she had a bad night with Thomas? The toddler was of an age when he'd be teething. Joe could remember how that felt, a child whingeing and refusing to settle, the exhaustion and the guilt because by morning you'd run out of patience and any sympathy you might have felt had long since gone. No partner and parents you didn't feel you could ask for help. No wonder if she'd felt she needed someone to talk to. But Joe thought the call had been prompted by more than that. Lorna Falstone had sounded seriously scared.

'Are you ready for the next message?' Joanne had her finger poised over the button. He set his phone and nodded. 'This was timed just after nine.'

So just before Lorna had gone to Constance and asked her to babysit.

'*Joanne, it's me again. Lorna. I'm sorry if I was a bit melodramatic before. I'm a bit calmer this time. Look, I've found someone to talk to. Someone who runs one of the groups. I still need to speak to you, though. I don't think anyone else would properly understand. You're the only person who can help. I know you're busy and you have other patients now, but please come back to me if you pick this up.*'

Joe looked across at Joanne and saw she was almost in tears.

'She'll have thought I didn't care enough to get back to her. She died thinking that.'

Joe shook his head. 'If she knew you, she'd have understood you'd have called her back if you could.' He paused. 'What was the group she was talking about?'

'It could be an informal group for sufferers of anorexia. Or a fellowship on the Alcoholics Anonymous model. When she left Halstead House, she'd have been given a list of meetings, a phone number to ring. Some people find that kind of support very helpful.'

'Could you give me the list that she had?'

'Of course.' Joanne seemed relieved to be given something practical to do. She went to her computer and the printer started whirring.

Joe scanned the paper. There was a list of venues with contact details next to each one. 'The closest seems to be in Newcastle.' *Perhaps that was where she was going on her bus trips to the city. To find support in her illness. A lot less glamorous than meeting the wealthy boyfriend invented by village gossip.*

'We try to keep the list updated. She might have been given slightly different information.' Joanne seemed to have calmed a little now. She glanced at the clock on the wall. 'Look, I'm sorry, I have to see another patient.'

Joe nodded and got to his feet. It would be afternoon before he got back to Kimmerston, but he'd have time to phone the leader of the Newcastle support group before the briefing. If Lorna *had* gone to that meeting on the day before she died and confided in the group, they might have a much clearer idea about the motive for her murder.

Chapter Twenty-Four

VERA SAT IN THE CUPBOARD OF an office, which she'd managed to cling on to even when the rest of the team had been forced to go open-plan. It was gloomy even in summer and this time of year the desk lamp was always on. She'd made coffee and wrapped her hands round the mug. The office was either sweltering or freezing and this was one of the days when the heating wasn't working. She was sitting in her coat. In her more paranoid moments, she wondered if the faltering radiators were part of a conspiracy designed by her unpleasant boss to force her into early retirement. Or into sharing a desk in the office like a goldfish bowl.

The news that Crispin had paid Lorna's hospital fees had shaken Vera, but it hadn't surprised her. She hadn't been convinced by Juliet's assertion that Crispin couldn't be Lorna's father. The response had come too swiftly and too stridently. Vera thought the relationship was a possibility that Juliet must have already considered for herself. Perhaps it had been so distasteful to her that she'd pushed it to the back of her mind, but it hadn't come as a new idea.

This had implications. Personal implications. If Juliet and Lorna had been half-sisters, then Vera would have been related to the lass too. A cousin of some description. Vera felt an unusual ache of familial responsibility. She couldn't have known about Lorna's problems but felt the pain of guilt all the same, a sense that she should have been there to protect the young woman. And now, it seemed, she might also be some kind of distant relative to Thomas. That too might bring with it unwanted obligations.

She was still sitting in her office, mulling over the day's events, when the team started to gather for the evening briefing. Vera was feeling odd. She was used to being alone in the world. She had her colleagues and felt no need for a family. She'd looked after Hector in his last months out of a sense of duty. Because she was all he had.

She'd known about Juliet and Harriet, of course, but had never thought of making contact, even after Hector's death. She had too much pride. If she'd made an effort to know them, they might have thought she was on the scrounge too. And it wasn't as if they needed her. They had the big house and centuries of entitlement and had never acknowledged her as part of the Stanhope clan. What could they possibly have in common?

Now, it seemed, there was that scrap of a child who might have a claim on her affections. The thought that there could be another generation of Stanhopes, as excluded as she had been, made Vera think differently about herself. Of course she couldn't care for the baby! That would never work. But perhaps she should look out for him in some way. Be a kind of mentor as he was growing up. Not let any bastard take advantage.

Vera picked up her notebook and made her way to the ops

room. Everyone was gathered. They must have been waiting for her. She looked at the clock and saw she was five minutes late.

'Sorry, everyone!' It was time to focus, to shut out any other emotion until the case was over. 'Right. What have you got for me? Joe, I got the message that you went back to the private clinic in Cumbria. What was that all about? Your psychologist friend wanted more of your scintillating company?'

There was a snigger from the back.

Joe explained about the voicemails from Lorna. Vera listened to the messages and then asked him to play them again. Joe switched off his phone and stood up so he was facing the room. 'Mrs Simmons Wright gave me a list of possible anorexic support groups, of people Lorna might have contacted. The nearest to Kirkhill is in Kimmerston. I've been trying to call the number on the list and I've just got through.'

'Is that where Lorna was on the Thursday before she died, the day Connie Browne was looking after the bairn?'

'Yes, at least there was no group meeting that morning, but they met up in the woman's home.' He paused. 'I couldn't get much out of her over the phone. She's called Olivia Best, she's a midwife and she was just rushing out to go on shift, but I've arranged to visit tomorrow morning. She lives just down the road from me.'

'Champion.' Vera felt a spark of optimism. It was clear from the voicemail message that Lorna had been frantic, that she had something important to discuss. They had to find out what that was. 'You've had a productive morning, Joe. For the rest of you, our sergeant here discovered that Crispin, father of Juliet, paid all Lorna's hospital fees. Now, he could just have been a charitable soul, with a sense of obligation to his tenants.

But as he had a reputation as a lecherous old goat, there's also a possibility that he was Lorna's dad.' She pointed at Charlie. 'I've warned Juliet that we'll need a DNA sample from her. Can we do that asap? I'm not sure how that'll move us forward in the inquiry, but it might explain Robert Falstone's coldness to his daughter, and that's one fewer thing to chase up.' A pause. 'How did you get on with the Blackstocks yesterday, Joe? And was your psychologist able to shed further light on any relationship between them and Lorna?'

'She remembered them both – Paul and Sophie – but my impression was that neither was particularly close to Lorna.'

'Just a coincidence then that they happened to be in Brockburn the night Lorna died?'

He shrugged. 'Maybe. Sophie job-shares with Mark, and he's running the place full-time while she's on maternity leave. That's why they came to be there.'

'They're just colleagues? Nothing closer?'

He shrugged again, unwilling to commit himself either way, and Vera turned her attention to Holly.

'You've had a day in the city, Hol. What have you got for us?'

'I've found out that Mark Bolitho's a liar.'

'Is he, now? And how do we know this?'

'He left home at six this morning. At that time of day, it wouldn't have taken longer than an hour to get into work, but he didn't get to his office until nine. He claims he had breakfast in a cafe near his flat. Avocado on toast.'

Vera wondered when that had become a thing. 'I'm not sure we need a breakdown of his breakfast preferences.'

'Trust me, boss, it's relevant. I checked with the cafe. This morning there was no avocado.'

'Oh, Mr Bolitho! If you hadn't been so clever, adding the details in the hope we'd believe you, so arrogant, we'd never have caught you out.' Vera gave a little chuckle. 'Well done, Hol. Any idea what he was doing in his spare two hours?'

'I'm checking CCTV in the city.'

'Check CCTV out to the coast too. Maybe he went to Tynemouth to see the lovely Sophie.'

Holly nodded. 'The guy in the cafe did say he went in sometimes with a skinny young woman. That could have been Sophie. She was a colleague.'

Vera considered for a moment. 'Or it could have been Lorna.' She had a brief tremor of revulsion. She hoped desperately that this lying city boy wasn't the father of the child, with whom she now imagined she had a connection. How unimaginative, how pathetic, if Mark had followed in his father-in-law's footsteps and slept with one of the Brockburn tenants! She couldn't think how Juliet might cope with the knowledge.

Holly was talking again. 'I spoke to Joshua Heslop's friends. He was definitely with them on Friday night, so we can rule him out of Lorna's murder. Even though he didn't join them until eight-thirty, he couldn't have killed Lorna and got to Newcastle in that weather. He must have left Kirkhill earlier in the day.'

'Did we learn anything more about him?'

'They admire his art. He has an exhibition in a small gallery here in Kimmerston. They were expecting him to bring a girlfriend with him, but she didn't show.'

That sparked Vera's interest. 'Had they met her? Was she Lorna?'

'They didn't know anything about her. He'd been very

mysterious. Friday was to be the evening when he'd finally introduce her to his arty mates.'

Holly paused, but Vera could tell there was something else. 'What's bothering you, Hol? Spit it out!'

'When Charlie and I looked round Lorna's house on Sunday, we saw her paintings. There was one subject that she painted over and over again. It seemed to haunt her. A cottage in the forest. I haven't been able to forget it because it seemed so important to her. I thought the image was imaginary, kind of symbolic. Only one was titled and that was wintry, the most recent. She'd called it "The Darkest Evening", and that seemed familiar. There was a book of poetry on her desk – a collection of Robert Frost's work. It's been inscribed inside by Constance. I did Frost's poetry at school and I still had the book at home. I picked it up on my way through from the Baltic Gallery.'

Holly paused. Vera could tell the others in the room were bored, but she was interested. She nodded for Holly to continue.

'One of the poems is called "Stopping by Woods on a Snowy Evening".' Holly stopped and opened the book. 'This is the second verse:

'My little horse must think it queer . . .' She was interrupted by a muffled snigger from the back of the room.

Vera turned to the offender. 'You're not in the playground now! How old are you? Go on, Hol.'

'. . . *To stop without a farmhouse near* /
Between the woods and frozen lake /
The darkest evening of the year.

'And it ends like this:

'*The woods are lovely, dark and deep,* /
But I have promises to keep /

201

And miles to go before I sleep /
And miles to go before I sleep.'

Holly looked up. 'She must have got the title of the painting from the poem, don't you think? There's a feeling of a fairy tale in it.'

The room was growing even more restless; poetry obviously wasn't their thing. Vera felt sorry for her.

'You think it's relevant that Constance gave her the book?'

'I don't know.' Holly ploughed on: 'But I wonder if the place she painted could be real. A real cottage. If Lorna needed somewhere to hide from the world . . .' She paused. 'And then she seems to have been very low recently, anxious. That would chime with the title. "The Darkest Evening".'

Now, Vera could tell, Holly was anxious, scared she looked stupid, or pretentious, or both. The lass cared far too much what other people thought. 'I assume you took a photo. Let's have a look. Kirkhill's my patch. I might recognize it.'

Of course, there wasn't just one photo, there were several, all turned into images that could be linked to Holly's computer and projected onto a screen. Vera could see why Holly might at first have thought that Lorna had imagined the place. There was something idealized about it, even when it had been painted as dark and brooding. The poem caught the essence of it. She shook her head. 'Sorry, Hol, it doesn't mean anything to me. Can you send it across? I've got a contact, a former Wildlife Liaison Officer. If it's anywhere local to Kirkhill, he'll recognize it.'

Holly nodded, relieved.

'Anyone else?' Vera scanned the room.

There was a brief silence before Joe asked, 'Did the CSIs

find a diary in Lorna's house? The hospital psychologist said she kept one and she'd talked about turning her experiences into a book or a blog.'

Vera looked at Billy Cartwright. 'Your lot come across anything like that?'

'Sorry.' Cartwright paused. 'No laptop either, which is a bit strange for a lass of that age. Especially if she was thinking about doing some sort of blog. And no phone.'

Vera thought about that. 'Are we saying she had them with her in the car and they were taken after she was killed? Or did someone go into her house and nick them?'

'It could have happened,' Billy said, 'but they'd have to have gone in early the morning after she died. It took us a while to get there because most of the team were tied up at Brockburn.' A pause. 'They'd have needed a key, though. The place was locked when we got there.'

'Someone worried about what she might go public with, perhaps?' Vera looked out into the room. The team were tired and edgy. Instead of an immediate result, or even a possible prime suspect, after two days they had nothing but more questions. And an elderly woman's disappearance.

'Fingerprints?'

'Four different individuals, beside Lorna. Nothing that matches anyone on the database.'

Vera nodded. 'One will be her mam, another Constance maybe.' She looked out into the room. 'You'll have heard that Constance Browne is missing. She's still not home and not answering her phone, so it's unlikely she's just been to town for a day's shopping. I've been asking around the village. Constance helps out at the village school once a week. Tomorrow afternoon is their Christmas show and she's supposed to be there. If she's not, we start worrying big style. There was no sign of a break-in or violence at the house. So, either something freaked her out and she's in hiding, or she's responsible for Lorna's death and she's run away.'

There was no response. They were all exhausted.

'Get home,' she said. 'Have some rest. You've got your actions for tomorrow. Charlie, let's chase that DNA analysis. It might not be relevant. I can't see that the Brockburn bunch would have any financial gain from Lorna's death even if they were related.'

They got to their feet as soon as she stopped talking, but she stood at the front of the emptying room, lost in space and time. Her mind had suddenly jumped back to her youth. Visits to Kimmerston library had provided welcome escape from home on Saturdays and during school holidays. As a teenager, Vera had loved reading traditional detective novels. Hector had thrown that back at her when she'd joined the police as a cadet. She could still remember the sneer in his voice and wondered now if there had been something else there too. A fear of being left alone? Or a fear of his daughter passing on information about his squalid criminality?

It won't be like Agatha Christie, you know. It won't be all country houses, vicars, butlers and wills.

This case was like that, though. The vicar was female these days and there might not be a butler, unless Dorothy counted as an updated version, but there was a country house. And there might be a will. Was it possible that, when Crispin had seen how Lorna was struggling with anorexia, he'd changed his will to leave something to her? Not the house, perhaps, because as Vera understood it, that had already passed to Juliet, but some income from the tenant farms or some savings. If that was the case, what might have happened to the will? Vera imagined a scenario like a scene from one of the books she'd escaped into as a teenager: Harriet coming across it before it could reach a solicitor and throwing it onto the fire. Vera smiled at the image, but she thought Harriet would be ruthless enough to do it. And perhaps Lorna had found out and was about to reveal all through her diary made public.

'Boss? What would you like from us?' Joe was bringing her back to the present. He and Holly were the only people left in the room.

'Eh, I'm sorry, you two. I'm having a senior moment. Or a flight of fancy. Hol, you talk to Josh Heslop. Away from Kirkhill, though. Why don't you get him to show you his exhibition here in Kimmerston? Get his trust. You're more on his wavelength than the rest of us. Nearer in age too! We've already ruled him out of Lorna's murder. He could just have killed Connie – he rushed into the art class at the last minute this morning – but I can't see two monsters roaming around the village. I don't see him as a suspect, but I do think he knows more about Lorna than he's letting on. See if he knows the significance of that cottage.'

Holly nodded. She seemed happy enough. Vera thought she was getting the hang of working with the woman. It didn't take more than a little bit of praise and recognition to keep her sweet. Vera didn't usually have the time or the energy to massage egos, but perhaps with Holly Jackman it was worth the effort.

'Joe, you're off to talk to that midwife, Olivia. I have high hopes of that interview.'

She waved them away then, and sat alone in the empty room, thinking again of Thomas, no mother and no father as far as the rest of the world was concerned. It seemed to her then that the child, present at Lorna's abduction, their only real witness, was at the centre of the case. The adults wheeled around him like planets round the sun.

Chapter Twenty-Five

Joe had arranged to talk to the midwife Olivia Best after she'd come off shift in the morning. 'I can't sleep as soon as I get home anyway,' she'd said when he'd phoned the day before. 'I need to wind down a bit. If you get to the house about eight-forty-five, my daughter will have left for school and we'll be able to talk.'

That meant he was around to see *his* kids off to school too and to give Sal a bit of a lie-in and a cup of tea in bed. Build up all the Brownie points he'd need if this case dragged on into the Christmas school holidays. Or if he had to miss the middle lad's nativity play.

Olivia had changed out of her uniform and was sitting at the kitchen table, looking as knackered as you would if you'd been pulling out babies all night. The house was on the same executive estate as the one where he and Sal lived and the interior felt much the same too. The furniture could have come from the same online company, though Sal would have cleared all the mucky plates into the dishwasher if she was expecting company. He thought he'd seen the midwife a few times in the school playground. She nodded as if she recognized him too. 'You're Sal's bloke.' No answer needed.

She pushed the pot and a mug towards him. 'Milk's in the fridge.'

He helped himself. He could tell how much effort it would take for her to get to her feet.

'Lorna Falstone,' he said.

'I hadn't heard about it. It's been a crazy few weeks. I couldn't believe it when you told me.'

'You saw her the day before she died?'

'Aye. Poor, poor lass.'

'How did you know her?'

She didn't answer.

'I know confidentiality's important,' he said. 'I won't ask for the names of the other group members, unless there's someone she was especially close to, someone she might have confided in.'

Still it seemed she couldn't bring herself to speak.

'Have you suffered from an eating disorder yourself?' He realized how difficult this was for her. It wasn't just exhaustion that was preventing her from speaking. 'You know I won't tell anyone. Not Sal or any of the other mams.'

'I have,' she said. 'So has everyone in the group.' A pause. She stared at him over the rim of her mug. 'Some of us had been close to death but we found our way out of it. And after Lorna had done so well – she was strong enough to give birth to a child and not everyone who's recovered from anorexia manages to get pregnant. Then to be killed like that. It's heartbreaking.' She was almost in tears.

'Lorna phoned you the Thursday before she died.'

'Yes. Early in the morning. I'd been working nights then too and I'd only just come off shift. She was in such a state I couldn't work out what the problem was over the phone. She said she'd tried to phone Joanne, the psychologist at Halstead House, but there'd been no answer. She sounded so desperate that I offered to go to Kirkhill, but she didn't want to meet there. She said she needed to get away from the place for a bit, so she'd get the bus into Kimmerston and come here.'

'She didn't say she'd borrow her friend's car and drive over?' Joe thought that was strange. The bus to Kimmerston might be quicker than the one into Newcastle but it would still take longer than the car.

'No. She said then she'd have to explain where she was going and anyway, she didn't want to trouble Connie with any more of her problems. She'd bothered the poor woman enough. This was a decision she'd have to make on her own.'

'So, she had a decision to make?' This was useful, Joe thought. If Lorna was close enough to Olivia to have explained that she was friendly with Miss Browne, perhaps she'd confided the name of her child's father to her too. It seemed that Connie had known more about Lorna and Thomas than she'd let on to Vera.

'Yes.' Still there was no real explanation. Joe sat quietly. Let the midwife tell the story in her own time. 'It was mid-morning before Lorna got here. She'd had to drop Thomas with Connie and then wait for the bus. I was shattered. It had been a hard night – on the ward we'd come close to losing a baby – and all I wanted was my bed. But other members of the fellowship had been there for me when I needed them, so I hadn't felt I could turn her away. That's how it works. There's an obligation. She was calmer by the time she got here. She said she was sorry for making such a fuss. She'd overreacted. Things would be okay.'

'She must have told you why she'd been in such a state, though?' Joe couldn't imagine that Lorna would have left her toddler and made the trek to Kimmerston without a good reason.

'Not really, and only indirectly. It was something to do with Thomas's father.'

'Do you know who the father was?' In his head, Joe was muttering a prayer to the God of his childhood, to the God of his lay preacher grandfather.

Olivia shook her head. 'No, that was always a complete mystery. One of Lorna's big secrets. I knew she was besotted with the guy, but she'd never really talked about him. Not in any detail, even at the beginning when she first told me. Just the things we all say when we're first in love – that he was gentle, supportive, that he'd make a perfect father.' A pause. 'Something must have happened between the frantic early phone call and Lorna turning up on my doorstep. When she got here, she'd stopped panicking. It was almost as if she was more worried about me than I was about her. I found myself talking about the shit night I'd had and the stress of being stretched too thin, and no time to care properly for my women.'

'She didn't give *any* indication of what was worrying her?' This was one of the most frustrating interviews Joe had ever conducted.

'She said she'd been having problems with Thomas's dad. He was being a rat and freaking her out big style. I assumed he was ducking out of his responsibilities, that he'd decided he wanted nothing more to do with her and Thomas. That was the impression she gave. I think she must have become dependent on him, since setting up home on her own.'

'But Lorna wasn't so anxious when she arrived here later that Thursday morning?'

'No, she said she'd talked him round. It was all okay after all. She thought she must have taken a couple of his comments out of context.' Olivia looked up. 'I think he was stringing her along and she was believing what she wanted to believe. We've all been there, haven't we? Even if we know in our hearts that our lover doesn't care any more, that they've moved on, we're so desperate to be with them that we persuade ourselves that they're telling the truth. But most of us grow out of that stuff. I thought she was still infatuated and I told her so.'

'What happened then? How did you leave it?'

Olivia didn't answer immediately. 'Perhaps I hadn't been very tactful. It certainly wasn't what she wanted to hear. She said I didn't have a clue what was going on, I didn't know the man and I didn't know what she had to lose.' The midwife hesitated again. 'You have to understand that I was shattered, dealing with my own shit. I wasn't even concentrating properly on what she was saying. I'm not proud of what I said next.'

Again, Joe said nothing and waited for her to go on.

'I told her not to be a drama queen. I told her if she wanted to keep the relationship secret, that was up to her, but she couldn't expect me to help if I didn't know all the details. She got up and stormed off.'

There was a moment of silence before Olivia continued. 'I went to the door and called after her. I offered her a lift back to Kirkhill. Goodness knows when the next bus would be. She shouted back that she didn't need a lift. Her bloke had arranged to pick her up in Kimmerston.'

'By her bloke she meant the father of her child?'

'Aye, well, that was what I took her to mean.' Olivia looked up at him again. 'I didn't know whether that was true or whether she just wanted to prove to me that he was a good man, that he'd put himself out for her.'

Outside, a young woman walked past the window, with a baby in a buggy. She waved in at Olivia, who lifted a hand in return.

'I was too tired to care by then. I told myself she was an adult and she should be allowed to make her own mistakes. I couldn't be responsible for her. I had my own stuff to worry about.' She put her head in her hands. It was as if it were too heavy to be supported by her neck. 'If I'd been more careful how I spoke to her, if I'd listened, properly listened, she might still be alive.'

Joe wasn't sure how to answer that. He didn't think easy words would help her. 'Until we find Lorna's killer, we can't know why she died. There seemed to be a lot going on in her life.' He thought he should end the interview; the midwife needed to sleep. It wasn't fair to keep her talking. He'd always thought *his* work carried huge responsibilities but he couldn't imagine what her working life might be like. Still, Lorna was dead and they were no closer to finding her killer. 'There's nothing else you can think of that might help identify her boyfriend? Might she have spoken to anyone else in the group?'

Olivia shook her head. 'There was always something reserved about her. She never properly engaged emotionally. I had the impression she didn't really get on with her parents, with her father at least. She said something like: *I never really knew him.*'

'She liked her teacher though. Connie Browne.'

'Yeah.' Olivia smiled. 'She thought Connie was brilliant. *She never judges and you always know where you are with her.* That was what she said.'

212

'So, a kind of surrogate mother, do you think?'

'No.' Olivia paused for a moment. 'More like an aunt or an older cousin. There wasn't that responsibility or obligation you feel for a parent.'

Joe nodded, waited for a beat. 'Constance is missing. Of course, we're checking with her friends, but Lorna didn't mention if she was planning to go away over Christmas?'

Olivia shook her head.

'Did you ever meet her?'

'Yeah, a couple of times. Before my daughter started school in September, Lorna and I would get together occasionally. Have a coffee, either in Kimmerston or Kirkhill. There's a lovely park there, right by the river. Once or twice Connie was there. It seemed a bit weird that Lorna didn't have friends of her own age, but Connie seemed cool.' A pause. 'She knew, like *everyone*, in Kirkhill. I suppose she'd taught most of them, knew their secrets.'

Joe nodded and got to his feet.

'I'm sorry I haven't been more help.' She looked up and there was a moment of confession. 'My bloke left three weeks ago. I'm only just holding it together. That's why I'm so wrecked – it's not just that we're manic at work.'

'I'm so sorry.'

'He found someone younger who works in an office. Nine to five. Always there to cook his tea.' She shook her head, a refusal to feel sorry for herself. She stood too and showed Joe to the door.

Chapter Twenty-Six

HOLLY ALSO SPENT THE MORNING IN Kimmerston. She'd phoned the Heslops' farm the evening before, a call to their landline. Vera had given the number to her: 'Use this. Mobile reception is crap anywhere near the forest.'

A middle-aged woman had answered. She sounded harassed, as if she was in the middle of something important, but her voice was pleasant enough. 'Yes?'

'Could I speak to Josh, please?'

'Who's speaking?' Classic mother, nosy about her adult child's calls. Holly wondered why Josh had moved back after years of freedom in Newcastle. Had the place really pulled him home as his friends had suggested? Or was the pull purely financial?

'Holly Jackman.' No need for her to know anything else, that she was part of the investigative team, though Holly wouldn't put it past her to eavesdrop. *Her* mother wouldn't be able to resist.

'Just a minute.'

'Hello.' Josh Heslop's voice, similar in inflexion to the

recording of Lorna Joe had played at the briefing. A rural Northumberland accent that was quite different from city Geordie.

Holly had explained who she was and asked if they could meet. 'I wondered if you'd mind coming into Kimmerston. Not to the station, it's not a formal interview. This is a bit cheeky, but I understand you have an exhibition in the gallery in the Chantry. I'd love to see your art. Could we meet there?' Not flirty exactly. Holly had never been able to do flirty. But interested and young men always seemed to like that.

'Sure.' An immediate response. Holly thought Vera might be a cow, but she was a wily cow. She knew how to reel in her witnesses. Holly had a brief image of Vera in thigh waders, standing in a river, a fishing rod in hand.

They'd arranged a time. The gallery had a coffee shop attached. Holly sometimes had lunch there. It was a solid stone building with its foundations in the river, a view over the water to the old houses on the other bank. She'd suggested that they meet in the cafe. 'You can show me the exhibition after we've chatted.' By the time the call had ended, Holly thought she'd had him eating out of her hand.

Tuesday morning, she got there early, bought herself a skinny cappuccino, and expected to wait, but he arrived soon after she did. Eager. She recognized him from the photo on the board in the ops room. Tall, fine-featured, dark-haired, dark-eyed. She had a moment of disappointment when she realized how young he was. Only twenty-three and not long out of university. Too young for her even if he hadn't been a witness. She thought he'd smartened himself up for the meeting. He had that scrubbed, just-out-of-the-shower look, the jeans were clean and there was an ironed shirt and a jacket. His mother would certainly have thought he was out to meet a new girl-friend, unless he'd told her who Holly was. She waved, offered to buy him coffee, but he insisted on going to the counter himself.

The place was quiet. A couple of women, of Connie Browne's vintage, were gossiping in a corner, but they were totally engrossed in their own conversation about plans for Christmas.

'I'm not really sure how I can help,' Josh said. 'I explained to the other woman.'

'My boss.' Holly gave a little grimace. Not out of real disres-pect to Vera. Of course not. But to encourage Heslop to talk, to make him feel she was different from the older woman, more on his wavelength.

'She does seem quite a character.' A shy smile because he didn't want to be rude about a colleague whom Holly might admire.

'That's one way of describing her!'

Now the smile was shared.

'Tell me about your home,' Holly said. 'The farm near Brockburn. I was speaking to your friends, the guys who work at the Baltic, and they said you loved it and wanted to get back as soon as you left university. I must admit I'm more a city girl. I live in Newcastle.' She paused and when he didn't answer immediately, continued. 'Isn't it a bit oppressive, living somewhere so small, so enclosed, where everyone knows you?'

Still, it took him a little while to answer. 'It doesn't feel like that to me. I find the city oppressive, claustrophobic. All those people. I love the space around Brockburn, the lack of noise, the dark skies. Even though the forest can make you feel closed in at times, that seems comforting to me. Or mysterious. And I get on very well with my family. I've never felt the need to escape from them.' There was a moment of hesitation and she thought he had more to say, but he remained silent.

'But that sense that everyone's interested in your business?' Holly was genuinely interested in his opinion. People celebrated the North-East for being friendly, but she felt the curiosity almost as a kind of assault. 'Doesn't that annoy you?'

He shrugged. 'I grew up with it. I suppose I'm used to it.' He paused. 'I think it just means that people care. And really, it's not that hard to keep the important things secret. If you need to.'

She gave a little laugh. 'Well, Lorna seems to have managed well enough. We still haven't managed to find out who Thomas's father might be.'

He didn't bite, so she moved on. 'Your old uni friends Ollie and Jon said you had a mysterious girlfriend. You managed to keep that to yourself pretty well too.'

He blushed. The colour rose from the collar of his shirt to his hairline. 'They've got good imaginations.'

'My boss, Inspector Stanhope, the woman who came to the farm the night of your sister's party, thought that might have been Lorna.' Holly raised her hands, palms up, a gesture of helplessness. 'Look, I know she's a bit eccentric, but she's in charge and she told me to ask. I'm sorry if it's intrusive, but you do see we need to know.' She thought again how young he was. He seemed so naive, hardly more than a schoolboy.

'Lorna was a friend,' he said. 'I saw her more often than I told your inspector, but that was because my mother was there when she asked. My mother disapproved. She thought Lorna would be trouble. Hard work. I don't know . . . I'm not sure why she took against her. Usually Mum's the first person to support folk on hard times.'

The cynic in Holly thought that *if* Josh was the murderer, this would have been clever. He'd know his fingerprints would be in Lorna's house, so best to admit to having been there at least once. But she couldn't see him as that calculating and he was admitting to Holly now that he'd been a regular visitor. Besides, he'd been in Newcastle when the woman had been killed.

'Perhaps the history of anorexia concerned her?'

He nodded, gave a wry smile. 'Mam said I didn't need that sort of responsibility when I was starting off, that I'd only get hurt. You know what mothers are like.'

'And you are her only son. And the oldest.'

He nodded again, pleased that Holly understood. 'Nettie and Cath seem to get away with murder.' The last word seemed to catch in his throat and the blush returned. 'I mean they can wrap Dad round their little fingers.'

'When was the last time you saw Lorna?'

'She was at the art class the Monday before she was killed. Afterwards I went back to her house for coffee.' He paused. 'She didn't want people to know we were getting friendly, so she left the village hall with Thomas and I went along when I'd cleared up. There's an alley behind her house and a back gate into the garden. I always used that.' He looked at Holly. 'I know it sounds ridiculous, but she'd been the subject of so much talk in the village – the anorexia and then being so secretive about the baby – that I could understand all the cloak-and-dagger stuff.'

'Maybe it made it a bit exciting?' Holly suggested.

'Yeah, maybe.' He paused. 'The best times were when we could get away together, leave everything behind. I'd pick her up with the baby and we'd head out somewhere miles from the village. Once we went out to the coast. It was one of those beautiful days you can get in September. We went to Druridge Bay, I put Thomas in the sling and we walked all the way along the beach, then stopped for ice cream in Cresswell on the way back.'

'That was what you wanted,' Holly said. 'To be a real family?'

'I wanted it more than anything.'

What a romantic he was, Holly thought. What did he picture? Himself and Lorna farming in the valley, just as his parents had done? More children perhaps? Or setting up some artistic venture together.

'Lorna wasn't interested?'

'We weren't even lovers.' There was a touch of bitterness in his voice. 'Sometimes I thought she was using me, because she was lonely, others we felt really close.'

'You aren't Thomas's father?'

'No! I was still at university when Thomas was born. I only started seeing Lorna regularly when I came home in the summer. She never talked about the man and I never asked. Really, I didn't want to know.'

Joe had phoned Holly just before she'd come out to the gallery: *Someone gave Lorna a lift back to Kirkhill after she had the meeting with Olivia on Thursday. Can you find out if it was Josh Heslop?*

'Lorna met a friend in Kimmerston the morning before she died. We know she got a lift back to Kirkhill from someone she knew. You're saying that the person who drove her home definitely wasn't you?'

'Definitely,' he said. 'I remember the last time I saw her.' A pause. 'I'd asked if she wanted to come to the party in Newcastle with me, to meet my friends. I thought she'd enjoy it. She never really had a chance to be young, to let her hair down.

Never did the whole student thing. I said we could take Thomas if she liked. I promised I wouldn't drink and I'd look after the baby, so she could have some fun.'

'You asked her on the Monday, after the art class?'

He nodded.

'What did she say?'

'That she'd think about it.' He paused again. 'And she smiled, as if she was glad to be asked. That was the last time I saw her. It was one of those clear, frosty days we had at the beginning of the week and the sun was shining through her living-room window, catching one side of her face, and she had Thomas on her lap. I let myself out of the house, and walked down to the village hall. There was still ice on the pavement.'

Holly saw that every moment of that last meeting was imprinted in his mind. 'Did she phone you to say she wouldn't be coming?'

'She sent me a text.' The bitterness of rejection was back in his voice. 'I'd been trying to call her all week, but she finally texted me on the Thursday afternoon, to say she wouldn't make it.' He got out his phone, clicked a few buttons and passed it to Holly.

Sorry. It's been a shit week. Can't make tomorrow, but all fine now.

'I thought it was the most self-centred message ever,' he said. 'It seemed as if she didn't care about me at all. It was probably my fault – I'd built the party up into something important, a chance for her to be part of my life away from the valley, and perhaps she hadn't realized.' A pause. 'But it wasn't all fine, was it? Now she's dead.' There were tears in his eyes.

Holly went back to the counter for more coffee, a chance

for him to regain control. When she returned, his eyes were dry and he was looking out over the river.

'How well do you know Constance Browne?'

He seemed surprised by the question, but he answered readily enough. 'She's always been there,' he said. 'A part of my childhood and my growing up. She's like that with all the kids in the valley. She's never had children and perhaps we're a substitute family. She certainly encouraged my art. When she was our teacher, she saw it as her mission to broaden our minds. She took us on trips to the theatre and to museums in the city. She said we might end up farming with our families, but we had to know there were options.'

'So, the special interest she took in Lorna wasn't unusual?'

Josh shook his head. 'Though perhaps Lorna needed her more than the rest of us.'

Holly framed the next question carefully. 'You were late arriving at the art class this Monday. Why was that?'

'Trouble with my car,' he said. 'It's clapped out and a nightmare.' He looked up. 'You can check with my mother. I needed to borrow one.'

'Were you surprised when Connie wasn't there?'

'Yeah, but she'd been so close to Lorna, I thought she might not be up to it.'

'Miss Browne seems to have disappeared,' Holly said. 'Any idea where she might be?'

He shook his head. 'Connie Browne's adventurous. Brave. Last year she travelled through India on her own. Not a trip with an organized group. She might just have wanted to go away.'

★

Later, they walked together round the gallery. Holly was impatient. She felt she'd got everything she could out of the man and she wanted to get back to the station to pass the information on to Vera. But it was almost as if she'd lured him here with her interest in his work, and she didn't feel she could just walk away. He was shy, awkward, and stood back, not soliciting any response. When she turned around, halfway through the gallery, he'd disappeared altogether.

The paintings were very different from Lorna's: small, detailed, domestic. Strange points of view and changes in perspective made Holly see the landscape where Josh and his family lived and farmed in a new light. Often, the forest provided the backdrop, circling, dense, overwhelming the buildings and the people. Holly wondered if this was some kind of message about the strength and importance of nature, but she was given to over-analysing and didn't want to ask Josh in case he thought the idea ludicrous. Occasionally a view was seen from the edge of the forest and then the light was startling, dazzling, a moment of revelation.

She walked round both rooms of the gallery, hoping that she might see the cottage which had featured in Lorna's paintings, but there was nothing that resembled it.

Josh was waiting for her by the main door into the building. He was wearing his coat and seemed in a hurry to leave before she could make any comment on his art, but Holly asked him to give her another couple of moments.

'Do these pictures mean anything to you? I assume you recognize the paintings?' Holly got out her phone and showed him the photographs she'd taken of Lorna's work. 'I found them in Lorna's spare room.'

'No,' he said. He sounded genuine enough. Sad. 'She didn't show me all her stuff.'

'Do you recognize the place? The building?'

He hesitated and she thought he might provide the answer, but he shook his head. 'No. Sorry.'

'She called one of the paintings "The Darkest Evening". Does that mean anything to you? I think it's a quote from a poem.'

He shook his head again.

'Well, if anything comes to you, do get back in touch. If I email the pictures perhaps you could ask your family.' She held out her hand. 'Thank you for meeting me.'

'It was good to speak about Lorna. It's hard to do that at home. My sisters are sorry she's dead, of course, but they didn't really know her and they're at that age when everything just seems funny. My dad's still traumatized by finding her and my mother just wants to pretend nothing's happened, for everything to get back to normal.' He paused. 'You know it was Cath's birthday party at the weekend. None of us really felt like celebrating, Dad especially after finding Lorna's body, but Mam insisted we go ahead. Maybe she was right. Things can't just stop because she's dead.'

Holly wasn't sure how to reply to that. 'If you think of anything that might help us find out who killed her, you will get in touch?'

He hesitated again and she thought he might be about to share something relevant, but he just shook her hand briefly and hurried away.

Chapter Twenty-Seven

IT WAS VERA'S FIRST VISIT TO Broom Farm, the place where Lorna had grown up. She must have driven past it a few times, on those trips to Brockburn with Hector, because it lay on the road between Kirkhill and the big house, but nothing stirred in her memory as she approached. It was low-lying, with meadows that would flood when the river was high, but the hill rose sharply behind the farmhouse, with rocky outcrops. To the west, the inevitable line of Sitka spruce broke the horizon.

The house seemed quiet. A child's clothes – sleepsuits, dungarees and vests – had been pegged on a washing line behind the house. Somewhere in the distance a dog was barking. Vera hoped that meant Robert Falstone was out on his land. This was a conversation she'd prefer to have with his wife on her own.

She found Jill in the kitchen with Thomas. The toddler was on a rug in front of the Aga playing with plastic bricks. Vera supposed they were new. The Falstones hadn't been given permission to go into Lorna's house in Kirkhill. Joe had

described this place as dirty, but Vera thought it was no grub-
bier than most farmhouse kitchens she'd known. Joe's Sal was
obsessive about housework. Vera thought she should find something better to do with her time.

Vera introduced herself. 'Your man not about?'

Jill shook her head. 'There's a fence that needs fixing down
by the river. He's just gone out.' She moved a kettle onto the
hotplate. 'Tea or coffee?' Her eyes were red as if she'd had
little sleep, but she seemed to be holding things together.

'Tea, please.' Vera nodded towards the child. 'How's it going?'

The woman smiled. 'He's good as gold.'

'Keeping you awake at night?'

'Nah, I don't sleep much, but that's grief. Guilt. Thinking
of all the things I might have said. Might have done.'

'Eh, pet, you have to let go of the guilt. That way lies
madness.'

Jill set the pot on the table, added mugs, a milk bottle and
a packet of shop-bought biscuits.

Vera felt at home. She'd never been at ease with perfect
housewives, perfect families. Home-made biscuits. 'Tell me
about your fling with Crispin Stanhope.'

The woman stared at her, frozen.

'Now, I'd normally say it was none of my business what you
got up to with the lord of the manor. Unless you'd been forced
into it. But this is different. Your lass was murdered and we
have to look into all sorts of possibilities. Her body was found
on Brockburn land, after all. You do understand?'

Jill nodded.

'*Did* he force you?'

'No!' At last the woman did seem able to speak. 'No, it was
nothing like that.'

'Because he did have a bit of a reputation.'

'I think he loved me,' she said quietly.

'But not enough to leave Harriet for you?'

Silence again. Jill bent and built a tower with the bricks. Thomas knocked them down and chuckled.

'It wasn't easy for him.' Again, the words seemed to take an age to be spoken.

'Eh, you don't have to make excuses for him after all these years.'

'He felt the responsibility, not just for Harriet and Juliet, but for the estate. For his position.'

'He always did care what folks thought of him.' Vera was muttering under her breath and hadn't realized Jill had heard her.

'You knew him?'

'He was a distant relation.' *Not that distant but there was no need to complicate things now.* Vera paused for a moment. 'Was he Lorna's father?'

'I'm not sure. He could have been.' The woman looked up and gave a twisted smile. 'I always thought Lorna looked more like Crispin than she did Robert as she got older, but that could have been my imagination.'

'Wishful thinking?'

Jill shook her head. 'Rob's a good man. Crispin was a year of madness. An infatuation. I might have left Robert and this place, if he'd asked me at the time, but later I was glad he never did. I'd have hated living in the big house and Crispin would never have left it. I had a good life here.' She paused. 'We ended things just before I realized I was pregnant. Just as well. It might have made things more complicated.'

'Did Robert know? About the affair?'

'Not at the time,' Jill said. She added, with the same twisted smile, 'Crispin had practice in being discreet.'

'Later?'

'Later, Rob might have had his suspicions because the lass looked a bit like Crispin's real daughter, Juliet. They *could* have been sisters. And there was gossip. This place there's always gossip. He never said anything.' Jill paused. 'By that time, we were settled as a family. He'd think there was no need to rock the boat. And he did love her as if she was his own.'

Vera thought of Connie Browne's words. She'd said the Falstones didn't speak of anything except sheep and the farm. Had that been a bad thing? They'd rubbed along happily enough even when Lorna had been ill, and that would have caused more stress than most couples could weather.

'What about Lorna?' Vera asked. 'Did she suspect that Robert wasn't her dad?'

Jill bent once more to build the pile of bricks for her grandson. 'Lorna might have heard things. Kids can be cruel. They might have listened in to the adults speculating and passed the rumours on as facts. She was an easy target.'

Vera nodded. 'Do you think that might have led to the anorexia?'

'I did wonder.' The woman straightened. 'Me feeling guilty again. It haunted me all the time she was ill. Impossible to get rid of.'

And you couldn't talk about it to your husband. Because in this marriage things don't get spoken of.

Vera thought they were an oddly matched couple. Now that Jill had started talking, she was articulate, what Vera's hippy friend and neighbour Joanna would call emotionally intelligent. Quite different from Robert, who dealt with problems by shutting down, hiding away from them. 'Where did you and Robert meet?'

Jill seemed surprised by the question, but she answered readily enough. 'At the Kirkhill show. I was working for a little craft brewery based on the coast, and we had a stand. Robert was showing his animals. He kept coming back for beer. I thought he was an alcoholic . . .'

'But it was you he came back for?' Vera paused. 'I've seen that photo of you as a lass.' She nodded to the picture on the mantelpiece. 'More than bonny. You must have had your pick of admirers. What attracted you to Robert? He wasn't much of a looker, even when he was young.'

'He was a farmer,' Jill said. 'I'd always dreamed of marrying a farmer and living in a place like this.'

'That wouldn't have been enough, though.'

'He was kind. My parents had been through a messy divorce. They were both a bit flaky and self-obsessed. It was all shouting and throwing things, and not caring that I was stuck in the middle. I couldn't see Robert behaving like that. Kindness is very attractive when you're not used to it.'

'But sometimes not enough?' Jill didn't answer and Vera continued. 'You must have fallen for Crispin's charms.'

'Maybe. For a while. But then I saw sense and just threw myself into the work on the farm. I love it here, love the place and the animals.' A pause. 'And I love my husband. Robert and I are partners in every sense of the word. We don't feel the need to bare our souls.'

Vera wasn't quite sure she believed that. Robert's dourness and reluctance to engage seemed like a kind of self-absorption to her. A selfishness.

Jill was talking again: 'Besides, we've got this little one to think about now. A new start.'

'I was wondering,' Vera paused for a moment, then looked directly at Jill, 'if that was a case of history repeating itself.'

'What do you mean?'

'There's another man at Brockburn now, lording it over the place. Juliet's bloke Mark Bolitho. He couldn't be your Thomas's dad?'

'No.' The response came slowly after she'd taken time to consider. 'I don't think he and Lorna ever met.'

'Seems she was quite arty, though, your lass. She could have met him at his theatre? Or one of his community arts days at the big house.'

Jill shook her head. 'She didn't mention it. And she never did go to Brockburn. Never went near the place. I think because she'd heard the rumours and she thought it would be too close to home. Embarrassing. I never went either for the same reason.'

'Apparently young Josh Heslop was keen on her too.'

'Oh?' Now Vera did have her attention. 'He seems like a good lad. And they're a lovely family. Rosemary called in yesterday just to offer her condolences. The rest of the valley haven't been anywhere near. She brought a casserole, thinking I wouldn't have much time for cooking.' The grin again. 'Not that I ever have much time for cooking.'

'According to Josh, Lorna didn't return his affections.'

Thomas was getting bored with the bricks. Vera could understand that. They didn't seem to provide much in the way of entertainment, and if he had Stanhope blood, he'd be easily bored. The child started to grizzle and Jill took him up onto her lap, reached out and gave him a biscuit. 'You've found out more about Lorna in the four days since she died than I had in the last three years. What sort of mother does that make me?'

'The sort of mother who respected her daughter's privacy, knowing that was the best thing to keep her well,' Vera said. 'I can't do that. My job's all about digging out information that other people would rather keep hidden.' She stood up. 'I'll leave you in peace to spend some time with the bairn.'

As Vera made her way to the door, Jill spoke again. 'I'm glad it's you looking into it. Lorna would have liked you. You'd have made her feel safe.'

Vera wasn't sure what to say to that. She started to feel herself come over all emotional, so she just nodded, and went outside.

She could see Robert Falstone, just where Jill had said he'd be, in a lower meadow, fixing a fence. He was almost done, but taking his time, looking for an excuse not to come back to the house, because he'd have seen her Land Rover in the yard. Not knowing who was calling, but imagining she was some other neighbour bringing pity and home-cooked food. He was two fields away but she decided to walk across the grass past the sheep, making sure to fasten the gates carefully behind her, instead of driving down the track. He must have been aware of her approaching, but he didn't stand and look at her until she had almost reached him.

'Are you one of them social workers, coming to check up on us?'

Vera was horrified. 'Do I look like a bloody social worker?'

'Who are you then? You don't look young or smart enough for a reporter. We've had a few of those and all.'

'I'm a police officer, the officer in charge of the investigation into your daughter's murder.' She held out her hand, but didn't give her name. The Stanhope connection might not be welcome here.

He stood for a minute, then wiped his hand on his overalls and took hers 'I can't chat. I want to finish up here.'

'No reason why we can't talk while you finish off.'

He seemed about to argue, then realized she wasn't about to shift, that she was as immovable as the hill behind them, and nodded.

'All people seem to do is talk. Gossip everywhere about my lass being killed. Why can't you *do* something to find out who did that to her?' A pause. 'That's all I can think about. Her, cold, in the snow. Scared. And I wasn't there to save her.'

'Folk are scared too,' Vera said. 'Murder coming so close. That's why they talk.' A pause. 'What do you make of Miss Browne? She seems to have gone missing.'

'Wor lass liked her well enough. I thought she stuck her nose in when it wasn't wanted.'

'Recently?'

'She came to the house a while ago. Just before Bonfire Night because the excuse was her asking if we had any wood for the fire in the village. Pallets, dry stuff that would burn. There's always a big firework display in Kirkhill. A community do.'

'But that wasn't really why she was there?'

He looked up from his work. 'Jill was taken in, but I wasn't.'

'What do you think was going on?'

'She was telling us that Lorna was struggling. *I think she's got into a relationship and is a bit out of her depth.* Something like that. Nothing useful. Nothing that would help us sort things out for Lorna. Just stirring. Making herself feel good by doing something. Shifting the load onto us.' He started packing away his tools. 'I know that Jill was visiting Lorna. Every Friday, regular as clockwork. Until this last week when the weather was so bad. She'd have seen if anything was seriously amiss.'

'Jill told my sergeant those visits were secret.'

'Nah,' he said. 'She might have thought that I didn't know what was happening, but I was glad for her to go. I just couldn't face the lass myself. I wouldn't know what to say to her. It's gone on this long.' He hoisted his tools into the back of his jeep. 'You'll have heard the rumours about Jill and old man Stanhope if you've been asking around about us all.'

Vera nodded.

'It hurt,' he said. 'I knew I was punching above my weight with Jill. She was such a beauty when she was younger. Lorna got all her looks from her mother. But I thought I was giving her what she wanted. What she needed. A bit of stability. Respect. It was a kind of bargain and I believed I was getting loyalty in return. Then along came old Stanhope, slimy as a toad, with his money and his fancy talk. I knew the affair wouldn't last. He'd had most eligible women in the valley at one time or another. I'd thought Jill would have more sense than to fall for him.' He looked up. 'I suppose it was my pride that was most hurt.'

'It can't have been easy,' Vera said. 'All that gossip again.'

'It was hard.' He fell silent for a moment. A skein of geese flew overhead, honking. 'I heard folk talking about how Lorna looked so like him. Like his daughter Juliet, at least. It hadn't occurred to me before then, but once it was in my mind, I couldn't shift the thought. I was reminded every time I looked at her.'

'You and Jill must have talked about it. She must have known you were hurt.'

He looked up at her. 'Of course she knew and she hated what she'd done to me. I knew she was sorry. What was the point of talking? It was over.'

'Except that Lorna reminded you.'

He started walking towards his vehicle, but turned back to face her. 'She was *my* daughter, and I loved the bones of her. I was a better father to her than that man would ever have been.'

'Crispin paid for her treatment in the clinic when she was ill.'

'He could afford to! It was the least he could do. He did bugger all else for her.' Falstone paused again. 'Except leave her alone.'

'He never tried to get in touch when she was growing up?' Vera wasn't sure where she was going with this, but she wanted to keep Falstone talking.

The man shook his head. 'I saw him watching her, though, when he thought nobody was looking.'

'What do you mean?'

'She was mad about horses when she was growing up.'

'Aye, your wife said she was a canny little rider.'

'Sometimes, at the local shows, when Lorna was competing on her pony, I'd catch Stanhope staring at her,' Falstone said. 'Looking kind of proud but sad. Usually he was there to open the event, give out the prizes, and if Lorna won, he'd be handing the rosette to her. But it was us she ran back to as soon as the ceremony was over. We were the people she wanted to congratulate her. Those times, I just felt sorry for him.'

'Lorna never suspected Crispin might be her dad?' Vera

wondered what that might be like. It had been bad enough being Hector's daughter. Hector, the black sheep, despised by his family and his respectable neighbours. Vera had been the object of pity and suspicion. But at least there'd been no denying her parentage. She might not have *liked* Hector, but she'd known where she'd come from.

'Not until she was a teenager. She heard stuff from the other kids when she got to the high school. They were a cruel bunch. I saw them sometimes when I was dropping her off for the bus. All pointing and whispering. No wonder it made her ill.' He paused. 'We should have taken her away, sent her to a different school.'

'Was there anyone specific making fun of her? The Heslop kids?'

Falstone shook his head. 'I think they were all as bad as each other.'

'Did she talk to you about it?' Vera asked.

'Do you mean, did she ask if I was her real dad?' He stood looking out at the river, brown and swollen with melted snow. 'No. We weren't that sort of family. We just got on with things.'

'And she'd not have wanted to hurt you,' Vera said. 'You'd always cared for her.'

'But I couldn't save her, could I? She still got ill. And she still got killed.' Falstone climbed into his vehicle, revved the engine and drove away. Vera walked back through the fields towards the house.

Chapter Twenty-Eight

JULIET WAS IN THE BEDROOM WRAPPING Christmas presents when Vera arrived. There was still no heating upstairs and she was wearing a thermal vest, two jumpers and a down jacket. No wonder, she thought, that she and Mark had few romantic moments at this time of the year; spontaneity was tricky when it took half an hour to undress. Dorothy had lit a fire for Harriet in the small drawing room, and now the housekeeper was back in the kitchen clearing up after lunch. As Dorothy and Harriet would be recipients of some of the Christmas gifts, Juliet had retreated into the freezing room upstairs.

She was still unsettled, anxious. Earlier, the older male detective had arrived, asking if he could take a DNA sample. No explanation, just that it was routine. She could refuse if she liked, he'd said, but really, she'd known there was no option and perhaps it would be a good thing to know, once and for all, one way or another. Her hands, cutting the shiny wrapping paper, were still trembling.

She heard the Land Rover first, wheezing and coughing down the drive, and was looking out of the window to see Vera descend, looking remarkably sprightly for someone of her build, approach the front door and ring the bell. Juliet left what she was doing and ran down the stairs, shouting towards the kitchen that she'd get the door. She knew Harriet wouldn't move from the fire and she thought that Dorothy would hate being treated as some sort of parlourmaid or female butler. Juliet was always uncomfortable that her friend, so much brainier than her, so much more competent, should be expected to wait on them. It was bad enough that she did most of the cleaning.

Vera was wearing mud-covered wellingtons, a woollen hat and a padded jacket. Juliet's heart sank at the thought of the mud that would be carried into the house. They stood for a moment looking at each other, while Juliet wondered how she could tactfully ask Vera to take off her boots.

'Were you just off out, pet?' Vera nodded at Juliet's jacket.

'I thought I might go for a walk. The sun's so glorious and it probably won't last.' A spur-of-the-moment decision and it did feel warmer outside than in her bedroom.

'Shall we go together? We can chat just as well outside and what I have to say's a bit delicate. I wouldn't want your mam earwigging.'

'Let me just let Dorothy know where I'm going and fetch some boots. You don't mind waiting here?'

'Not at all.' Vera smiled, as if she knew what Juliet had been thinking all along about the wellies.

Juliet called the dogs; she needed friends with her. The Labradors were mother and son. Wren was elderly, Dipper was younger, still lively, very randy. He went ahead, leading the way through the park and to the wild part of the garden by the river. There was a public footpath here that led along the bank and out through the forest towards the Pennine Way, but today it was empty. Few people ever used it at this time of the year. Harriet hated the intrusion in the summer: the families with their picnics and the hardened walkers with their leather boots and their shorts and their maps. She'd stood watching one party march along the path and exploded to Juliet and Mark who were with her, 'Can't we just block it off?'

Juliet had explained that would be impossible and that it was a legal requirement to keep the path clear. Harriet had muttered about privacy and invasion. Juliet didn't mind the walkers at all – it made her feel less guilty about having the house and the rest of the grounds virtually to herself – and Mark said it was a positive benefit:

'When we have the theatre and arts centre open, those people will be our customers. They'll look at the exhibitions, eat and drink in the bar. We'll open up a path to the house.'

Juliet allowed these thoughts and memories to run through her mind as a kind of distraction, because she suspected she knew what Vera was going to say next, and she didn't want to hear it. They came to a narrow stone bridge across the river. Once it might have been a wagonway; it had never been wide enough for a motorized vehicle. It stood in full sunlight, and the women stopped there, where it was almost warm, looking down at the water. The dogs were sniffing in the undergrowth.

'Your dad,' Vera said. 'What was he really like?'

'He was always rather lovely to me. Kind, gentle, generous.' *Quite different from my mother*, she was going to add, but that would have been disloyal.

'Seems he had a bit of a reputation for chasing the women.'

'I wouldn't know.' Juliet was already being defensive, but really, how could she defend Crispin? She knew he'd been a nightmare, charming and entitled. 'I never saw that side of him.'

'You know that some folk say he was Lorna Falstone's father?'

Juliet had been expecting the question, but still it came like a punch to her stomach, winding her. 'I'd heard rumours.'

'But you must have seen for yourself.' Vera was quite ruthless now. 'The pair of you looked quite alike. Until Lorna lost all that weight.' She paused. 'I did wonder if that was how the anorexia started. She wanted to shrink away until she was nothing like her former self. Until there was nothing to remind her of you and Crispin.'

'You can't blame my father for her illness. I know he wasn't a saint, but really, that's too much.'

'Maybe he blamed himself,' Vera said. 'He paid her hospital bills after all.'

'He was a generous man. He felt some obligation to all his tenants.'

'Eh, pet.' Vera turned and smiled. 'That sounds almost like your mother speaking.' She paused. 'You can't help but admire Harriet, though, keeping her dignity through it all, ignoring the gossip, keeping the show on the road.'

Juliet looked at her relative, suspecting sarcasm, but she saw that the admiration was real.

'We'll know soon enough anyway,' Vera went on. 'Charlie came and took the DNA sample earlier?'

Juliet nodded. A buzzard was sailing above them, the sunlight shining through the thinner feathers.

'It might take a while to come back, but we should know in a few days. What I was wondering . . .' Vera let her voice tail away. It was as if she wanted to choose the right words. She started again. 'I was wondering if Crispin felt an obligation to her. Might he have made some other financial provision for her? If she might have been mentioned in his will.'

Silence apart from the river, distant sheep.

Vera persisted. 'You must have seen the will?'

'He'd transferred ownership of the house to me some years before his death.'

'Oh, I know about that. A wheeze to avoid inheritance tax. But he had other assets. The rent from the tenancies. And there must have been savings, stocks and shares.'

Juliet wanted to laugh. 'There were mostly debts. Why do you think most of the house is so fucking Arctic?' Mark's phrase again, but she felt the need to shock Vera, to make her see that what she was implying was impossible.

'Did you see the will?'

'There was no need. Mother was my father's executor and a solicitor in Kimmerston drew it up and held it. I knew what was in it. Dad discussed it with me before it was all arranged. I'd just turned twenty-one and the house was transferred into my name. He still ran the estate, of course. The remaining assets would go to my mother for her lifetime and then to me and my children.'

'But you have no children.' Vera's voice was gentle now. 'And nor do I, and as far as I can see I'm the only other living relative. Officially. These men love the idea of family, don't they? Their family. Their bloodline. Like fancy race horses or prize cows. It occurred to me that Crispin might have changed his will, put in something about any child Lorna might have. If that child happened to be a boy. That he might have wanted any son to inherit a part of the estate, to keep it going. A man running the place again.' A pause. 'Unless you were planning to have bairns yourself?' She left the question hanging and the silence returned.

'I would love children,' Juliet said. 'It just hasn't happened.'

Vera looked at her, not shocked at all. 'I thought it might be like that. I could tell by the way you were with Thomas.' A pause and something close to a shiver of distaste. 'I've never fancied the idea of motherhood myself.'

Then Juliet found the words spewing out, gushing, and she was telling Vera about the tests and the IVF, the circle of hope and nightmare disappointment, of failure and early pregnancies and miscarriage. The realization that there was no way she could put herself through the stress of another cycle, the dull, empty ache. The panic of time passing, of approaching middle age. Suddenly, somehow, Vera had taken her in her arms, wrapped her up, and Juliet was crying, certain that there would be tears and possibly snot on Vera's coat, and even in that moment of embarrassment, it occurred to her that Harriet had never held her like this, not even when she was very young.

'What does your chap make of all this?' Vera asked. 'It must be hard for him too.'

Now the embarrassment did kick in. Juliet freed herself and moved away a little, found a tissue in her jeans pocket and turned so she could dry her eyes without Vera watching. 'I think it's different for men,' she said at last. 'Mark's disappointed, of course, but I think he sees it as a failure, in an almost professional way. Like a project at work that he couldn't quite complete or a play he's directed that has had bad reviews. Though I'm the problem, not him. He could father a child with someone else.' She bent to tickle Wren's neck.

'And your mother?' Vera asked. 'She'll have been some support?'

'Oh, Mother was a failure too,' Juliet said. 'In the eyes of my father, at least. Only one child and that was a girl. My father loved me, of course, doted on me even, but it was never the same as if I was a boy. I was a kind of indulgence. A boy would have been a responsibility. There would have been expectations – university or the army, then to be trained in the ways of the estate.' She paused. 'I think Mother would have been a different woman, their relationship might have been different, if there'd been more children.'

'Oh, hinnie, it sounds like something from another era. Something you see on TV on Sunday evenings. All long frocks and footmen.'

Juliet couldn't help laughing at that. There was, after all, still something very feudal about rural Northumberland.

'Your father will never have known that Lorna had a lad.'

Juliet shook her head. 'He died before Lorna was pregnant.'

Now Vera seemed almost to be talking to herself. 'I'm not sure where that leaves us then. I had some crazy scheme in my head about wills and inheritance. It's this place.' She nodded up the bank towards the house, which was half-hidden by trees. 'It drags you back into the past.' She paused. 'But even if your dad had left all his money and the estate lands to Lorna, none of you would get your hands on it now, because it would go to her lad. At least, I presume it would.'

'You think any of us would kill for this?' Juliet felt herself on the verge of hysteria just at the thought of it. 'Mother would rather a place in the city, close to her friends and the shops, Mark likes the idea of being lord of the manor, but the discomfort is already starting to bore him. And me? I'd give the whole place up in a second in return for a child.' She found that she was crying again and turned away. She'd made enough of a scene already. Harriet would be furious at the idea that Juliet had lost control in front of Hector's daughter.

This time there was no hug from Vera. Only a nod of

understanding when Juliet turned back to face her. 'I know,' she said. 'I know.'

They walked back towards the house then. Vera seemed deep in thought and didn't speak until they were nearly there. As they approached the door, she stopped, arms folded below the massive bosom. 'You and your Mark get on all right, do you? I mean, you're solid. All these problems with conceiving, I understand they can put a strain on a marriage.'

'Yes,' Juliet said. 'Of course we're fine.' Because she'd been well brought up and really, what else was there to say? The idea of Vera, who'd been single all her life, offering relationship counselling, made her grin, and when she went back into the house to continue wrapping presents, the dogs following behind, she felt lighter, almost cheerful.

Later that evening, Harriet announced that she was going out. There was a charity carol concert in the church in Kirkhill. She'd been invited to open it, to say a few words of welcome, and they couldn't keep running away from their duty. The last thing they needed was for the people in the village to think they had something to hide. Dorothy had given them an early supper in the kitchen and after Harriet went, she sat at the table with Juliet drinking coffee. The silence was companionable, easy, and Juliet was tempted to break it, to tell her about Vera's crazy ideas. But just as the thought appeared Dorothy started speaking:

'Do you mind if I go back to the cottage? I've hardly seen Duncan for days and Karan is going stir-crazy. He usually plays squash in Kimmerston with his mates on a Tuesday. You could come too, though, if you don't want to be here on your own.'

'Of course you must! And I'll be glad of a little time to myself.'

'Make sure you lock up behind me.'

For the first time, Juliet had a sense of danger, the notion that there might be a killer lurking in the forest, watching for somebody else to prey on. She imagined a shadow, sliding between the trees, peering into the house. Before that moment, the events of the last few days had seemed unreal, a fiction. 'You shouldn't walk up to the cottage on your own.'

'I won't. Karan's coming down to get me.'

At that, as if he'd been summoned, there was a tap on the door and Karan came into the kitchen. He was wearing a waxed jacket, a hat and gloves, and Duncan was in a rucksack on his back, only his eyes visible because the hood of his snow suit was pulled low over his face and a scarf was wound round his chin.

Karan gave his wonderful smile. 'It's freezing out there now. Sorry to drag Dorothy away, but I need to get her back before the wood-burner dies.'

By the time Juliet could answer, Dorothy had already pulled on her boots and her jacket.

'Lock the door behind me,' she said again, and Juliet felt the same panic. It seemed to scramble her brain, so she could hardly put together the words to say goodbye.

When Dorothy and her family left, the house was silent. It felt as dark and imposing as the forest surrounding it. Juliet's mobile rang. It was Mark, calling she thought from the theatre bar. There was conversation and laughter in the background.

'How are you?'

But she could tell that he didn't really want to know. It was a form of greeting; he could just as well have said hello. 'I'm fine,' she said. 'Will you be back tomorrow?' She thought now how unfair and thoughtless it was to leave her alone when there was a murderer on the loose, how unlike Karan her husband was.

'Yeah, I hope so. Should be back in time for dinner.' Then he started talking about the school matinee they'd had on that afternoon. 'It was bloody brilliant. The actors really got it, you know. So physical. And the kids responded big style. Then the writer led a discussion afterwards. I'll tell you all about it when I get back tomorrow. It's just the sort of performance I'd hope to do at Brockburn.'

'Great,' she said, but she could tell he'd already stopped listening, that his attention had shifted to someone more important, a reviewer, or one of the pretty young women he always seemed to employ. She switched off the phone and the house became silent again.

If the call hadn't made her so angry, she would have sat by the fire in the small drawing room, drinking tea and watching the television programmes that Harriet and Mark despised: soap operas and old murder mysteries. Instead she made her way upstairs to her mother's room. Towards the end of her parents' marriage, this had just been her mother's. Her father had slept in a smaller room on the other side of the corridor. Growing up, she'd thought the separate sleeping arrangements were an affectation, an aping of royalty; now she thought her parents had probably disliked each other intensely and couldn't bear to be in the same bed. She'd stood outside the day before, while Harriet was in Newcastle, trying to conjure the courage to go in. Now, she pushed open the heavy door.

The room was large, with two long windows covered with heavy curtains to keep out the draughts. The radiators seemed to work here and Harriet had left on an electric fan heater too. No wonder she was unmoved whenever Juliet tried to bring up the subject of a new boiler. The bed was large with a carved bedhead and a quilt in reds and golds. Regal. Juliet went to a desk standing against one wall. One of the drawers was locked, but Juliet had been a watchful, curious child and she'd known for years where her mother kept the key. It was in a little music box, which stood on Harriet's dressing table. The tune played 'Bobby Shafto', which seemed inappropriate for such a delicate object. The key was still there and Juliet opened the drawer, the tune tinkling in the background, becoming slower until it stopped and the deep silence returned.

She found what she was looking for almost immediately: an envelope in the heavy cream paper her father had favoured. The name on the front – Harriet Stanhope – was written in her father's hand. The envelope was unsealed and Juliet removed the single sheet inside. She'd suspected the letter's existence for years; her father had mentioned it obliquely a few days before his death in a whisper although nobody else was in the room. She'd thought later that perhaps he'd had a premonition that he was about to die. Harriet had never mentioned it, though, and Juliet had been too much of a coward to challenge her. Now Juliet read the contents with a rising anger that pushed fear of an anonymous killer out of her mind. She took a photograph of the letter on her mobile phone and replaced it in the envelope. She was just returning the key to the music box when she heard Harriet's car on the drive.

Chapter Twenty-Nine

HOLLY DROVE HOME FOR A COUPLE of hours before the evening briefing. In her sleek, clean flat, with its view of the graveyard, she made camomile tea and changed into her running gear. It was dark and the rush hour was over, so the streets were quiet. Running was a habit that was fast becoming an obsession. A ruling addiction. If she missed a daily run, because of the demands of work or because she'd come home exhausted, she felt guilty. She wondered if Lorna had felt like that when she was cutting down on calories, if each mouthful of food was followed by guilt then more exercise. Holly told herself this was quite different. Running relaxed her and it made her stronger and healthier. Running was an antidote to the irritation of working with Vera, it wasn't an illness. As she moved down the deserted streets, passing the flicker of television behind occasional uncurtained windows, she felt the stress leave her and her mind become clear again.

She returned to thoughts of the forthcoming briefing, and what she would say. Vera seemed to assume that none of the women linked to Lorna had a motive for killing her. Now,

Holly thought that was a false assumption. Apart from Josh Heslop, all the men with connections to Lorna had partners. Even Josh had a mother, who seemed anxious to protect him from harm. If any of the suspect men had been Lorna's lover, wasn't it possible that a woman could have murdered her? Out of jealousy if, as Lorna had implied in her last conversation with Olivia, the man in her life had been willing at last to acknowledge his son.

Holly's thoughts were interrupted by the screech of a police car driving too fast, the scream of a siren, but the rhythm of her running continued, and the beat of her training shoes on the pavement allowed her to concentrate on the case once again.

The faces of the women she'd come to know through photographs on the whiteboard, even if she'd not met them in person, came into her mind one by one. Could the gentle Juliet, who was apparently so anxious and timid, have killed Lorna? Or her mother Harriet, who seemed desperate to preserve the reputation of the Stanhope family, that branch of the family at least? Because surely, she'd see Vera Stanhope as beyond salvation.

Holly turned a corner and came into a less affluent street. There were fewer trees, tiny front gardens, a house gaudy with external Christmas lights. She'd never met Rosemary Heslop, though they'd spoken on the telephone. She'd sounded busy, pleasant. It was hard to imagine she'd kill anyone to save the reputations of the men in her life. And surely Jill Falstone couldn't have murdered her own daughter.

Holly was on her way home now. She was moving easily, her muscles warm, despite the chill air and the fact that her breath was coming in clouds. Another face came into her mind.

Dorothy Felling. Holly had admired her for her strength, for her courage in choosing an unconventional career path, had envied the close family in the small cottage, the easy relationship between man and woman.

In the shower, her mind was still whirring. She knew she was a competitive woman. It was pathetic, but she saw her colleagues as rivals and collaborative working had never come easily to her. Now she thought she'd do as Vera would want and check into the background of the male suspects of the case, but she'd do some of her own research too. Perhaps the ladies of the manor and the farmers' wives weren't as harmless or ineffectual as they first appeared, and *she'd* find the murderer before the rest of the team. Holly had never considered Dorothy to be ineffectual but now it occurred to her that the sudden decision to leave well-paid posts in law and accountancy could be seen as suspicious rather than laudable. Perhaps Dorothy and the charming Karan had something to hide. Would a woman who'd sailed through A levels and into Cambridge, then been sufficiently ambitious to pursue a career in the law, really be satisfied with a life of cleaning up other people's domestic messes?

Holly changed into her work clothes, made more tea, and looked out over the dead.

The call came just before they started the evening briefing. Everyone was there; Vera at the front was writing furiously on the whiteboard. She reminded Holly of some elderly, eccentric graffiti artist, arms flying in wide sweeps, occasionally balancing on her toes to reach the top of the board. Finally satisfied, the inspector turned back to face them, eyes narrowed, soft bum planted on the edge of the desk behind her, stretching the dreadful crimplene trousers, which were her go-to office wear, into wrinkles round her belly. 'Well, team, what have you got for me?'

Holly was thinking how she'd describe her encounter with Josh Heslop when there was a tap at the door and a constable stuck in his head.

'Yes?' Vera was fierce and irritable. She never liked being interrupted.

'There's just been a 999 call, boss.'

'Well?'

'A worker from the Forestry Commission driving back towards Kirkhill this afternoon. He's found a dead woman. Not far from Brockburn. They wondered if it could be your missing Miss Browne.'

'And why do we only know about it now?' Her voice was deceptively calm, her eyes fiery.

'The guy only found the body because his van broke down and he was wandering around trying to get a phone signal. He ended up walking to the road and flagging down a car.'

'Where is he now?' Vera was already on the way to her office to fetch her coat.

'At the Forestry Commission office in Kirkhill waiting for you.' The PC ventured a little further into the room and handed over a slip of paper with an address.

Vera took it, stopped at the door and looked into the room. 'Joe, you take over here. Let the CSI and Doc Keating know. I'll give an accurate GPS location when I have one. Continue with the briefing. I want a full report of everything discussed on my desk before you leave tonight.' A pause. 'Hol, you're with me.'

★

The forestry officer was Les Robson. He was wiry, one of those outdoor, weather-beaten men it's impossible to age, still in his uniform green trousers and jersey, a fleece. The commission office was in a wooden building close to Kirkhill community hall. He was sitting at his desk, his hands cupped round a mug of coffee. Holly thought it would take a lot to throw him, but he'd been thrown by this. He looked as if he was planted in his chair and hadn't moved since he'd got there.

Vera was uncharacteristically patient. 'Will you find the place again,' she asked, 'in the dark? I wouldn't blame you if it was a struggle. These commercial plantations all look the same to me.'

'We carry coloured plastic ribbons,' Robson said, 'to mark the edge of the clear fell. I tied those to trees as I made my way back to the van. Even in the light I wasn't sure I'd find my way back.'

Vera nodded. 'We'll need you to come with us. This is your patch. We couldn't do it without you. Wouldn't know where to start.'

He got to his feet and picked up keys from his desk. 'We can take one of the other vans. Mine's still out there. It won't get fixed until tomorrow.'

'No need,' Vera said. 'We'll go in my Land Rover. You can direct me.'

'Thanks.' He seemed grateful that he didn't have to drive.

The three of them squeezed into the bench seat at the front, Holly squashed in the middle. There were still street lights until the edge of the village and then it was perfectly dark. No traffic. No houses. Holly thought she recognized the road and the long wall that marked the entrance to Brockburn, then they took a turn into unknown territory, a lane surrounded by trees, which blocked out even the stars and the moonlight. They came to a barrier and Vera stopped.

'Is this us?'

Robson didn't answer. He was out of the vehicle and raising the metal pole that blocked the way. Vera drove through and they waited for the man to join them.

'It's not locked?'

'No need. Nobody drives here.' A pause. 'Walkers come sometimes. It's a public bridleway and locals grew up playing in the forest. You get riders occasionally.' There was a steep, sandy track only separated from the trees by boggy ditches, covered in ice, which glittered when the headlights swept over them. A sharp turn, another narrower track and then a small clearing where the green Forestry Commission van still stood.

'It's a walk from here.' Robson jumped down first. 'There's an area we cleared years ago and seems to have been forgotten. I thought I might get better phone signal away from the trees. The path's overgrown now. I couldn't have got my van through and I wouldn't risk your Land Rover.'

The air felt sharp and thin, turning their breath white in the torchlight. The only colour was on pink plastic ribbons, strangely celebratory, which marked the route through the forest. The path was rutted and pitted, churned by heavy machinery, the forest already encroaching on either side. Patches of snow lay under the trees. Holly walked easily, only missing her footing occasionally on the uneven ground, but Vera was already wheezing. She stopped for a moment and bent double to catch her breath.

'Is this the only way in?'

'Aye.' He stood. Holly could tell he was impatient, eager to get this over. 'As far as I know.'

'You could get a tractor down here, a quad bike?'

'I guess so.'

Vera shone her torch to the ground, looking for recent tyre tracks, but everything was covered by a new sheen of frost. Holly thought the boss wanted an excuse to rest a while longer before they continued. As they walked on, following the trail of the ribbons at junctions and splits in the track, Holly again ran through the women she'd been considering, earlier in the evening, as potential suspects. Would Juliet and Harriet find their way here? Even if they had access to an off-road vehicle? Yet they'd both grown up in the valley. Harriet would have seen the trees planted, watched them grow. She'd know the land beneath the forest. The same was true of the farmers, Rosemary Heslop and Jill Falstone. And of the next generation, the Heslop girls and Josh. This land-scape was strange to Holly, but it was probably their playground, a place to explore.

Holly was wondering how well Dorothy would know it, when they came to a gap in the trees. She stopped in her tracks, stunned by the scene laid out before her. When Robson had spoken of a clearing, she'd imagined a green space, light and grassy, a place for summer picnics.

This looked more like a war zone, a graveyard, not like the neat and ordered cemetery she saw from the window of her apartment, but a place of twisted limbs, everything dead and dry. The foresters had cut the pines, and stripped them of branches, so only the valuable straight trunks remained to be carried away for sale. Everything else had been discarded, left in heaps, grey now in the moonlight. The bones of the trees thrown into giant piles, the huge roots pulled out by diggers, upturned, so they looked like fingers reaching towards the sky.

The area of devastation was huge and the moonlight shone in.

Vera and Robson would have known what to expect and were unmoved. Vera stood, hands on hips, breathing heavily. Holly thought it was the most exercise she'd had for years. She felt a smug smile crawl across her face.

'Where's the dead woman then?' Vera asked.

'This way,' Robson said. 'I would never have seen her, but I was clambering round, looking for phone signal, and I almost fell over her.'

'Just stay where you are and point it out to us.' Vera was her imperious self again.

He pointed to the far edge of the clear fell. 'About ten yards in over there.'

Holly followed Vera. They made their way around the clearing, close to the surrounding trees, a longer distance but much easier than climbing over the piles of branches and roots.

Robson shouted over to them. 'I've marked it with a ribbon.' A pause. 'I think an animal has been at her. A dog maybe. They exercise the hounds up here.'

Holly, not usually squeamish, thought she would vomit.

The ribbon was motionless in the still air, and they found her easily once they knew where to look. She'd been pulled a short distance from the forest edge and covered with spindly branches, but a flash of colour showed through. A blue Gore-Tex jacket. Vera leaned over and cleared a few of the branches away so they could see enough to make a positive identification, though Holly thought there was no doubt that this was Constance Browne. She stared out at them. Part of her cheek had been nibbled away, but there was no head wound that Holly could see, no blood and bone. Vera was leaning over her, torch in her hand, muttering to herself.

'Eh, pet, what a place to end up. I think they strangled you. Look at this mark around your neck. What did they use? Not that scarf. A bit of wire or twine? I hope you fought back. Let's hope for a bit of skin under your nails. Something for us to work with.'

She shot a quick, defiant look at Holly. 'Don't mind me. I always talk to the dead. You get more sense from them than the living most times.' She straightened and shouted out to Robson. 'I'd like you and my colleague here to go back to the road in my vehicle. Holly will give directions to my forensic team and the pathologist and when they arrive, could you show them the way? They'll have their own four-by-four. We'll give you a lift home then.'

'What about you, boss?' Holly said. 'What will you do?'

'I'll stay with her.' Vera gave a little smile. 'Keep her company and scare off any other animals that might want to spoil our scene.'

'Would you rather I do it?'

There was a pause and for a while Holly was afraid Vera might agree.

'Nah,' she said at last. 'There's nothing to fear from the dead. They can't hurt us. And I owe her. If I'd been more patient when I first went to interview her, asked her the right questions, she'd still be alive. She was killed for the secrets she kept. Besides, you're fitter than me. I'd show myself up by not keeping pace.'

Holly didn't push the point. She could think of nothing worse than waiting here in the dark. She'd started walking back towards Robson when Vera called out to her.

'You'll find a hip flask in the dash. Best malt saved for special occasions. Bring it back with you. I'll need warming up by the time you get here.' She paused for a beat. 'And I reckon this was a woman who'd understand quality.'

Holly lifted an arm to show she'd heard and understood, and walked on.

Chapter Thirty

VERA WATCHED THE TORCH LIGHTS BOUNCING away until they disappeared. She'd switched hers off. The moon gave all the light she needed. She knew better than to explore the scene before Billy Cartwright got his mitts on it, though she'd already decided this wasn't where Constance Browne had been killed. The teacher had been brought here, either dragged from the place where Robson had left his van, or driven in a quad bike or tractor. She *could* have been dragged; she'd been a slight woman, not a peck of fat on her thanks to all that Pilates and healthy eating. She'd more likely been driven, though that didn't help much with the identity of the murderer. Neil Heslop had been driving a tractor the night he found Lorna Falstone's body, and his lasses whizzed around the place on quad bikes. Even the big house had a grand four-wheel-drive vehicle that would probably have made it if the driver had more nerve than Vera.

Vera was angry, and still mumbled under her breath to the frozen woman.

Chances are you'd never have been found. Left here to rot and to be pulled apart by animals. Leaving us all wondering what had happened to you. All those bairns you taught during your career, thinking you'd just run away and left them.

Vera had never felt at home in the forest. She liked open spaces and hills. She thought she needed a view across half the county as far as the Cumbrian border, and with the hint of the coast in the opposite direction. The rows of trees, uniform and without character, depressed her.

Hector had brought her here occasionally, when he was in the middle of his egg-collecting addiction. She saw now that was what it had been. The only order in the chaos of their lives had been the narrow shelves in the case that would have looked more fitting in a museum. He'd displayed the eggs in clutches, as if they were still in the nest. Perhaps that madness had been all about control too, just like poor Lorna Falstone's attempts to starve herself. It hadn't been about bragging, showing them off. The only people to see them had been his gang, his partners in crime: John Brace and his cronies. It seemed to Vera now that the beauty of the eggs, the order, the strange friendships, had been all that had held him together through the depression following her mother's death. Or maybe he'd just been a selfish bastard, with a weird passion for collecting and owning things that would have been better left in the wild.

Vera couldn't remember what species he'd been after here in the forest. Treecreeper? Nuthatch? She wished she *could* remember. She'd been smaller then, and Hector had sent her up a ladder with an empty eggbox to retrieve the bird's eggs. It had been a glorious spring day and the nest had been caught in a spotlight of sunshine. The eggs had been small, almost jewel-like in their beauty, and briefly she'd understood his obsession. Then fear had taken over, fear that she'd fall, or that she'd end up in prison, because she'd known all along that this was against the law.

She was sitting on a grassy bank at the edge of the clearing, and she felt the hoar frost seep through her coat and into her bones. If she'd known the night would end up like this, she'd have worn her thermals. Vera's thoughts wandered back to Constance Browne. The teacher was wearing a weatherproof coat, so it was unlikely she was strangled in her bungalow. She'd been outside somewhere. They'd checked her landline, but there'd been no phone calls that morning. They hadn't found a mobile. So what had made her leave her breakfast uneaten and rush away to her death? Vera had only met her briefly, but she knew in her bones that Constance hadn't been a woman for panic, for impulse. There must have been a good reason.

Vera stood up and stamped her feet, to bring some life back into them. A tawny owl called and was answered further down the valley. Across the debris of dead branches, she saw suddenly a pair of eyes, caught in the moonlight, then there was a scuttering and the animal leapt away. Badger, Vera decided, or insomniac roe deer. The thought made her think of venison, of the casserole in the freezer. She'd thrown it together on one of her days off. Something to do when she wasn't at work. She realized she was starving, felt in her coat pocket and found a bar of chocolate. Like any explorer she knew the value of emergency rations. She broke off a piece, let it melt in her mouth, and thought she'd never tasted anything so good. She looked at her watch and saw that it was Wednesday.

She was almost dozing when she saw them coming, the lights through the trees. By now she was freezing and the half-sleep had seemed a survival technique, a way of escaping the misery of the cold. Her brain felt like slush too, half-melted ice, not really functioning. She got to her feet again and almost stumbled, then pulled herself together. No way was she going arse over tit in front of the team. Some bugger would capture the moment on their phone and she'd never live it down.

Holly was in front, recognizable, even though the white scene suit over her outdoor clothes made her seem bulky. She moved easily over the rough ground, as effortless as the roe deer Vera had surprised earlier. Vera felt a moment of envy. *Why did I never look like that, even when I was young?* Then decided she hadn't cared enough to work for it. There were always more important things going on. The latest investigation. Looking after Hector when he'd stopped being able to manage on his own, and the drink had eaten away at his brain. As they got closer, Vera saw that Holly was carrying a little rucksack on her back. Holly set it on the ground near to where Vera had been sitting, took out a thermos, opened it. Vera smelled coffee and warmth and could have kissed her.

'Are you okay, boss?' Holly handed over the thermos lid filled with liquid. Even with gloves, Vera's hands were so cold that she almost dropped it.

'I am now.'

Also in the bag, she found a pack of sandwiches, not shop-bought, a bag of crisps, more chocolate. And the hip flask. Vera took a quick swig, then hid it away. She wasn't going to share the good stuff with them. Holly wasn't much of a drinker anyway and it would only be wasted.

Next came Billy Cartwright and two of his team, then Paul Keating the pathologist. Vera ate the sandwiches and drank the coffee well away from their focus on the heap of dead branches covering Constance Browne, a strange surreal picnic.

'Shall we go back, boss?' Holly had been hovering, close by. 'Leave them to it?'

The area of clear fell was suddenly brought to life by a series of bright, jerky images. It looked to Vera like an ancient black-and-white film; the CSIs taking their photographs, everything recorded, caught in the flashlights of the cameras.

'Yeah,' Vera said. She tried to get to her feet but didn't quite manage it. Holly reached down and took her hand. 'Why not? We'll only be in the way.'

Later, she couldn't remember that walk back to the Land Rover. It must have been slow because it was two o'clock by the time they got there. Holly must have slowed her pace to match Vera's, and was there to help her scramble down the frozen, potholed track, which at times felt more like an assault course. By the time they arrived at the posse of vehicles, Vera was wiped out.

'I'll drive, shall I?' Holly said. She had the keys in her hand.

For a moment, Vera was tempted. 'Nah, bugger off,' she said. 'You only want me freezing my arse off again, getting down to lift the barriers.'

She heaved herself into the seat, switched on the engine and the heat full power, and felt her brain starting to work again. 'Let's get some padlocks organized for those barriers. Stop the gawpers and the press driving in. Get on the phone to Joe, tell him to get it sorted as soon as.'

'Won't he be asleep?'

'If he is, wake him up! The idle bugger's been in the warm all night. Fill him in with all we know. Let's get this investigation under way. I'll drop you at the station for your car, then we can both get home for a hot bath and a couple of hours' shut-eye. We'll put the briefing back for an hour to give the forensic-science team some time to see the wood from the trees . . .' Vera gave a chortle. Holly joined in. Vera felt a moment of triumph. Usually Hol saw it as a point of honour not to laugh at her jokes. 'Tell everyone to be there at nine. Sharp.'

Chapter Thirty-One

JOE HADN'T BEEN IN BED WHEN Holly called, though he was dozing, in the armchair downstairs, covered by a fancy throw that Sal had bought to keep the new sofa clean. He thought Vera should have taken *him* to the crime scene with her. He wasn't sexist, but some situations were best dealt with by a man.

The phone call wasn't unexpected. Vera always did need him, his reason and his common sense. He was surprised that it was Holly who called.

'The boss is driving.'

'Is it definitely Browne's body?' Sometimes the public called in a pile of bones that turned out to be hundreds of years old, or which had once belonged to a horse or a cow.

'Oh, yes.' A pause. 'It was all a bit Gothic, actually. This place in the middle of the forest. If the forester hadn't found her, Miss Browne could have been there for years.'

Joe didn't think that sounded like Holly. She wasn't usually given to fancies. 'Cause of death?'

'The boss thinks she was strangled.'

'Different from Lorna Falstone, then?'

He heard Vera shouting in the background, above the incessant rumble of the Land Rover's engine. 'So? What's he going on about? Does he think there are two killers in a place like Kirkhill? Just because there are different causes of death.'

'No,' Joe said. 'Just making a point.' He thought Vera would be feeling bad because they hadn't managed to prevent Constance's death. Guilt always made her ratty.

Then there came a list of instructions, all sent via Holly, about grid references and padlocks, and keeping a lid on things until they could think properly about a media release. Later he got a text from Holly. *The boss stayed with the body on her own while we fetched the team. I think she was knocked by Browne's death. She seemed very frail when we got back to her. We need to keep an eye on her. You know what she's like.*

He was in the station before the rest of them, making sure all the demands had been met. Vera breezed in, bright-eyed and eager.

'Eh, pet, do me a favour. Pop out and get me a bacon stottie. I had nothing in the house. Don't forget the brown sauce.'

She seemed her normal self. If it hadn't been for Holly's text, Joe would have been angry; he thought that sometimes Sal had a point about Vera taking the piss. As it was, he just had a few words of complaint for appearance's sake and then he went. He brought back coffee and a doughnut too.

Vera looked at him with suspicion. 'What's this then? You not feeling well?'

Joe didn't know how to reply. He thought Holly was making

a fuss about nothing. 'Thought you might need a sugar and caffeine boost after a night in the cold.'

'Aye, well.' A moment of silence. 'Poor woman. Nobody should be left like that. Let's find the killer, shall we?' She bit into the stottie, and brown sauce squirted onto her chin.

Joe sat at the back of the room and watched Vera take them through the details of Constance Browne's death.

'As I see it, she got up on Monday morning as usual, expecting to go along to the art class. The CSIs have been into her house and are protecting it as a potential crime scene but I don't think she was murdered there. She was wearing a thick waterproof jacket when the forester found her, and she wouldn't have been dressed like that if she was in the house. She'd laid the table for breakfast and the curtains were open, she'd put out food for the cat, so I think she was preparing for a normal day.'

'Could she have been killed on the Sunday?' Joe had stuck up his hand and was responding to Vera's nod. 'I don't think any of the team saw her that day.'

'Nah, when I went looking for her on the Monday morning the kettle was still warm. Not hot, but it had been used that morning.' Vera paused. 'That's a good point about Sunday, though. Let's track down what she was doing. I think she was a churchgoer. Let's check with the vicar. There was a priest at the party at Brockburn the night Lorna was killed, so we've got her contact details.' A pause. 'The folk from the big house were at church too that day. Did they spend any time with Connie? Share any information about Lorna's murder?' She looked around the room. 'Joe, that's for you.'

'Okay.'

'The way I see it, she was disturbed early that Monday morning. Either by someone she knew knocking at the door or a phone call. CSIs in the forest still haven't found a mobile, though we know she had one. It's interesting that Lorna's mobile and laptop have disappeared too.'

'You think the killer has them all?' Joe asked.

'Or has disposed of them, if they've got any sense. We're trying to track down the suppliers for both victims. Connie was an organized woman, so there should be records in the bungalow, receipts, or bills. The CSIs haven't found anything like that in Lorna's house, so it's possible that they were taken at the same time as her devices. Which would indicate a certain level of planning and intelligence.' Vera paused for breath. 'Let's hope the killer still has them, stashed away somewhere. There was no break-in at Connie's and the door to the bungalow was locked when I got there. So, as I say, it was most likely someone she knew.'

Joe looked at his colleagues, all intent, all taking notes. They understood how important it was to Vera that this end quickly. The case had been personal for her from the beginning. It seemed even more personal now.

'So,' Vera continued, 'Constance either left the house with the killer, dressed for outdoors in a waterproof jacket and walking boots, or she'd arranged to meet him somewhere. If she drove away from the bungalow with him, did someone see them? Or a car parked close by? If she met him elsewhere, where might that have been? We know her own car is still being investigated as a possible murder scene in the lab, so she didn't drive herself. She was a fit woman, but she wouldn't have walked all the way to the middle of Brockburn forest.

They're a nebby bunch in Kirkhill. I can't believe nobody saw her.' She stopped and looked out at them. 'So that's for the rest of you. Let's have you all in Kirkhill talking to the locals. We know that any sighting of Constance Browne on the Monday morning will be significant.'

She was just about to send them on their way, when Holly stood up. 'You talk about the killer as *him*,' she said. 'Could it have been a woman, do you think? Wouldn't Constance have trusted a woman coming to the door, or phoning and asking to meet, more easily than a man? We think she might have been killed because Lorna had confided in her, perhaps about the identity of her son's father. Surely, she wouldn't have gone off with the man she suspected of being Lorna's killer.'

There was a moment of silence. Joe thought Holly had a point and was about to speak up in support, when Vera answered, her voice more conciliatory than he would have expected. Usually, she hated to be challenged. 'You're right,' she said at last. 'Of course Constance would have been less wary of a woman than a man. We think she was moved from the place where we parked to the patch of clear fell. She could have been driven by someone with a four-wheel-drive and a strong nerve. I wouldn't have wanted to do it in the Land Rover, but it would be possible. Or she was dragged. A strong woman could have done that as well as a man. So, no closed minds here, please, everyone. Thanks for pointing that out, Hol.'

Joe thought that perhaps after all the night in the cold had transformed Vera. As Holly had said, they should look out for her.

But Vera hadn't finished yet. 'And on the point of strong women, this morning I've been doing a bit of digging into the history of Dorothy Felling. It seems she wasn't the brilliant lawyer we've been led to believe. Apparently, she made a monumental cock-up on an employment case and cost her client, and so her chambers, an eye-watering sum in compensation. She was forced to resign. So, while she might enjoy skivvying at the big house, her move to the country wasn't entirely voluntary.'

They stared at her. 'Well, I had to do something while Joe here was taking so long to organize my bacon stottie, so I got on the phone to her former boss. Again, you were right, Holly. We should have done that earlier.' She sighed. 'I'm not quite sure how that could be relevant to Lorna's murder, though.'

As they were leaving the room, Vera spoke again. 'While you're in Kirkhill, Hol, drop in to Brockburn and speak to Harriet. That's another strong woman, with secrets to hide. I got off to a wrong start with her and she'll not confide in me. I'm too much of a pleb. See if you can get her to admit her husband was having an affair with Jill Falstone. The rest of the valley knows, so I'm sure she does too.'

Holly nodded – as shocked, it seemed, as Joe was.

The vicar was hard to pin down. Joe knew that her name was Jane Grant and she was in charge of four parishes. One church she only visited on the first Sunday of the month; others had more regular services. He had a mobile number for her, but it took five attempts before she answered his call: 'Sorry! I seem to spend most of my time on the road and this time of year is a nightmare. Every primary school in the county is holding its nativity play this week and they all expect me to be there.' There was no stress in her voice, though. She seemed to delight in the activity.

'Where will you be today? It is rather important that I talk to you.'

In the end they agreed to meet at the vicarage in Kirkhill at lunchtime. 'If I'm not back by the time you get there, my husband will let you in.'

Joe had been expecting to find her in a large Victorian building close to the church, but it seemed that had been sold and turned into apartments. A new and smaller house had been built in the former vicarage grounds. It was square, functional, and rather ugly. He arrived at the same time as the vicar, who was younger than he'd been expecting, in her thirties, bristling with the kind of energy that got things done. He parked next to her and waited while she pulled a bag out of the boot. She was wearing a soft dog collar under a hand-knitted sweater and a heavy parka.

She must have guessed his thoughts. 'Most of our churches are freezing and I haven't got any formal services today. Come in. There'll be soup if you're hungry. I'm starving.' A pause. 'I suppose you're here about Lorna Falstone. Poor little thing. We gave a statement to your colleagues the day after she died, but we couldn't help much.'

It seemed the news about Constance Browne hadn't reached her yet. The team would be starting to canvass Kirkhill now and Vera had asked comms to put out a media release. Soon the information would be everywhere.

Joe followed her into an untidy house. A couple of small kids' bikes stood in the hall and they climbed past them into a big kitchen. An older man sat at a scrubbed pine table, a pile of papers in front of him. He got up when they came in, seemed genuinely pleased to see her, gave her a hug and a kiss.

'This is Doug, my rock. He's an academic, semi-retired. He holds all this together.' She waved an arm around the kitchen, taking in the clothes horse, the laundry basket, the ironing board, the washed dishes piled on the draining board. 'This is a detective. Joe Ashworth. I promised him soup.'

Doug got to his feet and cleared the papers into a tidier pile. 'You're in luck then. There *is* soup.'

'Are you okay talking in front of my husband?' They were sitting at the cleared end of the table. Doug had ladled vegetable soup into big blue bowls. There was a loaf of home-made bread too. Joe felt swept along by the flow of her energy and had found it impossible to resist the hospitality. 'If it's confidential we can go into the office afterwards.'

'I'm happy to talk here,' he said. 'Doug might be able to help.'

'It is about Lorna?'

'Did you know her?'

'I knew *of* her, of course. I visited a couple of times, once when she was pregnant and once when she was back home with the baby, but she was resistant, prickly. She saw me as an interfering do-gooder, which I probably was.'

Joe paused. 'We're trying to trace the father of her child. Do you have any idea who that might be?'

Jane shook her head. 'I didn't ask. I wasn't there to judge, just to offer help and support.'

'You'll know the farming families in the valley,' Joe said. 'What do you make of Lorna's parents?'

The vicar shrugged. 'I don't know them well. They're not church members and they don't take part in village functions.'

'What about the Heslops?'

'Ah, I know them better.' Jane smiled. 'They're not regulars

– I suspect that church for them is more a matter of tradition than faith, something to hold the community together – but they're always here for the big festivals. I saw Rosemary in the village yesterday and I know she's worried about Neil. He's not slept properly since he found Lorna's body. Sometimes we forget that there's often more than one victim of a crime.'

'You were at Brockburn the night Lorna was found. Are you close to the Stanhopes?'

Across the table, Doug gave a kind of snort. Jane grinned. 'You'll have to excuse my husband, Joe. He doesn't enjoy the social obligations of being the partner of a country vicar. We were invited, I suspect, because the family has always asked the parish priest to these occasions. A kind of tradition. Harriet would have preferred an elderly man, of course, but I had to do. Perhaps the Brockburn clan likes the sense that they have God on their side.'

Joe wasn't sure what to say about that. 'You left early?'

'As soon as we decently could. Immediately after dinner. We had an excuse because of the weather. We were walking.'

'Isn't it a long walk back into Kirkhill?'

'It would be by road. Not by the footpaths.'

Joe finished the soup in his bowl and set down the spoon. 'Did you see anything unusual?' He thought nobody else would have been out that night.

'We saw nothing at all. It was rather beautiful.'

Doug began to pile up the bowls. Joe spoke before the man left his seat. 'Yesterday Constance Browne's body was found in Brockburn forest. She'd been murdered.'

There was a shocked silence. 'Are you sure it's Connie?' Jane asked at last.

He nodded.

'It's just that she always seemed indestructible. I never saw her tired or upset or vulnerable. She was one of those women who can face anything the world has to throw at her.'

'We know she wasn't married and that she lived alone,' Joe said, 'but was there a partner? Someone special we should notify?'

Jane shook her head.

'Connie's been single for as long as I've known her. We've been here for five years. She mentioned men she'd known in the past – there was someone she met at university and they were engaged for a while – but I had the impression that she'd been alone for ages.' Jane paused. 'I think she had admirers, but she always said she was too long in the tooth to put up with another person's mess.'

'When did you last see her?'

'On Sunday. It was ten-thirty Holy Communion in Kirkhill and she never missed if she was home.'

'Did you have a chance to talk after the service?'

'Only briefly.' Jane got to her feet and switched on the kettle. 'It was a foul day. Nobody felt like chatting and I had another service to go on to.'

'I had a word with her.' Doug had hardly spoken throughout the exchange and now he seemed diffident, uncertain. 'She and I were on sides duty and we put out the hymn books, greeted people as they came in.' He looked at his wife. 'She asked if she might pop round sometime. There was something she needed to discuss with you.' He paused, stared into the distance. 'I'd forgotten all about it. I said Sunday was always manic but she'd be very welcome on Monday. I invited her to come for lunch. When she didn't turn up, it just slipped my mind.' He turned to Joe. 'If I'd raised the alarm then, might you have been able to save her?'

Joe shook his head. 'We think she was killed early on Monday morning.'

'I still feel dreadful.'

Jane reached out and put her hand on his arm.

'She didn't tell you what was worrying her?' Joe said.

'No. She was just about to explain a bit more, when the family from Brockburn came in, Harriet, Juliet and her husband. Connie saw them coming and said she'd tell us on Monday.'

'Did Miss Browne talk to the Brockburn family at all? Before or after the service?'

'No,' Doug said. 'She seemed actively to avoid them. It seemed rather odd, because they'd always been on good terms.'

'But Connie hadn't been invited to the Friday-night party?'

'No,' Jane said. 'I think we were there to represent the whole community. And it was a fund-raising event really. Connie only had her teaching pension.'

'So not worth bothering about,' Doug said.

'Are the family at Brockburn regular worshippers?'

'Oh, yes.' Jane broke in, before Doug could answer. Joe thought that was a pity. Doug might have been more honest.

In the end the man spoke anyway, muttering under his breath. 'Bloody parasites.'

'You'll have to excuse my husband.' Jane grinned. 'He disapproves of inherited wealth. I'm afraid he's a bit of a socialist.'

'As was Our Lord.'

They smiled at each other. Joe had the impression that there was no real argument between them. This was a kind of dance, a ritual. 'Are they really wealthy? I thought they were dreaming up schemes to keep the house from falling down.'

'It's all relative,' Doug said. 'If they sold Brockburn, they'd make a fortune.'

'What would the village make of that?'

'They'd hate it.' Jane was definite. 'This is a place where tradition matters.'

Chapter Thirty-Two

HOLLY WAS ON CANVASSING DUTY IN Kirkhill. She stood for a moment in the main street. Despite being dressed for the weather she felt the wind slice through her clothes and chill her bones. She felt spacy with tiredness. The night before now seemed like a nightmare; occasional images would explode in her brain, monochrome and weird. The twisted roots of the abandoned area of clear fell felt like a dystopian background to a horror film. The memories had disturbed what little sleep she'd managed.

She turned and climbed the bank to the old people's bunga-lows beyond Lorna Falstone's house, and knocked on the door of Matty Fuller, the elderly retired shepherd. The light inside flashed and after a moment it was partially opened. Matty's face appeared at the gap in the door. He seemed almost embarrassed.

'Eh, lass, it's you. You'd better come away in. Don't mind the mess.'

There were underpants and socks drying on the radiator. Awkwardly he cleared them into a laundry basket.

'No point putting them on the line, this weather. They'd just freeze.' He picked up the basket as if it were something to be ashamed of. 'I'll make us both a cup of tea. You'll need warming up.' And he disappeared into the kitchen, taking the offending underwear with him.

Holly stood at the living-room window and looked out over the valley. There was a view of the village and the hills beyond. A view down to Constance Browne's bungalow. Because of the angle of the slope, she could see over the fence and into the dead woman's garden. Matty returned with two mugs of tea, a packet of biscuits in his cardigan pocket. 'I've not put in any sugar,' he said. 'Most young folk don't take it these days.'

They sat for a moment. He opened the packet of biscuits and passed it to her.

'Have you heard about Constance?' She turned towards him so he could read her lips.

'The schoolteacher? What about her?'

'We found her dead in the forest last night.' Holly paused. 'Murdered, like Lorna.'

There was no response. She was surprised that he seemed so little shocked or upset.

'Didn't you know her?' Holly asked.

'Oh, aye, I knew her. I couldn't keep her away. She was one of those women who think they know what's best for you.' He looked up. 'I didn't mean she deserved to die, like, but she could be interfering. One of the women who don't have bairns to boss about, so they boss the rest of the world.'

'You think she was killed because she interfered?'

'I suppose not,' he said. 'That's no reason to kill a woman. But she could be irritating, all the same. That confidence, you knaa, that she was always right.'

This sounded personal. 'Did she try to boss you about?'

'She succeeded, didn't she?' He gave her a sad smile. 'She was the one to persuade me I needed to move closer to the village. She kept on at me. And then when I was here, she was in every day about the old folks' lunch club and bingo in the hall.' He paused. 'I told her I didn't want company. I needed my lass Lizzie, but that's something different. In the end, she gave up and left me alone.'

There was a silence. Holly didn't know what to say. She'd never met anyone with whom she could spend her life, couldn't imagine what it would be like to be alone after a lifetime's company.

'We think Constance left home on Monday morning, maybe with her killer. You've got a good view of the village from here. Did you see anything unusual?'

He thought. She could see he was taking the question seriously. 'I sit by the window for a couple of hours every morning. A cup of tea and watch the world go by, until I feel ready to go down to the Co-op for my shopping. Watch the weather on the hills. Maybe the woman was right and I'm better here. There'd not be much to see from my old place. Monday is the art class in the hall. Constance walks there. Gets there before the rest of them.' A quick grin. 'So she can boss *them* around too.'

'But not this Monday?'

'No,' he agreed. 'Not this Monday. I wondered about that.'

'I don't suppose you notice what time she draws her curtains in the morning?'

'Early,' Matty said. 'Six-thirty on the dot, even if it's dark. She's an early riser. In the summer, she's out walking.'

Holly thought the boss would be pleased to hear that. It was a bit of concrete information. Matty was still thinking about Holly's original question.

'A car pulled up outside her house that morning. Seven o'clock, maybe. I didn't see Constance, though.'

'What sort of car?'

He shook his head. 'It was still pitch black and it parked between the street lights. All I could see were the headlights and then the shape. A van or a jeep.'

'You didn't see anyone get out?'

Another pause. 'I think the door of her house opened. I remember a sudden light on the path. But whether someone went in or she came out, I can't say. Not for certain.'

'What happened next?'

'The car drove off,' he said. 'Not fast. Nothing suspicious. I thought maybe it was someone delivering to her door. A parcel. It's that time of year.'

'Is there anything else you can tell me? Did you see the colour of the vehicle when it drove off?' *Anything to make Vera proud of me.*

He turned to her. 'I'm sorry. I just didn't take much notice.'

Holly was about to go when she had another thought. 'You can see Lorna's house from here, and you're up early, looking out. We're interested in Saturday morning. The day after she died, but it was before the news got out, before the forensic guys could get to her house. I don't suppose you saw anyone go in?'

He sat back in his chair. 'Someone was there, but I didn't see anyone go to the door.'

'What do you mean?' Holly tried not to sound too excited. She didn't want to spook him, or for him to elaborate on the facts to please her.

277

'There was a light downstairs. Early. That was unusual, so I noticed. The bairn was a good sleeper and young people don't get up so early as us old folk. I hoped there was nothing wrong, that the lad wasn't ill.' Matty stopped abruptly. 'But Lorna was already dead by then, wasn't she? They found her body at Brockburn the night before.'

Holly nodded.

'I'm sorry.' He sounded distraught. 'I should have remembered last time you were here. I'm a foolish old man. I didn't think.'

'Really,' she said. 'Don't worry about it. You're telling me now. Do you think somebody had let themselves in before you were up, if you didn't see anyone come in from the street?'

Matty shook his head, definite. 'I was up before the light. Here, looking out over the village. I would have seen.' He paused. 'But there's a lonnen at the back. Someone could have gone in that way.'

The way Josh Heslop always went to visit Lorna with nobody seeing.

'Did Lorna have a laptop in the house?' Holly asked.

'Oh, aye. The young are always online, aren't they? Once she got me a train ticket on it, so I could visit my nephew down in York.'

And now it's disappeared. So we were right. The murderer went in the morning after they killed her to cover their tracks.

Holly sat for a moment in her car outside Brockburn, planning her conversation with Harriet. Part of her admired the woman, her style and her confidence. Her pragmatism. Because after all, Harriet was allowing Mark to transform the place. She'd married into the Stanhope clan, expecting a life of privilege and comfort, and now she was coming to terms with the possibility of a very different life, of sharing this place with strangers. Holly thought she'd have an empathy with Harriet which Vera would never manage. Vera's father had been cast out by the family, or had turned his back on them. But still it wouldn't be easy, talking to the woman about her late husband's affairs.

Juliet opened the door to the house before Holly rang the bell. She was wearing outdoor clothes and had car keys in her hand. 'I've just heard about Connie. Isn't it dreadful?' But despite the words she seemed distracted, unfocused. 'Look, I'm just on my way into Kirkhill. Can it wait until later?'

'I was hoping to speak to Mrs Stanhope.'

'Oh!' A moment of surprise. 'Yes, Mother's there.' She raised her voice. 'Mummy, there's a detective here to speak to you.'

Juliet ran off down the grand steps to the drive. Holly was left standing awkwardly in the hall, not sure whether she should wait for Harriet to appear, or wander on in to find her.

At last, there was a voice. 'Well, do you want to talk to me or not?'

Holly followed the sound and arrived into a small sitting room, with a view of the formal garden. There was a coal fire, and two armchairs pulled up very close to it. Harriet was sitting in one, almost hidden from view. She turned, but didn't get to her feet. 'Come on in and shut the door. This place is all draughts.'

Holly did as she was told. Harriet nodded towards the empty chair. 'Is this about Constance? Poor woman. Have you got the killer yet?'

'Not yet.' Holly paused. 'Do you have any idea why anyone would have wanted to kill her?'

Harriet seemed to consider. 'I found her a little irritating – she was one of those rather self-righteous women with a heightened belief in their own moral superiority – but I can't believe she would have driven anyone to murder. I suppose it must be related to Lorna Falstone's death.'

'Did you know that your husband was having an affair with Lorna's mother? At the time, I mean.' Holly tried to keep her voice sympathetic, despite the bluntness of the question.

There was a moment of silence, then an outburst of scorn. 'Of course I did. I'm not stupid.'

'It must have been very hurtful.'

'Oh, please! Now you're sounding just like Constance. I take it you're not married.' A brief pause to check that her assumption was correct. 'Well, of course not and neither was she. So how could either of you understand? Crispin and I had a perfectly satisfactory marriage. An arrangement. He would only have broken the terms of the agreement if he'd caused embarrassment to me and my daughter.'

'Did he ever do that?'

There was another moment of stony silence. 'He came close to it,' Harriet said at last, 'with the Falstone woman.'

'Because she had his child?'

'Because he allowed that rumour to develop and grow, to sour our reputation in the community here and with the rest of the county.' Harriet stood up. 'It gave people the right to pity me. And in my opinion, there is nothing more degrading than pity.'

Holly got to her feet too. She didn't know what else to say.

'Now, if that's all, officer, I'm sure you can see yourself out.' Harriet stared out of the window so she wouldn't have to watch Holly go.

Chapter Thirty-Three

VERA SAT IN HER OFFICE AND brooded. About an elderly, educated woman who filled her life with good works and trips to the theatre. About a young lass who'd stopped eating to bring some order to her existence. About her own strange family, landed gentry, who, despite being lords of all they surveyed, seemed fraught, anxious and not at all at ease with themselves. About a young boy named Thomas, who was growing up without parents. It was the child who filled her thoughts in the end.

The phone call jolted her back to the present, to the small overheated room.

'Ma'am, there's a woman on the line for you. Her name's Bolitho. She says you'll want to speak to her.'

It took Vera a moment to realize who the woman might be. Of course, it was Juliet. She'd taken her husband's name. Vera wondered about that. Didn't most women hang on to their own, these days? Would Vera herself be the last remaining Stanhope?

Juliet sounded nervous. But then she usually did. 'Do you

think we could meet up? I've found something which might be helpful.'

'Of course, pet.' Vera thought she always treated the woman as if she were a shy child, who needed reassurance. 'I'll come over to Brockburn, shall I?' She was glad of an excuse to leave the police station and to breathe a bit of fresh air.

'No!' The reply came quickly. 'I don't want to put you out. I can come to you.'

So, you don't want the rest of the Brockburn mafia to know that we're meeting.

'Tell you what,' Vera said. 'I've got to be in Kirkhill anyway. Why don't we meet there? Gloria's caff. It's usually quiet at this time of day and if there are people around, we can go for a stroll.'

Juliet was there before her, sitting in the back, close to the counter. Nobody walking past in the street would be able to see her, but the windows were so steamed with condensation that she was invisible anyway. Vera joined her, and Gloria brought coffee, then made herself scarce in the kitchen. They were the only customers.

'What's all this about then?' The same motherly tone.

Juliet looked up at her and for the first time, Vera wondered if she was being played here. There was something calculating in the woman's glance. Something steely. Perhaps Juliet wasn't the shy innocent she pretended to be. 'This is rather awkward.'

'More than awkward,' Vera said, 'for Lorna and Constance. You did know that we found Constance last night in the forest? She'd been murdered too.'

Juliet nodded. '*So* dreadful.'

'Now, why the cloak-and-dagger stuff? Why couldn't we meet at Brockburn?'

'You'll understand when you see this.' Juliet put her phone on the table, tapped the screen and enlarged the photograph so Vera could read the print.

It was a very brief letter addressed to *My dear wife*, and was obviously from Crispin Stanhope to Harriet. The language was stilted and formal. This was intended for possible public consumption. The apology was brief. Perhaps Crispin had been more fulsome in person, though Vera suspected not. This was an entitled man, who had easily found justification for his hurtful behaviour.

> *My dear wife*
> *This is to inform you that Lorna Falstone, the daughter of Gillian Falstone, is entitled to some claim on me and my estate. In the event of my death, I ask that you ensure she is provided for in a manner commensurate with that status. Out of respect for you and to save our family from possible embarrassment, I have not made a legal arrangement through our lawyers, but out of respect for me, I trust that you will follow my wishes.*
> *I apologize for any distress this might cause.*
> *Yours,*
> *Crispin Stanhope*

The letter had been printed but the signature was hand-written.

'Where did you find this?'

'In an envelope in my mother's room.'

'You knew all along that Lorna was Crispin's daughter, your half-sister?'

'I still don't *know*,' Juliet said, 'but yes, I suspected. I suspected that something like this might exist. My father was kind to the people he cared about, but he ignored the rest of the world. I couldn't believe that he would pay for Lorna's treatment out of an altruistic benevolence.'

'Why didn't you tell me earlier?' Vera tried to contain her impatience. What was it with these people, who thought that the rule of law didn't apply to them?

'I didn't think it could be relevant. I thought you'd find Lorna's murderer quickly and none of this would have to come out.' Juliet paused. 'I still don't think it could be relevant. What reason could any of us have for killing Lorna? There's nothing legal in this. My father left it to my mother's discretion to provide for Lorna. Her death changes nothing.'

'If it came out that Harriet had ignored your father's wishes, it might change the way your neighbours, all these people who treat you as superior beings, look at you.'

Vera wondered why Harriet had hung on to the letter. Was it guilt or a kind of superstition that had stopped her from destroying it?

'You won't go public on this?' Juliet sounded alarmed. 'That's why I came to you. You're family after all.'

Vera didn't answer that directly, but still she spoke:

'Lorna might have decided to go public. She was building a new life for herself. If she knew what Crispin intended, she might have put pressure on Harriet to comply with his wishes.'

Especially if she was in danger of losing her man. A payout from the Brockburn estate might have persuaded him to stay.

Vera thought she wouldn't sink so low as to bribe a bloke

to stay with her, but then she wasn't sure she'd ever been in love. People in love, it seemed, had no pride.

'How could Lorna have known?' Juliet was sounding seriously scared now.

'Perhaps your father told her,' Vera said. 'We know that Crispin paid the bills of the private hospital. And an elderly man visited her once. Perhaps that was him, wanting to make his peace. To tell her that she'd be cared for even after his death.' There was a moment of silence. 'You do know,' Vera went on, 'that we'll have to ask Harriet about this.'

'Oh, God, no! She'll realize that I went into her room. Nobody else could have told you about the letter.'

'You'd better warn her then. Tell her what you did. It'd be better coming from you.' Vera couldn't understand Juliet. Did she really think a police officer could keep this information quiet in the middle of a murder investigation? 'I'll give you until six this evening. I'll be round at Brockburn then to speak to Harriet.'

'But you're family!' This time it came out as a scream.

Another silence while the accusation hit home, then Vera spoke very quietly:

'But I'm not really, am I, pet? Only when it suits you. And even if I were, I'll always be a cop first.' She stood up and held both empty mugs in one hand. Gloria appeared miraculously from the kitchen and took them. Juliet remained where she was and watched Vera stamp out into the street.

Vera walked. It was what she did when she needed to think. She walked and when she stopped walking, she ate. The cold snap seemed to be lasting. It was late morning now but there was still frost on the ground and ice on the river. She followed the path along the bank, passed the school on the slight rise in the land where Constance Browne had taught for her career. The playground was empty, but there was a light on in the classroom. Suddenly, there floated over the clear air the sound of children's voices, singing a carol. 'In the Bleak Midwinter'.

She was thinking that this valley, surrounded by hills on one side and the forest on the other, was its own complete world. There were rich people and the self-satisfied middle classes and the poor sods who did most of the work. Though Vera hadn't met many of those: the cleaners, the care workers who wiped old people's bums. The farmers – Neil Heslop and Robert Falstone – grafted, but they went home at night to a comfortable home. The domestic work at Brockburn was done by Dorothy Felling, who could hardly be described as down-trodden. Vera decided these musings were bonkers and would lead her nowhere.

Her thoughts turned to Juliet. The letter from Crispin only told them what they'd already suspected. It was good to have the confirmation, but it didn't do much to move the investigation on. What *really* interested Vera was Juliet's motivation. Why bring the letter to Vera's attention? She can't have been so stupid as to believe that Vera wouldn't follow it up. She was still thinking that over when she came to the Falstones' place. She was close to the fence Robert had been mending on her previous visit, but there was no sign of him now.

On impulse she took the track to the farm. Jill must have been at the kitchen window and had seen her coming, because the door was opened before Vera could knock. The woman stood there with the boy on her hip, looking better than when Vera had seen her before, less worn down and worn out.

'Come away in.' A smile.

Even since her visit on the previous day, the kitchen looked different. A colourful rug on the floor had replaced the brown mucky one, and a painting made from a child's handprints was stuck on the fridge.

Jill saw Vera looking at it. 'We've started going to the parent-and-toddler group in the village. I'm not the only gran going along with the bairns. It's been a chance to meet up with old friends.'

'Did Crispin promise that he'd look after Lorna? Even after he'd died.'

Now Jill looked wary. 'He said we weren't to worry.'

'Were you surprised that there was nothing in his will?'

Jill gave a little laugh and shook her head. 'Nah, the rich always look after their own. And we never really belonged to him. Besides, I wouldn't have wanted it.'

'It might come in handy now, with little Thomas to care for.'

'I suppose it might. But we can manage.'

Jill set the child down on the rug and offered coffee, but Vera shook her head. She hadn't finished thinking. There was more walking to do.

She was tempted to make her way back to Kirkhill, to her car and then on to a pile of ham, eggs and chips in Gloria's. Her legs were aching. She'd walked further during this investigation than she had for years, since long before Hector had died. When she'd been looking after him, there'd been no time for walking for pleasure. It was all work and then thankless grind at home. But her brain was firing on all cylinders now and she had the sense that if she went further, she might make the links that would bring her close to a solution.

In the distance, she could see the high wall that surrounded Brockburn. Before that, there was the Home Farm where the Heslops lived, almost in the shadow of the Stanhopes' palace. Away from the roads, the three houses were closer than she'd realized before. Broom Farm, Home Farm and Brockburn, all linked through history and obligation. Vera thought she'd go as far as the entrance to Home Farm and then turn back. As she approached, she saw the two girls, Nettie and Cath, sloping down the lane towards the house. They were dressed again in black: skinny black jeans and Kimmerston High School hoodies. Both skinny themselves, and they must be freezing. No real coats and not an ounce of flesh on either of them. Vera met them just by the gate that led to the farm.

'Why aren't you two at school? It's only lunchtime.'

'Last day of term.' That was Nettie, the older one. 'They let us high school kids out early.'

'Did the bus drop you up by the cottages?' Vera thought she should place Dorothy and Karan's cottage on her mental map too. They were part of the Brockburn estate.

'Yeah. Josh was going to pick us up but he's having car trouble again.'

'Do either of you drive?'

'I was too young until my birthday.' Cath sounded resentful, then smiled. 'But I've got my test booked now. I've been driving round the farm for years.'

'I passed my test a month after I was seventeen,' Nettie said, 'but the parents are making me wait until my next birthday until I can get a car.' A pause. 'That's *so* mean. I only need an old banger.'

Vera leaned against the gate to catch her breath, her mind still fluttering with ideas. 'Did you hear about Miss Browne?'

'Of course.' Cath this time. 'It's all over social media. A serial killer on the loose in Kirkhill. We were warned at school not to wander about on our own.' She didn't sound scared. Excited, if anything. The invulnerability of the young.

Vera thought that when she made it back to the Land Rover, she'd get Holly to check social media and see what was being said.

'You still doing extra classes with Karan Pabla?'

'Yeah, no real holiday for me.' Cath didn't appear upset, though.

Vera looked up the track towards the farmhouse. 'Is your brother at home?'

'I guess,' Nettie said, 'unless he could con Dad into lending him a vehicle. He's stranded without his car.'

Vera followed the girls up the track in the hope of talking to Josh Heslop, but when they got there, it was Neil with his head inside the bonnet of the car, looking at the engine.

'Shouldn't that be Josh's job?'

The girls had sloped off into the house. Neil emerged, wiping his hands on a bit of rag.

'Ah, well, he's not exactly practical, my lad. Which is why he let his vehicle get into this state.'

'Is he around?'

The man shook his head. 'He's gone into Newcastle on the bus to catch up with some of his mates.'

'Did you know he was friendlier with Lorna than he first let on?'

'She was a bonny lass,' Neil said lightly. 'No doubt there were a few lads in the village had their eye on her.'

'Do you think Josh could be the baby's father?'

'No.' Now the man was definite. 'My son's a good man. If he was the father there'd be no need to be secret about it. He's single and free. He'd have taken responsibility for the bairn and we'd have supported him, welcomed Lorna and the boy into the family if that was what they all wanted.' He closed the bonnet. 'That's patched up for now. It'll last a while longer. I'm heading into the house for a bite and you'd be welcome to join us.'

Vera hesitated for a moment. No doubt there'd be home-made cakes, maybe a pan of soup. Rosemary, Neil the Viking and the two girls would be sitting round the table together for lunch. But she decided she wasn't in the mood for happy families and her brain was still whirring with ideas. The walk back to Kirkhill might clear it.

She'd almost reached the village when her phone rang. The sound startled her. There was so little mobile reception here that it was the last thing she was expecting. She didn't recognize the number but answered anyway.

'Vera, it's Ernie. You're a tricky person to get hold of.'

Ernie was the retired Wildlife Liaison Officer. She remembered she'd sent him the photo of Lorna's painting. 'You know where that cottage is?'

'Of course.' His voice was smug. 'I'm surprised you didn't recognize it yourself. It was close to one of your father's old haunts.'

Cocky bastard.

'Well, don't keep me in suspense.'

'It's on the Brockburn estate. Only a couple of miles from the big house, but you'd not find it if you didn't know it was there. I'll send you the grid reference.'

Vera thought she had no map with her and the GPS on her phone wouldn't work out here, even if she knew how to follow it. 'Why don't you meet me in Gloria's? I'll buy you lunch and then you can show me yourself.'

He pretended to think about it before answering. 'Could do,' he said at last. 'There's nothing on this afternoon that won't wait for another day.' She could tell, though, that he was delighted to be asked.

Chapter Thirty-Four

ERNIE WAS WEARING A WAXED JACKET, corduroy trousers and leather boots, and until he opened his mouth, he could have been a member of the gentry he claimed to despise. He was a small man, slightly hunched with a rat-like face and thin hair. Vera thought he had a wife at home, but couldn't remember her name and Ernie had never mentioned her.

Once they'd finished eating, he spread an ordnance survey map over the table. The lunchtime rush was over and they had Gloria's cafe to themselves.

'It's down here by the burn.' He pointed with a thin finger. 'It was a water mill once. Jinny's Mill, the locals call it. But only the shell of the miller's cottage is left. When I was a lad, walkers used it as a bothy, but then the forest grew up around it and nobody goes there any more.'

Lorna went there. Over a long period of time if she painted it in the winter and also in midsummer when the flowers were in bloom.

'So how do we get there, Ernie? We'd best be quick or the light will have gone.' Vera didn't fancy another walk in the dark and the cold. Thoughts of the night she'd spent keeping vigil with Constance Browne still gave her the creeps, still appeared on the edge of her consciousness.

'We can drive to the back lane that leads down to Brockburn and take it on foot from there.'

They went in the Land Rover and parked not far from Dorothy and Karan's cottage. Vera thought again how compact the area of the investigation was and how connected the leading players were to each other. They made their way towards the big house, but before they reached it, Ernie turned off down a grassy path. Vera noticed tyre tracks had flattened the grass in places and remembered her meeting with Nettie Heslop the day after Lorna's murder. Perhaps the girl had come this way on the quad bike, and hadn't been driving from the big house or to feed sheep as Vera had thought then. Perhaps all the young people of Kirkhill used the cottage as a meeting place, but Vera couldn't imagine that Lorna would have been part of that group.

The track narrowed to a footpath. The forest here wasn't formed of the ubiquitous Sitka spruce; this was a patch of deciduous woodland, bare enough now to let in the afternoon light. It didn't feel as sinister as the dark pines of the Forestry Commission plantation. Vera thought Lorna had captured the magic of the place in her painting. In the spring, it would be beautiful, a pool of bluebells. The path led downhill and at last opened into a clearing very different from the one where Constance Browne's body had been found. The sun was very low now and slanted through the bare trunks onto a meadow. The almost derelict cottage faced them with its back to the water. They stopped for a moment to look at it. The stone walls were crumbling and covered in lichen. Most of the windows were cracked and covered in cobwebs, and ivy grew out of the chimney. The corrugated-iron roof was as rusty and multicoloured as Lorna had painted it.

Vera walked across the grass towards the house. Ernie reverted to his role as subordinate officer and followed at a distance. If it had ever been possible to lock the cottage, that time had long passed. The door was sagging on large metal hinges and propped shut with a stone that might once have been part of an outbuilding. Vera moved the rock, pulled open the door and looked inside.

The building was surprisingly watertight. The roof hadn't rusted to the extent that the metal had worn through into holes. Vera had been expecting a dump – piles of beer cans, evidence of drug use, the occasional used condom – a place where the bored young of the community might gather to pass their spare time. But as her eyes grew used to the gloom, she saw that it was tidy, more adults' den than teenagers' hangout.

There were two rooms. This must once have been where the family lived and ate. There was still a small cast-iron range against one wall. The floor was of cracked stone flags, but had been recently brushed. In one corner, a pile of sheepskins provided a makeshift day bed. Someone must have carried them here, unless there was another way into the clearing, because there was no access for a vehicle; not even a quad bike could have made it down the narrow path through the trees. The scrubbed pine table, with the drawer in one side, the settle and two chairs might have belonged to the place, been used by the miller or whoever else had lived here, but they'd been cleaned and mended. There was nothing but the paintings to link the cottage to Lorna, but

Vera was convinced that this was where the young woman had met her lover.

She turned to Ernie. 'Do you know the place where we found Connie Browne's body?'

'Aye. I met Les Robson, the forester, in the Stanhope yesterday. He was talking about it. He and I go back a way.'

Of course you do.

'How far is this place from there? As the crow flies.'

'Be more likely the buzzard round here.' Ernie must have realized she wasn't in the mood for that kind of comment, because he continued speaking immediately. 'A mile at the most, but you'd probably have to fight your way through the trees. And know where you were going. Quickest would be back along the path, then the road and the forest track.' A pause. 'What are you saying? That she could have been killed here?'

'No reason for thinking that.' But Vera *did* think it. 'I'll get Billy Cartwright and his team to take a look, though. Just in case.' She was itching to look through the sheepskins, in the table drawer, to explore the further room she could only glimpse at from here, which had probably once been a bedroom, to search for Lorna's diary, love letters, any scraps of information which might be hidden, but she didn't want to contaminate the scene.

She looked at her watch. The light was fading now and she had an appointment at the big house. Then she got out her phone and saw there was a bit of reception.

'Are you okay to stay here until the cavalry arrives, Ernie?' It was against all the rules but Ernie had been wedded to the job and was more reliable than most young PCs she knew.

Anyway, there was no evidence that this was a crime scene. Just a feeling in her gut that the place was significant.

He grinned. 'It'll cost you a pint or three.'

She nodded her agreement to the deal. 'Cheap at the price, Ernie.' Then she got Joe Ashworth on the phone.

Chapter Thirty-Five

WAITING FOR VERA TO TURN UP, Juliet was feeling rattled and indecisive. She hadn't felt able to confide in Mark, though he was back in Brockburn, still giddy with the triumph of his play. He'd arrived earlier than Juliet had expected. She'd hoped to talk to Harriet before he got home, to prepare her for Vera's visit, but the afternoon had passed without Juliet quite finding the courage for the confrontation. Then Mark was there, elated and beaming. Usually she'd have been happy for him. She enjoyed basking in the reflected glory of his professional successes. She'd never been very good at anything and admired his confidence, felt somehow that his competence rubbed off on her. Today, though, his first words on coming through the door seemed to strike the wrong note:

'It's a sell-out all week. The website crashed this morning because so many people were after tickets. We got a review in the *Guardian* and it went crazy after that.'

Nothing about the killings. No anxiety about Juliet, knocking around in this house with a murderer not yet caught, out of her mind with worry. He'd heard about Connie, though:

'I saw about it on Twitter and then the phone calls started.' A little chuckle. 'Perhaps we should start running Murder Mystery weekends before we get the theatre project up and running. With all this interest we could make a bomb.'

'I really don't think this is something to joke about.' Tension made Juliet's reply sharper than she'd intended. Part of her suspected he wasn't joking at all. Perhaps he did see the killings as a money-making opportunity, a chance to get even more publicity for his projects.

Mark looked immediately chastened, a schoolboy repri-manded by a favourite teacher.

'You're right, of course.' He took her into his arms and held her for a moment. 'That's in very poor taste. Constance was a sweet old thing and I know you were very fond of her. It's so sad and we'll all miss her. Do the police have any idea what might have happened?'

'They're still trying to discover the identity of Thomas's father.' Juliet paused, looked at Mark for a reaction but there was none. She pushed away the moment of suspicion. Of course Mark couldn't be the boy's father. 'Vera will be here in half an hour. She might have more information then.'

'Vera's some sort of relative, right? The one who looks like a bag lady. Do they really think she's competent to run the investigation?'

Why do you think she might not be? Because she's a middle-aged woman who doesn't dress to please men?

But Juliet said nothing. She didn't have Vera's courage to be herself. 'I need to speak to Mother before Vera arrives. I'll be down in a moment. Dorothy's gone home but she's left a casserole in the Aga for dinner.'

Mark seemed not to hear. He was looking at his phone, smiling as he scrolled through the admiring tweets and messages from his theatrical friends.

Juliet knew that Harriet was in her room. She knocked on the door and went in, was hit by a blast of heat.

'It's very cosy in here.' Resentment made Juliet braver than she might have been.

'Darling, you know I'm not like you. I can't do the cold.'

'Vera will be here soon and I need to speak to you before she gets here.'

'Oh, Vera!' Harriet dismissed the woman with a wave of her hand. 'She reminds me of dreadful Hector every time I see her. One of her subordinates was here this morning. Rather brighter than her boss, I thought.'

'She's a clever detective, Mother, and you need to listen.' Juliet sat on the other comfortable chair in the room. Mark must have switched on the lights on the cedar. She saw them through a gap in the curtains, thought they made the tree look ridiculously inappropriate, almost flighty, like a flashily dressed woman at a funeral. She took a breath. 'I know about the letter Father wrote to you about Lorna Falstone.'

Harriet's only reaction was to straighten her back and raise her chin a little. 'I'm not sure I know what you're talking about.'

'He showed it to me before he died.' Juliet had planned the lie as soon as she'd realized this conversation was inevitable. And it was only half a lie. After all, her father had hinted about the content of the letter. She thought Vera would go along with the fib, but that would mean getting to the inspector first to explain. No way could Juliet confess to Harriet that she'd been snooping in this room in her mother's absence.

There was a silence, as icy as the temperature in the rest of the house.

'That was unfortunate,' Harriet said at last. 'I'd have thought he'd have had more decency. More honour.'

'You didn't have the decency to carry out his wishes.' Juliet had raised her voice and felt suddenly liberated from a lifetime of politeness.

'How could I,' Harriet said, 'without telling the world our business?'

'Well, I've told the police. I thought they had the right to know.'

'You did what?' Now Harriet was seriously shaken. She was on her feet. The colour had drained from her face.

Juliet thought her mother might faint, but the sense of power was intoxicating and she continued almost joyously. 'I met Vera this morning and I told her. Two women have died.' A pause. 'Besides, she'd already guessed that Crispin was Lorna's father, though she *was* a little surprised that you hadn't carried out his last wishes.'

There was another silence, while Harriet regained her composure. She returned to her seat and stared at Juliet.

'What is this about? You never previously had any sisterly feelings for Lorna Falstone. I don't recall your suggesting that she should share your inheritance. When she was ill, you didn't visit or invite her to Brockburn to recuperate. So why these sudden scruples? Is it revenge? Have I really been such a poor mother that you delight in causing me embarrassment?' She paused. 'Or do you have something to hide? Is this a way of turning the police's attention away from you and Mark and your intellectual friends in the cottage? It would be much more convenient for you all if I weren't here to stand in the way of your grandiose plans for my home.'

Juliet felt herself become light-headed and confused. The flash of confidence had already disappeared. How could she have ever thought she might get the better of her mother in any situation? She was stumbling her way towards a reply, some sort of apology that might improve the situation, when she heard the sound of a growling engine, the crackle of scattered gravel. Vera had arrived.

She left her mother's room and almost ran down the stairs, tripping on the last step. Through an open door she could hear Mark talking on his phone to someone from the theatre and in that moment, she hated him. She wished she could recapture the courage that had allowed her, at least for a moment, to challenge her mother, and throw him out. How could he not sense how tense she was, how scared? She should be able to share with him the nightmare of her twisted, tangled family. Just as Vera started ringing the bell, Juliet opened the door to let her in. The detective stood there, legs slightly apart, as solid as the hills from which she'd grown. Behind her the lights on the tree twinkled, seeming to mock them.

'You have to know something.' Juliet spoke quickly before moving aside to let Vera in. 'I told Mother that Crispin explained about the letter, asking her to take care of Lorna, before he died. I couldn't admit that I'd been in her room. You do understand?' Because surely this woman, who had been so comforting when she'd confided about her inability to conceive, *would* understand.

'Well, I'll do my best, but two women have been killed. I'm not prepared to play games.'

Then she was inside, stooping to take off her wet and muddy boots, puffing with the effort of bending to untie the laces, grabbing on to Juliet for a moment when she nearly toppled over.

'Where is she then?'

'In her room.' Juliet came halfway up the stairs with Vera and pointed it out, but Vera stood for a moment in her stockinged feet.

'I want you there too,' she said. 'I don't have the time to repeat myself.' She stomped on up to the landing, assuming that Juliet would follow. And of course Juliet did. Because Juliet had always done what she was told.

Vera tapped on the door, but went in before Harriet could answer. Juliet stood behind her.

Harriet was standing too, prepared for the onslaught. 'We'll go downstairs, shall we? I don't think my bedroom is the place for any kind of official discussion.'

'Oh, I think we'll stay here,' Vera said, moving in, looking around. 'Plenty of room and it's nice and cosy. I've been freezing my tits off outside for most of the day.' She landed on a small silk chaise longue that stood under the window.

Juliet saw Harriet wince, but whether she was offended by the language or anxious that the furniture might not withstand Vera's weight, it was impossible to tell.

'Why don't you both take a seat?' Vera went on. 'This might take a while.'

Harriet seemed about to object, but she went back to the armchair where she'd been sitting earlier. Juliet perched on the end of the bed.

'You know I could charge you both with wasting police time.' Vera was staring at them, her conker-brown eyes hard and cold. There was silence.

'There are some things,' Harriet was at her most imperious, 'that should remain private.'

'Not in a murder investigation!' Vera had raised her voice so she was almost shouting. Juliet thought she was genuinely angry. 'Do you think Lorna's family want people in the village gossiping about her? Speculating about who her father might be? Her illness? The father of her child? Of course they don't. But there's gossip all the same. What makes you so different?'

Another silence.

'You've known from the start that Lorna was most likely Crispin's child.' Vera spoke more quietly now, but Juliet found the tone of reason and logic even more chilling. 'But you both pretended that you hardly knew her.'

'We did hardly know her,' Harriet said. 'We didn't have her round every week for tea on the lawn.'

'Ah.' Vera sounded suddenly wistful. 'Tea on the lawn. Scones and strawberry jam. Meringues.'

Harriet stared at her as if she was mad.

Vera's attention seemed drawn back to the present with a jolt. 'You must have realized it was important for my investigation to understand the lass, to know all about her. You deliberately hindered my work. That's an offence.'

Harriet said nothing.

'Let's see this famous letter then. The one Crispin told Juliet about before he died.'

Juliet almost fainted with relief. At first, she thought Harriet would refuse to comply. Her mother sat, stony-faced.

'Look, pet, if you want to be difficult, I can always get a warrant, fetch my specialist search team in to look for it.' A pause. 'And if you've destroyed it, I'll charge you with hampering a police investigation.'

Without a word, Harriet got to her feet. She fetched the key from the music box and unlocked the drawer, took out the envelope and handed it to Vera. The jaunty music died away. Vera looked at the letter as if she were reading it for the first time, slowly, taking in every word. Now, Juliet felt not only relief, but gratitude.

Vera stretched her legs so her feet were no longer touching the floor; she seemed beached on the fragile chaise like a whale. 'Had Lorna found out about this? Had she come to you making demands?' She waved the letter in her hand.

'No,' Harriet said. 'How could she possibly have found out about it?'

Vera seemed not to hear. 'Because it seems a strange coincidence. Just as you're all making plans to turn this place into a money-making venture, the lass who could ruin the family reputation and claim the right to a heap of your cash is suddenly found dead on your property.'

Juliet expected an explosion of outrage from her mother, but Harriet's response was strangely subdued, dismissive.

'You must think what you like, Vera.'

'Did either of you have any contact at all with Lorna Falstone in the weeks running up to her death?'

Juliet almost put up her hand like an eager child in the classroom, but Vera had already turned to her, waiting for her to answer. 'Really, I haven't,' Juliet said. 'Not on her own, at least. I saw her about a fortnight ago in the Co-op. She had Thomas in the buggy and I couldn't help stopping to look at him. He's probably my nephew, after all, and of course I was interested.'

'You had a conversation?'

'Only the sort of chat you have with a young mum. *Hasn't he grown? How are things going?*'

'How did she respond?'

'Just as you'd expect. There was nothing meaningful. Nothing to suggest she knew about the letter and was about to make a claim on the estate. We were in a queue for the till – some poor elderly woman couldn't remember her PIN so everyone was having to be patient. Then Karan came in with Cath Heslop. He's been tutoring her to get her through A levels and he'd given her a lift into the village. Lorna lost patience then. She was only there for milk and she said she'd come back when it wasn't so busy.'

Vera hesitated for a moment. 'Did you have the impression that Lorna was running away? That she didn't want to speak to Karan?'

'No,' Juliet said, though she wasn't sure now. She played the scene in her head. Perhaps Lorna's ending of the conversation had been a little abrupt and her scurrying out of the shop a little odd. 'No, I don't think so.'

Vera turned her attention to Harriet. 'What about you? Have you had any contact with Lorna in recent weeks?'

'Not to speak to.'

'What does that mean?' Juliet could tell that Vera was losing patience now, that soon there would be an explosion of anger.

'I drove past her one day,' Harriet said. 'She was walking up the back drive from the house towards the cottage, where Dorothy and Karan live. It's not a public right of way and I was tempted to tell her so.'

'But you didn't. Because she was Crispin's daughter and she had as much right to be there as you.'

'No.' Now Harriet was contemptuous. 'Because I was in a hurry to get home and I couldn't be bothered.'

'When was this?'

Harriet shrugged. 'About a month ago.'

Vera swung her legs round until her feet were on the carpet and she stood up. Juliet slid off the bed and opened the door for her. They were hit by a blast of icy air from the landing and walked down the stairs together. Vera stooped to put on her boots.

'Thanks *so* much,' Juliet said.

Vera replied with a kind of snort. No words. In another room, Mark was still laughing.

Chapter Thirty-Six

AFTER SPEAKING TO HARRIET, HOLLY WENT back to Kirkhill, but she had little luck with the other residents she talked to. They expressed shock at the death of Constance Browne, but gave no helpful information. She was making her way to the car, thinking that she'd head back to Kimmerston and the evening briefing, when she saw Karan Pabla walking down the street, a woven shopping bag in either hand. She shouted a greeting. The light was fading and for a moment he seemed not to recognize her. Then there was the beautiful smile, the sense that she was just the person he was hoping to see. She crossed the road to join him.

She nodded to the bags. 'Stocking up?'

'Dorothy sent me out for supplies. Apparently, there's more snow forecast. Though she's always got enough in stock to feed an army. She's the most organized person I know.' He set down the bags. 'How's the investigation going? Poor Connie.'

'You knew her well?'

'She helped me get a couple of voluntary placements in schools. Teaching practice before the PGCE starts in September.'

He paused. 'She must have been an awesome teacher. So interested in all her pupils.'

'And her former pupils. She was very kind to Lorna.'

'Do you think that was why she was killed?' Karan said. 'Because Lorna had shared information about her killer?'

Holly was tempted to reply. There was something in Karan that invited confidence. But she only shook her head. 'You'll understand that I can't talk about an ongoing investigation.'

'Of course.' He picked up the bags. 'I shouldn't have asked. Good luck, though. When all this is over, you'll have to come round for supper.' He walked away in the gloom towards his car.

It was the evening briefing. They sat in the ops room, where one of the strip lights flickered occasionally, giving Holly a headache. The ancient radiators were pumping out the heat. Vera was at the front, there before the rest of them, perky as if she'd just woken up from a good sleep, so Holly knew that she had information, or an idea, or that maybe she'd cracked the case without the rest of them. The others just looked tired.

Vera slid her bum from the table she'd been resting against and called for order. The background chatter ended.

'Let's catch up,' she said. 'Lots of information this evening so I hope you lot are taking notes.' A quick grin. Vera was famous for *never* seeming to need notes. 'First, we now know that Lorna was indeed Crispin Stanhope's daughter.'

Charlie got to his feet. 'Sorry to interrupt, boss.' Something in his voice made Holly think that he wasn't at all sorry. 'But we don't know that.'

'I realize before it was only a suspicion,' Vera said, 'but since we last met, I've seen a letter from Crispin to Harriet telling her that Lorna was entitled to a portion of his estate.'

'Well, he might have written that letter,' Charlie said, 'and he might have believed that he was the lass's dad. Or hoped that he was, maybe, if he'd fallen for her mother. But the DNA's just come through and he was no relation.'

Vera looked deflated. Physically smaller, like a balloon with a pin stuck in the side. Holly enjoyed the moment, then couldn't help feeling sorry for her.

'Well,' Vera said at last. 'That'll teach me to make assumptions. All that gossip – folk saying how Juliet and Lorna looked alike. Jumping to their own conclusions. Just because it made a good story, but ruining the lass's life. Nearly killing her with the anorexia. And ruining the lives of her parents, tearing them apart.'

There was silence in the room. Everyone knew better than to speak.

'I'll call on the Falstones on the way home.' Vera was talking to herself. 'Let them know. After all these years . . .'

Joe stood up. He was the only one who could move her on when she was in this mood. 'Does it make any difference to the investigation? If everyone *thought* she was Crispin's daughter, the motive's still the same.'

'Maybe.' Vera was still lost in thought.

'I spoke to the vicar and her husband.' Joe could be persistent when it was needed. Holly thought he knew Vera better than anyone else in the world. If he left the team, the boss would be lost. Maybe that was the only thing that would persuade her to retire. 'Connie was at church the day before she went missing. So was the family from the big house. She didn't speak to the vicar, but she did talk to Doug, the husband. He said something was troubling her and she asked if she could have a chat with them. He invited her to lunch on the Monday but of course she didn't turn up.'

He'd managed to pull Vera's attention back into the room. 'Did Connie talk to the Brockburn lot at church?'

Joe shook his head. 'Doug doesn't think so. The family rushed away almost as soon as the service was over.'

'So, what did Connie know?' Vera looked around at them all. 'What was the secret that killed her?'

Holly waited long enough to allow that particular question to remain unanswered before standing up to speak.

'Yes, Hol? What have you got for us?'

'I spent some time in Kirkhill, chatting to the residents about Constance Browne. One elderly guy saw a car outside her house on the morning she disappeared. He thought someone either went in or out of the house and then the car drove away.'

'A credible witness?'

Holly thought of Matty Fuller. 'Oh, definitely. A bit deaf but sharp as a tack.'

'He'd have noticed if she'd been screaming and struggling?'

'Yes,' Holly said. 'I think he would. That would have taken more time. The guy only saw shadows and he didn't get any details of the vehicle, but if that was when Connie left the house, I'd say she went willingly.'

'Did you get a chance to talk to Harriet?'

Holly nodded. 'She definitely knew about her husband's affair with Jill Falstone at the time and was furious that it had become public knowledge, but after all these years I can't see she had any motive for killing Lorna, even if she believed she was his daughter.'

Vera nodded, then looked up at them. Holly could tell the

boss was about to share the information that had excited her. 'I've found Lorna's cottage. The one that she painted. It's in a bit of deciduous woodland on the Brockburn estate, not very far from the house, or from the patch of clear fell where Connie's body was found, but you'd probably never find it if you didn't know it was there.' She paused. 'Someone's been using it recently.'

Holly felt a moment of anticlimax. She'd been expecting something more relevant.

Vera turned to the senior CSI. 'Billy, your team has been in there. Have they found anything to make an ageing detective very happy?'

Billy smiled his weasel smile. 'Lorna Falstone's fingerprints. Will that do?'

'Oh, it certainly will. Buy them a drink from me.'

Billy muttered under his breath that he'd need to see her money first.

Holly stuck up her hand. 'But we know Lorna had been there. She must have been if she painted the place.'

'They were everywhere,' Billy said. 'On the pieces of furniture. You won't have seen the bed, Vera, because you were a good girl and didn't go further than the front door, but Lorna's fingerprints were on the brass headboard.'

'And you needed to be there to tell it was important to Lorna.' Vera had turned back to Holly. 'You could see it was a love nest.' She pinned a couple of pictures onto the board.

Holly saw a pile of sheepskins, some ancient wooden furniture. It didn't look much like a love nest to her, but she knew better than to say so.

'Got any photos of the other room, Billy?'

'It just so happens . . .' He moved to the front of the room, added half a dozen images to the board.

Holly saw the brass bedstead he'd mentioned. Tarnished, but clean, with proper bedding, not a manky sleeping bag of the sort a dosser might use. She moved closer to the board and pointed. 'What's that?'

'A wooden cradle. An old-fashioned thing with rockers.'

'That's where they'd have put the bairn,' Vera said. 'Harriet said she'd seen Lorna walking down the back drive towards Dorothy's cottage. She would have come from there. They call it Jinny's Mill, by the way. You can still see the old mill wheel in the burn.'

'Did you find Constance's fingerprints?' Holly thought Vera was making assumptions again.

Cartwright shook his head. 'No matches. We checked.'

'And if Constance was killed there, we wouldn't find prints.' Vera seemed carried away by her theory. 'It was early morning, bloody freezing. She'd have been wearing gloves.' She turned back to face the room. 'Did you find anything else, Billy? Lorna's missing diary, for instance? Her phone or her laptop?'

Billy shook his head. 'Unfortunately not. They're still searching the surrounding area, but there's nothing like that in the building.'

In the end, it was Joe who said what Holly was thinking. 'I'm sorry, but I don't see how this takes us much further forward.'

'Because I'll bet my pension that there were other prints in the place,' Vera said. 'The lass didn't go there for quiet contemplation and to further her art. And if we can find out who fathered her child, we'll have a decent idea who killed her.' She turned back to the CSI. 'I am right, aren't I? You did find other prints?'

Billy gave a little bow. 'Of course you're right, Vera. We all know you're always right. There was one other set of prints all over the place. We haven't got a match yet, though.'

'Well, in the morning we'll invite all the men involved in the case to give us their fingerprints. And then we'll have these murders cracked.'

There was a cheer. Holly couldn't bring herself to join in. Most of the men in the community could have had reason to go to the cottage over the years. No way would a case based on a flimsy coincidence stand up in court. Vera might well be right that they'd get a suspect from her discovery today, but she'd need more evidence than some fingerprints in a derelict cottage to prove their guilt. And Holly still thought they should keep an open mind about the gender of the killer. This was a community of strong women, and one of them might have been provoked so far that she could contemplate committing murder.

Chapter Thirty-Seven

VERA DROVE SLOWLY INLAND TOWARDS THE hills. She needed time to think and to process her reaction to the news that young Thomas Falstone wasn't a relation after all. She was alone in the world again, with no blood relations except Juliet, who was an adult and had no need of her. No obligations. She'd never liked kids and she should have been pleased.

Yet there'd been a sudden emptiness when Charlie had passed on the news that Lorna couldn't have been Crispin's daughter. Vera had found the idea that she could be a guardian angel for Thomas, at a distance of course, and a mentor as he got older, strangely appealing. She understood the Falstones, liked their reticence and she admired their determination to carry on with their lives without wallowing in self-pity. She'd hoped that they might have become family of a sort too.

She pulled into the track that led to Broom Farm and parked the Land Rover. When she opened the door, the wind was northerly cold. No moon and no stars. Low cloud shut out the lights from Kirkhill. Inside the farmhouse, the couple must be in the kitchen, because there was a bright square marking the uncurtained window. Vera checked the time. It was nearly eight o'clock. Perhaps the bairn would already be in bed and she could talk to the couple without distraction.

Vera knocked at the door and pushed it open without waiting for an answer. Jill and Robert were just finishing a meal at the kitchen table, watching the old television mounted on a shelf in the corner as they ate. A plastic container on the bench showed they were eating a microwaved lasagne. She thought how different they were from the Heslop family. In Home Farm there'd be laughter and silly chat, a home-cooked dinner.

'Sorry to disturb you,' Vera said, 'but I've got some news. I thought you'd want to hear it from me.'

'You know who killed Lorna?' Robert reached out for the remote control and turned off the TV.

Vera shook her head. 'But I don't think we'll be long now.' She paused. 'This is about your lass.'

They stared at her, waiting. Neither spoke.

Vera looked at Robert. 'She *was* your lass. Your daughter. We took DNA from Juliet Stanhope and they weren't related.'

She wasn't sure what she was expecting. Tears, perhaps, joy, anger at all the years of uncertainty. *She'd* have been angry. Lorna might not have starved herself nearly to death if it hadn't been for the rumours, the cruel jeers from the teenagers who should have been her friends.

But in the end, there was a moment of silence as the couple looked at each other. Robert reached out and took his wife's hand. 'She always was *my* lass. It was other people who had the problem with that.'

Vera waited while Jill cleared the plates and put on the kettle.

'Did Lorna ever show you her paintings?' The three were all sitting at the table now, mugs of tea in front of them.

Jill shook her head. 'I knew Connie Browne persuaded her to go to the class, but I never saw what she did there.'

'Josh Heslop taught the group. I told you before that, he and Lorna had become good friends. Apparently they'd become very close.'

'Oh, that's lovely! I always hoped she'd make friends in the village.' Jill's face lit up. 'Friends of her own age at last. I know she was close to Miss Browne, but that's not the same, is it?'

Vera thought about that for a moment and had the whisper of an idea. 'She never talked about Josh to you?'

Jill shook her head. Robert reached out again and took her hand. This time he didn't let go.

'She did lots of paintings of one particular building, a little house in the woods not far from the big house at Brockburn. Is it somewhere she might have gone as a child?'

The couple looked blank.

'I think at one time it might have been part of a mill,' Vera persisted.

'I've heard of it,' Robert said. 'Jinny's Mill. But I've never been there and I don't remember Lorna talking about it. She didn't stray much from the farm when she was younger, except for the riding.'

Vera nodded to show she understood. 'Maybe she took to exploring more when she was on her own with the bairn.' But she couldn't see Lorna pushing a buggy down the final narrow path to the cottage, not on a whim, just to go exploring. The woman must have been taken there by the man who'd made love to her. The man, with whom, it seemed, she'd still been infatuated, who she'd been desperate not to lose. Vera got to her feet.

'Thanks for coming.' Now Jill was standing too and she gave Vera an awkward hug. 'It means a lot. We're so pleased. So pleased.' Jill pulled out of the embrace and stood behind her husband, then put her arms around him too, stooping because he was still in his chair. She bent and kissed his hair. Vera let herself out of the house.

Her next stop was at Brockburn. She supposed they had the right to know the truth too, though she was tempted to let them stew for a bit longer, to think that Lorna's son might have a claim on the estate. It was quicker from Broom Farm to take the drive to the front of the house, but Vera went on and turned down the back lane past the cottages. Dorothy's car was outside their place, but Vera drove straight past. Billy's team must have finished because there were no vehicles at the fork in the track where the path led on to Jinny's Mill. Vera parked at the back of the big house. There was a light in the kitchen window and she knocked.

'Who is it?' A nervous voice. Juliet. Perhaps they were all nervous with a murderer still not caught, though the Falstones hadn't bothered locking their door.

'It's me. Vera.'

There was the sound of a key turning, a bolt rattling and the door opened.

Juliet was on her own in the room. She looked as if she'd been crying.

Vera felt a stab of impatience. Of irritation. *And I thought you were an adult!*

Juliet took a tissue from her pocket and wiped her eyes. 'Don't mind me, I'm just being silly.'

'What's happened?' Vera made no effort to sound sympathetic. The last thing she needed was to be dragged into the emotional entanglements of the family at Brockburn. No way was Juliet her responsibility.

'Oh, just Mother being beastly as always and then Mark and I had a bit of a row. Nothing serious. It's the stress. Nothing feels normal at the moment.'

'I've got some news.' Vera didn't sit. She didn't want to be here for very long. She was dreaming of a beer, a fire and her bed. 'We've had the DNA results back. We fast-tracked them.'

And that took a chunk out of my budget.

Juliet looked at her, fragile, doe-eyed. She was wearing a loose black dress that seemed to swamp her.

'You're no relation to Lorna. You're not half-sisters. Crispin wasn't her father.' Hoping to make it clear, all in one sentence, so there wouldn't be questions, uncertainty. When the woman didn't respond Vera added, 'Thomas isn't your nephew. He has no claim on the estate.'

'Oh.' Juliet's voice expressed shock, confusion, but no real sense of relief. In fact, Vera thought, Juliet was feeling the opposite. A sadness. Perhaps Juliet too would have welcomed a connection with the child. 'Mother will be pleased. Do you want to talk to her?'

'No need for that.' The last thing Vera thought she needed was an encounter with Harriet. 'I'll leave you to pass on the good news. I just thought you should know.'

'Have you told the Falstones?'

'Yes, I've just come from there.' Vera paused. 'They were pleased.' She turned to walk out, but stopped at the door. 'Do you know a cottage called Jinny's Mill?'

Juliet smiled. 'Of course. I used to play there when I was little. It was a place my father took me to. I treated it as a sort of Wendy house. In the summer, you can dam the burn and make a pool deep enough to swim. The water was straight from the hills and freezing, but I loved the wild swimming. Even Dad came in sometimes. Just paddling, his trousers rolled up to his knees. Then Dorothy and I hung out there when we were teenagers and wanted to escape the adults.' A quick grin. The memories seemed to have cheered her. 'It was where I first got drunk. On sherry we nicked from my father's drinks cabinet. I've never been able to touch the stuff since.'

'Did other youngsters in the area use it too?'

'I expect so. Occasionally we'd find empty beer cans, signs that someone had lit a fire in the range. I don't remember us bumping into anyone else there, though.'

There was a moment of silence and Juliet seemed lost in memory. 'I took Mark there too, when he first came to Brockburn. It was the end of May, and it's very beautiful then, with the meadow in front of the cottage full of buttercup and clover.' There was another brief pause. 'It was where Mark proposed to me a few months later. It was September and the leaves were starting to change colour. All very romantic.' Now there was a sour note in her voice.

'Have you been back there recently?'

'No.' She gave a little laugh. 'Not for ages.'

'Would Mark have a reason for going there?'

'Oh, I shouldn't think so.' Juliet's tone was light, brittle. 'Unless it featured somehow in his plans to turn Brockburn into a theatre and arts centre. That's been his main preoccupation in the last six months. We don't go walking together these days.'

Now Vera did open the door to leave. As she walked towards the Land Rover, she could hear the bolt slammed shut and the key being turned in the lock.

At the cottage, Vera locked her own door. She'd been more careful about security since the fire earlier in the year, when work had come far too close to home and the place had been wrecked. The wind rattled against the house and battered the windows. She could hear the roar of it even after she drew the heavy curtains. A sound like the sea in a storm. She put a light to the wood in the grate and put on the kettle. The beer could wait and she'd been yearning for tea and digestive biscuits all the way back from Brockburn. She also needed a clear head, because she was groping her way towards an idea, a solution of sorts. This whole case, even the murder of spinster Constance Browne, was about families, about what held them together and what ripped them apart.

The call came just after midnight. Vera was still dressed, dozing in front of the embers. It came on her work mobile and made her start, the sound jerking her awake, making her aware of every pulse of her heart. Who phoned at this time of night if it wasn't an emergency?

She didn't recognize the voice at first, because the words were tumbling over each other, jumbled, and because she was still caught in the place between sleep and wakefulness. She only heard the panic.

At last the words made more sense. 'He's gone! We were in all night but someone must have got in and taken him. We can't lose another child.' It was Jill Falstone, beyond herself with fear.

Chapter Thirty-Eight

HOLLY WAS IN BED BUT STILL awake when Vera rang. She never slept well. At night, the control that made her life ordered and predictable during the working day slipped away and she was overcome by unwelcome anxieties, jumbled misgivings. Her muscles tensed and her thoughts raced. She'd started running in the hope of stilling her mind, becoming physically tired, but even so most nights she struggled to sleep.

When her phone rang, she knew it would be about work. She had a few friends, but nobody sufficiently close to call her in the early hours of the morning.

It was Vera, speaking as she was driving. The signal cut out occasionally and Holly could hear the background rumble of the Land Rover's engine.

'I need you to go to see the Falstones at Broom Farm. The little lad's gone missing. Thomas, Lorna's bairn. I was only there this evening and now it seems he's vanished into thin air.' A pause. 'Get Joe Ashworth out too.'

'Are you on your way there?'

There was a moment of silence and Holly thought she'd

lost phone reception. In the end she caught the end of Vera's reply.

'I'm better looking for the boy. I think I know where he might be.'

The line went dead. Holly tried to return the call, but there was no answer. She dressed and hit Joe Ashworth's number. She thought Vera had phoned her first so *she'd* be the one to disturb him at home. There was a delay, then his voice.

'Yes?'

In that one word she could tell he'd been asleep. 'I've just had a call from the boss. She wants us at Broom Farm, the Falstones' place.' Holly was already running down the stairs to the lobby, car keys in hand.

'Why?'

'The little boy, Thomas, has gone missing.'

'How did that happen?' Now he was wide awake.

'I don't know. I can't get through to Vera for more details.'

Holly heard a muttered conversation in the background. Joe must be explaining to Sally what was happening. Holly heard him raise his voice, a response to something Sally had said. 'How would you feel if one of ours had disappeared?' There was a brief silence before he came back onto the line. 'I'll be there.'

When Holly arrived at the Falstones' farm, Joe was already in the house. He'd been there before and the satnav had taken her a long way around, but still he must have driven ridiculously fast to have arrived ahead of her. She saw him through the window, sitting at a farmhouse kitchen table. As she got out of her car, she felt a sting against her face, tiny darts of ice, more like hail than snow. She knocked and went straight in.

Joe introduced the Falstones to her. They were still in the clothes they'd worn during the day. 'This is my colleague, DC Jackman. Holly.'

She sat next to him. 'I know you might already have explained to Joe, but could you tell me what happened?'

The couple sat opposite, radiating tension. Rigid. Holly could almost taste their anxiety, bitter on her tongue.

'I put Thomas to bed at seven-thirty,' the woman said. 'He's a good little sleeper. Usually he doesn't move until morning. Your boss turned up not long after and we chatted for a bit. Robert and I watched the ten o'clock news and were about to go to bed ourselves, but somehow, we got to talking. Things maybe we should have said a long time ago. It was gone eleven-thirty by the time we made a move. I love looking at Thomas when he's asleep.' She gulped back a cry. 'But he wasn't there.'

The man was making an attempt to hold things together. 'The lad's been sleeping with Jill and I moved out to the spare room. Not for any reason other than that we thought he needed to be with someone.' He looked at them both to understand they got the message: *There's nothing wrong with our marriage.* 'We thought if he woke and found himself in a strange place, he should have his gran there. We couldn't get his cot from Lorna's house until your forensic chaps had finished and then it didn't seem urgent right away.'

'So, he could have climbed out if he was in your bed and not in a cot?' Holly tried not to turn the words into an accusation. The couple were obviously distressed and guilty enough.

'That's what we thought at first,' Jill said. 'But he's only just started toddling and the doors were all shut. We'd put pillows on all sides so he couldn't fall out. Where could he have gone?'

'You've searched the house?'

'Of course! Everywhere.'

'The front door was unlocked,' Robert said. 'We don't lock up until we go to bed. Someone could have got in.'

'Could you show us?' Joe was already on his feet.

Robert Falstone led them through a painted door to the rest of the house. It was clear the kitchen was where the couple spent all their time and this was like entering a different world. An abandoned film set. They walked down a corridor and in the hall light, through an open door, Holly saw a living room, furnished with a faded sofa and armchairs, an upright piano against one wall. On the other side there was a formal dining room with a large, ugly table and four chairs.

'They were my parents' things,' Robert said. 'We don't use them much.'

The air was chill away from the Aga. A heavy curtain covered the front door. Robert pulled aside the curtain and opened it. The small spiky snowflakes had grown larger and the ground was already speckled white. They looked out on a garden, a lawn and borders. Again, the only light came from the house.

'Jill's the gardener,' Robert said. 'In the summer it's glorious. We were thinking we'd get a swing for the bairn.' This time he was the one almost to lose control.

'Would you still park in the yard if you were coming to this side of the house?' Holly tried to picture the place with the sun shining. There was a patio with a wooden table, the chairs tipped into it, so the snow slid off.

'Aye, then walk round the house. Once you could drive right

round to the front, but we put up a barn, so there's no access now.'

'Did you hear a vehicle this evening?'

Robert shook his head. 'But then, I don't think we would. The wind was so loud and we had the telly on all night. We didn't hear your boss until she knocked.'

'And you wouldn't have heard this door being opened?'

'I don't think we would. Not from the other end of the house.'

Holly was thinking it would have taken some nerve to come in and snatch the boy. The couple might have been deep in conversation in the kitchen, but the abductor wouldn't have known they'd stay there, that they wouldn't come regularly to check on the child or use the bathroom. 'You never thought to lock this door? After two murders close by?'

Robert shook his head. 'We have our way of doing things. A routine. It would never occur to us to change.'

Holly could see that was true. The everyday rituals held them together, even with the arrival of the child.

'Usually I went to see Thomas every hour or so,' Jill said.

The start of another ritual? Holly imagined the woman marking the time, by a specific programme on the television, getting up from her seat, climbing the stairs to enjoy the sight of her grandson. 'But not tonight?'

'No! Tonight, we were so wrapped up in our own affairs.' There was a pause, then she wailed, 'I should have checked.'

'Can we see where he was sleeping?'

The stairs went up at an angle, close to the front door. The four climbed them in silence. There were three bedrooms and an ancient bathroom. All the doors were open, all the lights on, evidence of the frantic search which had taken place. Holly saw into a small room which they must be preparing for the baby. Wallpaper was being stripped and there was a dust cover on the floor. She wondered if once Lorna had slept there. They walked on.

'This is our room,' Jill said. 'Thomas has been sleeping here with me. As I told you, I'd put him in the middle of the bed with pillows at each side to stop him rolling out.'

It was a big square space. The furniture was the same vintage as the stuff in the formal rooms downstairs, heavy, solid, built of a dark wood. A wardrobe with a brass key and a dressing table. The bed had sheets and blankets, not a duvet, and two bolsters still sat with a space between them, where the boy had been sleeping. A sash window looked out over Jill Falstone's garden. It had been covered by a red velvet curtain. The floor was bare, apart from a rug close to the bed, the boards stained almost black. Standing at the entrance Holly saw a set of footwear prints, faint but muddy on the wooden floor.

'You don't wear outdoor shoes in the house?'

Jill shook her head. 'We leave our mucky boots in the porch.'

Holly had thought as much; they were both wearing slippers, shabby sheepskin affairs.

'It seems that somebody has been in.' Until then Holly had thought they'd find the boy hiding somewhere in the house. Now she saw that Vera had been right to react as she had.

'What can we do to get him back?' Robert turned so he was facing the detectives, determined. 'We'll do whatever it takes.'

'Of course.' Joe paused. 'You haven't had any message on your phone? Any threats or demands?'

'I don't know!' Panic seemed to be robbing Jill of all reason. Holly was pleased Joe was there. He would keep them both calm. She wasn't sure she'd have the patience or the sympathy to see the couple through it. 'Not on the landline. I'll check my mobile. Not that there's much signal in the house.'

'I'll go,' Robert said. Holly thought he was pleased to have an excuse to leave the room. He was finding this unbearable.

'Can you check if any of Thomas's clothes are missing?' Joe asked.

'His outdoor things were on this chair.' Jill was crying now, large tears rolling down her cheeks. 'I should have noticed before. Then we wouldn't have wasted time looking before calling your boss.' She paused. 'Where is she? Where is Vera?'

'She's looking for Thomas, of course,' Joe said. That seemed to satisfy the woman and to stem her panic a little. 'Why don't you come downstairs into the warm with me? I'll need a description of what the lad was wearing and we'll check your phone for messages. We'll leave Holly here to see if she can find anything else that might help.'

Jill followed him down the stairs, pleased to have someone to take decisions, to tell her what to do. Holly was left alone. The house seemed to echo around her, but the stairs were carpeted and she didn't hear them leave.

She took a photo of the footwear prints and tried to put herself in the shoes of the abductor. This wasn't a time to think about motive, but perhaps she could track his movements. She imagined him opening the front door, seldom used in the winter. He'd walk straight into the heavy curtain. Would that have freaked him out? The dusty cloth in his face, almost suffocating him? It occurred to her suddenly that she was thinking of the abductor as male now, but that wasn't necessarily the case. The footwear print could belong to a tall woman. She should follow her own advice and keep an open mind.

The kidnapper would have parked somewhere out of sight,

down on the road, and walked up the track, through the yard and to the front of the house. Had they known that the door would be open? They would have turned the handle and pushed it, and there might be prints. So, were they there by chance, hoping that they might get in? That implied a kind of desperation. They hadn't stopped to take off mucky shoes, but had climbed the stairs quickly. Speed had been more important than not leaving evidence of their movements.

Had they gone straight to the main bedroom, which was at the end of the corridor? Holly went back into the hall and looked in the other rooms. The small one, half-decorated in preparation for the child, seemed untouched. Certainly, there were no footprints on the dust cover on the floor. Robert had been sleeping in the third bedroom and Holly saw that clearly this had once been Lorna's. The couple had decided not to give Thomas his mother's room. Not yet, at least. There were rosettes on a board, photos of horses, whitewood furniture, a single bed under the window. Holly couldn't imagine what it must have been like for Falstone to sleep in his daughter's bed. Perhaps he'd welcomed the opportunity. It could have made him feel closer to Lorna. Or perhaps he'd seen it as a kind of penance. Here too, there was no sign of any intruder.

Holly stood for a moment, putting off the time when she'd have to join the couple below. She paused, silent, going through the possible suspects in her head, trying to imagine who would have been so desperate or foolhardy to take the child, to scoop him up and run with him down the stairs and into the night.

Chapter Thirty-Nine

VERA WAS DRIVING THROUGH THE SNOW, talking out loud to herself, because what did it matter if she sounded like a batty old woman when there was nobody to hear?

'We got the whole thing the wrong way around. I should have realized from the start. At least when I saw that picture of the cottage. Lorna was nowhere near as needy as we all thought. It was the illness that put me off-track, and all that bollocks with Harriet and Juliet.'

The road towards Brockburn was familiar now, and she chuntered away without having to think too much about directions. Closer to the big house, she started to plan her move. There'd been a number of calls from Holly, messages and texts coming and going according to reception, but she'd ignored them all. The last thing she wanted was to go into this mob-handed. That would only put the lad in more danger and things had already got out of hand. Besides, she could have the whole thing wrong and she'd never liked making a fool of herself.

Vera stopped on the road, just after the track that led to the back of the house past Dorothy and Karan's cottage. She pulled into the verge, hoping there wasn't a ditch, and climbed out, hit by the cold. It was still snowing but in flurries, nothing like the blizzard on the first night she'd come back to Brockburn. She needed to go the rest of the way on foot. Usually, she avoided any form of exercise unless it was essential, but you could hear the Land Rover a mile off, and this was a time for discretion.

Before she left the vehicle, she sent a text to Holly and Joe, explaining where she was and what she had planned. Not with any sense of urgency. They were more use where they were. *Just checking. I'll call if I need you.* She pulled on wellingtons, made sure her flask was in her pocket, and that her torch was working properly.

By now, it was past one in the morning, but there was a light on in the living room of the housekeeper's cottage. She could see a sliver of silver where the curtains didn't quite meet. She wondered who was up, and thought as she walked past the building that this other family, Karan, Dorothy and Duncan, was still a mystery to her.

She paused by the turn in the track that led to Jinny's Mill, and looked down to the big house. The house itself was dark, but a security light outside shone past the outhouses and bins, so she could see the way onto the path towards the mill without using her torch. The grass was clear of snow, sheltered by the trees, boggy in places. Here the darkness was deep and dense and occasionally she stumbled. The trees were closer together than she'd remembered and in places she had to push her way through.

She'd forgotten how far it was to the mill and had a moment of anxiety, thinking that she'd wandered away from the footpath,

that she was lost in the forest. It was a kind of claustrophobia
– she'd never been good in enclosed spaces – and the same
panic as when she'd been waiting alone with Constance Brown's
body. She was just thinking that she'd retrace her steps when
there was a dip in the path and she came to the clearing, with
the mill beyond.

There *was* snow on the ground here, blown around roots
and plants into tiny drifts, like ripples on a pond. No footprints,
but that might be because the snow had started to fall after
they'd arrived here. Because there was somebody in the mill.
A light flickered in the window and Vera could smell woodsmoke.
She switched off her torch and waited for a moment, partly
because she was knackered after the walk, partly because she
wanted to decide the best way to deal with the situation. She
hadn't planned much beyond getting to the place. Brown
clouds parted and suddenly there was moonlight. If anyone
looked out of the mill, she'd be visible. She moved back into
the shadow of the trees and waited for the clouds to blow over
the moon again. In the brief moment that it was caught in the
moonlight, the cottage had looked idyllic, an illustration from
a children's fairy tale. Except in the story Vera was remem-
bering, 'Hansel and Gretel', a child had been held captive and
put into a pot over the fire to be eaten.

She stood, motionless, for ten more minutes to be sure that
nobody had seen her, then made her way carefully towards
the mill. She kept away from the windows at the front and
slid to the back of the building. It was so close to the burn
that she was in danger of ending up in the water. She could
hear the stream moving under the ice. It was dark here. No
windows. She listened, hoping to hear a child crying, some
sign that Thomas was in there and safe. There was complete

silence apart from the wind in the forest beyond. She moved around the building, feeling her way, close to the wall. She was wearing gloves but the stone was still chill against her fingertips. She needed to know if there was a back door, some other way in, but there was no change in the texture of the surface.

She'd reached a corner and was making her way to the side of the building when she was hit on the cheek, just below her eye, a sharp stab that almost sent her into the water again. The pain was so intense that she couldn't help crying out. She put her hand to her face and felt blood. She froze, stunned and confused, a moment of panic when she almost stopped breathing. She'd heard nobody approaching and still there was silence. She stood for a moment, then ran her fingers over the wall again, felt rusty metal, and risked switching on the torch.

She'd walked into an ancient hook, fixed to the house, some remnant from the mill's working days, part of a winch perhaps. If there'd been anyone in the building, they'd surely have heard her cry out, but nobody had appeared to check. She moved to the front of the cottage again, and looked through the window into the room where she'd been the day before. A candle stuck in a bottle lit the space. The range had been lit. There was coal in a bucket and logs piled to one side. On the battered table stood a loaf of bread and a bottle of wine. This stirred in Vera ideas that were faintly religious. Hector would have said religion was another form of fairy tale – he'd been a raging atheist – but she liked to keep her options open. Nobody was there.

She moved past the door to the other window that looked into the room she hadn't seen on her visit. No candle here, but light filtered through from the kitchen beyond. She saw the bed with the brass headboard Billy Cartwright had described. Beside it was the wooden cradle on rockers that she'd seen in the photograph. It was handmade, beautifully painted. Very recently painted, she thought. It hadn't looked like this in the picture. It was larger than she'd thought; not a small crib for a tiny baby, but big enough for Thomas, who was lying inside it, still in his bright red snow suit.

He was motionless, pale. She stared, holding her breath until he stirred in his sleep. There was no sign of anyone else. He was alone in the place. Vera felt the anxiety drain away. It would be hard to carry the boy all the way back to the Land Rover, but not impossible. She was picturing the relief on the Falstones' faces as she walked with him into their kitchen, when there was a shout from the edge of the clearing and somebody was running across the meadow towards her.

She turned towards the person, who was too far from the house for her to make out in any detail. Then the clouds cleared again and she saw a figure covered in outdoor clothes. A shotgun.

'It's me,' she shouted. 'Vera Stanhope. Police.'

A crack as the gun was fired and the pellets bounced off the wall behind her. She started to run, because she was a perfect target, caught in the candlelight coming from the mill, and close enough for the gunman to hit her with accuracy. But also, because she needed to pull the shooter's attention away from the cottage where Thomas lay. The killer was unpredictable now, desperate, and Vera had no idea what might follow. She ran away from the figure, who was blocking the only path she knew, the one that led back to Brockburn, and headed into the cover of the forest. Here the dark was as deep as water and she felt she was drowning in it. It was impossible to move quickly, so once she'd stumbled away from the clearing she stood quite still, listening, half-hoping and half-fearing that the killer had followed her. Here, they'd be as blind as each other and if she made no sound, surely she'd be safe.

There *were* sounds. Scuffling sounds in the undergrowth. Animal sounds, somehow comforting. Followed by a more regular beat of heavy boots crushing twigs, roots and frozen leaves. The snow hadn't penetrated the canopy to deaden the noise. Then a sudden white light from a powerful torch, its beam sweeping through the lines of trees. She was dazzled, held like the birds Hector caught in his flashlight, when he'd gone raiding nests for eggs in the middle of the night. Exposed.

In the moment the torch beam got to her, there was another shot, and again there was a near miss. Perhaps there was no real attempt to kill her. Perhaps the killer was losing nerve, or losing heart. They should have hit her that time. All the same, she wasn't prepared to risk it and she started running again, dodging between the trees. The forest was dark once more. Had the shooter given up? Thought she'd been scared away? But still she heard the pounding beat of boots behind her. Perhaps the torch battery had run out, or she was being played, taunted; though, unless she'd got things seriously wrong, she didn't think that was really the killer's style.

She chanced upon a straight path between two lines of conifers. It was still hard going, impossible to maintain any speed, because the ground was uneven and boggy. At one point she fell into a ditch, got a boot full of freezing water. She stopped for a moment to pull herself out and listened. All she could hear was the wind in the trees. No footsteps. Perhaps she should go back to make sure the child was safe, but she feared her presence would only put him in more danger, and besides, she wasn't sure she'd be able to find her way. That was when she remembered she wasn't sure anyone knew where Thomas was. She'd told them where she was looking, but not that she'd found the boy.

She sat to catch her breath, leaning against the straight trunk of a spruce, and fished her phone from her pocket, pressed in the passcode. One bar. When she dialled Joe's number, there was a ringtone, but nobody answered and even the ringtone sounded hesitant and uncertain. She left a message. *Thomas is in Jinny's Mill. Take care and take backup. I'm* . . . But before she could continue the phone cut out. Now there were no bars and reception had disappeared altogether.

This seemed to be a path of sorts and she continued, reaching out with her hands on each side, to make sure she was following the line of trees. Perhaps eventually it would come to a road or a Forestry Commission track, she'd pick up reception again and she could use her phone to find out where she was through GPS. Perhaps. Holly had shown her the trick once, but Vera had never quite worked out how to do it.

Time seemed not to move. Every step was the same and she could have been on a treadmill, moving but motionless. At last the path grew wider. Vera started to be aware of falling flakes, icy on her skin, and there was snow beneath her boots now. It creaked as she walked on it: dry not slushy. Her eyes had got used to the lack of light and could make out the contrast between the straight white path and the rigid line of conifers on either side. Then the trees stopped and she was in a wide space, leaving behind the rustle of branches. The clouds parted once more and she saw that she was in the area of clear fell where Constance Browne's body had been found. The place of her nightmares. But the place too where pink plastic ribbons would lead her back to the track and at last to the road.

She was exhausted. She'd never been one for exercise, even when she was a lass, and this was new to her. Her doctor would be delighted, but she needed to rest before she started back. She wondered what was happening at the cottage, if Holly and Joe had picked up her message about Thomas, if they'd had the sense to act on the earlier text she'd sent. She sat on a pile of branches and closed her eyes.

Perhaps she fell asleep. Certainly, she didn't hear the approach and there must have been footsteps, even though they'd be deadened by the snow. It was the voice that brought her back to the present, made her suddenly alert. A voice that was intimate, very close. Then the barrel of a shotgun, colder even than the falling snow, against the side of her head, just above her left eye.

'Did you really think you could escape? I grew up here. I've known this place since I was a child. I could find my way blindfold and I knew where you were heading, even if you didn't.'

Chapter Forty

THEY FOUND VERA'S LAND ROVER PARKED close to Karan
and Dorothy's cottage. Charlie had turned up to sit with the
Falstones. Holly and Joe had both needed action by then, to
escape the couple's misery, and they were desperate to find
out what had happened to Vera. They pulled to a stop outside
the Brockburn cottage, thinking perhaps she might be there.
There was a light at the window, although it was two in the
morning. Joe knocked on the door, not caring that they might
wake up the baby, not caring much about anything, except
that they'd had a mumbled message from Vera that they couldn't
make out at all. That the boss had sounded disorientated,
almost scared.

Karan came to the door, still dressed despite the hour.

'Have you seen Vera? DI Stanhope?'

The man looked confused, shocked. Joe thought that was
only to be expected. The couple wouldn't usually have visitors
so late at night.

'No, no, I'm sorry. What is this all about?'

'Is your wife at home?'

'No, she took Duncan to her parents' home this evening and decided they should stay over because of the weather.'

The man made no move to ask them in. Through the open door behind him, Joe glimpsed two coffee mugs on a table, the wood-burner still lit.

'You're up late. A visitor?'

'No, not now.' Karan gave a little laugh. 'I don't clear up if Dorothy's not here to chivvy. I'll make sure it's all tidy before she gets back. Cath Heslop was here earlier. I'm coaching her for her exams.'

Joe paused. What else was there to do here? Nothing. Perhaps it was strange that the man was still up in the early hours of the morning, but even if he'd had a guest who wasn't his student, that was none of their business. 'Sorry to disturb you.'

Holly was waiting impatiently on the track. 'Vera's first text said she was checking out Jinny's Mill. That's where she'll be.'

He nodded. He was still anxious about the more recent voicemail. The words had been blurred, but he'd picked up the panic, the exhaustion. Vera never panicked.

'Why don't I go on to the mill?' Holly said. 'I'll run, get there faster. In case she was right and the boy's there. You check out for Vera on the way.'

He nodded again, because he could feel himself overwhelmed by panic too and he was glad Holly was willing to make a decision. He watched her set off, fleet-footed into the night, wearing a headtorch to light her way. Of course, he thought, she would have come suitably prepared. In comparison, he felt leaden and inadequate.

When Brockburn came into sight, he hesitated. Should he go to the big house to check if Vera was there? It seemed dark and silent and the people who lived in Brockburn intimidated him. He could imagine how angry they'd be if he woke them with no real reason. But this place seemed at the heart of the investigation. Lorna's body had been found very close to where he was standing. He paused for a moment looking at the bulk of the house, lit by the security lights, then he walked on down the path towards Jinny's Mill. Vera had said that was where she'd be. All the same, he continued shining his torch through the trees on both sides of the track looking for signs of the boss. Holly might be quick, but he was thorough.

He saw nothing to cause him anxiety when he approached the cottage. Everything was quiet. There was snow on the roof and the window ledges, a candle at the window. A Christmas-card scene of warmth and welcome. He imagined Vera inside, the child awkwardly on her knee, a strange middle-aged Madonna. Then he thought this was all *too* quiet. Holly should be here by now and if the boy was in the mill, they would want to get him back to his grandparents. They wouldn't be waiting for Joe before carrying him back through the forest. There was something sinister in the calm and the stillness. It was the stuff of horror movies: the picturesque scene was hiding something monstrous inside. His heart raced and he felt every beat.

He still had his torch as he approached the house. The beam trembled and he held it more firmly. As he got close to the building, he saw something metallic shining dully in the light. He knelt and picked up a few pellets of shot, visible because there was a bare patch of ground in the shelter of the wall. Searching, he collected more.

He waited and listened at the door. Nothing, then a faint cry. He pushed it open and saw Holly, not Vera, holding the baby. He could tell it was her first time with a child that age and that she was terrified she'd drop him. She was standing close to the range and he felt the heat from the fire as he walked through the door.

'The boss was right. He was here all the time in a cradle in the room next door. Alone. I've checked him over. He seems fine.'

'Have you told the Falstones?'

She shook her head. 'No reception.' A pause. 'There's no sign of Vera, though.'

He held out his hand and showed her the pellets. 'Someone's been here with a shotgun. Recently. I found more that had gone through the snow and left a mark.'

There was a moment of silence. 'I think you should take Thomas home,' Holly said, 'away from danger and back to his grandparents. They'll be frantic.'

'You could take him, leave me here.'

She shook her head. 'There's a child seat in your car and anyway I don't do kids. As soon as you get reception, call for backup.'

'What will you do?'

She looked at him as if the answer was obvious. 'I'll see if I can find the boss.'

For the second time that night, Joe did as Holly suggested. He carried a sleeping Thomas in his arms back towards his car. It took longer than he'd expected and he struggled to manage the torch and the child. The dark closed around him as he left the light of Jinny's Mill and he stopped every few yards to check that he was on the path. All the way he was worrying about Vera, running through scenarios which might explain her absence. He couldn't see how she would have left the boy behind unless she was in some danger. Even then it would be out of character. Occasionally, he thought he heard noises, footsteps, a distant shout, but when he paused to listen, there was nothing at all.

At last he reached the track behind Brockburn. He shifted the weight of the boy onto his shoulder. Walking past Dorothy Felling's cottage, he saw that there was a light still on inside. The curtain was pulled aside and Karan Pabla looked out, as if he were waiting for someone. Perhaps he was expecting his partner to return. The curtain dropped back into place immediately, even though Karan must have seen Joe walking past.

When he reached the car, there was mobile signal. He strapped Thomas into the seat and called the Falstones. Robert answered immediately and Joe heard the man sobbing at the other end of the line. Then he phoned the station, demanding action, every available officer.

'There's someone armed with a shotgun and the boss is wandering around in the forest on her own.'

Chapter Forty-One

VERA SAT QUITE STILL FOR A moment and tried to control the panic. She didn't want her career, her life, to end in this place that reminded her of a war zone: dead trees like twisted limbs and animals ready to eat her flesh when she was gone. She had never before been so certain that she wanted to live to boring old age.

'You do know it's all over, pet. My chaps will have found Thomas by now and he'll be back safe and sound with Robert and Jill.' She'd aimed at jaunty, but her voice sounded tight and scared.

Still the barrel of the shotgun was icy against her skin. She could feel the weight of it, the round imprint burning like a brand. But it shifted a little and that gave her the confidence to continue.

'What good will it do, shooting me? Another dead woman to add to your tally? You're not that sort of person. Not a psychopath or serial killer. Not a monster.'

'He's my boy!'

'I know he is, but Lorna would never acknowledge you as the father, would she?'

'She said once that she loved me.'

'Aye, well, she was a young lass looking for some kind of father figure.' Vera paused for a beat. 'Tell you what, why don't you give me the shotgun? I've got a flask of whisky in my coat pocket. I reckon we both deserve a nip to warm us up and then you can tell me all about it, how it all fell apart.'

She could hear him breathing, smell the waxed jacket and the leather boots. She felt in her pocket for the flask. The clouds cleared and she held it so the moonlight reflected from it. 'Just as well I filled it up after I spent the night here with Constance Browne.'

'She was an interfering cow.'

'Well, I did get that impression myself.' Another pause. 'What do you say? Give me the gun. I'd say that was a fair swap.' Vera thought how ridiculous this was, bartering her life in return for whisky, and she felt a snort of hysteria rising from her stomach. But this man would hate to be laughed at and he'd already killed twice. She pushed back the impulse to giggle.

The cold steel moved from her skin. Now he was standing with the gun at his side.

'Pass it over,' she said, 'and sit down. You've had a dreadful week. What was it you called it when I saw you at your daughter's party? A nightmare. It must all seem like a nightmare.'

He raised the gun and she thought she'd miscalculated. She hadn't played him right at all. But Neil Heslop flung the shotgun away from him. She heard the crash of twigs snapping as it landed in a pile of dead, discarded wood. In the silence the noise sounded like gunfire. She thought it would take the team an age to find it again. He got down on his knees, then twisted his body so he was sitting beside her. She unscrewed the flask, took a sip, then handed it over to him.

'How did it start?' she asked. 'Some sort of mid-life crisis. Your son all grown up, but back home and reminding you he still had a life ahead of him, and your daughters suddenly independent young women, with lives of their own. Planning a future away from you. Your wife a domestic goddess, but without much time for you. Life a bit of a boring routine.'

'Something like that,' he said. He spoke very slowly, as if he was still in a sort of trance. 'And then Lorna was so bonny.'

'She was,' Vera said. 'She took after her mother. How did you meet her?'

'She was working in the pub in Kirkhill. I'd go occasionally for a break, a bit of time to myself. I'd ask Rosemary to come along but she always had something better to do. A floor to mop or biscuits to bake . . . Important things. More important than me or our marriage.' In his voice, there was resentment mixed with a thread of self-pity.

Vera was tempted to tell him what she thought about the self-indulgence of a middle-aged man who had a life most people would envy, but that could wait until she was somewhere warm and safe and she'd already heard his confession.

'We started talking,' he said. 'I'd find myself hoping Lorna would be there when I went into the bar. I worked out what shifts she was working, dropped in when it was quiet. Not thinking it would lead anywhere, like, just enjoying her company. But dreaming about her when I was working the farm. Not able to get her out of my mind. One night there were a few rowdy guys in the pub, bikers, full of ale and hassling her. I helped her clear them out at last orders and offered to walk her home to make sure she got in safely.' A pause. 'She asked me in for coffee. That was when it started.' He turned towards Vera. The moonlight caught his face. 'I was her first. Her first boyfriend. That made it special.'

Oh aye, it would do. Every middle-aged man's fantasy. 'Then she found herself pregnant.'

'I wasn't upset,' he said. 'Not angry. I was pleased. Pleased when she decided to keep him. I could see how it would all work out. We'd be a family. A proper family. I told her I was willing to leave Rosemary and the children for her. I'm good with bairns when they're young, so trusting and full of life. I'd have made a fine father.'

Vera could see that a baby might be easier than an arty grown-up son and a couple of bolshie teenage girls, but still she didn't challenge him. Best to let him carry on talking.

'I went to see her as soon as she was home from the hospital with the baby. I told Lorna then that I wanted to marry her, that I wanted us to set up home together. I explained that I'd just have to sort things out with Rosemary. It hadn't been much of a marriage for years. That was what I told Lorna. She said she'd wait. She wanted me then as much as I wanted her.'

'But it didn't last, did it, pet? The passion and the excitement. For her at least. Lorna was growing up, getting a bit more confidence. She didn't need you in the end.'

'She was young,' he said. He sounded as petulant as one of his kids. 'She didn't know her own mind.'

Again, Vera bit back a reply. For a moment the forest was silent again. 'Then she started going out with your son. The lovely Josh. I rather think my DC has a soft spot for him. Even *I* can see the appeal.' Vera turned to him. The sky was quite clear now and the stars seemed so close she felt as if she could reach out to grab a handful. 'And you never had found the courage to tell Rosemary you wanted to leave and split up the happy family. No wonder Lorna lost patience and preferred a boyfriend her own age.'

He tensed. She sensed the hostility coming from him.

'Thomas was *my* son.'

She was glad he'd thrown away the gun, but he was still bigger than her and very much stronger. There was anger in his voice; she should be more careful how she spoke to him. Then she remembered Lorna and the way Heslop had tried to own the young woman, a brave young woman, who'd survived an eating disorder and who was making a life for herself and her child. At that moment, anger took over and thoughts of self-preservation flew away.

'I got it all wrong,' she said. 'We all got it wrong. We thought Lorna was trying to hold on to her lover, to persuade him to stay with her. Not that she was trying to escape from a toxic relationship, a relationship that wasn't working for her any longer, with a man who was becoming more and more controlling and obsessive.'

He tensed again, but she continued talking all the same. 'Did you feel that she'd used you? That she was keen to see you while she was still frail and needy, but once she was stronger, she wanted someone closer to her own age?'

'I *made* her stronger!' He thumped the icy ground beside him with his fist.

'You did,' Vera agreed. 'But if you'd loved her, you should have let her go. Not bullied her into staying as your bit on the side.' She turned to him. 'You wanted it all, didn't you? Happy families at home, and an illicit young woman to spice up your love life. You couldn't bear it when Lorna started to see sense.'

'Thomas was *my* child.' It had become a refrain. She thought he'd repeated it over and over in his head until it had become an obsession, a belief in the justice of his actions. The words had convinced him that Lorna had been planning to steal what was rightfully his.

'Was she going to tell Josh?' Vera asked. 'Not just that you'd had the relationship, but that you were stalking her? Is that why you had to kill her?'

'She was going to take everything away from me.' The voice was implacable, without emotion.

'So, you arranged to meet her at the lay-by looking down over Brockburn. You had the tractor and came over the field. What I don't understand is why she agreed to be there that evening, in the dark and the snow, the bairn in the car when the driving was dangerous. And what had panicked her the day before?'

'She wasn't fit to be a mother. The anorexia proved that, and the way she treated me wasn't rational. I told her I was going to apply for custody of the boy. Rosemary would have understood, she loves kids and would have taken him in. He'd have been part of a loving family. Happy. When I picked Lorna up in Kimmerston the day before, I told her access might be enough for me. If she met me that night, we could discuss it. Maybe we could come to some arrangement . . .'

At that, Vera forgot all sense of caution. 'She was a much better parent to Thomas than you'd ever be.' The words came out strong and slow and as soon as they were spoken, she knew she'd pushed him too far. Still she went on: 'And it wasn't an arrangement you wanted, but some crazy idea of revenge.'

He turned slowly towards her. The blue Viking eyes were piercing and a little mad. There was ice on his beard. He got up onto his knees, pulled off his big mittens and put his hands round her throat and began to squeeze. Vera tried to fight back by tugging at the giant fists and kicking out. But she was still sitting and her movement was restricted. He was strong and used to handling struggling beasts. As Vera began to lose consciousness, she thought this was her fault. She should have kept Heslop sweet until she'd got him to the station. She thought it was her pride again, making her think she was indestructible. Some words from the poem Holly had read out at an earlier briefing repeated themselves in her head.

But I have promises to keep. And miles to go before I sleep. And miles to go before I sleep.

Then the world went black.

Chapter Forty-Two

HOLLY RAN THROUGH THE FOREST, HER pace even, jumping across the roots that occasionally blocked her way, ducking to avoid branches. She was following a line of boot prints. She told herself she couldn't possibly recognize them as those she'd found in the Falstones' house, not in this light, but she was certain that they belonged to the person who had abducted Thomas. She'd picked up the trail close to the cottage and by now the snow had stopped and the sky had cleared, so the marks were uncovered and intact, frozen. There was no sign of Vera's prints, but if she found the killer, she'd find Vera too. Holly understood Vera; the boss had acted as a decoy, leading the abductor away from Thomas, so the child would be safe in the cottage for them to find. No thought for her own safety or for that of her colleagues who might need to come to her rescue.

Holly's breath was coming in puffs of white mist, but she hadn't reached the point of exhaustion yet. She'd run the Kielder Dark Skies marathon in October and it seemed to her now that the race had been training her just for this moment.

When she came to the edge of the clearing, she recognized it at once. This was where they'd found Constance Browne. The blue-and-white police tape remained, though the woman's body had been taken away. Holly stood, silent, and watched the scene playing out in front of her.

She saw the man first. Neil Heslop. So, Vera had been right all along and it had been a man who'd killed Lorna and the teacher. He was kneeling, his back to Holly. She couldn't see what he was doing.

'Move away!'

He got to his feet but he didn't move. He was as still as the dead branches that littered the clearing. She saw a pile of clothes at his feet. No, not a pile of clothes, Holly thought. That was Vera, lying in the snow, looking smaller than Holly would have thought possible.

She ran towards them. 'Move away from her!'

No response. Heslop seemed barely to register Holly's presence. All his focus was on the woman. Holly continued, her voice sharp and fierce. 'Move away. You're surrounded. There are armed officers with their weapons trained on you.'

Now Heslop did turn. He walked a couple of steps in Holly's direction. 'On your knees,' Holly shouted. 'Put your hands on your head.' She fixed him in the light of her torch, willing him to obey. He was bigger and stronger than she was and she knew she wouldn't be able to take him on. The bluff about the armed officers would only work for so long. He hesitated for a moment and she thought he might run. She *hoped* he might run so she could give her full attention to Vera. They knew who he was now and he wouldn't get far. But all the fight seemed to leave him. He crumpled back to his knees in the snow and when she got to him, he followed her instructions in silence. She tied his hands behind his back with the plastic restraints she had in her pocket. 'Stay where you are.'

He still didn't speak. He seemed lost in a world of his own.

Holly ran to Vera. The woman seemed lifeless and cold. There were livid marks on her neck where the man had tried to strangle her, just as there'd been on Constance Browne's body. For the first time since leaving the Falstones' farm, Holly was frightened. From the moment she'd joined Northumbria Police, this woman had ruled her life, and Holly wasn't sure, now, how she'd manage without her. Joe would never forgive her if she didn't take Vera back to him, alive and well. She tried to remember all she knew about CPR, but her thoughts were scrambled and she realized that tears were running down her face. She lay Vera on her back and unbuttoned her thick jacket so she could start pressure on the chest. All the time desperately trying to remember all that she'd been taught on the first-aid course, knowing that she was too late.

'What on earth are you doing, hinnie? I'll catch my death.' The words were very faint, scratchy, as if it hurt the woman to talk. As if she was learning to speak again after years of silence. It was the voice of a ghost. The shock of the sound sent a rush of adrenaline through Holly's body. She began to shake uncontrollably.

'I thought you were dead.'

'Well, so did I.' Holly helped her into a sitting position and Vera continued, her voice still strained. 'I lost consciousness for a bit and only came to when I heard you shouting. He'd have finished me off, though, if he'd realized.' She looked across at Heslop who was still kneeling in the snow. 'Two women dead, he'd have nothing to lose.'

'I need to call it in.' Holly's hands were still trembling as she reached for a phone. 'Get you an ambulance.'

'Where's the cavalry then?'

'Still halfway between Kimmerston and Kirkhill, as far as I know.'

Vera nodded towards Heslop. 'So you were bluffing then.' There was a strange choking sound, which made Holly anxious again. Then she looked at the woman more closely and understood that Vera was laughing.

'Eh, lass,' she said, 'I didn't train you so badly after all.'

Chapter Forty-Three

VERA WOKE UP IN HOSPITAL AND saw Joe sitting by her bed. She was glad it was him and not Holly. Holly had saved her life, and Vera had never enjoyed feeling obliged to anyone. Besides, Joe was her lad. Her man. She was pleased to see him. She'd been dozing on and off all day. Now it was mid-afternoon and she was itching to be sent home.

'How's the boy?' It was still painful to talk, but nothing that honey and lemon with a good slug of Scotch wouldn't heal. They'd kept her in because of the hypothermia rather than the attempted strangulation. In the ambulance they'd wrapped her up in a foil blanket so she'd looked like a turkey ready for Christmas.

'He's absolutely fine. Back with the Falstones.'

'And Heslop?'

'Holly and I interviewed him this morning.' A pause. 'He didn't give much away, but he'll plead guilty. Save his family the trauma of a trial.'

Vera nodded her approval. 'You okay to drive me home? I can get a taxi if Sal wants you back.'

'Nah,' he said. 'I've told Sal it'll be a late one and I promised I'll take a few days off once this is all over. As long as I'm there for the kids' nativity tomorrow afternoon . . .' He paused. 'I've got your Land Rover outside.'

'Champion.' The words of the poem of Holly's rattled round her brain again, as much of an ear worm as some trashy pop song. *But I have promises to keep.* 'We'll make sure you keep your promise and get back in time for that play.'

He insisted on driving and she didn't put up too much of a fight. When they arrived at the cottage, she took a key from her pocket. 'You've not seen the place since I rebuilt after the fire.' She opened the door. 'Ta da!'

Joe followed her in. 'You didn't bother getting central heating when you refurbished? It's bloody freezing in here.'

'Nah,' she said. 'It'd have meant oil-fired up here and I'm doing my bit for global warming. Besides, I told you, I'd forgotten to renew the insurance so it all had to come out of my own pocket.' She bent over the fire, which had already been laid, and set a match to it. 'It'll soon heat up.' She stood up, felt her head swim a bit and grabbed hold of the back of a chair.

Joe left his coat on. 'The place doesn't look very different. I thought you might have added a few mod cons.' He looked at her. 'You sit down. The hospital said you should be resting. I'll stick the kettle on.'

She decided not to insist and closed her eyes for a moment. When she opened them, he was there with tea in her old black pot, milk in a bottle and two mugs. A packet of chocolate digestives. She saw him sniff the milk and decide it would do.

'I'm staying tonight,' he said. 'The hospital would have kept you in until tomorrow if you'd been on your own. I've taken a casserole out of the freezer. Joanna said I'd find something there.' He paused. 'She wanted you to go and stay with them.'

Joanna was her hippy neighbour. She was as kind as it was possible to be, but Vera needed her own bed tonight. 'Joe Ashworth, you're a lifesaver.' She looked at him over the rim of her mug. 'Did Heslop explain why he took the lad?'

'Not in any way that made sense.'

Vera thought sense hadn't come into it at all, not by then. After killing Lorna, Heslop had sat in Home Farm, pretending at happy families, and brooding. His wife and kiddies must have known he was losing it, but they'd put his strange mood down to the shock of finding Lorna's body.

'Heslop saw Thomas as his link to Lorna,' Vera said. 'The lass wouldn't let Heslop own *her*, but he decided he could possess his son.' She paused. 'I was scared he might attempt to kill the boy too. You've read those stories about jealous men who kill their wives and kids and then themselves.'

Joe shook his head as if it was beyond his understanding. 'If he'd just sat tight and let the boy be, he could have got away with two murders.'

'Oh, I don't think so.' Vera couldn't let that go. 'He'd already given too much of himself away. I was already on to him. I've never believed in happy families.'

They sat for a moment in silence.

'There's a bottle of Scotch in that dresser behind you,' Vera said. 'Dig it out and I'll tell you how I knew Heslop was our man. Give you the benefit of my wisdom. Listen and learn, Joe Ashworth. Listen and learn.'

She poured out the whisky – she knew his measures would

be pathetically small – before she started speaking again. 'I wasn't *sure* until after Constance Browne died, but in the end Heslop was the only one with means and opportunity. When I found Lorna's car, that night in the blizzard, it had been left by a gate leading into a Home Farm field. We know now that Heslop had arranged to meet the lass there with his tractor. He'd just be the other side of the wall, waiting for her. It was his land, anyone seeing him would think he had every right to be on it and a good reason to be there.'

Vera thought that image would haunt her for the rest of her career: the young woman in the cold, the child in the car. She didn't want to dwell on it and started talking again:

'That's why Lorna didn't bang on the door at Karan and Dorothy's cottage and call for help. That bothered me right from the start. The road from the abandoned car to where her body was found would have taken her right past their house. So, either Karan was lying – and I did have my doubts about him for a while – or Lorna got to Brockburn over the field. She wouldn't have done that on foot. Not in the pitch dark and leaving the bairn behind. So that set me thinking about the bunch at Home Farm.'

She beamed at him. 'Just common sense really. And a bit of logic. Of course, Heslop had to go back to Brockburn to pick up his lasses later in the evening, so even if the snow hadn't covered his tracks, he'd have had an explanation for them being there.'

'But he left Thomas in the car with the door open.'

Vera could tell that in his head, Joe was back on the narrow road, the forest behind him, in the blizzard and the dark. This case would haunt him too.

'I think Lorna left the door open,' Vera said. 'She would

ANN CLEEVES

have been anxious about the meeting and ready to make a quick getaway. Heslop didn't check the car. Besides, he always planned to come back for the boy. Jinny's Mill was waiting for them, all snug and tidy. His and Lorna's special place.'

'But then you came along,' Joe said.

'Then I came along, out of the snow, to play the Good Samaritan,' Vera said. 'I left my business card in the car. It must have been a shock to the system to see that the police had come along to spoil all his plans.'

'You know we found Lorna's devices in Heslop's office? We've been checking her texts and emails.'

Vera nodded.

'In the beginning, Lorna *was* infatuated with Heslop,' Joe said. 'He was her first real love. Then she started to be less dependent and things got nasty. The relationship might have started out as consensual but it's clear the man was harassing her big style. He was cyber stalking in the last few months when she was trying to break free from him, and some of the messages suggest that he was following her physically too.'

'Bastard.' Vera reached out for the bottle and topped up the glasses. She took a sip before continuing. She was warm and content. She'd sleep well tonight; she was already drowsy. 'The poor lass must have felt entirely alone when Heslop threatened custody proceedings to take the boy off her. No wonder she panicked. Because she was so screwed up about her own parents – she still believed that Crispin was her natural father – she didn't feel she could talk to Robert and Jill. And while she dropped a few hints to Constance, she was so scared of Heslop by this point that she couldn't even confide properly in her.'

They sat for a moment. Vera felt her eyes closing. If she'd

been here on her own, she'd have fallen asleep in the chair, warm as toast until morning, but she couldn't do that with Joe in the house. She had a position to maintain.

'Are you going to heat up that casserole then? I told you, I'm supposed to rest.' Now she did lie back in the chair and allow herself to nap.

She woke to Joe's voice, almost shouting into his mobile because phone reception was so bad. He was talking to his wife, making his excuses for another night away. Sal was giving him a hard time. Vera kept her eyes shut until the call was over, then she stretched.

'Are we ready to eat? I'm clamming.'

They sat at the table she'd picked up for a tenner in a charity shop to replace the one she'd lost in the fire. Vera pointed Joe to the sideboard where there was the good bottle of red she'd been saving to take to her neighbours on Christmas Day. 'We can't eat one of Joanna's casseroles without a decent glass of wine.'

'So,' Joe said. 'Let's hear why Constance Browne had to die.' His role had always been to act as her stooge, to feed her the lines.

Vera settled back in her chair. 'I think Connie must have guessed that Neil Heslop was Thomas's father. She struck me as a perceptive woman. Curious too. And willing to meddle. Constance had been to warn Robert Falstone that his daughter was seeing someone inappropriate, but he'd just thought she was an interfering cow and took no notice.'

'Why didn't Constance speak to us?' Joe asked. 'To you when you went to interview her?'

'She wanted to talk to Heslop before accusing him of murder. In a close community like Kirkhill, you don't go to the police unless you're sure of your facts and she'd known Heslop since he was a boy. Holly found out from his phone records that Constance spoke to him on the Sunday evening. I think they arranged to meet before the Monday morning art class, but he turned up earlier than she was expecting.'

'How could she just go off with a man she suspected could be a killer?'

'Because she really didn't believe that a man she thought she knew well could act like that. Because she was a strong woman of a certain age and she thought she was indestructible.' Vera gave a strange little smile. 'She'd taught all the bairns in Kirkhill and Brockburn and sorted their problems. She probably thought she could sort this out too. She might have realized Heslop was desperate, depressed, suicidal even, but she was arrogant enough to think she could deal with the situation, maybe persuade him to hand himself in. I'm sure she went willingly.' That smile again. 'Pride and curiosity. A dangerous mix.'

'I still don't understand how you could have been so sure that Neil Heslop had taken her.'

Vera took a large mouthful of wine, and thought it was better than any of the painkillers they'd given her in the hospital. 'It was Josh turning up late for the art class that clinched it. He said his car had broken down and he'd had to wait for his father to get in, so he could borrow his van. There was no explanation for where his father could have been on a dark winter's morning.'

'Do you know where Connie was killed? Heslop wouldn't say when we talked to him yesterday.'

'I'm sure it would have been in Jinny's Mill. They probably walked in from the back drive close to Dorothy's cottage.

Nobody would have taken any notice of his van parked near Brockburn. It was often there.'

'And after dumping her body in the clearing, he drove back to the farm,' Joe said, 'just in time for Josh to borrow his van to get into Kirkhill to teach the oldies' art class.'

Vera nodded. 'Heslop kept a cool head. There he was, playing the fiddle and the proud father at his daughter's birthday celebration on the Sunday night, only two days after killing the mother of his child. But it was all on the surface – the strain must have been taking its toll.' She shook a little more coal onto the fire. The embers still showed through, glowing red.

She lifted her glass and clinked it against his. 'A toast,' she said, her voice ironic. 'To happy families.'

They smiled and Joe thought Vera gave him a little wink, but the fire was smoking and he couldn't be entirely sure.

Chapter Forty-Four

THE NEXT MORNING, VERA DROVE JOE back to Kimmerston and told him to go home. 'Or head into town for a bit of Christmas shopping. I bet you've still not bought anything for your Sal. She deserves something special, putting up with you.' Vera stayed in the Land Rover and watched him go into the police station. She couldn't face going in herself: all that sympathy and she knew there'd be the inevitable lecture from her superintendent about putting herself in danger. Given half a chance he'd probably order her on a risk-assessment course, but if she stayed out of the way until after the holiday, he'd have forgotten all about it. He had a very small brain.

There were loose ends to be tidied and she drove back to Kirkhill. Vera couldn't abide loose ends. She was supposed to be off sick, but it was almost on her way back to the cottage, after all, and these would be informal chats. Hardly work at all. Her first stop was to Home Farm. Best to get the most unpleasant visit over first.

She found them all sitting at the kitchen table, a cafetière of coffee going cold in the middle; Nettie and Cath sitting

very close together, their arms around each other, Josh white
and silent. Their mother alone at the end of the table. Vera
didn't know what to say to them, but in the end, she had to
ask. That curiosity again, getting the better of her.

'You didn't suspect?'

The question was directed to them all, but it was Rosemary
who answered. 'That my husband's a murderer?' Her voice
was shrill and hysterical. 'No, I didn't suspect.'

Or you didn't want to.

'That he had a lover,' Vera said gently. 'Did you suspect
that?'

Rosemary turned away and refused to reply. They were all
frozen in their grief, like sculptures of ice. Vera let herself out
of the house. On the doorstep she paused and turned back to
the group at the table. 'He'll plead guilty,' she said. 'No trial
and the press should soon lose interest. He's done that for you
at least.' She could hear one of the girls sobbing as she walked
towards the Land Rover.

She moved on to Broom Farm. An officer should have been
in touch with the Falstones with the basic details. They'd know
Heslop was in custody, but they deserved more explanation.
On the way, Vera wondered if it might be possible for her to
keep in touch with the family after Heslop had been convicted,
once the fuss had died down. It was about time she made a
few friends away from work and it would be interesting to see
Thomas grow up. She might not be related to him, but there
were no other kids in her life. She might be able to help out
from time to time. Not babysitting. She wouldn't go that far.
She was so cack-handed she couldn't contemplate changing a
nappy. But when he was older, she might be there for him.
Money if he needed something the couple couldn't run to.

Driving lessons. Advice. Then she thought Robert and Jill would probably want to put the investigation behind them and the last thing they'd need was Vera butting in.

She found them in a living room that she'd never seen on her previous visits. It was at the back of the house full of big, dark furniture. There was a fire in the grate covered by a mesh guard, and they were putting up a tree. Thomas was on the floor, crawling through tinsel, chuckling. There was a smell of pine needles and old-fashioned furniture polish. Lavender or beeswax. Vera wasn't an expert, but either Robert or Jill had been cleaning.

'We've never bothered much with Christmas since Lorna left home,' Jill said. 'But when she was a bairn, she always liked a real tree. We tried to persuade her that an artificial was less mess, but she wouldn't have it.'

'Your liaison officer will have been in touch, kept you up to date with what's going on?'

'Aye.'

'How's he been?' Vera nodded towards the toddler.

'Canny. He seems to have had no ill effects at all.'

'And he'll be too young to remember,' Robert said. 'That's a blessing.'

'Hard for *you* to forget, though.'

Robert nodded, but didn't dwell on the idea. 'We can't thank you enough for finding him. For getting him back.' He turned away so she wouldn't see that he was close to tears. 'The officer said you ended up in hospital.'

'Just doing my job.' Vera paused. 'I'll be interested in seeing how he turns out.'

'You'll be very welcome here,' Jill said, 'at any time.' She smiled. 'An honorary auntie.'

Vera wasn't sure how to respond to that, but she gave a little laugh. 'I can't guarantee I'll remember his birthday.' There was a slightly awkward silence before Vera continued. 'How would you feel if the Heslops stick around in the valley? Would that be difficult for you?'

The couple didn't answer immediately. They looked at each other. 'I wouldn't like to think they'd lose their home.' Robert paused. 'Not if they knew nothing of what was going on. What's that saying about the sins of the father? I don't think guilt can pass down the generations.' He nodded towards the child. 'If it did, this one would be tainted too. And whatever we might think of it we're all related in a way now.'

'That's a charitable way to look at it.'

Falstone seemed embarrassed. 'Soft, you mean? Aye, well, I suppose it's that time of year.' He looked away. They watched Thomas pull himself up on the sofa and walk a few steps towards the piano.

'Could you manage a mince pie?' Jill said. 'Shop-bought. Obviously.'

'Eh, hinnie,' Vera smiled. 'That's just how I like them.'

Chapter Forty-Five

AT BROCKBURN, JULIET STOOD AT HER bedroom window and looked out at the garden and the forest in the distance. She thought she was always an observer, always looking out. It was as if this grand house was a prison or a cage and she couldn't quite take the step to freedom, to break away.

Mark had gone into Kirkhill early to buy a paper and returned to say that the Co-op had been full of the news of Neil Heslop's arrest. She supposed *he* would be spending the rest of his life behind real bars, locked gates. The life that he'd known before with Rosemary and his children was over. It seemed ridiculous to turn *herself* into a virtual prisoner when she had the opportunity to do whatever she wanted, just because she didn't have the confidence to strike out on her own.

The trouble was that she wasn't quite clear in her own mind *what* she wanted. A child, of course. That was always in her mind and the babies that might have been still haunted her. But there were children who needed homes and she had the space and the love to give them. Mark had tried to bring up the subject of adoption in the past but she'd always put him off; she'd seen it as a second-best option, not enough. After holding Thomas in her arms in this room, she wasn't sure now that was true.

Perhaps, she thought, she should escape this altogether: the house, her mother and her marriage. She could run away, travel, take a university course, see a bit of life away from the valley. She had a brief image of a sunlit hillside with the sea in the distance, the smell of salt and thyme, the taste of olives and oranges.

Juliet knew that would be an empty gesture, though. It might do as a holiday but not a long-term proposition. She belonged in this place and wanted to be here. She needed to stand up to her mother, not allow herself to be bullied, and she should make a real effort to work with Mark and make his project a success. There could be excitement enough in that. After all that had happened, Harriet was no longer in any position to call the shots. Perhaps she could be persuaded to move to a comfortable flat in the city, somewhere close to her friends and the shops. Without the woman's interference, she and Mark would have more of a chance to build a proper marriage. Only then could they consider a child. The possibilities made Juliet feel suddenly joyful, dizzy. A new year would bring new possibilities. Perhaps Vera was like a crotchety fairy godmother, who had opened Juliet's eyes to a different world.

As if on cue, there came the distant sound of the ancient Land Rover's engine, and Juliet watched as it stopped in front of the house and Vera climbed down.

Chapter Forty-Six

VERA ARRIVED AT BROCKBURN BY THE grand drive. When she'd left the Falstones, she'd sat in the vehicle for a moment, the low winter sun shining straight into her eyes, making them water, planning her last visit of the day. It was a week since she'd first driven this way to Brockburn and parked by the cedar tree, scattered with fairy lights, the toddler in the Land Rover beside her. Today was the winter's solstice, the longest night of the year. Lorna's 'Darkest Evening'. She'd felt then a bit like Cinderella, peering through the window at a different world. She knew better now and she didn't envy them their house or their fancy parties. She got out of the Land Rover and rang the bell by the front door. Dorothy opened it almost immediately.

'Are the family in?'

'They are. Juliet's upstairs, but I've just shouted to let her know there's coffee in the kitchen.'

'Perfect timing then. You'll join us, pet? It'll save me having to repeat myself.'

'Of course.'

Juliet appeared beside them and then they were all there. Harriet sat at the head of the table, immaculate in a cashmere sweater and silk scarf, grey trousers. Juliet looked pale and skinny, but for once she wasn't wearing black. Instead she was in a bright red sweater over her jeans. Mark, at the other end of the table, was still dressed like a country gent in wool sweater and cord trousers. Dorothy poured coffee and passed around a plate of brownies. The coffee was strong and good. Vera thought there were compensations to mixing with the gentry.

'I wanted to let you know that we've arrested a suspect for the murders of Lorna Falstone and Constance Browne. Only fair that you should know before the press gets wind.'

'Oh?' Harriet showed slightly more interest than she had on any of Vera's previous visits.

'We'd heard,' Juliet said. 'Mark was in Kirkhill this morning and everyone was talking about it.'

'You didn't tell me.' Harriet turned a stony stare on her daughter, but Juliet didn't seem cowed. Harriet looked back at Vera. 'Well? Who was it?'

'Your tenant from Home Farm. Neil Heslop. It seems he was the baby's father.'

'Ah.' Harriet seemed almost pleased. 'A domestic situation. I suppose that makes sense.'

'Poor Rosemary,' Juliet said. 'To have a husband capable of that! Of murder! I've been thinking I should go round.' She looked at Vera. 'Or do you think that might make things worse?'

Vera didn't think anything could make things worse but she didn't reply.

'You're sure he was the culprit?' Harriet said.

'He's confessed. There'll be a guilty plea. No need for a trial.'

'Ah,' Harriet said again, and Vera could sense the relief, the satisfaction. 'I suppose we'll need to find a new tenant.'

'Not yet.' Juliet was firm. 'The Heslop girls are still at school and we can't ask them to leave Home Farm. Not now. We can keep things ticking over for a while, even if we have to get contractors in. I suppose it would be awkward to ask Robert Falstone to help.'

'Perhaps you should ask Josh Heslop if he wants to take over the tenancy,' Vera said. 'It's in his blood. If the family can face staying.'

'You're right,' Juliet said. 'We should offer at least. Rosemary and the children will need all the support they can get.'

'I'm not sure.' Harriet poured herself more coffee. 'Joshua's rather young. And would we really want the family staying on the land? Think of the scandal there'll be, all the media interest when the case comes to court.'

Vera stood up. 'As you say, it was a domestic situation.' A pause. 'It happens in the very best of families, as you know yourself. I'm sure you wouldn't want to be accused of hypocrisy.'

Harriet made no reply. She stared once more at Juliet, then got up and left the room. Vera turned to Dorothy. 'You knew the family well. You were at the daughter's birthday party in the barn. You didn't suspect that there were any problems there?'

There was a moment of silence. 'Karan thought Cath seemed nervy, preoccupied. She didn't seem to be enjoying time at home and turned up at the cottage even when she didn't have a class scheduled. I thought she just had a crush on him and told him to take care.'

'Wise words,' Vera said. 'That was how the relationship

between Lorna and Neil Heslop started. She fell for an older man, looking for security.' She smiled. 'Good for the ego, eh? But a dangerous game.'

'Oh, I'm sure Karan knows he's got too much to lose. Besides, he's far too sensible to go down that route.'

'I'm sure he is.' But Vera remembered Joe's description of knocking at Pabla's cottage the night before, while his wife and child were away, two coffee mugs on the table. 'And Cath will have more on her plate than A levels now.'

Dorothy nodded. 'Of course. And Karan has to focus on work for his post-graduate teaching qualification. It's probably a good time to give up the classes.'

Vera smiled again. She thought the message had got through. No need to mention Dorothy's own mistake and her reason for leaving London and the law. She was about to stand up when Juliet reached out and took her hand.

'You will keep in touch, Vera? Now we've been in contact again, we should get to know each other a little better. Don't you think so? There are so few Stanhopes left.'

Vera said nothing for a moment. 'Well, with coffee as good as this, you'll not keep me away.' No promises. Nothing specific.

Mark had been watching the exchange with confusion and a little amusement, like a member of the audience following a piece of theatre he didn't quite understand. He seemed about to speak, but Vera got to her feet before he had a chance. 'Perhaps you'd see me out, Mr Bolitho.'

They stood together at the top of the stone steps leading down to the formal garden.

'How's the arts centre project going?'

'Well,' he said. 'Arts Council England has made some very encouraging noises about our application.'

'It's never wise to lie to the police, Mr Bolitho.'

'I wasn't aware that I had lied.'

'The morning of Miss Browne's death. You told my officer that you spent a short time in your flat and then went out for breakfast.'

'Ah.' He paused. 'So I did.'

'Where were you exactly?'

'This is rather awkward, Inspector.' He paused again and looked back into the house to be sure that nobody was listening. 'My full-time contract at the theatre is covering for maternity leave. My colleague had a little girl a couple of months ago. You met her here. Sophie Blackstock. She and Paul came to the party that night.' He looked up at Vera and seemed to guess what she was thinking. 'Really, the baby's absolutely nothing to do with me. Sophie's happily married. And I love my wife. But I'm a bit soppy about babies and I went for a visit. To take a gift and steal a cuddle. It's a sensitive subject for Juliet. I didn't want it getting back to her. She already thinks she's letting me down.'

'Maybe she'd understand.'

'Perhaps. I've been so wrapped up in work that I've stopped saying anything important to her.' He paused. 'I don't want to hurt her.'

Vera wasn't convinced. She thought Bolitho was telling her what she wanted to hear. But perhaps she was just a cynical old bat and besides, as Robert Falstone had said, it was the time of year to be charitable. She nodded and patted Mark Bolitho's arm. 'You talk to her,' she said. 'I'm her relative after all, so I've got a right to interfere, and I want her to be happy.' She paused for a beat. 'I don't envy you taking on this lot, mind.' She made a gesture which included the house and the people inside. 'Good luck with it all.'

She stamped back to the Land Rover feeling suddenly energized. She'd had a flutter with mortality, and lying in the hospital bed she'd wondered if it might be time to retire. But there was plenty of life in the old dog yet. Again, some lines of Holly's poem came back to her. *And miles to go before I sleep. And miles to go before I sleep.*